I0778246

CHILDREN OF THE SHADOWS

THE CROOKED TALES SERIES

In reading order:

The Rising

Night Of The Witch

Children Of The Shadows

Dawn Of The Demon

The Reckoning

(Coming: June 2026)

CHILDREN OF THE SHADOWS

CROOKED TALES
BOOK THREE

CHRIS HARRISON

WICKED INK

PUBLISHING

Children Of The Shadows (Crooked Tales Series) : Book 3
Copyright © 2025 by Chris Harrison

Published by Wicked Ink Publishing Ltd.
www.wickedinkpublishing.com

Cover and book design © 2025 by Wicked Ink Publishing Ltd.
Editors: Raymond Griffiths & Adam Bamford

First Edition: June 2025
Printed in Canada

Library and Archives Canada Cataloguing in Publication

Title: Children of the shadows / Chris Harrison.
Names: Harrison, Chris, author.
Description: Series statement: Crooked tales ; book 3
Identifiers: Canadiana (print) 20250211963
Canadiana (ebook) 20250219476
ISBN 9781998278176 (softcover)
ISBN 9781998278183 (EPUB)
Subjects: LCGFT: Horror fiction. | LCGFT: Novels.
Classification: LCC PS3608.A78 C45 2025 | DDC 823/.92—dc23

For Winnie

When darkness falls, evil will rise…

CHILDREN OF THE SHADOWS

PROLOGUE

Wrestling with the remnants of sleep, Doctor Singer prised his bleary eyes open. He groggily surveyed the murky on-call room in search of whatever woke him, but the room was empty. Feverishly rubbing the five o'clock shadow framing his narrow jawline, he waited for the reliable hum of idle gossip to come from the ward outside, only to find it was eerily absent.

Instead, all he could hear was the gentle ticking of the oversized wall clock as its flimsy plastic hands gradually edged their way closer to 4am.

"*Where is everyone?*" He wondered, shuffling his way to the edge of the tiny bunk bed to investigate.

It was a long, draining shift, and having pulled yet another 'all-nighter', he decided to get a few hours' rest before attempting the long drive home. Servicing three neighbouring villages, Chase Side Hospital always had a steady flow of patients throughout the night, but as he peered through the narrow window into the corridor, all he saw was its stark pale-green wall staring back at him.

Something felt off, beyond the unfamiliar silence, but he couldn't quite put his finger on it.

The air was warm and stuffy as he tiptoed closer to the door, and it carried a strange, sweet odour that reminded him of fresh candy apples at the fairground. He waited a moment, hoping to see the familiar flash of blue scrubs rush past, but nothing came, and so he continued to creep closer.

As he felt the cool chrome door handle in the palm of his hand, the hairs on the back of his neck stood to attention, causing him to hesitate.

"Creeeeaaak!" The silence outside was suffocating, and the moment he allowed it into his room, a heavy knot of dread formed deep down in the pit of his stomach.

"Stop being ridiculous Terry!" He grumbled as he ventured out into the abandoned hall.

Glancing up towards the reception desk, he flinched as the knot in his gut tightened with a sharp twist. The entire third floor was empty. No porters, no nurses, and no patients. Shuffling forward, he noticed the sweet, sickly smell somehow followed him, overpowering the hospital's signature scent of disinfected lemons.

"Jenkins..." He muttered, as his memory kicked in.

She was sucking on a lollipop when she entered his office earlier that day, and he smelt it on her breath for the entire examination. It was nauseating and did nothing for his patience with the girl. An obnoxious eight-year-old suffering from bad dreams wasn't exactly the best use of his degree in medicine and he made no secret of it either, being intentionally forceful whenever she refused to cooperate.

"Brat!" He grunted. But that didn't explain why he could smell her now, out here in the hall.

"*Buzzzz!*"

Ahead of him, the fluorescent lights flickered, peppering the derelict corridor like a malfunctioning strobe.

"*BANG!*"

Doctor Singer jumped as the light furthest from him exploded like a firework, showering the floor with radiant sparks and broken glass.

"*BANG!*"

Burst after burst, the lights succumbed to a menacing surge of darkness. A surge that was heading straight for him. Slowly retreating, Doctor Singer frantically rattled the door handle of the on-call room behind him, only to find it was now locked.

"*BANG!*"

Before he had a chance to think, the last light shattered above him, and prickly shards of broken bulb rained down over his balding head. The metallic aroma of singed electrics amalgamated with the thick saccharine stench clogging his lungs as he fought to catch his breath. His asthma was about to rear its head.

Gasping, he hurriedly patted down the pockets of his white coat in search of his inhaler, but he left it beside the bed. Doubling over, he wheezed as the air continued to elude him. He knew what he had to do; he just needed to stay calm, but the growing tightness in his chest was all he could think about, and within a matter of seconds that tension had congealed to form a dull and heavy ache.

"Not so tough now, are you, doctor?" The child's voice came to him like a thought.

A trespasser infiltrating his neural pathways, and from the shadows emerged Valerie Jenkins. She appeared ethereal, shrouded by an unearthly glow shimmering like a sapphire in the darkened corridor.

Her chestnut brown hair was tied neatly into pigtails on

either side of her chubby face, and she wore a royal-blue princess frock as if she was on her way to a party. In her hand was the same glistening red lollipop she was sucking on earlier, only now she wielded it like a magic wand.

"Va...Valer...ie..." Doctor Singer rasped, still fighting for his breath.

Valerie raised her arm in response and revealed a purple bruise in the shape of a handprint wrapped around her triceps.

"You were mean to me today, Doctor, so now I'm gonna be mean to you." Her menacing tone reverberated in his head as if it had come from within.

Coughing and spluttering, Doctor Singer's strength ebbed away, and he collapsed to his knees.

"P...plea...se!" he choked, tears streaming down his face. But the girl continued to watch him suffer, wide-eyed and gleefully sucking on her lollipop.

"You're going to wake up dead, doctor." She grinned through gappy teeth. "Just like nana Quinn did. She was mean too..."

Valerie leaned in closer as he floundered on the cold hard floor, her warm breath tickling his ear as she softly whispered.

"Bye-bye Doctor." With that, she triumphantly skipped away down the empty corridor, giggling as she disappeared into the shadows.

"*Kaff kaff...*" Alone, eyes bulging, Doctor Singer forced a slow, sore blink only to find himself back on the staff bed in the on-call room. He never really left it.

Caught in the web of a deadly nightmare, he awoke deep in the throes of a fatal attack. His body was rigid and riddled with pain. The weight on his chest was unbearable, as billions of capillaries cried out in unison for their precious lifeblood: oxygen.

Beyond the door, he heard the inaudible chatter of the night team as they ignorantly went about their rounds, but try as he might to call out, his seared lungs were spent. There was no last-ditched scream, or final cry for help. All that remained was the muted sound of his own heartbeat slowly grinding to a halt.

As death loomed, and the room faded, there was no lost loved one waiting to greet him. No divine light eager to guide him home. His convulsing body painfully wrung out the last vestiges of life, leaving only darkness, until Doctor Singer was no more.

I

Meridia anxiously twiddled with the seatbelt as her mum pulled up outside the Jackson house and turned off the engine.

Still shell-shocked from their ordeal at Crooked House, the uncomfortable silence steadily building between them amplified every awkward squeak and creak as they both wearily clambered out of the tiny white Fiat Pander.

Dusk fell, painting the muted houses on Forest Road a murky shade of blue as Meridia and Emily grudgingly reconvened on the footpath outside number 36.

The evening chill offered welcome relief from their hot, stuffy car journey, and Meridia's rosy cheeks tingled beneath the gentle caress of the icy breeze as it rushed to greet them. Loosening her coat, she caught the smell of rain hanging in the air and noticed a band of thick, black, ominous clouds gathering overhead.

"I'm scared mum..." she whispered, "it's bad, I can feel it."

Lacking the courage to look directly at Zach's deserted house, she fixed her bright blue teary gaze on the far less daunting paving slabs at her feet. Having left Izzy and Peter at the hospital to take care of Father Alexander, there had been no word from Kane or JJ since they both left in search of Zach. Regardless of her gift, it didn't take a seer to know something was seriously wrong.

"Why don't you wait here while I go see what's going on..." Emily draped an arm around her daughter's shoulder and gave her a tender squeeze. Head hunched over, Meridia didn't answer as the tears she was holding hostage finally broke free, and leapt into the arms of gravity. Tucking a flyaway lock of thick auburn hair behind her ear, she watched silently as the tiny droplets splattered on the cold, hard concrete.

"No." She sniffed. "I need to know..." Cuffing her tears, she forced herself to gaze up at her best friend's house and her heart immediately sank.

The charcoal-grey street door she merrily skipped through so many times now stood ajar, as if the house itself was rendered slack jawed by whatever tragedy it now concealed within. There was no movement inside, and darkness and dread replaced the warm, familiar amber glow that always radiated from its windows.

Meridia caught another earthy waft of rain as she inched forward, then felt the first spot hit her forehead as the heavens wept. The knot of anticipation in her stomach tightened with each reluctant step as the house pulled her in like an insidious vacuum, desperate to share its terrible secrets.

"S...stay behind me." Emily stuttered. "It might not be safe."

Meridia felt the padding of her mum's winter coat as she gave her another squeeze before edging a fraction ahead. The closer they got to the doorstep; the quicker any vestige of hope abandoned them. Continuing along the garden path, they came face to face with early warning signs of a struggle through the gap in the door.

Directly ahead of them, they saw the soft cream entrance rug strewn across the hall, with shards of shattered glass twinkling dimly on the wooden floor beneath it. Meanwhile, to their right, Mr Jackson's silver Kia sat idly on the drive, and it dawned on Meridia that whatever occurred, it most likely involved Zach's parents.

"Look!" Meridia trembled, pointing at the coarse brown welcome mat at their feet. "It's blood!"

A smattering of crimson flecks decorated the concrete step leading into the house, and both Wilson girls froze in terror. Meridia wrestled to regain control of her imagination as dozens of gruesome scenarios laid siege on her mind all at once.

Before she did anything more, her mum pressed a finger to her lips and then signalled for her to listen by tugging at her earlobe.

"THUD! THUD! THUD!"

Overcome by a sudden queasiness, a cold sweat broke out across the back of Meridia's neck and fear took hold. Someone was thundering down the stairs towards them.

2

Peter's knee nervously bounced up and down as he fidgeted in his seat. He and Izzy had now been waiting impatiently for over half an hour, and he could already feel the early onset of cabin fever.

Chase Side's minor injuries unit was much less crowded than A&E, and home to fewer coughs, but the skeleton staff on hand all seemed far too aloof for Peter's liking. It was a modern wing compared to the rest of the aging hospital, with sparkling clean pale-blue laminated flooring and a cozy refreshment area offering free tea and coffee.

There were a dozen other patients dotted around, and one by one, he systematically scrutinized them all for the slightest hint of suspicion. For a whole twenty minutes his jade-green eyes fleeted back and forth like a magpie on the lookout for something shiny to justify his misgivings, but all he found was an assortment of worried faces.

The sinister swarm of hooded assailants pouring out of the woods surrounding Crooked House left him understandably rattled and on edge, but Izzy's shocking discovery of Valerie Richards further stoked his paranoia.

In his search for a viable explanation, he kept circling back to the idea that Valerie might not be another hapless victim of Crooked House as they first suspected. His gut was telling him her presence in Crooked House was part of something far more disturbing, but what that was, he couldn't yet fathom.

With only a solitary image of her on file, they had very little information to go on until now, and it was all he could do to stop himself marching up to the fourth floor to confront her. How could he, though?

He clearly underestimated the cult's resurgence, and they outnumbered them greatly. For all he knew, Chase Side was teeming with Children of the Shadows right now, watching him in plain sight, just waiting for the right moment to attack.

"Hey...any news?" Izzy plopped herself down in the seat next to him.

She was munching on a bland looking granola bar she bought from the hospital vending machine.

"Nothing yet." He replied, glancing at his watch. "Have you checked your phone? I'm worried about the others. Meridia and Emily should be there by now."

He watched as Izzy, a mousy and rather timid child prodigy, held her snack between her teeth and fumbled around in her jacket pockets.

"Still nothing." She grumbled, staring back at him blankly from behind her tortoiseshell glasses.

"*She'd make an excellent poker player,*" he thought, as he struggled to gauge her level of concern.

Her thick wavy hair was pulled back tight into a neat and tidy ponytail, as it often was, leaving her slender face completely exposed as she locked eyes with him, but still he had no idea what was going on in that brilliant brain of hers. Peter took another glance at his watch.

"I'll give them another five minutes, then I'll chase the receptionist again for an update. The longer we're stuck in here, the less help we are to everyone out there." He swept his silky dark blond hair away from his face and restored it to its effortlessly tousled shape.

Too tall for the blue bucket seat he was awkwardly perched on, he decided it was time to stretch his legs and grab another cup of coffee. The last thing he needed was the day's events to catch up with him, and being cooped up waiting for an update on Father Alexander's condition wasn't exactly helping.

As he rose, an intense waft of lemon scented disinfectant tingled his nostrils, rendering him giddy and nauseous from its chemical aroma. In an instant, Peter was transported back to his last visit there as an inpatient. The daunting memory instantly raised the hackles on the back of his neck and cranked up the urgency of getting as far away from Chase Side Hospital as humanly possible.

"Wait here. I'll be back in a sec, Izz." He whispered, and then strolled over to the coffee station next to the reception desk.

When he arrived, the young receptionist had her head buried in a patient file, meticulously studying a page of scrawled handwritten notes. Over her shoulder, through a tiny window on the far side of the glorified cubbyhole she was sitting in, he could see the corridor leading to the treatment rooms where he left Father Alexander.

He watched for a while, waiting for any sign of life on the other side of the glass, but there was no trace of any doctors, or the eager-to-please male nurse who initially showed them in.

Satisfied nobody was watching, he quickly flipped the bowl full of sugar and sweetener sachets into the plastic bin beneath the coffee station and mooched to the front of the reception desk.

"Excuse me..." He probed. "Sorry, I know you're busy, but is there any chance I can get some sugar for my coffee?"

He flashed a half-smile as he raised the empty bowl above the counter for the receptionist to see.

As humble as he was, Peter was aware of his looks and knew how to turn on the charm when needed. The nurse blushed upon peering up at him and nervously cleared her throat to answer.

"Oh...yes. Give me a minute and I'll run and get you some." The woman, an attractive brunette in her late twenties, stood up and made her way over to the door behind her.

Within a matter of seconds, she stepped out from behind a side door connecting the treatment area to the waiting room, and Peter walked over to greet her.

"Thank you...Alice." He said, glancing at her name tag, and handed her the empty bowl.

"Gosh, you're tall!" She smiled, blushing again before adding. "I'll be back in a jiffy." She briskly exited through the electric door leading back to the main hospital.

The moment Alice disappeared out of sight, Peter made his move and quietly slipped through the side door to the treatment area. Another blast of hospital disinfectant washed over him as he tiptoed along the shiny, pale-blue corridor towards treatment room 3. It was unexpectedly quiet for an overburdened hospital, and his paranoia immediately bubbled back to the surface.

Once again, he mulled over the siege of cult members who chased them out of Cold Christmas, and he couldn't help but wonder if any of its members might be hiding here in plain sight.

His brief stint as a patient already left him contemplating the possibility something sinister was going on at Chase Side, and judging by how clammy his palms were right now, his body was clearly in agreement.

"Squeak!"

The high-pitched sound of scuffed rubber reverberated down the hallway, announcing his arrival as it cut through the eerie silence. Cursing his shoes, Peter froze for a moment in case a member of staff came to investigate.

Whilst holding his breath in anticipation of being caught, he felt his heart thumping against his ribcage as if it wanted out. Despite every fibre of his being telling him to run, he held his ground until the sensation passed and he was satisfied it was safe to move on.

Each door along the corridor was firmly closed, including the one Father Alexander was wheeled into. He tried to recall if that had been the case when they first arrived, and his uncertainty led him to question if he heard the receptionist call any other patient names since their arrival.

Again, he couldn't be sure and wasn't entirely clear why it suddenly felt so important, but something in his gut continued to niggle him, turning the screw on his apprehension as he edged his way forward.

"Perhaps I need that coffee after all." He muttered, stopping outside room 3.

Placing an ear to the door, he listened for any noise on the other side. Nothing. With his back to the corridor, he could feel the uneasy silence creeping up behind him, slowly skulking its way up and over his shoulder until it was all he heard.

Something was increasingly off with this place, and it extended way beyond a staff shortage. The more he deliberated, the more he was convinced none of them were safe here.

If he was right, then he needed to find Father Alexander and get everyone the hell out of dodge.

"*Click!*"

Peter turned the handle and warily crept inside.

3

Emily forced herself between Meridia and the door, acting as a human shield against whoever was charging toward them. Meridia winced, bracing herself for what was to come as she clung onto the back of her mother's arm. The moment she saw their aggressor's shoes, she let go of the lungful of air she was holding onto and allowed her shoulders to relax.

"Kane!" she cried. Overcome with worry and relief, she pushed her way past her mum and into the hallway to reach him.

"Stay there!" He screeched. "Don't come inside!"

As he came into her view, Meridia's entire body seized up as if she was playing an involuntary game of musical statues. Kane was a mess. Red-eyed and distraught, his elfin face looked like thunder as he raced down the remaining steps towards her.

When he broke free of the shadows, Meridia saw his chocolate-brown hair was matted to his forehead, as if he just ran a marathon.

Stopping a few feet in front of her, Meridia swallowed a

mouthful of the metallic air he was carrying with him. The taste reminded her of the copper pennies she and her mum collected in a jar at home, and then she noticed the kitchen knife in his hand. White knuckles gripped the handle as if he was ready to attack.

"They're gone!" He raged, through melancholy tears of anger. "They're all gone!"

"*Clang!*"

Kane dropped the knife and howled as he collapsed into Emily's open arms. Over his shoulder, JJ staggered down the stairs behind him. Head hung low, the peak of his signature LA cap covered his face.

He appeared almost drunk at first, wobbling and weak at the knees as he gingerly navigated each step. Meridia watched his trembling hands tentatively feel their way along the banister until he reached the bottom.

"It's true..." He mumbled. "Zach...their mum and dad... they're all gone."

JJ raised his head, and Meridia noticed his bottom lip quivering as he continued.

"W...we were too late. There's so much blood...*sniff*...it's everywhere!" JJ looked completely broken.

As he drew closer, his bright hazel eyes were now puffy and bloodshot, awash with more tears than his emotions could carry. While Meridia grappled with the enormity of what she just heard, she noticed he also wielded a blade, shimmering under the fading light.

"ZACH!" she wailed, springing to life as the catastrophic news pried its way in.

Pushing past the shell-shocked statues in the hall, Meridia darted into the living room. She needed to see with her own eyes.

A nauseating wall of coppery stench stopped her in her

tracks seconds before she saw the blood. The yellow armchair in front of the bay window was caked in crimson like a Jackson Pollock painting, as was the adjacent sofa.

The room was a bloodbath, as if someone murdered the house and smeared its innards around in gruesome jubilation. Slashed cushions and spattered blood decorated the plush beige carpet, but the bodies of their loved ones were nowhere to be seen.

"Oh god!" Emily quickly caught up with her daughter and tried to shield her from the carnage, but Meridia wriggled her way free and ventured further into the kill room.

"This can't be..." she trailed off, wide eyed in morbid wonder. "Where is Zach?" She turned to face Kane, finding him stooped in the doorway.

"WHERE IS ZACH?!"

"W...we can't find him..." JJ stepped forward to speak for his grief-stricken friend. "We've looked everywhere... he's gone, M."

Meridia became lightheaded as the room spun around her. A swirling vortex of murder and mayhem encircling her as she fought to regain control of her balance.

"This can't be!" she argued, dizzy with denial. "I would know...if something happened...like at the hospital, remember?! He's got to be here somewhere!" She turned and raced towards the stairs.

Once again, she gave her mum the slip as she zigzagged between Kane and JJ before grasping the banister.

"Wait!" Emily called out after her. "It might not be safe..."

By the time her mother's anxious plea caught up with her, Meridia had already reached Zach's room. The door was ajar, and all she made out from the hall was the corner of his white desk.

Taking a step closer, she caught a faint waft of his favourite body spray. It was a warm scent of ginger and cinnamon that always reminded her of Christmas. She remembered telling him that one summer before they moved up to secondary school and he wore it every day since.

"Zach?" she whispered, shakily reaching for the brass knob to forge a better view.

Meridia didn't even make contact when she sensed the tiny prickle of electricity tickle her palm. At first, she thought it was static, but as her hand drew closer to the shiny metal handle, there was no sudden snap or spark, only a growing tingling sensation pulling her toward it like a magnet.

"Huh!" She yelped as her hand eventually made contact.

A warm surge of energy raced up her arm and down her legs, rooting her to the spot as a blanket of hazy white light softly descended over the room, shrouding everything in its ethereal glow. Pushing the door open, she caught sight of Zach perched on the edge of his bed, cradling his phone.

"ZACH!" she beamed, her heart leaping at the sight of him.

It didn't take long for the rush of excitement to dissipate when Zach remained unmoved. This was another of her visions. He had an eerie, translucent quality to him, as if he was the product of an old movie projector being cast into the room. Head down, his thick brown mop of hair draped over his eyes like a set of curtains as he continued to ogle the screen in his lap.

Meridia glanced around the room, and everything else seemed solid. The assortment of action figures posing on the shelf above his desk, the gaming temple he worshipped for hours at a time, they all appeared real, albeit iridescent under the mysterious light. This felt unlike any of her previous visions. A window into the past, perhaps, which meant Meridia was just a hapless passenger along for the ride.

"AARGH!"

A bloodcurdling scream snatched Meridia from her trance with a start as a synthesized cacophony of piercing cries whistled violently past her ears from somewhere downstairs.

Zach jumped in unison at the distorted sound springing to his feet in panic, and Meridia realized it was all part of the augmented reality she was now immersed in. She saw the look of fear in his eyes as he hesitated, caught in flux, as the crash and clatter of a scuffle broke out downstairs.

"Aargh!" Another muffled cry followed, filtering its way upstairs.

This time it was a man's, lower in pitch. It had the same clunky electronic tenor as the previous scream, as if it was coming from a glitchy sound system.

Silence ensued.

A dreadful, deafening silence that spelled the end for both Zach's parents and Meridia felt helpless. She wept again as she watched Zach quiver on the spot, eyes wide and gripped by indecision. Was she about to witness her best friend's murder?

"*THUMP! THUMP! THUMP!*"

The killer marched up the stairs behind her. A slow, triumphant march toward their next would-be victim.

"RUN!" Meridia turned and screeched at Zach, but it was no use.

He continued to dither, his head in a spin, as he desperately searched for somewhere to hide.

"*THUMP! THUMP! THUMP!*"

The killer continued, closer now, and Meridia glanced over her shoulder to catch a glimpse of his face. The murky figure loomed menacingly at the top of the stairs, slowly turning toward her. A shadow, in the shape of a man, or so she thought, but beyond that she couldn't tell. It reminded her of the horsemen at Crooked House, only this was human in form.

A faceless silhouette, flickering and glitching as it drew ever closer. Squinting and straining, Meridia tried to peer beyond its gloomy veil, and for a moment she thought she saw the darkness conspire to form a wry smile, but in an instant, it was gone.

Heart in her mouth, she turned to face the room again, half expecting to find Zach still faltering next to his bed; a sitting duck. To her surprise, he was nowhere to be seen.

"*Tap...Tap...Tap...*"

The window was now wide open, and the heavy navy-blue curtain rattled against the wall as it frolicked in the gentle breeze blowing into the room. In his rush to hide, Zach dropped his phone on the floor. A shiny black beacon in a sea of sky-blue carpet, just waiting to be seen.

Meridia gasped when she noticed his trembling hand reach out for it from beneath the bed, then quickly reconsidered and withdrew.

"No! Not there!" She pleaded. "You idiot! That's the first place he'll look!"

The killer was upon them now, and she sensed a draft

as he silently drifted past her in the doorway. With it, she noticed a sudden burst of another odour, but it wasn't Zach's.

It vaguely reminded her of Sunday morning cleaning duty with her mum, but the familiar aroma eluded her before she could place it.

The killer marched past her and across the room, stopping at the open window. All Meridia thought about was how scared and alone Zach must have felt hiding under his bed.

Why didn't she see this coming? Was the witch simply a distraction? A sacrificial pawn to allow someone else to get to Zach?

She forced herself to face the killer as he turned back toward the room and could feel the rage coursing through his abstruse frame. Although bathed in light, he remained dark and ambiguous, as if he was blocking her power with one of his own.

"Who are you?!" She breathed, and the killer rushed at her as if he heard her voice.

Meridia gasped as another wave of electricity rippled through her body, gluing her to the floor, as the sinister assassin stood toe-to-toe with her.

Paralyzed by an invisible force, she tried with all her might to recoil as the strange lemony stench returned, this time stinging her nostrils. Then he spoke.

"*I know you're in here...watching.*" His voice was deep and distorted like a cliched slasher, and it sent a cold, sharp shiver up her spine.

"*Your time will come, seer.*"

For a moment she thought she saw a sneer deep within the shade of where his face should have been, and then he lunged towards her at speed. Meridia flinched, hard this time, jarring herself free from the virtual prison of her belated gift.

All light faded as the room returned to its natural gloomy state and the killer, along with any answers she hoped to glean, vanished without a trace.

4

THE MOMENT PETER STEPPED FOOT INSIDE THE treatment room, the automatic lights dazzled him. Four bleached walls and a slender metal cabinet on wheels were waiting for him when his eyes adjusted, but there was no hospital gurney, and no Father Alexander.

Taken aback by the priest's disappearance, Peter massaged his stubble whilst pondering his next move. He knew it was perfectly normal for a patient to be transferred from one part of the hospital to another when needing treatment, but in his experience, whenever that happened, the friends or relatives waiting were always informed. On top of that, as far as he knew, there was only one corridor linking the minor injuries ward to the main hospital and he would've noticed if a bed was wheeled out.

"CLICK!"

Peter jumped as the soft-close door snapped shut in his wake, sealing him inside. Unsure how much time he had before the receptionist returned, he quickly made his way to the cabinet on the far side of the room.

Crouching on one knee, he opened the solitary drawer

and riffled through its contents. In there he found a dead smart phone, an old leather-bound prayer book, a small crucifix, and a shiny bunch of keys. Peter instinctively pocketed the keys, assuming they would grant access to the church.

Given the magnitude of what they were up against, he figured St Peter's could provide them with a place to lie low while they came up with a plan. As his own house and Meridia's were already compromised, he didn't want to involve any more parents for fear of putting them in harm's way.

He still couldn't reconcile with the sheer number of people involved with the cult and did not know who else they could trust going forward.

Satisfied he learned all he could from an empty room, Peter quietly closed the cabinet and made his way back to the exit. Peering through a gap in the door, he noticed the corridor was still empty, so he seized his chance and slipped back out.

The stillness of the ward bothered him. With a sizeable number of patients still waiting to be seen, he expected there to be more staff working behind the scenes, but this felt more like a mortuary than a hospital.

Up ahead, the remnants of daylight leaked through the window blinds, decking the floor in washed-out stripes. There were a couple of desks, both unattended and swamped in paperwork, reminding him of his days at university. Insipid but functional, they had all the hallmarks of a hospital short on money.

Maybe it was why they were so understaffed?

Checking the coast was still clear behind him, Peter ventured on to find out where everyone was. When he reached the open plan office at the end of the corridor, he found it somewhere between empty and abandoned. Home to three desks crammed in one half with a printer and medical cabinet taking up the other, the room was only fractionally wider than the hall he just tiptoed down.

The farthest end had wall-to-wall windows, and beyond it lay a fenced plot of grass backing onto the road leading into the carpark. There were no other exits or access points as he had suspected, which begged the question.

How did they move Father Alexander without him or Izzy noticing? Peter sensed the butterflies in his stomach coagulate and form a knot.

This was quickly becoming more than a fishing expedition, and he was now concerned something sinister might have happened to the injured priest. There was a disconcerting energy to the room's composition that told its own story, and Peter wondered if everyone was called away to tend to an emergency.

Chairs were left haphazardly adrift from their desks, while unfinished cups of coffee sat idly watching the trio of screensavers weave vibrant geometric patterns on repeat.

"Hello?" Peter called out timidly to break the tension.

"Get a grip Peter!" He grumbled, trying to quieten his nagging paranoia.

He closed his eyes and took in a deep breath. The suffocating, citrusy aroma stifled every inch of the hospital, and made his throat tingle as he swallowed another mouthful before exhaling.

"Ahh!" As soon as he opened his eyes, Peter gasped in horror.

There, bold as brass and staring straight at him from the other side of the window, was a disciple of the cult. The shock contrast of his dark and ominous presence against the room's blanched interior was jarring and sent Peter spiralling headfirst into total panic.

Stumbling backwards, Peter's heart furiously pounded against the inside of his chest as if it were trying to break out.

"Thump thump! Thump thump! Thump thump!"

Each frenzied heartbeat was deafening, ringing in his ears, as his body sounded the alarm and readied itself for a fight.

Outside, his face shrouded in darkness, the tall and powerfully built man continued to ogle Peter like an obstinate predator stalking its prey. Wearing a heavy, dark brown cloak that stopped just short of his ankles, the hooded tormenter remained stock-still. His arms flexed at either side, fixed by rage.

Dry mouthed and gripped by fear, Peter took another faltering step back and collided with something solid.

"Gotcha!" Peter jumped at the stranger's voice behind him and spun round, fists clenched and ready to swing.

"Woah! Easy there Rocky. I didn't mean to make you jump...I was just kidding around." Nurse Grady held his hands up as a sign of surrender.

His bright blue eyes sparkled beneath the halogen lights, and he was grinning from ear-to-ear. Peter glanced back at the window, but the disciple had vanished.

"You're Father Alexander's friend, aren't you?" Grady continued as Peter turned his attention back to the room.

He still felt the cortisol coursing through his veins, and it took a while to register what the young nurse was saying.

Nurse Grady, or Silas as he insisted on Peter calling him, was one of the first to see Father Alexander when they arrived. He was decidedly average looking in his dreary blue scrubs, average height, average build.

What he lacked in his physical presence, he more than made up for in gusto. Bordering on patronizing, his unwavering enthusiasm really grated with Peter when they first met, and he was glad to see the back of him when Father Alexander was eventually wheeled away on a gurney.

"I've been looking for you. I have an update." Silas continued, oblivious to the weird energy Peter was giving off.

He self-consciously dabbed his slicked, jet-black hair before getting to his point.

"Your friend went into surgery. His wrist was pretty banged up and needs a couple of pins inserting. It's a routine procedure and shouldn't take more than a couple of hours. We can call you when he's ready to go home?"

"Thanks, nur...er...Silas. I was beginning to worry..." Peter trailed off, still preoccupied with the disciple lurking outside.

His mind scrambled to figure out why the fanatic was at the hospital. Did the cult follow them all the way there?

"Izzy!" He blurted, and then brushed past Silas in his rush to get to her before anyone else did.

"You know you look a little tired and beat up yourself, Mr Higginsworth." Silas called after him as he left. "Might want to get some rest while you still can..."

There was a hint of menace in his parting remark, and it was enough to make Peter pause and glance back once he reached the waiting room door.

Silas was watching him intently. Arms folded across his chest and still grinning, he seemed more intimidating than he was up close.

The harsh fluorescent lighting shone down from above, exposing an athletic frame beneath his scrubs, and transformed the soft contours of his face into something altogether sinister. Silas's electric blue eyes twinkled eerily beneath the dark shadow cast by his brow, while his toothy grin slinked into a sneer.

He appeared more vampire than human as he continued to eyeball Peter from afar and an icy chill tickled Peter's spine as he tried to reassure himself it was just a trick of the light. Turning his back on Silas, he pushed his way out through the exit. He needed to find Izzy and get the hell out of there.

"Bang!"

The heavy door slammed shut behind him, stirring everyone from their collective trance. As he surveyed the sea of startled patients, he noticed there were no changes to their ranks since his absence. The same assortment of glum faces sat scattered around the room like hired extras on a reality tv show.

Peter sensed their eyes on him as he searched for Izzy amongst the crowd, but she was nowhere to be seen. A festering feeling of dread rose from the pit of his stomach as he wrestled with the possibility something bad happened whilst he was busy playing detective. Trembling and wracked with guilt, he teetered over to where he left her.

"No..." He shuttered at the busted remnants of her half-eaten granola bar that now lay strewn across the floor.

One thing he knew he could always rely on was Izzy's compliance. There was no way she would have wandered off without telling him first, and no way she would have left such a mess on the floor.

Peter sensed the room begin to swirl and spin around him as the burgeoning reality swept him up in a whirlwind of panic.

The cult abducted Izzy right from under his nose.

5

Zach lay face down on the floor, eyes clenched and body trembling. He was that way for hours, frozen in absolute terror. Sweat drenched his back, and every muscle screamed at him to let go, but he couldn't, even if he wanted to. His limbs were completely seized up, numb from exertion, but that wasn't the reason he couldn't move.

He knew if he moved, his entire world would collapse and fall apart. If he just held on a little longer, until the warm mess he made in his boxers was closer to drying and the smell of wee dissipated, then he might find the courage to face what was waiting for him.

"Zach...please Zach..." Meridia was whispering his name for a few minutes now, but he couldn't bring himself to look at her. He didn't want anyone to see him like this, least of all her.

Silent tears of heartache relentlessly rolled down his freckled cheeks, and he wondered if his eyes would ever heal. He could still hear the screams from downstairs echoing in his mind.

First his parents' agony, and then his brother's despair.

He would never forget those sounds as long as he lived, nor would he forget the harrowing sensation of sailing so close to the jaws of death.

"Please, Zach...you can't stay under there forever. I'm here now. Please come out..." Meridia continued to plead with him, and Zach's hand quivered in contemplation.

"That's it..." she softly urged. "It's time Zach. We need to get the others and get out of here..."

She was right, of course. He couldn't spend the rest of his life cowering in the crawl space beneath his bed. Propped up on his elbows, Zach winced as he tried to lower himself to slither out from under his mattress, but the pain of all the pent up trauma tore its way through his biceps and he collapsed in a heap. He closed his eyes, exhausted.

All he wanted to do was lay there and pretend this was all a bad dream. A tiny part of him, somewhere deep within, still desperately clung to the hope that might be the case, like a battered piece of driftwood floating blindly downstream.

"M...what are you doing down there?" Emily's voice snapped him out of his fantasy and forced him back into his fortress of solitude.

"Shh!" Eyes closed once more, he sensed Meridia's frustration having been so close to coaxing him out.

"It's ok...I...I'm coming..." He stuttered.

They were the first words he had uttered in what felt like forever, and the sound of his voice seemed alien to him. Broken like his heart. However, true to his word, he wriggled his way out like a beached seal.

"Oh, you poor thing..." Emily made a fuss as he continued to writhe on the floor.

"Give him some space, mum..." Face firmly pressed to

the carpet, he heard Meridia gently fending her mum off somewhere overhead.

"Why don't you go check on the others for a sec, and we'll meet you down there?" Zach paused for a moment as he waited for Emily's response, but the next voice he heard was Meridia's again.

"Let's get you up and out of those clothes, your back looks soaked through." As he scrambled to his feet, he was instantly greeted with an enormous bear-hug.

"I was so scared I lost you," Meridia's voice trembled in his ear as she smothered him in her green winter coat.

The subtle scent of lemon and mint filled his nose, and he savoured every delicate note.

"I'm so sorry." She finally broke. "I...I couldn't save them..."

Zach's knees buckled under the weight of her words as the slender shred of hope he was holding onto finally snapped irrevocably. As he collapsed to the floor, and everything around him faded, his thoughts were flooded by vivid memories from a happy childhood that felt like a lifetime ago.

Walks along the beach eating ice-cream and movie nights sandwiched on the sofa sharing pizza. Bike rides in the park and backyard ball games all weaved their way through his mind like a technicolour tapestry of his life. He heard every laugh, sensed every loving touch, until his heart could take no more.

His parents were gone, and his world shattered, Zach finally succumbed to his overwhelming grief and passed out.

6

Gasping for breath, Izzy stopped sprinting for a moment to get her bearings. Hunched over with both hands on her knees, she wrestled to regain control of her breathing and snuff out the fire that was raging inside her lungs.

The stench of hospital disinfectant wasn't exactly helping matters, and for a moment, she teetered on the brink of hyperventilating. Eyes watering and wheezing, she glanced around for a signpost, but all she found was a solitary pink line painted on the floor, which meant she was headed towards the Oncology department.

The hospital was unusually quiet, and apart from the odd elderly wandering the halls, she didn't cross paths with anyone of note, which was a godsend given what she'd just left behind.

At first, she thought she imagined him, but when the mysterious hooded figure skulked past a second waiting room window, she knew the cult somehow caught up with them. Panicking, she fled in search of Peter, only to realize she had no clue where he snuck off to.

With no phone signal to call him, she instinctively ventured deeper into the hospital, but with each empty corridor she raced past, the fear she may already be too late grew harder and harder to ignore. The hospital itself wasn't too difficult to navigate.

Aside from the tacked-on minor injuries ward, it followed a simple grid system, but with five stories, there was too much ground to cover for one person, which made Peter the proverbial needle in a concrete haystack.

"Think Izzy!" she grunted, cuffing the sweat from her forehead.

Glancing back down the hall towards the main entrance, she wondered if she might have been a bit too eager to bolt, but there were only two doors in the room she was sitting in, and one of them was marked 'Staff Only'.

Izzy groaned, rolling her eyes as the penny dropped. Taking in another big lungful of sterilized air, she marched back in the direction she'd just come from.

Each intersecting corridor on the ground floor of Chase Side featured heavy, navy-blue double doors that were power assisted. Whilst they made it hard for Izzy to see more than fifty yards in front of her, they provided cover, allowing her to suss out each department before entering.

When she arrived at the doors of the imaging department, she saw Peter racing towards her from the other end of the corridor and felt a tremendous wave of relief.

"Peter!" she blurted, barging her way through the slow-moving door.

"Thank god! I thought something happened to you!" He began, meeting her half-way. "We need to get to the taxi rank and get to the others. They're here Izzy. The Children of the Shadows are here."

"I saw one...at the window. That's when I ran and came looking for you. But what about Father Alexander? We can't just leave him." Izzy could see the conflict raging behind Peter's bright green eyes as he paused a moment.

"He's in surgery for a couple of hours. That gives us time to find the others and come back for him with a plan. We have no idea what's going on beyond these walls. There could be a hundred disciples waiting for us outside, or the disciple you and I saw, might just be someone acting alone. The best thing we can do...no, the only thing we can do is fall back and regroup. Despite my misgivings about this place, I can't imagine they are going to storm the hospital. It's too exposed, too public. We need to find the others and come back better prepared. It's our only option." Izzy couldn't argue with Peter's logic, so nodded in agreement.

"I saw a sign for the carpark two doors back." She gestured over her shoulder, half-turning to look at the door, but what she saw made her blood run cold.

A tall, dark shadow suffocated the door's windowpane, and it didn't take her or Peter long to recognize the familiar brown cloak that was the cause.

"This way Izzy. We'll have to go out through the front..." Peter trailed off when he spotted a second disciple blocking the other end of the passage.

They were trapped.

"Go!" He whispered, gesturing subtly toward the imaging department to their left. "We have to hope there's another way out down there. Now run, and I'll be right behind you."

Izzy didn't need telling twice and raced off down the only path available to them. True to his word, Peter was hot on her heels.

"*Bang bang!*"

The ominous clatter of heavy doors bashing against the corridor walls echoed behind her as the disciples took up chase.

The hunt was on.

7

Peter tried desperately to avoid tripping over Izzy's flailing legs as they both galloped down the corridor in search of a way out. Glancing over his shoulder, their rear view remained empty, and he wondered if they should stop and take stock of their surroundings.

He felt the words forming on the tip of his tongue when the two disciples turned the corner in unison and resumed stalking them. Their dark cloaks ebbed and flowed weightlessly behind them as they swept down the corridor like phantom apparitions. Beneath their ghostly exterior, their movement was robotic as they marched onwards like relentless killers in a B-movie slasher.

As brisk as they were, they were clearly losing ground, even at Izzy's sluggish pace, yet the disciples seemed unperturbed. Their determined, yet extremely measured approach raised an alarm bell in Peter's mind as he contemplated the possibility they knew something he didn't.

"WAIT!" Izzy interrupted his train of thought and slammed on the brakes, causing Peter to bundle into her.

"A fire exit!" She pointed. "But I think it might have an alarm."

Peter wasted no time deliberating and gave the metal panic bar a firm shove. The door immediately gave way to the cold winter air, and they both poured out onto the gravel forecourt beyond.

"Where are we?" Izzy's eyes bulged as her tortoiseshell glasses fogged up in response to the sudden drop in temperature. Heavy rain clouds gathered overhead, smothering whatever remained of the afternoon light and ushering in nightfall.

The icy chill was welcome relief from Chase Side's close corridors, and within a matter of seconds Peter could smell the faint earthy aroma of car engines.

"This way, Izz!" He hurried her away from the door and into the direction of a narrow footpath he spotted up ahead.

"Scrunch! Scrunch!"

The gravel was like quicksand, slowing them down as they traipsed and trudged their way onward, but Peter knew they had to break free from the shadow of the building's imposing structure if they were to see a way out.

"W-which way?!" Izzy stammered once they reached the pavement.

There was still no sign of the disciples, so Peter hesitated as he weighed up their options. With only one of two ways to go, he had no choice but to aim for the front of the hospital. Regardless of who or what might be waiting for them there, the alternative risked running into a dead end.

"That way!" Peter nudged Izzy onward as he glanced back at the open fire exit.

Still nothing. A smattering of pale-yellow streetlights perforated the gloom as they rushed along the path, and it didn't take long for the dreary roadside to emerge in the distance. The path, framed by the thorny remains of knee-high hedges, was wide and looping, straying away from the hospital at first, only to loop back the closer they got to the building's edge.

"We're almost there, Izz." Peter assured, overtaking her for protection as they reached the final stretch.

Chase side's exterior was a hotchpotch of uninspiring upgrades, with each lazy extension diminishing the hospital's overall aesthetic. The main wards they had narrowly escaped from, were all crammed into a five-storey cube that looked as if it was built in the seventies using nothing but Lego.

Wall to wall glass held together by red brickwork was a valiant attempt to match the original building's colour, if nothing else. Now serving as an oversized lobby, the oldest and more grandiose part of the hospital provided a nice focal point from the roadside and set a lofty expectation the more modern components failed to live up to.

With its perfectly pitched roofs and quaint window frames, it carried all the hallmarks of an architect who took great pride in their work, cutting a distinguished shape amongst the banal suburban landscape.

Then came the minor injury unit. Resembling a giant portacabin, its bright white paintwork not only stuck out like a sore thumb but also created a blind corner as it sat further forward than any other building. Slowing to a walk, Peter shielded Izzy as they gave the corner a wide berth.

There was a good chance the disciples doubled back and were lying in wait for them somewhere around the bend, ready to pounce. Until now, he assumed the Children of the Shadows were regular human beings, devoted lackies who were the eyes and ears of Crooked House and its malignant undertaking. However, now faced with the daunting prospect of confronting them, he wasn't so sure.

The only thing he knew was if they were going to make it to the taxi rank, they needed to get to the opposite side of the building, past A&E and beyond the ambulance bay.

"Stay close, Izz...just be ready to run the rest of the way." Peter reached into his jean pocket and pulled out a crumpled twenty-pound note.

"Here, take this in case you have to go on without me. That will cover the fare to Kane's house, and I'll meet you there as soon as I'm able."

"What do you mean? Without you?!" There was a twinge of panic in Izzy's voice.

"They could be waiting for us around this corner. If they are, then I'll buy you enough time to get away. I'm hoping it won't come to that, but if it does, you need to promise me you'll run to the nearest taxi and not look back."

"But..."

"I mean it, Izz. Promise." Peter stood firm as Izzy reluctantly accepted the money and huddled closer behind him.

Tiptoeing to the corner, Peter kept Izzy at arm's length to his rear while he cautiously peered around the edge of the architectural eyesore. Squinting, he could only make out a fraction of the easy access ramp leading into the main reception, but from what he could tell, the coast was clear. Too clear, in fact.

Most hospitals had a steady stream of patients and loved ones either ambling about or sneaking the odd cigarette break, but Chase Side was abnormally quiet ever since they arrived. Something was gravely awry with this place, and his gut was telling him it went way beyond a couple of fanatics running around in fancy dress.

A chilly breeze corkscrewed around him, and he could feel the dampness in the air as it gently brushed against his cheeks. Realizing how exposed they were, he decided it was time to make a run for it.

Behind him, he sensed Izzy's anxiety bubbling to the surface as she hopped nervously from one foot to the other like someone in desperate need of the toilet.

"Tap tap...tap tap."

Her incessant bouncing up and down cranked up the tension like a ticking clock, counting down every second it took for Peter to find the courage to move.

"On three Izzy." He whispered. "Just run as fast as you can. I won't let anything happen to you. I swear."

His words helped stoke the fire in his belly and so he started the count.

"One..."

"Two..."

"Three!"

8

Izzy's legs turned to jelly as Peter broke cover and took the corner wide. She'd never seen this side of him before, fists clenched and ready for war. He was an imposing figure, towering over most, but athletic rather than stocky.

She hesitated a moment, still clutching the corner of the building as she watched and waited while Peter ventured out ahead of her. He only took a few paces when he stopped, dumfounded.

"Quickly Izz. There's no one here..." Feeling the strength return to her legs, she made a run for it and they both charged across the face of Chase Side Hospital, uncontested.

Heavy drops of rain splashed against her glasses as she ran, muddying her view, and the aroma of petrichor and petrol fumes began flooding her lungs as she got closer to the ambulance bay.

Peering over her glasses, she saw the hospital was completely desolate, as if it was long abandoned. There were no lights permeating through its narrow window frames, and its usual bright, red-bricked veneer was now dull and dingy under the heavy onslaught of rain.

"Where is everyone?" she exclaimed, half to herself.

"Keep moving, Izz. We're almost there." Peter uttered back, and he was right.

Within a matter of seconds, they reached the vibrant red canopy of the emergency ward and slowed to a stop. Wiping away the rain from her glasses, Izzy perched them back on her nose and took a quick glance around.

The emergency ward was a beacon of light in the gloom. A wall of glass with two large double electric doors at its centre which were fixed wide open. Neon-red signage hung over every windowpane like a warning, but inside all appeared to be normal.

A slew of patients sat scattered around the waiting room while a young couple stood patiently in front of yet another unoccupied reception desk. It was a window into the waking world, full of ordinary people going about their ordinary lives while Izzy and Peter stood marooned in a murky nightmare outside.

"This way, Izz..." Peter snapped her out of her inertia, gesturing to an assortment of vacant ambulances to their left.

Neatly parked under an illuminated glass shelter. The fluorescent yellow paintwork gave off an eerie supernatural glow beneath the lights, and Izzy felt another surge of apprehension as she watched Peter round the back of the first ambulance and disappear.

"Wait!" she gasped, hurrying to catch up.

Peter had come to another stop when she reached him. The torrent of rain was deafening as it rattled the glass roof above them, making it hard to hear anything. Crouching low, Peter craned his neck from side to side to see between the undercarriage and the tarmac.

The second row of vehicles were tightly parked against the hospital wall, bumper to bumper, forcing them to navigate the rest of the bay like a maze. Izzy waited anxiously until he gave her the thumbs up, and they both stealthily crept along to the next ambulance in line.

Once again, Peter stooped low to check underneath before waving Izzy forward. The air was thick with tension as they cautiously edged their way around the bay, one vehicle at a time, never quite knowing what might lurk around the next corner.

Overhead, the downpour had intensified, making it difficult to hear her own thoughts, but then it suddenly dawned on her. They were both preoccupied navigating the path ahead that neither of them thought to look over their shoulder.

A searing wave of warm sticky panic washed over Izzy, leaving her queasy and weak at the knees as she clung to the side of the cold hulking ambulance they were both hiding behind.

She wanted desperately to grab Peter by the sleeve and have him look for her, but her trembling hands wouldn't move. Glued to the icy metal wall at her back, she was forced to watch in silence as he continued to creep away.

The further Peter got, the higher Izzy's shoulders bunched around her ears as she imagined the hooded maniac's hands creeping around her throat. Dry-mouthed and gripped by a newfound sense of dread, she held her breath and slowly turned to check behind them.

"Phew..." Her entire body wilted when she found there was no one there.

Taking another gulp of air to steady her nerves, she

scuttled to catch up with Peter, wobbling all the way on quivering legs. When they reached the end of the fourth ambulance, it signalled the end of the line, so they shuffled their way to its rear so Peter could peek around the corner.

"I can see a taxi up ahead," he whispered. "Still no sign of our friends though."

Izzy wanted to believe the sense of relief as it began knocking at her door, but she knew deep down this was far too easy. Why would the cult members risk being seen in public only to retreat at the first opportunity? They didn't even put up much of a chase. As Izzy knew full well, she wasn't a natural sprinter.

"What if it's a trap?" She asked, as they continued to wait in the wings.

"Only one way to find out now, I suppose." Peter concluded and tentatively stepped out into the open.

The rain ricocheted off the asphalt beyond the shelter as Izzy reluctantly made her way to the edge of the ambulance, still lacking the confidence to break cover completely. She too could see the yellow taxi waiting enticingly in the centre of the hospital's open plan carpark.

It had to be a trap. There was no way an organization that had been operating in the shadows for centuries could be so lax.

"Let's go Izz. Be sure to keep your eyes peeled. First sign of trouble, you run to that taxi." With that, he set off into the pounding rain, slowly at first, his head on a swivel, looking for any imminent threat.

"*Click!*"

For a second Izzy thought she heard something else hiding within the relentless rain clattering above. Using that as her cue to follow Peter, she took her first step forward, and that was when she felt an arm coil around her from behind.

Its grip was vice-like, pinning both arms to her sides. The cloth followed, clamping her mouth shut and covering her nose before she could scream. It was a sweet, pleasant smell she could neither resist nor escape.

Within a matter of seconds, her shoulders relaxed and her limbs fell limp. Eyes heavy, Izzy succumbed to her captor and everything around her faded to black.

9

"It's ok Izz, we can make it now if we move qui…" Peter turned back to where Izzy was standing and felt the colour drain from his face. She was gone!

"Izzy?!… Izzy?!" He yelled.

The ice-cold rain lashed at his face, clouding his vision as he rushed back under the shelter of the ambulance bay. His head was pounding, a cocktail of stress and saturation as he frantically retraced his steps in search of Izzy. He only turned his back for a matter of seconds, and yet she somehow vanished into thin air.

"Izzy?!" He called once more in desperation, checking underneath the first ambulance in case she was hiding. Nothing.

How could he have lost her? There had been no one around. He made sure of it, and yet somehow, someone snatched her right from under his nose.

"*Click!*"

Peter spun around towards the rear of the ambulance just as its back door squeaked open. A rush of adrenaline sent his heart racing as a disciple skulked into view, slow and deliberate, corrupting the yellow and grey haze with his menacing silhouette. Peter held his ground for a moment, sizing him up.

Hidden beneath the heavy brown robes of his cloak, it was difficult to get an accurate measure of the man, but Peter had a significant height and reach advantage in the event of a fight.

On top of that, he also had some training under his belt. A lifelong boxing fan, he spent the best part of a year sparring in his local gym to stay in shape, working on his strength, reflexes and stamina.

Of course, he never hit more than a pad or a bag until now, but he was reliably informed he possessed enough speed and power to prove a handful in the ring if he ever chose to pursue the sport further. Based on the disciple's aggressive stance, Peter guessed he was about to find out what truth there was in his trainer's claims.

"Who are you?" Peter demanded, trying his best to be heard over the beating rain.

"What have you done with the girl?" The disciple remained motionless, his face shrouded in darkness beneath the shadow of his hood.

Whoever it was hiding under the ghoulish façade, they bore an unsettling air of menace as he defiantly stared Peter down in silence. Caught in an ominous deadlock, Peter watched the breeze coil around his mysterious adversary, causing his inky robes to flap and hiss as if the wind stirred something evil within them.

"*Bang!*"

With a flick of his arm, he closed the ambulance door and took a step forward. As he approached, Peter noticed the man's shoulders rise and fall beneath his cloak as if he was huffing. He was nervous.

"*Whirr click click...vroom!*"

Suddenly, the ambulance started up beside them both.

"Izzy!" Fists clenched and raised around his chin, Peter marched towards the disciple, and that was when he saw the knife.

It was a short blade, jagged and rusty, like an ancient relic from a museum.

Peter broke out in a hot sweat as his fight-or-flight response kicked in, but he refused to waver. He knew he had to hurry if he was to stop the ambulance from getting away. Now was not the time for second guessing himself, he had to be assured.

The moment he stepped within range, Peter bounced on his toes, flustering his opponent. His assailant froze for a moment, taken aback by Peter's unflinching approach.

In a moment of panic, the disciple made a sudden lunge and wildly thrust his knife towards Peter's chest, but it was telegraphed and lacked any genuine conviction. Peter instinctively sidestepped to his left and unloaded with a solid left jab to the side of the disciple's head.

"*Thump!*"

He felt his knuckles connect flush with the soft tissue of the man's temple and watched him wobble on his feet. It was a peach of a shot, dazing his opponent and giving Peter enough time to plant his feet and wind up for his next punch. He let fly with a right hook which landed firmly in the centre of the stunned disciple's hood.

"*Crack!*"

Peter felt the man's nose break on impact and his knife went clattering to the tarmac. Another sharp, hard jab to the side of the head finished the job and sent the disciple crashing into the side of the ambulance, speckling it with blood on his way down to the ground.

High on adrenaline now, Peter left the man on all fours and raced to the back door of the vehicle. Flinging it open, he found Izzy unconscious on a stretcher, with another unsuspecting disciple behind the wheel ahead of her.

"Izzy!" Peter cried, scooping her up from the gurney and whisking her out of the ambulance.

"*Click!*"

He heard the driver's door open over his shoulder, but Peter wasn't about to risk another fight, so he raced off toward the carpark. Izzy bounced and flapped around in his arms as he fled through the pouring rain, adrenaline still pumping while his long legs ate up the ground between him and the taxi.

The cold air nipped at his throat, stinging his lungs as Peter fought to catch his breath following his violent encounter. Lucky for him, Izzy weighed next to nothing, and in a matter of seconds he arrived at the window of the yellow A1 cab.

"I...*gasp*...I need to get to 36 Forest Road right away! It's an emergency!" Peter's sudden arrival startled the middle-aged man behind the wheel as if he was dozing.

Before he replied, Peter already propped Izzy up in the passenger seat behind him and was busy fastening her seatbelt.

"Er...Is she ok?" The driver asked, checking his rearview.

"*Click!*"

Peter closed the door, then hurried around to the other side to join her in the back. There was no sign of either disciple, or anyone else for that matter, but Peter wasn't about to relax now. He subtly checked Izzy's pulse before replying to the cab driver.

"Yes, she's fine. I just need to get her home...it's been a

very long day." Fastening himself in, Peter waved a damp twenty-pound note between the two front seats.

"Hopefully that will cover it?" The driver paused before taking the money and nodded back in the mirror.

"We really need to get a move on, though. Please."

The driver started the ignition while Peter arched and craned his neck in search of any unwanted followers, but the disciples were still nowhere to be seen. Slowly pulling away, Peter kept watch all the way down the snaking slip road that led back to the streets of Shawbrook.

As they passed the bay, he saw the ambulance he rescued Izzy from, but its doors were now closed and there was no trace of the two men in hoods. Allowing himself to let go of the tension he was carrying in his neck and shoulders, Peter slumped back into his polyester seat and let out a tremendous sigh of relief.

Outside, the rain continued to rattle against the windscreen as they weaved their way free of the hospital grounds and made their way to Kane's house. Closing his eyes for a moment, Peter breathed in the smell of fresh pine courtesy of the green, tree-shaped air freshener tied to the rear-view mirror.

As he gathered his thoughts, he noticed a light throbbing pain coming from two of the knuckles on his right hand and wondered who's nose he broke.

For whatever reason, their assailants wanted to take Izzy alive. This also puzzled him. Was he so preoccupied with protecting Zach that he missed something?

Whatever their motives, he only hoped the Children of the Shadows didn't find the others before he did.

10

Silas Grady's blood boiled as he stood with his nose pressed against the window of the insipid monochrome office on the hospital's fourth floor. Fists clenched, he watched the yellow taxi exit through the carpark barrier and then disappear out of sight.

"Fuck!" he spat through gritted teeth, steaming up the glass, unable to contain his thirst for blood after watching his brethren's painful incompetence play out below him.

Shifting his focus from the depressing forecourt to his own reflection, Silas glimpsed the contemptuous sneer smeared across the bony contours of his washed-out face. It was a look that was often likened to a vampire over the years.

His pasty white skin and sparkling blue eyes made for an unsettling spectacle under the right lighting, particularly when taking his jet-black hair into account. The sight of his clear disdain only poured more gasoline on the fire raging within him.

"Idiots!" he fumed.

All they had to do was kill the teacher and grab the girl.

How hard can it be? It was virtually two against one. Silas knew he should have done it himself. He even told his master as much. He dedicated his entire life to becoming the ultimate killing machine, so why was he now pushed aside in favour of a pair of untrained idiots?

Ok, he might not have spared the girl, but that was neither here nor there. You can't make an omelette without breaking a few eggs. Besides, what use was she, anyway? What use were any of them beside the boy?

Spiralling into rage, he fantasized about the taxi driver having a sudden change of heart and delivering its precious cargo back to him so he could satisfy his urge to kill.

The teacher was an unexpected dark horse, and not to be taken lightly, but he needed more than a couple of lucky punches to escape Silas with his jugular still intact. Perhaps his master underestimated him?

As for the girl, it was clear she would never be turned. It would make much more sense to cut their losses with that one and hunt her down with the other vermin. Silas took a deep breath and counted to five. His appetite for murder was insatiable, and the longer he was forced to keep up this ridiculous charade, the more he struggled to control it.

It had only been a matter of hours since he butchered the Jacksons, and he was already craving more violence. Sometimes, when he felt suffocated underneath his preposterous nurse's costume and fake smile, his hunger for blood would grow so intense he would draw some of his own, just to take the edge off.

As he waited in the private office on the fourth floor, he felt the skin on his forearm tingling beneath his sleeve, begging for him to make another cut to add to his collection.

He took great pleasure in observing the blade in his hand as it effortlessly cut through his smooth, taut skin. Silas could sit for hours, squeezing a fresh wound and watching the blood trickle slowly down his arm. There was something about its movement and warmth that always soothed him.

The Jacksons were different, however, gushing and spraying the walls with crimson. Still, with all that blood, he wished he could have spilled the boys instead of leaving him trembling under the bed like a coward! Alas, the master had other plans for him.

"*Click!*"

The door behind him opened and two men sheepishly slipped inside. Silas continued to gaze out of the dripping-wet window as they both lowered their hoods. Glancing at their reflection under the light, he saw one was a bloody mess as the other opened his mouth to speak.

"Brother Grady, th..."

"Save your snivelling excuses for the master!" Silas snarled, cutting the disciple off. "I saw the whole shit show!"

"The teacher...he caught us by surprise...he...he was more capable than we thought."

"Capable? *Scoff!* He made you both look like fools!" Silas was relishing scolding them and spun round to look them in the eyes. Both men flinched.

"Haha! Look at you both...the master should have sent me in your place. Two grown men and you couldn't take care of a bookworm and a little girl! Not just any little girl either, brother...your own meddling daughter!" Robert Di Salvo glanced down at the floor in shame as Silas approached both men.

"Don't worry, brother, I know you're not to blame. You did your part." The temperature in the room went up a few notches since the two disciples had entered, and Silas's neck was now flush with anger.

"You have a lot to learn, brother Alman!" He growled, singling the youngster out.

Both men were soaked to the bone, and the smell of their sodden robes tussled with the citrus scented disinfectant that dominated the room. Somewhere in the mix, however, Silas smelled Alman's blood in the air. Slathering his mouth and chin, it didn't take a doctor to realize his nose was badly broken.

Silas guessed the teacher's blow must have struck him squarely in the middle of his face, and his once slender, ski slope nose was now bulbous and bent off-piste. His eyes were already dark and puffy as the bruising forced its way to the surface.

Silas noticed Alman's bottom lip was trembling too as he got closer, and it gave him a kick, seeing him in so much pain. The least he could do was suffer for his incompetence.

"It needs resetting. Bite down on something," Silas sneered. "This is going to smart."

He cupped Alman's face in his hands and pinched his nose between both thumbs.

"Argh!" Alman winced the moment he made contact, and tears began streaming down his face.

"There..."

"*Crack!*"

"There..." With a forceful, short, sharp jerk and a sneer, Silas snapped Alman's nose back into place.

Thick, gloopy blood gushed from both nostrils, glazing his mouth and chin with claret. Licking his lips, Silas watched obsessively as all the colour drained from the boy's cheeks and oozed down his face.

"Now now...don't be a baby..." He snarled, clenching his jaw.

As Alman's legs wilted from the sudden jolt of pain, it

took Silas every ounce of self-control to resist taking a knife to the boy's throat and putting him out of his pathetic misery.

"Stop your snivelling!" he spat. "You're lucky I have somewhere more important to be, otherwise I'd spend the rest of the afternoon slicing up your worthless corpse to see if you actually have a spine."

Alman curbed his whimpering instantly and took a nervous step back towards the office door. Silas circled both men, like a sergeant major dressing down his subordinates.

"Hopefully you won't make such a mess of things next time...if there is a next time, of course." Circling back to face them, Silas bore a hole into Alman's skull with his eyes as he delivered his ominous warning.

He saw the boy was fidgeting awkwardly on the spot as he tried to stifle a shiver scampering up his spine. Once more, Silas felt all control ebb away, seduced by the steady flow of blood oozing down Alman's face and seeping into his robes.

"I suggest you get out of my sight before I change my mind. I must go deal with the priest downstairs. As for you, brother Di Salvo, I suggest you control your daughter before I do!"

II

"Zach! Pizza's here!" Zach blinked his way free from the clutches of the hypnotic blue loading circle spinning at the centre of his TV screen and glanced down at the Xbox controller in his hands. He must have been spacing out again.

"Coming, mum!" Zach hollered back and turned the console off.

Guessing the internet must be on the fritz again, he tucked his chair under his desk and made his way into the hall. Overcome by a strong feeling of déjà vu, he hesitated at the top of the stairs as a gauge sense of foreboding tiptoed through his thoughts, then evaporated before he had a chance to fathom it.

At the bottom of the stairs, a narrow shaft of light extended across the rug, bleaching the soft creamy pile with its lambent rays.

"Why is the front door open?" Zach thought as he continued down.

A gentle breeze drifted in, ruffling his thick brown fringe, and carrying with it the warm, captivating aroma of melted mozzarella and sizzling pepperoni. The familiar, comforting smell swept away any lingering trace of apprehension, and within a matter of seconds he reached the bottom step, excited by the feast that was no doubt waiting for him in the dining room.

As he skipped into the hall, a series of jagged crimson streaks caught his attention, seeping down the glossy white door frame. Stopping him in his tracks, it seemed as if the room was fatally wounded and left to bleed out.

"Mum?" A dry knot of dread tightened in the pit of Zach's throat, desiccating his voice as he croakily called out. Nobody answered.

Edging closer, his pizza-fuelled euphoria was now nothing but a distant memory, as the trepidation that was choking him clambered its way up inside his brain, filling his head with terrible thoughts.

The moment Zach turned the corner and stepped into the living room, a jarring spectacle of violence greeted him, and all his worst fears suddenly came true.

The hollowed carcass of his dad's favourite yellow armchair lay upended. Its innards strewn across the beige carpet like the victim of a vicious axe murderer. Deep red gore stained and smeared the walls above the royal-blue sofa in the far corner, with each scarlet streak punctuated by a bloody handprint that glistened beneath the sepia-toned sunlight pouring in through the broken window.

"MUM! DAD!" Zach cried out, his voice drowning in a sea of anguish as he soaked up every brutal detail.

Sick to his stomach, he stumbled clumsily towards the dining room. A cacophony of agonizing screams came flooding back to him, like distant memories of a past life, as the enticing smell of pizza made way for one of death and decay. It had to be a dream, a terrible nightmare he just needed to wake from, but it was all so vivid, assaulting his senses and overloading them with heartbreak and tragedy.

Zach's wails echoed through the empty house as a torrent of tears streamed down his cheeks. Each inconsolable sob felt like a serrated blade ripping through his chest and clawing at his heart, as his entire body trembled beneath a weight of grief and loss too large for him to carry.

Staggering into the dining room, he could stomach no more and promptly barfed in the doorway, peppering his shoes in vomit. Retching and heaving, he doubled over coughing the rest of his guts up while his family sat on ceremony around the large mahogany table, as if they were part of a macabre art exhibition. His belly empty, Zach cuffed the tears from his eyes and looked up at the grisly arrangement before him.

Both parents sat lifelessly at either end of the table with their throats slashed wide open. Heads flung back at full tilt, they stared vacantly at the ceiling with empty sockets where their eyes once were.

Grisly scarlet sinkholes circled by coagulated blood that streaked halfway down their sunken cheeks. Mouths aghast, they were both dressed in long brown hooded robes that were drenched in their own blood.

The air was thick with a bitter metallic odour as a handful of flies buzzed around their gaping wounds, gorging on their pallid flesh. Between them sat his brother Kane. Head bowed and arms dangling at either side, a long ceremonial knife nailed him to his chair. Driven to the hilt in the centre of his chest, all that was visible was an intricately sculpted bronze handle depicting an angel with an animal's head.

There was a rotten pizza sitting in the middle of the

table. Overrun with flies and maggots, it completed the gruesome staging of a family mealtime. A family Zach now ached to be reunited with.

"Ka..." Zach trailed off as he went into shock.

Cold and clammy, he started shivering as the room spun around him like a twisted merry-go-round of waxen corpses. Three empty husks of everyone he ever loved. As the room continued to spin, an impenetrable fog descended on his brain, rendering him totally inert.

With his senses dampened, every move he attempted seemed heavy and sluggish, as if he was sinking in quicksand. Whilst his body refused to cooperate, his muddied mind whirred like a radio station drifting out of range as he fought to break free from the static devouring all his thoughts. In his daze, he failed to notice the ominous shadow skulking towards him on the ceiling above.

"*Thisssss is all yooour fault, Zach!*" The sinister whispery voice slinked its way up Zach's spine and slithered into his ear.

He was trembling now, unable to stop his teeth from chattering as the temperature plummeted below zero. Quaking and quivering, he grappled with the icy chill and forced his gaze upward.

The horseman swamped the ceiling like a giant octopus, its robes gracefully ebbing and flowing like writhing tentacles as it inched ever closer. Its skeletal face was a malevolent mosaic of corroded bone and teeth like broken glass, savage and razor-sharp as it sneered at him from above.

Eyes black as night, stared him down and deep within them, something beautiful and bright sparkled like flickering stars trapped inside two dusky orbs. Zach clenched his eyes tight the second they made contact. He saw first-hand the hypnotic effect the horseman's deathly gaze could have.

"*How many mooore must die Zach?*" The monster's rasping voice continued, drawing closer with each word.

"*It doesn't haaave tooo be thisss way Zach! Yooou can stop thisss...you can spare yooour friends...*"

Eyes still clenched, Zach could feel the creature's rancid breath tickling his ear, but his legs remained rooted to the spot, paralyzed with fear.

"*Come toooo meee Zach...you cannot escaaape your destiny...*" Zach sobbed as the last of his resolve abandoned him. All he wanted to do was be with his family.

"*Come Zach...before it's tooo late!*"

———

"Zach...Zach! Wake up...c'mon Zach, we need to get you cleaned up and out of here!"

Kane's voice floated into his consciousness on a cloud of confusion and Zach was no longer sure if he was standing or sitting. He was suddenly warm. Too warm, in fact, and wet where he shouldn't be.

Gingerly risking one eye, he squinted through his long lashes and saw a familiar crowd of worried faces looming over him. Kane's was front and centre, riddled with pain and worry.

Then it all came hurtling back to him. Zach jolted awake and sat bolt upright, reaching for his crotch, only to find a blanket preserving his dignity.

For a fleeting moment, he thought his parents might still be there amongst the crowd, alive and well. Then his eyes widened as he gasped.

"They're back! The horsemen are back!"

12

The words made Kane's blood boil and brought a hush down on everyone as they stood piled together in Zach's bedroom. It was almost dark outside now and the motion nightlight had kicked in, bathing everyone in its eerie green glow.

A gentle breeze blew in through the window Meridia opened when Zach fainted, and the earthy smell of rain helped mask the stench of his brother's pee-soaked joggers.

"What do you mean they're back?!" he fumed, cutting through the uneasy silence.

"Did they do this?! I'll kill them! I'll fucking kill them for what they've done!" Emily placed an arm around him, but Kane's rage consumed him, and he shrugged her off. His hands were shaking.

"I saw one...downstairs, with mum and dad...and you." Kane baulked at his brother's claim.

"What do you mean you saw me?!" He was fizzing with anger and frustration. "I wasn't..."

"What did you see?" Meridia interrupted, placing a

soothing hand on top of Zach's and Kane realized he needed to cool it.

Tears began streaming down his brother's cheeks as he sat like a rabbit in the headlights and Kane became aware he wasn't helping matters. Without another word, he swooped in and hugged his little brother with all the strength he had, binding them both together in the hope he could share the load of unbearable loss.

Until now, they didn't have an overly tactile relationship beyond the odd play-fight and occasional teasing, but something told Kane that had to change. Zach needed him.

"I'm so sorry..." Kane whispered in his ear. "I thought I lost you."

He was so wrapped up in his own fury that he lost all sight of how scared and confused his brother must be feeling.

"Are they really gone?" Zach whispered back.

Kane nodded, and both brothers broke down together, wrapped in each other's arms.

"Th...*sniff*...this is all because of me," Zach bawled, and Kane squeezed him tighter.

His arms became a fortress as he gathered his kid brother closer to his chest and allowed Zach to melt into him. Clinging to each other in a sea of tears, neither boy moved as they took comfort in the unspoken strength between them.

"It's not...this is all on them. All of it! Those fucking... things! This is on all of them, and I'm gonna make them pay...I promise." Kane felt his hatred simmer back to the surface, so he pulled away, locking eyes with Zach.

"It's just you and me now. I'm not gonna let anything

happen to you. We're gonna beat those bastards. Together, we're gonna find a way."

"We're all in this together, guys." JJ joined them on the floor, throwing his arms around them both and resting his head in the gap between theirs.

"You're my family too." Meridia joined them, then Emily as Kane battled the urge to break free.

Restless in his rage, he felt suffocated by the act of solidarity when all he wanted to do was lash out at something, anything, just to make the pain stop. He felt beyond broken. Disconnected, and barely able to recognize his own hate-fuelled thoughts, he felt as if the fun-loving Kane of old was now lost irrevocably.

"We need to get out of here. It's not safe." He finally surrendered to the mounting claustrophobia and wriggled free from the pack. "Whatever it was you think you saw, it was just a bad dream...a nightmare."

"But it spoke to me...it was right here in our house!"

"It wasn't!" Kane snapped, losing his cool again before softening his tone.

"Meridia saw what happened...someone was here, but it wasn't a horseman. At least she doesn't think it was. Besides, how would they have done this? It was broad daylight when...when..." Kane couldn't finish his own sentence. "Right now, we need to get our shit together and go."

"Go where?" Zach asked.

"I don't know yet...anywhere but here. We still don't know what's going on at the hospital and none of us can get hold of Peter or Izzy so perhaps we start there...or maybe we go straight to the police, or somewhere public so we can come up with a better plan?" Kane rose to his feet and backed away from everyone; he needed room to breathe.

"Why don't you get cleaned up while I pack some of

our stuff? We're sitting ducks if we stay here. We need to get moving and..."

The sound of a car pulling up outside interrupted Kane's train of thought and he stepped across to the window. A yellow A1 taxi pulled up to the curb beneath the streetlight and Peter clambered out of its back seat, then stepped around the other side to help Izzy out into the road.

"Who is it?!" Meridia probed impatiently.

"It's Peter and Izzy. Izzy looks like she might be hurt! He's half carrying her. We've got to stop them from coming inside!" Kane blurted and made a move for the door, but Emily stopped him.

"We'll go." She whispered. "You boys do what you need to up here while M and I tell them what's happened. C'mon hon."

She ushered Meridia out in front of her and then they both disappeared downstairs to intercept Peter.

"Thanks..." Kane mumbled after them before turning back to Zach and JJ.

"Zach, get a quick wash and change. Leave out another set of clothes you wanna bring with and I'll pack them with mine while you're in there. I don't know if we'll ever be able to come back here once we leave..." Kane's voice broke under the weight of his own words, and his bottom lip quivered uncontrollably.

Composing himself, he sensed the tears rising inside again, blurring his vision as he wrestled to reconcile the burgeoning reality. They lost everything, and yet somehow had to find the strength to go on.

"Sniff...ahem..." He continued, lowering his voice to a crackly whisper to mask the pain.

"You do that, then we'll join the others downstairs and figure out our next move."

13

Gathered in the downstairs hallway, Meridia couldn't believe what she just heard. Still struggling to process the murder of Zach's parents, she now learned someone also attempted to harm Peter and Izzy at the hospital.

It felt as if the walls were closing in around them as the Children of the Shadows tightened their grip on the town of Shawbrook. Since her mum and Peter brought each other up to speed, her head was buzzing with a million different questions.

Perhaps the most perplexing was how Valerie Richards could be an echo at Crooked House if she was still alive in a ward at Chase Side? It made no sense.

Meridia watched intently as the adults continued to debate their next move. The usually unflappable Peter Higginsworth was now fraught with worry, his chiselled face carved into a solemn frown. Her mum still hung on his every word, but not so much as to hold back from sharing her own opinions.

Like an intense game of tennis, they batted the idea of

going to the police back and forth between them, neither knowing for sure how far the deadly cult's influence stretched in their sleepy town.

Given the attacks, Peter urged JJ and Izzy to check on their parents, which they both did. JJ's were out at a local pub enjoying an impromptu date night, whilst Izzy's mum assured her they were both safe and sound at home.

For a moment, Meridia had a surreal out-of-body experience as she observed the activities unfolding around her. It was as if she was part of an elaborate social experiment where everyone was forced to swallow a paranoia pill. Peter and her mum were questioning the integrity of the police, scared that a centuries-old apocalyptic cult somehow compromised them.

Kane and JJ were busy in the kitchen rifling through knife drawers, searching for weapons to exact their revenge with. Zach, fresh from his shower and completely spaced out, was flinching at the slightest noise as if he was a combat-weary soldier battling PTSD.

Meanwhile, Izzy slouched in a chair by the open door, still feeling woozy and shaken from her ordeal. Whilst some of the colour had returned to her cheeks, Meridia saw she was still in shock. Eyes-closed and foot nervously tapping the floor, she appeared deep in thought, no doubt reliving the nightmare she narrowly escaped.

Each time they faced down Crooked House, their situation worsened, and the daunting task ahead of them seemed more and more impossible. Meridia's thoughts drifted back to their first encounter with Zach's echo and his warning about their involvement in an invisible war. None of them understood what he meant back then, but it was becoming clearer with each new confrontation. What other horrors might lurk on the horizon?

The rain paused outside, but the wind had picked up in its absence, softly howling at the door as it tried to force its way inside. Each time the breeze skimmed her cheeks, Meridia caught another subtle whiff of the oddly sweet chemical aroma that she noticed on Izzy when they hugged. Briefly lost in its curious allure, Meridia snapped back to the Jackson's crowded hallway as her mum and Peter finally agreed.

"Ok everyone, this is the plan." He announced, gesturing for the group to gather in.

"Today has been the most terrible of days... unimaginable...but I fear we are not safe here in Shawbrook anymore. We do not know who else may be involved in the cult, and so we cannot afford to rule anyone out, not even the police. I underestimated the Children of the Shadows...I dismissed them as a couple of fanatics trying to resurrect an urban legend, but the truth is they are highly organized, and they have a vast number of members. A group of that size would not come out in the open unless they had some form of protection, which is why we have decided to set up camp at St Peter's church until we can gain a better understanding of our adversaries and their affiliations." Peter jangled Father Alexander's keys so everyone could see.

"The church is like a fortress, so we'll be far safer there. It's also home to a collection of historical documents which might help us. Now I know it may seem crazy not to involve the police considering what's happened here today, but until we know who we can trust, we can't risk involving anyone else."

Meridia glanced around at the worried faces surrounding her and wished she could offer some assurance. Her gift remained more of a curse in her eyes. Never accessible on demand, and never the bearer of anything positive.

She needed more time to get to grips with it, but ever since the witch arrived, they were all trapped on a terrible relentless rollercoaster. Meridia's mum interrupted her thoughts.

"We know we're asking a lot, but Peter's right. This is the only way we can protect you all from whatever's out there. Izzy...JJ...we think it might be best for everyone if you come with us. We'll square it away with your parents if needed. Izz, we can tell them you're having a sleepover, and JJ, you can do the same..."

"What about our parents? What if they're in danger?" JJ was quick to question the plan.

He was still a bundle of nervous energy, shifting from one foot to the other as he stood sandwiched between his adopted brothers.

"That's a good question JJ." Peter was the first to answer.

"We have no way of knowing the cult's agenda, or who they might go after next. Now there's no easy way of saying this guys, but we don't know who else might be involved. The male nurse at the hospital was definitely odd when I bumped into him, and the disciples were wandering the corridors in plain sight. I know your mum works there, JJ, and I'm not saying she's involved, but we don't know who she might be connected to..."

"My mum?!" JJ snapped back. "She would never be involved in this! So, what am I supposed to do...just sit back and hope they leave her alone because she might work with some of them? I can't do that!"

Meridia felt the temperature rising in the room as JJ

blew a gasket. From the outside, she could see it was an impossible situation, filled with risks on both sides.

"Surely we have to let them know?" She blurted. Putting herself in JJ's shoes and deciding it had to be a chance they were all willing to take.

"NO!" Izzy bellowed from her chair. "We can't tell anyone! We can't trust anyone!"

Meridia had never seen her so emotional. Her cheeks were aflame, and her eyes were full of tears.

"It was my dad!" she screeched, taking everyone aback. She lowered her head and sobbed.

"It was my dad...*sniff*...the one who tried to take me...it was my dad..."

14

JJ WAS GOBSMACKED. IZZY'S BOMBSHELL INSTANTLY shattered any lingering irritation at Peter's remark.

"W...what are you saying Izz?" He stuttered, thinking he must have misheard her.

"It was my dad...at the hospital...I saw his ring...when he grabbed me *sniff*. It's a gold signet ring with a black onyx stone. It was my grandad's...I...I recognized it right away..." JJ's skin turned hot and clammy, as if Izzy's revelation sucked all the air out of the hallway.

His palms were sweaty, and he became restless again, fidgeting on the spot while he struggled to process what he just heard.

"Wait...how do you know it was his ring? I mean for sure..." JJ heard the flicker of desperation in his own voice as he tried to play devil's advocate.

Meanwhile, the rest of the group waited in stunned silence for Izzy's reply.

"It's a pentagon." She answered curtly, glazing over as she retreated within herself to curtail her emotions.

JJ tried to ignore his churning stomach as he persisted in pulling at the loose thread. He had to be certain.

"Sorry, maths ain't really my thing...how many sides is that again?" He realized how absurd his question sounded the second he uttered it, but he had to know.

"Five. It's a bit like the shape of a house...only my dad's is always upside down." Izzy answered lethargically, as if in a trance, but her words struck JJ with the force of a sledgehammer.

His knees buckled beneath him, and he stumbled into Kane, who also looked shellshocked.

"What is it? What's wrong?" Meridia begged, picking up on the weird energy both boys were giving off.

"It...it can't be..." JJ mumbled, staring into space.

"What?! What can't be?!" Meridia's impatience got the better of her as she moved within JJ's line of sight, forcing the issue.

"My dad...my dad has the same ring..." A chorus of gasps rang out around him, and JJ wobbled once more.

His own admission broke the dam to a million questions that all came pouring out at once, drowning him in a sea of doubt.

Without saying another word, Kane brushed past him and hurriedly bounded up the stairs, but JJ hardly paid any attention, too engrossed in his own thoughts as his world unravelled.

"Where are you going?" Zach shouted up to his brother, but by then the incessant racket in JJ's head had taken over, reducing everything around him to white noise.

How could he have been so blind? Were all those evenings schmoozing clients merely a cover for something diabolical? He teetered on the edge of denial, trying to vindicate his father, but the more he pulled on the thread, the more everything he believed in came undone.

"Like this?!" Kane's words shook him from his stupor as he thundered back down the stairs and thrust a ring under JJ's nose.

It was a thick gold band with a shiny black pentagon at its centre, exactly like the one Izzy described.

"This was my dad's!" Kane declared, before JJ's eyes had a chance to fully adjust to what he was seeing.

"He used to wear this when I was young...but stopped a few years after Zach was born. I remember being fascinated with it as a kid...I'd never seen a black jewel before and always used to fiddle with it on his finger like a fidget toy. For years, I thought he was some kind of sorcerer, and the ring was magic...ha...idiot." A sadness returned to Kane's eyes as he continued.

"I noticed it in mum's jewellery box a while back but forgot to ask why he stopped wearing it." Kane stared down at the ring in his hands, mesmerized by its shimmering surface.

"Is this the ring, mate? Izz??" Once again, a hush fell upon the group as they waited on the edge of their seats for someone to answer.

"It's the same Kane..." Izzy conceded, also transfixed with the ring in his outstretched palm.

"That means...that means..." Izzy faltered as Kane took over.

"It means you and Peter are right, Izz. We can't trust anyone anymore. I'm sorry guys, but we need to get out of here!"

15

It was approaching 6pm by the time they all arrived at St Peter's and a thin layer of fog descended on the town of Thundridge. They agreed to shelve any further talk of conspiracies and mysterious rings until they were all safely reunited inside, which made for an uncomfortable silence the entire journey there.

Meridia, her mum, and Izzy followed the boys in a taxi to the hotel where Peter's car was still parked, and from there, their convoy continued to the church. Peter suggested parking their cars on Hereford Lane, which was a short walk from the church's entrance and would hopefully reduce the risk of arousing any suspicion.

As expected, darkness shrouded the church. The only light came from a solitary Victorian streetlamp, which illuminated a modest graveyard on the left side of the building. Its waning yellow bulb painted an eerie picture fit for a horror movie as the assortment of decaying headstones threw long sombre shadows onto the misty ground.

Venturing through the wrought-iron gates, Meridia locked eyes with an angelic memorial as the light skimmed its mournful face, and for a split-second she mistook it for a ghost.

She found churches creepy at the best of times, and with tensions at an all-time high, this was the last place she wanted to be spending the night. How she longed to be back in her room, safely snuggled under her marshmallow duvet and basking in the amber glow of her luna nightlight.

Deep down, Meridia knew she might never see her home again. They were now on the run from a very real and sinister threat which loomed beyond the confines of Crooked House and had them vastly outnumbered.

"Just a sec..." A small security light switched on beneath the arched doorway of the church as Peter thumbed through a set of keys in search of the right one.

"*Creeeak!*"

He opened the door and quietly ushered everyone inside. Meridia held onto her mum and Izzy's hands as she edged her way forward into the musty church hall.

"Keep going while I find the lights." He whispered, closing the door behind the shuffling crowd. "We'll be safe here...for now."

"*Click!*"

While Peter made sure the door was locked and secure, a row of understated sidelights gently flickered to life and chased away the gloom.

St Peter's elegant interior seemed vastly at odds with its weather-beaten limestone shell. Uplifting magnolia walls intermingled with a series of exquisite archways that stretched all the way to the ceiling, whilst polished oak flooring provided the perfect contrast, grounding its celestial design with warm, earthy shades of brown.

A gallery of vibrant stain-glass windows on either side of the building injected a smattering of blues and reds, breaking up the neutral hues and imparting a sense of tradition with their mosaic stories of old.

The church was modest, reflective of its humble beginnings in the town of Cold Christmas, but at the opposite end of the hall was a grand-looking alcove that was home to a hexagonal shaped altar.

"What if someone sees?" Meridia asked, taking in the vivid lead-lined artwork looking down on them.

"It's pretty normal for churches to have their lights on in the evening, honey." Emily assured. "Father Alexander lives here, remember, so I'm sure he spends lots of evenings either tidying up or preparing for his next sermon."

"Your mum's right. We're safe here guys." Peter added and then glanced at his watch.

"Now, before we get into things here, I need to call the hospital and check on Father Alexander. He should be out of surgery soon and we need to figure out the best way to get him back here without running into any more trouble." Peter set his bag down on the nearest pew and began wandering toward the altar, phone in hand.

"Make yourselves comfortable." He called back. "We have a lot to talk about."

16

When Peter rejoined the group, they were all huddled together in stony silence on the pew where he left them. The church was cold inside, and they were all too exhausted to talk.

"I've just been told Father Alexander's surgery was a success, and he is now in the recovery ward waiting for the anaesthetic to wear off. The receptionist said they should be ready to discharge him in the next hour or so."

Meridia felt an immense wave of relief at the news he was ok. Although she didn't know him long, she owed him her life. In fact, they all did.

"How are we going to get him out of there after what happened earlier?" Kane asked.

"We'll come to that, but suffice to say the sooner we can get him back here with us, the better. Whilst there's a genuine chance he's in danger at Chase Side, I don't believe for one second the entire hospital are cult members... although Grady definitely gives me the creeps. Along with ensuring his safety, I expect there are records here that can help us better understand what we're up against, and nobody will know where to look better than Father Alexander. We need him if we're going to get through this... but make no mistake, getting him out of there is going to be risky." Peter sighed as he wearily perched himself on the pew next to theirs and continued.

"I don't know how long we'll be staying here, so we'll need supplies. Whilst I was on the phone, I found a storage room out back which had blankets and pillows. This place may have doubled up as a homeless shelter from time to time, so I suggest we use these benches for beds tonight. I've brought a couple of chargers from my car, so you can all charge up your phones, but please do not contact anyone for the moment until we figure out what we're going to tell your parents. We must assume they don't know we're onto them yet, and we need to use that to our advantage for as long as we can."

"Do you reckon we might be jumping the gun a little?" Emily mused. "I mean, could there be some other explanation for the rings? Something we've missed?" Peter stroked his chin in contemplation.

"I think there could be several explanations for the rings, but until we know more, we must assume the worst. I don't believe in coincidence, not as far as Crooked House is concerned, and if Izzy thinks it was her dad who tried to take her, then I believe her. Kane, whilst we're on the subject now seems as good a time as any to inspect your dad's ring...if that's ok with you?" Kane nodded lethargically as he wedged his hand inside his jean pocket.

Meridia watched him thrash about in his seat as he wrestled to fish it out.

"*Clang!*"

The ring slipped from his grasp and ricochetted across the herringbone floor.

"Shit! Sorry!" He fizzed, lumbering to his feet in a strop.

"It's ok, I see it." Meridia rushed over to where she thought it landed.

Skimming the polished floor, the ring wound up under another pew closer to the altar. Stooping down, Meridia reached into the shadows beneath the long oak bench and fumbled to retrieve it.

"Gotcha!"

Warmth radiated between her thumb and forefinger, and as she rescued it from the gloom, its onyx stone shimmered seductively under the soft glow of the church lights. Meridia remained there for a moment, on one knee, spellbound, as if she was about to propose.

The gemstone was liquid night, an inky bottomless pit of darkness drawing her in closer and closer. Hypnotic and captivating like the horsemen's eyes, the ring continued to twinkle in Meridia's hand, all the while compelling her to gaze into its glossy surface.

It took a conscious effort to tear her eyes away from its magnetic pull, but she eventually managed and got to her feet.

"Found it!" She exclaimed triumphantly, but when she turned to face the rest of the group, they had all vanished.

17

Alone in the church hall, Meridia felt a sudden surge of icy electricity prickle her skin. Now wasn't the time for practical jokes, so she knew it had to be a vision, or worse.

"Hello? Guys?" She murmured tentatively into the empty chamber and heard her whispery voice echo its way up to the altar behind her like a rattlesnake. It had to be the ring.

Everything was fine until she touched it. Meridia contemplated letting it go. Her gift handed her enough nightmares to last a lifetime, but deep down she knew with each ominous card it dealt, there was always a vital clue to their survival concealed somewhere within.

She took a deep breath and braced herself. The mossy aroma of dusty oak filled her nose and throat as she soaked up her surroundings, anxiously waiting for something to happen.

"It's not real M...whatever happens, it's not real." She tried in vain to settle her nerves, knowing all-to-well whatever was waiting around the corner could have very real consequences.

"*Click!*"

A wall-light suddenly went out behind her, dimming the room and making her jump.

"*Click!*"

Another light flickered out, then another, and then another, until darkness engulfed half the hall. The chasmic shadow continued to advance like a ravenous mouth, ready to devour Meridia whole, as she shuffled out from behind the pew and anxiously backed away.

A discord of inaudible whispers erupted from the gloom as dozens of voices echoed and swirled around her. Watching her. Judging her.

"*Die...kill...scum...*"

The venomous chatter was dizzying as it hounded her from every angle, goading and prodding her down the aisle toward the altar.

"*Click!*"

The light directly overhead went out and suddenly she saw them all, as if the darkness was a bridge between two worlds. A horde of disciples lurched toward her, sneering from beneath their hoods and armed with an array of knives and clubs.

All Meridia could make out clearly through the gloom were their spiteful mouths and poisonous tongues, lashing the air with evil menace, whilst the rest of their faces remained cloaked in shadows.

Thrust into a sinister twilight version of St Peter's, the magnolia walls grew mouldy and decayed as they became slowly infected by the horde's presence. Meanwhile, each additional step of their relentless approach gradually reduced the plush, polished floor to a patchwork of loose bricks and shingles.

An arctic chill swept aside the little warmth there was before, cutting to the bone, and the jumble of whispers crystallized into malevolent threats.

"Catch her, kill her!"

"Slit her throat!"

"Crush her skull!"

"Pluck her eyes out, filthy seer!"

Meridia reeled backwards, pupils dilated with terror at the angry mob as they skulked their way ever closer. Through the murk, she saw something among them shining like stars. Rings just like the one she was holding.

Did someone summon these vile monsters from the shadows to reclaim it? Having seen enough, she needed to get back to her own world, and fast.

Turning on her heels, Meridia raced towards the altar up ahead. It was now floating in a ball of brilliant white light, a window into her own world. Its seared sepia-toned edges bleeding into the surrounding twilight. The faster she ran, the faster her only means of escape withdrew.

"Help meeeee!" She screamed at the shrinking portal of light, but it made no difference.

The nightmare ruthlessly snuffed out the last remaining slither of hope, rescinding Meridia's only means of escape and trapping her inside.

18

Kane rose to his feet again, perplexed as he tiptoed to see over the rows of benches up ahead of him.

"M?" He called out, then turned to JJ and shrugged. "Where did she go?!"

A wave of panic swept its way along the bench and within a matter of seconds, the others were all up on their feet and scrambling toward the pew they watched Meridia duck behind only moments earlier.

"M?! Honey?! Where are you?!" Emily's voice was brittle and teetered on the brink of shattering as she called out for her missing daughter.

Kane and the others knew all too well where Meridia had gone the last time she vanished, and an avalanche of dread came crashing down on them.

"Wait, she has to be here somewhere..." Kane tried to temper the rising swell of fear. "This is a church! It's a safe place! What if it's the ring and she's invisible?"

"This isn't Lord of the Rings, mate!" JJ quipped, getting on his hands and knees to look beneath the benches.

"What if there's some kind of trap door here? Some of these old churches are full of secret tunnels and hidden rooms from back in the day. I saw a show on Discovery about it."

"M? M!" Emily was bordering on neurotic as she frantically searched under each bench.

"Maybe Kane's right," Peter finally spoke up amid the chaos.

"Not about her being invisible, but perhaps the ring has got something to do with it. Objects trigger her visions remember. So, none of us have ever been with her when she's had one, apart from Izzy, and even then she was asleep."

"That's right!" Izzy exclaimed. "She cut her head that time and we couldn't figure out how...then there was the other time she woke up covered in dirt!"

"Exactly!" Peter continued. "Perhaps her visions are more than dreams and she actually travels somewhere during them?"

"What about her first vision? The one at Crooked House? I was standing right next to her then and would've known if she'd gone missing..." Zach challenged Peter's theory.

"True, but that may have been because you were all watching me as I drew circles in the dirt. Didn't she vanish right next to you in Kane's room? How long was she gone before anyone noticed then?" Zach shrugged in response.

"If she is travelling somewhere else, then it may only last for a few seconds, and therefore hardly noticeable unless she gets stuck somewhere, the way she did in room 6." Peter's idea was gathering momentum and it dawned on Kane how little they knew about Meridia's gift.

"So, what if she's stuck now? How will we know where

to look for her?" Emily was weeping now and fearing the worst. Kane knew if Peter's theory was right, it might take a time machine to find Meridia.

"We need to keep looking guys!" He exclaimed. "There's got to be a clue in here somewhere!"

19

MERIDIA HAD NOWHERE LEFT TO RUN. THE INCESSANT whispering stopped the moment her only way out evaporated, and the bloodthirsty swarm of disciples gathered around her, weapons at the ready. Silently creeping over old, battered church pews like spiders closing in on their prey, they surrounded her in the middle of the old church hall.

As they came within touching distance, the pungent stench of body odour choked her, and Meridia saw the filth and dirt covering them, as if they crawled out of the church graveyard. Their rings, however, were spotless and sparkled amidst the shadows like stars on a clear winter's night.

"Argh!" Meridia screamed as someone behind snatched at her wrist, a man with a vice-like grip she had no chance of wriggling free from.

"Ow!" she cried out in pain as he spitefully twisted her arm halfway up her back, overpowering her resistance.

The rest of the horde then closed in, drowning her in a sea of soiled robes and grubby hands. In a matter of seconds, Meridia found herself hoisted aloft on her back, a reluctant crowd surfer being pinched and gouged by the sadistic swarm below.

"Stop! Let me go!" She cried, battling against her restraints, but her captors held firm, marching her up the aisle in stony silence.

Arching and craning her neck, Meridia tried to see where they were taking her. Upside-down, the unfamiliar altar teetered and wobbled its way toward her.

A large rustic stone table took centre stage, whilst amber flames from a smattering of black candles danced and flickered on the ground below it. Squinting, Meridia could see a series of shadows stretched across the floor.

A network of grooves carved into the craggy ground. At each intersection was a candle, and then she realized she'd encountered the shape before. A pentagram, similar to the one she discovered beneath Crooked House, although that one was buried under a pile of decomposing bodies and its canals filled with blood.

Was she about to meet a similar fate? Overcome with dread, Meridia's stomach churned, and a hot prickly sweat engulfed her body as if she was about to throw up.

"Stop! Please stop!" She sobbed, tears racing past her temples, as she tried once more to wriggle free, but all her struggling proved futile in the face of the overwhelming brute force holding her prisoner.

"Stop..." she whimpered once more in defeat, and this time, they did.

The procession came to an abrupt halt at the foot of the table as disciples to her left and to her right all broke formation and filtered into the stalls on either side of her.

"Welcome child!" A man's deep and bellowing voice boomed out from the shadows as she was contemptuously tossed onto the table.

"Restrain her!" He barked. "We don't want our guest to miss out on all the fun now do we…" The mysterious voice was sonorous, rattling Meridia's eardrums as if he was right beside her, but with all her twisting and turning she couldn't see him anywhere.

"Yes, Grand Master." The robotic chorus of obedience echoed around her, while someone flung the knotted end of a heavy rope at her stomach, delivering a sickening gut-punch.

"*Oof!*" Winded, Meridia coughed and wheezed, as the rope was wrapped around her from head to toe, pinning her to the stone table.

Its fibres were coarse and unforgiving, chafing at her throat as it was pulled tighter and tighter until she could barely breathe beneath its weight.

"That's tight enough!" The Grand Master snapped. "We want to hear her screams now, don't we…"

Gasping for air, Meridia's vision was a blur of sorrow and pain as she struggled to make out the shadow looming over her. Completely incapacitated, yet desperate to see, she tried blinking her tears away to get a better look. There was no escape from this, she knew that now, and no one was coming to save her either.

Meridia's only hope was that this was another of her twisted visions, and in her silent prayers, she pleaded for the strength to capture every detail before she awoke, or before she met a grisly end.

"Why are you doing this?" She begged, trying to coax the Grand Master out of hiding.

"You already know why, child!" He roared, stepping into the flickering candlelight. "Did you really think your god was going to save you?"

Meridia's blood ran cold beneath the heavy mountain of

rope as she came face to face with her oppressor, and a hostile shiver forced its way up her spine, rattling every single vertebra as it gripped the back of her neck with its icy fingertips.

The Grand Master was a mesmerizing spectacle of unequivocal menace. His face was concealed behind a terrifying goat's head, forged from twisted metal and embellished with a string of arcane symbols that spanned the length of its muzzle. Gnarled razor-sharp horns glistened as they coiled their way out from under his black, silver-encrusted hood, like deadly serpents ready to strike.

Among its elaborate engravings, Meridia noticed a pentagram in the middle of the forehead, and below that were two contemptuous eyeholes, shrouded in darkness, underlining the mask's air of disdain.

Steering away from his macabre face as far as her eyes would allow, Meridia saw he was dressed different to his followers. Just like his hood, his robes were jet-black and decorated with elaborate silver markings which lost themselves in the folds of his cloak.

"Let me go!" She pleaded, staring up at the church ceiling.

The altar was centred in a turret of sorts with manky, dilapidated brickwork spiralling its way up above her into obscurity. Coalescing with the smell of sweat and grime that was choking the room, another scent tickled her nose. A warm, sweet smell that reminded her of incense.

"You have meddled for the last time, seer!" The Grand Master snarled, leaning in closer.

"You thought you were clever, didn't you, bringing the law to Cold Christmas? Well, we are the law! The prophecy has already begun, and there's nothing you or anyone else can do to stop it!"

The Grand Master stood upright and reached towards the rafters like a reverend rallying his flock. He raised his voice by several decibels, and Meridia heard his cryptic words vibrate inside his metal mask before echoing up the tower above her.

"As below, so above!"

"As below, so above!" They chanted back in unison, like a choir of brainwashed zombies.

Meridia closed her eyes and tried to take in a long, deep breath to calm herself, but the ropes were throttling. Why had her gift brought her here? What was it trying to show her?

She opened her eyes to a glint of metal as the Grand Master waved a long, serrated dagger over her head. It glistened in the soft amber light, just enough for Meridia to catch a glimpse of the elaborate etchings along its blade.

The style matched those of his mask, but before she could look any closer, the Grand Master took the knife firmly in both hands and held it, point down, above his head.

"Wake up...wake up...wake up..." Meridia scrambled to break free from her hallucination, but it all felt so real.

The oppressive ropes, the suffocating stench, the cold hard steel hovering ominously overhead, all sent an emphatic signal to her brain that she was in real physical danger.

"Elizabeth Cooper!" The Grand Master's thunderous voice quashed her mental mantra, forcing her to gaze up.

"You have been declared an enemy of the temple of shadows. Your sentence is death!"

"Wait..." Meridia gasped, but it was too late.

The Grand Master brought his knife down with all his might, plunging it deep into her chest. Eyes bulging in shock, Meridia's ribs vibrated beneath the brute force of the blow, as her shell-shocked brain clambered to process what was happening.

Beneath her heavy cocoon, her hands tingled and twitched erratically as a warm river of blood slowly made its way up her throat. There was no pain, only icy numbness. She couldn't even feel the blade inside her, only an intense weight pressing down on her torso.

"*Kaff!*"

Blood erupted from her mouth like a volcano, spattering her face with thick, crimson gore. Its taste was pure copper, and then it was all she could smell.

Why hadn't she woken up yet? Had this been real, after all?

Her own gurgling interrupted her thoughts as she battled to breathe against the onset of death. She sensed every tiny blood-bubble expand and pop in the pit of her throat until the sensation slowly faded into an ice-cold nothingness.

A hazy white fog clouded her sight as she gazed blankly into the turret above. The last thing she heard was the Grand Master's voice reduced to a low whisper.

"You belong to the demon now..."

20

"Gasp!" Meridia sat bolt upright, clutching her chest with both hands.

"M!" JJ shouted, "Guys, she's over here!"

Terrified and confused, Meridia swivelled onto her knees whilst trying to catch her breath. Now crouched on the altar of St Peter's church, she saw JJ bounding up the aisle towards her.

"Oh, thank god!" She heard her mum's fretful voice reverberate from the other end of the hall, followed by the clattering of footsteps on the oak floor as everyone flocked around her.

"Wh...what happened?" She asked woozily.

A dull pain resided in her chest, and the metallic taste of blood lingered on her tongue.

"One minute you picked up the ring, and the next you were gone!" Zach's voice cracked under the strain of his emotions as her mum swooped in and held her.

"Where have you been?! We looked everywhere..." Emily trailed off as she tenderly swept one of Meridia's auburn locks away from her face and gasped.

"What happened to your neck?!" Meridia instinctively reached for her throat and winced.

"Ow!" That's when she noticed the pink rope burn on her wrist.

"How long was I gone?" She asked, loosening the collar of her bottle green jumper.

"A minute...maybe two." Peter replied from somewhere behind the crowd of worried faces.

Meridia thought she had been away far longer, however, and the sudden revelation brought about another hot flush.

"Ok guys, you can stop stroking me like a cat now...I need some air." Wobbling to her feet, Meridia's legs were like jelly. Zach and Emily both leapt to her aid.

"Guys, I'm fine!" she snapped. "I just need some air."

Her chest still ached with each breath as if she was punched in the ribs, and the sweat leaking from every pore was aggravating her phantom rope burns. She was sick to the stomach of her cursed gift and wondered just how close she came to death in that dingy church tower.

As the group sheepishly backed away, it gave her a chance to survey the altar. It bore little resemblance to where she was sacrificed moments earlier. This was more hexagonal, and not nearly as high as the one she was tied to.

"What is it?" Zach asked, sensing Meridia's confusion.

But without saying a word, she parted the pack and wandered down the aisle, her head still on the swivel, taking in every little detail.

"I picked up the ring over there, and when I stood up, you had all vanished." She started.

"It was the same church, only different. As the lights went out, it was as if I was seeing it before all this..." She gestured at the pristine walls and polished pews.

"It was stripped bare...old and creepy. They grabbed

me...the men in hoods and they carried me here." She turned and pointed back at the altar.

"Only it was different...the rest of the church was the same, only older, but this part...this part was completely different. It was round and tall." Her bright blue eyes glazed over as her mind wandered back to the stone table.

"There was a table there...in the middle. They tied me to it and...and..." Warm tears snaked down her cheeks as she struggled to find the words.

"He killed me...there on a table."

"Who did?" Peter probed.

"He called himself the Grand Master...or that's what the others called him...he had this horrible metal mask with horns and a long knife...The others, they all watched on as he stabbed me..." Still in a daze, Meridia put her hand on her heart.

"You're safe now, hun." Emily took a hesitant step forward and tried to placate her.

"Am I mum?! Are any of us safe, really?" Meridia fumed, holding up her wrists for all to see.

"I was just tied up and murdered, right under your bloody noses! What's next, eh? Who's next?!" Her hands were shaking now, and her cheeks pulsating in patchy red anger.

"Woah, hang on a sec!" JJ interrupted, giving Meridia a chance to cool down. "Back at the park, Father Alexander told me there was a turret that was left behind. The crooks in Cold Christmas wanted it to keep it..."

"That's right!" Peter added. "He said the same when we came here earlier. I bet it was the altar!"

"Exactly! That means M might have gone there, not here. I thought it was weird when he mentioned it. Why didn't they build their own church?" JJ was right.

There was a fire in his belly that Meridia hadn't seen in a while. It reminded her of when this all started.

"It's still there guys...or its ruins, at least. I bet that's where those hooded nut jobs are right now!"

"The Grand Master called it the temple of shadows. He said I was their enemy right before he..."

"We need to go there now!" Kane demanded, his knuckles white with rage.

"I'll burn them all for what they've done!" He paced, red-faced and full of fury.

"I'll kill every last one of them. You just watch me! I'll burn their temple to the fucking ground!"

All Meridia wanted to do was burst into tears. She had never seen him like this. So aggressive as he marched back and forth, painting the stuffy church hall blue. She glanced over at Zach and felt a pencil-thin crack form in her heart. He appeared completely withdrawn by comparison, staring at the floor as his brother continued to spiral out of control.

Despite her ability to see, she still had no idea what it felt like to be either of them in all this. Orphaned and on the run from god only knows what.

"Settle down Kane." Peter put a comforting arm around his shoulder.

"We need to come up with a plan. Rushing in half-cocked will only get us all killed. They will pay, I promise, but not like this. We need to be smart. We have Meridia, remember? Her gift is the key to all this. I just know it, and perhaps for the first time since this started, we have a level playing field. I think that's why the cult has come out of hiding. We have them worried."

"Elizabeth Cooper..." Meridia mumbled.

"What?" JJ asked.

"That's what he called me...right before he stabbed me.

Guys, I don't think I'm the first seer they've come up against..."

21

Meridia's shock revelation winded the room. Izzy had been quiet until now, listening intently while she processed the shifting dynamics of the group. There was a clear hierarchy cementing itself now, and she struggled to see where she fit within it.

Glancing at Zach, she guessed he might have felt the same, even though he remained at the centre of everything.

The realization her parents were involved in all this madness, that they somehow were responsible for Zach being orphaned, sickened her to the point she could no longer look him in the eyes.

As for Kane, seeing him explode in his quest for vengeance only alienated her even more. He had essentially just declared war on her parents and expressed a burning desire to murder them. An eye for an eye. She wondered what JJ thought of his little outburst, and what it might mean for his family.

If Meridia was right, and there was another seer before her, then what made this group of would-be-heroes any better than those who had come before? They were already threatening to come apart at the seams, riddled with anger and grief.

"We need a plan." She blurted, ripping away the gag Meridia had slapped on them all.

"We need to get Father Alexander and figure out what we do next." Izzy knew they couldn't afford to spiral now.

Regardless of what each of them were dealing with, they needed to find the strength to put it all aside and think clearly.

"Izzy's right." Peter sat down on the edge of a pew.

"We can't afford to lose our heads. As impossible as it seems now, there will be time to grieve later, but if we're going to get through this, we need to focus. I know this is asking a lot...perhaps too much. I often forget how young you all are, and I know the weight on all your shoulders is immense...but I believe in you. All of you. I still have faith there is a reason we've all been thrown together, and despite what has happened in the past, I still believe we can turn the tide on Crooked House and all its monsters."

"How are we going to get Father Alexander out of the hospital?" JJ asked.

"They could be waiting for us there. They could be waiting for us here. I sent him a message earlier, but it's still showing as undelivered. I can't even ask my mum..." JJ teared up as he ran out of steam.

"Perhaps it's finally time to involve the police." Peter mused.

"NO!" Meridia snapped. "The vision I had...the Grand Master said the last seer involved the law and that the cult *was* the law. Maybe that was a sign...that we can't trust the police here." Emily wrapped an arm around her and interjected.

"I know someone in the police. I think he's a detective

now. I can call him?" Peter rubbed his chin with deliberation.

"No, I think Meridia's right. We can't afford to make a wrong move. I'll go. I can call ahead and pull up in the collection point out front. If I time it right, I can be in and out in a matter of minutes. I'll need to make sure no one follows us here, so I'll drive around with him for a bit before circling back."

"What about the nurse?" Izzy asked. "And what about Valerie? Maybe one of us should go with you?"

"I'll go!" Kane was quick to volunteer, still seething.

"No, it's too dangerous!" Peter curtailed any debate. "You're all safer here with Emily. If I get a bad feeling, I'll drive through the collection point and come straight back."

"I think I should go with you." Meridia asserted.

"No way!" Emily cut her off.

"Wait mum, hear me out. If anyone is going to get a 'feeling' about anything, it's me. I can stay in the car and keep watch while you go inside." Izzy watched as Peter pondered Meridia's offer.

"I'm sorry, but the answer's still no. It's too risky. I won't let you!" Emily dug her heels in.

"Meridia's right." Izzy declared. "Peter needs a lookout. If Meridia's gift can make a difference, we need to let her use it."

Izzy tried to stifle the butterflies in her stomach as she continued to speak up.

"We're all in danger, no matter where we are...even here. You all heard what just happened to Meridia. We need Father Alexander, and he needs us...he might be in real trouble. You protected me, Peter...I know you can protect Meridia, too. If we did all come together for a reason, then we all need to start believing in each other."

"Emily, it's your call." Peter concluded. "In my opinion, we're all in danger, no matter where we are at the moment. Particularly Meridia, as we've just seen. Izzy makes a valid point, though, we can't hide forever."

"What if that's exactly what we need to do...hide, I mean?" It was Zach's turn to speak up.

"If they need me to finish whatever the prophecy is, then why can't we all run and hide somewhere they won't ever find us?"

"That might well be the answer, Zach." Peter conceded, glancing at his watch. "It doesn't change the fact we still need to get Father Alexander, so it's time I hit the road."

Izzy kept her eyes on Emily as Peter rose to his feet. She was still clinging onto Meridia as if her life depended on it.

"He needs me, mum," she pleaded. "They both do. I promise, I'll stay out of sight..."

Peter patted Meridia's shoulder and flashed a weary half-smile as he made his way towards the door.

"You might want to make up the beds while I'm gone. I'll grab us some supplies and something to eat on my way back..."

"Wait!" Just as Peter's hand reached for the door handle to leave, JJ jogged down the aisle to meet him. "I'll come and be your lookout. Nobody knows the hospital better than I do, and it was me who got Father Alexander into this mess. I wanna do my bit to help."

"But what about..." Izzy quizzed.

"My mum?" JJ finished her sentence. "She's on a date night, remember...or at least that's what she said. Don't worry, I'll stay in the car and promise to just keep watch. It'll be fine."

"I'm..." Emily didn't even start her sentence, let alone finish it as she gazed longingly at Peter.

A crinkle formed in the centre of her forehead, and Izzy saw she still felt torn about her decision to keep Meridia behind.

"It's ok Emily, I understand..." Peter assured her. "We'll be back before you know it."

22

JJ WATCHED THE UNRELENTING DOWNPOUR THRASH against the windscreen while Peter waited for his phone to connect. Dazzling white street lamps coalesced with the coursing rain to paint a mesmerizing kaleidoscope of speckled shapes and colours on the laminated glass.

It was full dark now and barely a few degrees above freezing. They were both soaked from the minute or two it took for them to run from St Peter's to Hereford Lane, where Peter parked, and his Audi was now steaming up faster than the air conditioner could handle.

The earthy smell of muddy shoes and soggy coats overpowered the tiny lemon air freshener hanging from the rearview mirror, so Peter wound his window down a little to help clear the air.

"*Bluetooth connected*" the female voice robotically announced through the car speakers, making JJ jump.

"I've put the heated seats on to help dry us off. If it gets too hot, just push that button next to the little red light." Peter gestured to the controls for JJ's seat and resumed scrolling on his phone.

"I'm going to call the hospital now, so Father Alexander is ready by the time we get there. I'm a little worried we've not heard from him, but I guess if his phone is dead, he won't have access to your number."

"I guess." JJ shrugged.

He could feel the warmth slowly filtering through the back of his joggers now and wished Audi made beds.

Peter hit the call button, and within a few rings, a woman picked up.

"*Chase Side minor injuries! How can I help?*" Her voice was bright and bubbly, like a sales rep, as it bellowed through the speakers.

"Hi, I'm calling to confirm the collection of a patient there. Martin Alexander? He was in recovery when I called earlier, and your colleague told me he'd be ready to leave around now."

"*Please bear with me while I check.*" The tip-tap of manicured nails on a keyboard followed, mimicking the rattling rain outside.

"*Can you confirm your relationship with the patient, please?*" She quizzed.

"I'm a friend who agreed to collect pick him up." Peter replied, non-committal.

"*I'm afraid I can't find any patient here by that name. Let me check against the other departments in case they have moved him. My shift only started 20-minutes ago.*" The tip-tapping in the background became louder and more feverish, and JJ felt a pang of worry in his chest as questions mounted.

"*I'm sorry, we haven't got any patients here by that name, and there are no records of him being discharged either. Are you sure you have the right hospital? This is Chase Side in Shawbrook.*"

Bemused, JJ opened his mouth as if to speak, but Peter was quick to shut him down, answering over him.

"Sorry, my mistake. I must have my hospitals mixed up." And abruptly disconnected the call.

"What did you do that for?!" JJ quizzed. He couldn't understand why Peter hadn't pushed harder.

"The cult is up to something." Peter put the car into gear and pulled away from the curb. "Arguing the toss with that receptionist would only have drawn more attention. When I called earlier, they found Father Alexander's details instantly and gave me a full update. That means someone has removed him from their system since my last call."

"But why?"

"I'm not sure yet. Perhaps they got to him after I left, or this is just an attempt to flush the rest of us out of hiding?"

"I think it's time we call the police." JJ couldn't think of anything else to suggest.

If Peter was right, they were already too late to save Father Alexander. A knot of guilt formed at the back of JJ's throat as he mentally assumed full responsibility for the priest's safety. After all, it was his chance encounter that brought him into this mess, and possibly the same encounter that ultimately signed his death warrant.

"We can't risk it." Peter reminded him. "What if that's exactly what the cult wants us to do? To go running to the police and give ourselves up. Meridia's visions never happen by chance. Maybe this is what she was being warned about all along? The cult is used to operating in the shadows, remember, they've done it for centuries. We, on the other hand, are not. I'm sure this is all part of their plan. To tie us in knots and keep us second guessing our every move."

"So, what are we going to do, then?"

"The one thing they won't be expecting. We're going to the hospital."

23

FATHER ALEXANDER'S EYELIDS FELT AS IF THEY WERE super-glued together in his sleep. He was desperate to see where he was, but try as he might to prise them open, the most he could muster was a murky slither of light slinking in between his tangled eyelashes.

A strange mechanical humming sound drifted in and out of his groggy consciousness, and he did not know if he was sitting or lying down. Both his legs were completely numb. In fact, he couldn't sense much of anything beyond the unpleasant chemical taste dominating his nose and mouth. It was an overpowering sensation that permeated every breath. A revolting cocktail of minty aluminium.

"*Anaesthetic!*" He thought.

He experienced the strange sensation once before following surgery, and it took him a whole day to rid himself of its nauseating aftertaste.

"Wh...where am I?" He slurred, hoping he wasn't alone.

"*Ding!*"

The cheery sound of an elevator bell announced his

arrival, swiftly accompanied by a slight judder. Wherever he was, he had been travelling down.

Straining to open his eyes again, he managed a little more this time, but the gloomy blur told him nothing of any consequence. He felt a light breeze against his cheeks as he was wheeled forward. The ground was bumpy, and every tiny vibration suggested he was sitting, most likely in a wheelchair or gurney. Still, he couldn't feel the rest of his body.

"Where...are you taking me?" Each word required a concerted effort to force through his tingling, uncooperative lips. If he could only get rid of this awful taste infused in his brain, then he might be able to concentrate.

He felt his carriage come to a stop and tip back a little as it turned to the right. Definitely a wheelchair. Twitching his eyelids to rouse them from their slumber, Father Alexander kept them at half-mast. He was coming to. Blinking away the blurry remnants of his anaesthesia, he could just about decipher the edges of a windowless room. Wherever he was, it was no longer the Chase Side recovery ward.

As his drowsy eyes struggled to adjust to the dark, he noticed the décor here was more in keeping with a dungeon. Surrounded by yellow-grey limestone, it reminded him of the secret chamber they had stumbled upon beneath Crooked House.

Although he couldn't smell it, he sensed the moisture in the air, tugging at his lungs with every breath, and upon closer inspection, what he first thought were shadows on the stony walls were, in fact, water stains. In the room's centre was a huge white granite table decorated with candles flickering dimly against its freckled veneer.

"We meet at last holy man..." His mysterious host was a man, lurking somewhere out of sight.

His voice sounded deep and hollow, as if he was cupping his mouth.

"That will be all, brother Grady." The order to leave was received with petulance, as Father Alexander felt the rubber handles of his wheelchair vibrate and creak beneath the strain of his pusher's grip before being brusquely released.

"As you wish, Grand Master," Grady replied with a delayed response that sounded as if he had forced the words through gritted teeth.

"You must forgive brother Grady...he longs to slit your throat and watch you bleed out. I trust your arm is more comfortable in its cast?" In his lethargy, Father Alexander hadn't even noticed the thick white plaster clinging to his wrist.

Nor had he felt the leather restraints shackling him to his chair. His inertia felt too acute to be caused by a routine anaesthesia. All sensation from the neck down abandoned him.

"Oh, that's right, I forgot. You can't feel anything, can you? The wonders of modern medicine! Haha...nothing permanent, just a nerve block. We wouldn't want you missing out on all the fun once you have served your purpose and brother Grady finally gets his way with you..."

"P...purpose? What...purpose?! Wh...who are you?" Father Alexander was still slurring his words, drunk on numbness.

A prisoner in his own heavily sedated body, he was already teeming with fear as he sat helpless in the gloomy dungeon, and then out from the shadows stepped his oppressor. Even though a chilling silver mask of a horned goat's head concealed his identity, Father Alexander knew all too well what his assailant symbolized.

"Baphomet…" He murmured, transfixed by the esoteric markings decorating the mask's nose.

The cyphers shimmered in the murky candlelight. An intricate web of a language long forgotten, and whilst Father Alexander was not versed in their meaning, the inverted pentagram amongst its ranks was irrefutable.

"Satanists…" He blurted.

The Grand Master took a measured step closer, towering above the priest in his wheelchair.

"An ignorant misconception!" He snorted.

"Over the centuries, Baphomet has been plagiarized by heathens, and those robbed of their voice by the societies that enslaved them. In the days when religion reigned supreme, he provided the perfect nemesis to your false god. A persuasive recruitment tool, driving the gullible in their masses to one deluded faith or another, else the boogeyman would claim their souls. How convenient…that the self-proclaimed 'light' somehow earned the right to define the dark. Naturally choosing to vilify it… and all the while they spread their manipulative lies, the church quietly amassed power and wealth; whispering in the ears of rulers across the land. So no, we are not the Satanists you have been brainwashed to believe. We represent the union of opposites…the yin to your god's yang. We are here to restore balance and harmony…"

The Grand Master's revelation left Father Alexander reeling. Was his faith so fragile it could be challenged by the ramblings of a masked lunatic?

Yet something about this twisted counter-perspective struck a nerve, rekindling a lapse in faith he suffered long ago when his wife passed.

"You are not restoring anything! Innocent people are

being murdered. You're nothing but animals!" He roared back.

"That's all any of us are, is it not? Animals playing dress-up..." The Grand Master stroked his twisted, metal face as if it were his own.

"After all, that's how your kind have stayed in power so long. Convincing us we are something we're not. Guilting us into suppressing our true nature with your trite commandments and rules. Seducing us with plastic trinkets and empty promises. Like all good magicians, your kind have done well to distract us from the truth. You have kept the masses furiously pedalling their little hamster wheels, feeding the machine you have created. But don't you worry, priest, all of that is coming to an end now. The war is almost over, and the tide has turned in our favour. Your sham of a society will soon be reduced to rubble, and then from the ashes, darkness shall rise."

"Who are you...really?" He probed.

"Who I am is no concern of yours, priest!" The Grand Master barked, agitated, and Father Alexander felt a slight flutter in his chest. Perhaps his feeling was returning.

"I am merely a symbol. A humble servant of darkness, here to usher in the day of reckoning. But enough about me! That was quite the show you put on at the house. Poor, simple Molly. If you only knew what you have condemned her to with your desperate prayer. You see, the gates of heaven are now closed for business. Your god has no dominion there, or here. That brief stay of execution he granted you was merely a parting gift on his way out the door. All things must end, you see, and the light's reign is no exception."

The Grand Master stooped until he was face to face with his prisoner. Behind his menacing facade were piercing eyes, black as night, and Father Alexander could feel them boring into his soul.

"There is no escaping what is to come, holy man. The reckoning is almost upon you. Soon your kind will make way for the Children of the Shadows. No seer, nor band of misguided children, can stop the inevitable. Go ahead, pray to your god, see what he has to offer you now! It's over, priest! It is our time. We are the children who shall inherit this earth..." The Grand Master backed away and disappeared into the shadows like a ghost, his long black robes shrouding him in darkness.

"All the darkness in the world cannot extinguish the light of a single candle..." Father Alexander whispered the words of St. Francis of Assisi under his breath before calling out after the Grand Master.

"They will come for me...and for you!"

"Of course they will...why else do you think you're still alive?" His sonorous voice echoed around him.

"*Bang!*"

The door slammed shut, and Father Alexander was condemned to his gloomy prison cell.

24

PETER PULLED INTO THE PATIENT COLLECTION BAY AT Chase Side Hospital and switched the engine off. Neatly sandwiched between two other cars, it provided the perfect cover from prying eyes whilst conveniently placing them a few yards from the main entrance. All appeared normal as he and JJ watched from the warmth of his car.

The rain eased to a drizzle, and their clothes were almost dry. Outside, a smattering of mini floodlights hung from the hospital's eaves, bouncing broad beams of light off its sodden redbrick walls and illuminating the tarmac below.

Waiting patiently, they observed a steady footfall of patients and staff roaming the grounds, which was exactly what they were hoping for. The more people, the better, in fact.

Having arrived at a plan quickly en route, they had then spent the last fifteen minutes of their journey debating who got to execute it. To his surprise, JJ had eventually come out on top and was quick to undo his seatbelt.

"Now remember, this is just a recon mission. I'll be in

your ear the entire time and ready to come in at the first sign of trouble. If you get a sniff of something unusual, anything at all, then you need to hightail it out of there. Understood?" JJ nodded in agreement whilst tucking an AirPod in his right ear.

"Like I said, most of the evening staff know me, so if anyone asks, I'm in there looking for my mum. Nobody knows where I've been today, including my parents, so I shouldn't run into any trouble. I'll be in and out as quick as I can." JJ tugged the visor of his cap down tight on his head and reached for the door handle.

"I'm calling you now. If you lose signal at any point, get out of there, ok?" Peter was strict with his instructions.

"It's fine, my phone connects to the Wi-Fi there automatically, so I should have a signal the whole time." JJ answered Peter's call and tucked his phone back in his pocket.

"Testing one, two, three..." He quipped.

Peter let out a deep sigh, clearly uncomfortable with their arrangement despite the overwhelming logic that supported it.

"Ok, I hear you. Visiting hours end in the next half an hour, so nothing too adventurous, and if you happen to see that weirdo Grady, turn around and come straight back out!" JJ agreed and left Peter in his car to play the unlikely role of overwatch.

He thought it was odd he'd never seen nor heard of this nurse Grady character, and it gave him some sliver of hope his mum might not be tangled up in all this madness.

"Ok, I'm going in," he whispered, imagining he was the lead in a spy movie, as he warily crept inside.

25

The front desk at Chase Side's main reception was unusually quiet as JJ approached. He was praying for a queue of people to duck behind on his way to the central corridor, but alas, he found himself totally exposed. He knew if anyone was going to recognize him, it would be a receptionist.

The desk, made of polished cream MDF and curved like a giant kidney bean, dominated the otherwise sparse room. A protective PVC screen was all that stood between JJ and the two middle-aged women stationed behind the counter.

The abrasive smell of chemical infused lemons wedged itself at the back of JJ's throat as he loitered in the doorway, trying his best to avoid eye contact.

"Shit!" he whispered under his breath, forgetting about the open line to Peter outside.

"*What is it?*" The unexpected response buzzing in JJ's ear gave him a fright and exposed how on edge he was.

"Nothing...sorry, I forgot you were there for a minute. I'm ok. It's empty in here and my mum's friend Jenny is on the desk. She's bound to stop me if she sees me." JJ couldn't believe he was about to be rumbled within the first minute of entering.

'*Some spy!*' he thought.

Backing up a little, he bumped into a metal box screwed to the wall and jumped again.

"For fu...dge sake!" He blurted.

"*What is it now?!*" Peter was back on high alert in the carpark.

"I'm ok...sorry. I think I've got an idea. Bear with me a sec." JJ swiped a face mask from the dispenser he just clattered into and quickly put it on.

Between that and his signature LA baseball cap, he looked like a ninja, and there was no way Jenny would spot him as he sauntered past.

"Can you hear me?" He asked Peter, as he casually breezed his way into the main corridor.

"*It's faint, but yes, I can still grasp what you're saying.*"

"Great! I'm in the main corridor. That's the hardest bit over with...now all I have to do is make my way to minor injuries." JJ felt a touch of relief as he put Jenny firmly in his rearview and turned right into the corridor.

Chase Side was a bit of a maze to most. A hotchpotch of interconnected buildings of all different shapes and sizes, but JJ knew the place like the back of his hand. Well, almost.

They agreed to start their search at the minor injury unit where Father Alexander was last seen. From there, JJ would swing by the recovery ward next door. This was a small area of the hospital, comprising a handful of cubicles. If that turned out to be a dud, he would head to the main ward at the back of the hospital and check the patient names on the whiteboard there.

Peter remained unconvinced the Children of the Shadows had infiltrated the entire hospital, so it stood to reason Father Alexander might still be there somewhere, blissfully unaware they were even looking for him.

"I'm approaching the door to minor injuries now..." JJ breathed.

He was already overheating from the mask, and the visor on his cap was keeping a lid on all the hot air he was pumping out.

"*Can you see who's at the desk?*" Peter asked.

"Hang on, just stepping inside...." JJ slipped through the door and pulled some change out of his pocket.

He knew there was a vending machine in the far corner, so he kept his head down as if counting his money and ambled towards it. The illuminated display of crisps and chocolate bars proved too tempting, given his empty stomach.

"*Clink! Clink!*"

"*What was that?*" Peter quizzed in his ear.

"It's my cover for being here." JJ explained feebly as he hungrily entered the code for a Chocolate bar.

"*Thump!*"

The bar landed in the collection drawer, giving JJ a chance to look around while he picked it up.

"*You're at the vending machine aren't you...*" Peter finally twigged.

"All part of my cover...trust me." His words were lost in the fury of the crackling sweet wrapper as he hastily tore into his snack.

"Ok, so there's a girl at reception. She's young for this place, anyway. Dark hair and kinda pretty."

"*Can you make out her name tag from there?*"

"Not from here." JJ squinted as he unhooked his face

mask from one ear and took a huge bite out of his Chocolate bar.

"Nope...*nom*...*nom*...not from here anyway. I'll try on my way out." He could hear the tension in Peter's voice at every interaction and so figured he best get a move on before he had a coronary.

"I don't think I'll be able to get into the treatment rooms; there are too many nurses around." JJ had already seen at least two come and go from behind the reception cubicle and the last thing he wanted to do was get busted by the creepy nurse Peter kept banging on about.

"There's only a handful of people waiting to be seen. I guess the rain's been keeping everyone inside and away from hurting themselves. I'm going to check the main ward now and see if his name is on any of the lists...*nom*...*nom*..." JJ stuffed the rest of his Chocolate bar in his mouth, then hooked his face mask back on.

The blue fabric wormed its way closer to his eyes with each chew, but he figured he would ride out any discomfort. He hadn't recognized the receptionist on his way in, but that wasn't any great surprise. The minor injuries unit was pretty specialized and had a separate roster of staff to the rest of the hospital.

"It's Alice." He mumbled, stepping back out into the main hall. "The receptionist was called Alice."

"*I thought I recognized her voice on the phone! That's the same woman who was on duty when I was there. She even signed Father Alexander in! I think you should get out of there now JJ...it's too risky!*" Peter's anxiety threatened to bubble over, but JJ had already done all the hard work getting inside undetected.

"But I'm so close now. I'll ride the lift and check the different patient lists for his name. It'll only take a few minutes. I'll come straight out after. I promise. He might be up there somewhere, waiting for one of us to come find him..."

There was a long pause at the other end of the line, so JJ continued toward the main corridor until he reached the second elevator down. This one came out right in front of the mini-reception desks so he could literally step out and back in once he'd checked the whiteboards on each floor.

"Ok...but be quick."

"I'm at the elevator now. No sign of him on the list here, so going to try the first floor. I may lose signal when I get in the lift...not sure if the Wi-Fi stretches that far. If I do, then don't panic. I'll call as soon as I'm back on the ground."

"Just be careful. You've got ten minutes, and then I'm coming in." JJ agreed and disconnected the call as the elevator doors opened.

26

JJ WAS OVERHEATING AGAIN AS HE ENTERED THE mechanical steel prison. The last time he stepped foot inside an elevator was with Izzy, and on that occasion they were both being stalked by the evil spirit of a witch. As much as he was eager to find Father Alexander, he clearly underestimated how afraid he would feel returning here alone.

"Click!"

With the lift empty, he pressed the button for the first floor and unhooked his face mask. Letting out a deep sigh, he lifted his cap and cuffed away the sweat from his forehead. The chemical cleaning agent saturating the hospital's halls took on a tinny guise in here, so between that and the inside of a face mask, JJ was craving some fresh air.

"10-minutes..." He muttered to himself nervously, foot tapping, as he willed the number 1 to illuminate above him.

JJ knew most people used the elevators closest to the main entrance when visiting patients and so this one only came into play when their time was up.

Glancing at his watch, he saw there was another 20-

minutes left before visiting hours ended. That left him plenty of time to get up and down all 5 floors uninterrupted.

"*Ding!*"

The soft sound of the elevator arriving at its destination startled JJ way more than it should have. Things were about to get real. In his mind he was no longer the lead in his own spy movie, but more like the expendable extra in a horror. He reattached his mask and, with clenched fists, braced himself in the centre of the metal cubicle while waiting for the doors to slide open.

"Phew!"

The only thing waiting to greet him was an unmanned desk. JJ took one step into the corridor and kept his trailing leg in the lift's doorway to hold it open. Checking the coast was clear, he scanned the names on the board, but there was no sign of Father Alexander.

Similar to the main reception, the first floor was unusually quiet, with only a janitor in the distance mopping its floor.

"One down, four to go!" He breathed, stepping back into the elevator, and pressing the next button.

The second floor was a different story, and when the doors parted ways, a wave of relief washed over JJ at the sight of what he considered another typical day at Chase Side. An elderly woman breezed past him in her wheelchair. A look of determination on her face, like she broke out of jail.

Meanwhile, a flustered nurse wrestled to control her own temper as she tried to pacify an irate visitor at the front desk.

Stepping forward, JJ bobbed and weaved to read the patient list beyond the gesticulating man who stood between him and the whiteboard. Still no Father

Alexander. His heart sank as he contemplated coming up empty again. For all they knew, their newfound friend may have met a similar fate to Kane's parents. The realization dragged him back down into the murky weeds of guilt as he slinked back inside his stuffy carriage.

Three more tries, he thought to himself as his finger hovered reluctantly over the next button. Along with the nagging sense of dread that still lingered from his last trip to the third floor, he also knew it represented something of a tipping point. The higher the floor, the more serious the patient's condition. If Father Alexander wasn't on the next one, it spelled bad news either way.

"*Ding!*"

The metal curtains opened on the third floor to reveal a barren stage. Noticeably darker than his previous stops, a flickering light overhead gasped and sputtered as if in its final throes of life.

The front desk beneath it showed no signs of activity, and an eerie silence swept along the empty hall in front of him. The murky reception brought memories of his last visit flooding back, drowning him in apprehension as he contemplated skipping ahead to the next floor.

With his mouth bone-dry with fear, JJ shuffled closer to the patient list. The trembling light made it harder to see the smudged names on the whiteboard, coaxing him all the way out of his steel bunker. The air seemed cooler here, and JJ welcomed the gentle draft from the air conditioning as it softly caressed his eyes and neck.

"*Clunk!*"

The sound of the elevator closing behind him was like a starter pistol for his heart, sending it into a sprint, and JJ froze like a rabbit in the headlights, not knowing whether to advance or retreat.

"Suck it up, man!" He grumbled to galvanize himself.

Forcing his leaden legs forward, he stepped closer to the board and squinted to read the list of names.

"Damn it!"

Dejected after coming up empty yet again, he turned back towards the elevator and that was when he caught a shadow from the corner of his eye. At the opposite end of the corridor, a man stood deathly still, watching him from afar like a predator sizing up its prey.

Dressed in blue scrubs with slicked black hair that glistened beneath the fluorescent lights, there was no doubt it was the creepy nurse Peter warned him about. In a state of panic, JJ furiously bashed the lift's call button.

"C'mon...c'mon..." He moaned, waiting for the doors to open so he could escape.

The nurse started walking towards him. Slow at first, like a machete-wielding psycho straight out of an 80s slasher flick, but the closer he got, the more he upped the pace.

Petrified, JJ shuddered at every glimpse he caught of the nurse's sinister grin as he marched beneath the long line of tubular bulbs.

"Finally!"

The doors opened and JJ launched himself inside, instinctively hitting the number 4 button as quickly as he could. Beyond the door, he heard the nurse's hurried footsteps chasing his own ominous shadow along the blue laminated corridor towards him, but he was too late.

The doors closed and JJ was on his way up again, but he knew he wasn't out of the woods yet. If the nurse was a part of all this, he wouldn't give up that easily, so JJ's decision to go up instead of down could prove a costly mistake.

27

"C'mon, think JJ!" The lift seemed to take an eternity to reach the fourth floor and in that time, all JJ could imagine was nurse Grady taking a leisurely stroll up the stairs and beating him with time to spare.

With no signal on his phone, he couldn't call Peter for help and his ten minutes were nowhere near up. His only chance was to make a run for it the second the lift doors opened. If he could get to the elevators at the other end of the corridor, he would be home and dry, but it proved a tall order if the nurse already beat him there.

"*Ding!*"

Adrenalin pumping, JJ began rocking heel to toe like an Olympic sprinter in the blocks. No matter what was waiting for him, he had to run.

Standing a shade under 5'8", he was confident he had enough size and weight to barge his way past most people if he put his mind to it. If Grady was waiting for him, his best chance of escape would hinge on the element of surprise. Knock him down and run.

"C'mon JJ, you got this!" He asserted.

As much as they all owed Father Alexander, it was time to abort and get the hell out of Chase Side. JJ would be of no use to anyone if he was captured, or worse.

"*Whirr...*"

It was do or die, as the sound of metal brushing against metal filled the elevator and the doors slowly opened. As soon as the gap was wide enough, JJ charged out, head down and shoulder first into the corridor.

"Squeak!" He slammed on the brakes once he realized the corridor was empty.

"Hey! No running in the hallway!" A middle-aged nurse growled at him from behind the front desk as she scowled disapprovingly over her glasses.

Glancing around, JJ saw they were alone. Perhaps Peter was being paranoid about Grady after all, but he was done taking chances.

"S...sorry!" He muttered back to the cantankerous woman giving him daggers.

Keen to break free from her glare, JJ allowed his eyes to wander up towards the whiteboard on the wall behind her.

"Richards!" He whispered in awe, remembering what Izzy told them all.

The only known living echo was in cubicle 5, just a matter of yards from where he now stood and en route to the second set of elevators. Although his search for Father Alexander was a bust, the chance of seeing Valerie in the flesh proved too tempting to resist, so JJ briskly set off in her direction.

Wall-to-wall with thick blue fabric, the fourth floor was home to some very poorly patients, and each cubicle curtain was tightly drawn to shield its residents from the outside world. Warmer than the previous floors, JJ pulled his face mask down under his chin to cool off as he hurried along the stifling corridor.

It only took him a minute or two to reach Valerie, but that proved ample time to concoct a host of reasons for her being there. Yo-yoing between an innocent prisoner and a bedridden monster, JJ came to a halt and placed an ear to her curtain, all the while keeping a watchful eye on the corridor for any sign of danger.

There was a serenity to this floor that was akin to a public library, and somewhere buried within the muted electronic beeps, he heard the rhythmic whooshing of breathing apparatus. Satisfied there was no other sound coming from inside the cubicle, JJ skimmed his hand across the folds of its curtain in search of an opening.

"*Ding!*"

Down the corridor, the lift announced another arrival and JJ's legs went rigid with panic. Gripping the hem, he wasted no time finding out who was about to gatecrash his little detour and swiftly ducked behind the curtain. He hadn't so much as glanced in Valerie's direction when he heard a man's voice echo down the corridor.

"Did you see a boy wandering around up here? About this tall, wearing a baseball cap and a face mask?" It was Grady, the creepy nurse!

"Yes, as a matter of fact, I did!" came the woman's crabby voice. "He came charging out of the lift...you just missed him."

"Which way did he go?" JJ held his breath as he waited for the receptionist's damning reply.

"Thanks." Just like that, she threw him under the bus.

JJ backed away from the curtain a little as the slow and steady sound of Grady's footsteps approached. His only option was to run, but when?! Did he go now and hope he could outrun him, or stick to his original plan of bowling him over to buy himself more time to get away?

JJ knew he wasn't the quickest, and Grady looked young and wiry from a distance, so could easily be a recreational runner. The footsteps drew ever closer, providing a countdown to JJ's indecision until it was eventually too late.

Grady's baleful silhouette snaked its way along the pleated curtain and then stopped directly in front of him. With bated breath, JJ watched the nurse's shadow deliberately turn and face him. The game was up, as he was surely caught. Shifting his weight to the balls of his feet, JJ braced for impact. There was no way he was going down without a fight. All he needed to do was make it to the elevator, or even the stairs.

"Pft!" Unmoving, Grady let out a sigh of resignation before calling back to the nurse on the front desk.

"I must've missed him. Shame...if you see him again, can you let him know I'm looking for him? I have a message for him."

"Will do!" The croaky voice echoed back, but Grady lingered for a moment as JJ silently stewed in his own juices.

What message? Was this a rouse to flush him out of hiding?

Again, before JJ could arrive at any conclusion, the looming silhouette continued down the corridor and disappeared out of sight.

"Phew!" JJ hunched forward, hands on his knees, as he tried to compose himself.

His face tingled from the blood rushing to his head as he listened out for the faintest sign of the nurse's return. With only a nylon curtain separating him from a potential killer, this had all been way too close for comfort, and it was time he worked his way back to Peter.

Amongst all the tension, JJ almost forgot whose cubicle he was hiding in when he heard the frail, whispery voice call out behind him.

"You should've run when you had the chance..."

28

Fear prickled the hairs on the back of JJ's neck, sending an icy shiver scuttling down to his tailbone. The intimidating silence that followed was short-lived, and soon the only sound JJ could hear was the pounding of his heart as it reverberated like an alarm bell in his inner ear.

Swamped by a cold, clammy sweat, he rummaged inside himself to find the nerve to turn around and face the patient in cubicle 5.

Beneath the tangle of tubes poking out of every airway, Valerie Richards was a withered old woman who appeared lost in the middle of her hospital bed. In the flesh, she was far frailer than her photo suggested.

Thick, blue-green veins besieged her scrawny neck and arms, whilst dark-brown liver spots covered her gaunt face. Valerie's emaciated body was barely noticeable under the white bed linen, but JJ could just about discern the rise and fall of her shallow, machine-assisted breathing.

If it wasn't for that subtle movement and the monotonous beeping of a heart monitor, JJ would have said he was looking at a corpse. With thinning white hair that lay matted to her bony forehead, her bulbous eyes remained closed in their dark and saggy sockets, rebuffing her bleak surroundings.

"H...hello..." JJ whispered, unsure how the creepy voice could have come from the shrivelled old woman laying before him.

As he spoke, he took in a mouthful of the stuffy cubicle air that was steeped in ammonia. Its sharp taste made him gag, forcing him to cover his mouth with his sleeve. Shuffling towards her, JJ leant in a little closer, studying her intently.

"Poor cow!" He breathed, feeling sorry for the bag of bones clinging on to her last tendril of life.

To her right was a small gunmetal cabinet that was home to a family photo. It looked well over a decade old.

Valerie and her husband were all smiles for the camera in what appeared to be a restaurant. JJ picked up the brass frame for closer inspection, but the background was too dark to make out beyond the glare of the white tablecloth they were sitting behind. The couple looked like a picture of happiness, coyly smiling as they held hands across the dinner table.

"So, you must be mean old mister Richards..." JJ muttered. "You both look like butter wouldn't melt..."

Sighing, he carefully returned the photo to its rightful place on top of the cabinet.

"Another dead-end!" He didn't even notice the subtle increase in the heart monitor over his shoulder.

"Argh!"

JJ jumped clean out of his skin as an icy, skeletal hand latched onto his wrist like a slap band. Spinning around in angst, he turned to stone the moment he locked eyes with Valerie.

Like Medusa, she held him in her gaze, mesmerizing and terrifying. Haunting, milky white eyes glistened beneath the fluorescent light overhead, devoid of any irises or pupils. Mouth agape, her reedy lips revealed a smattering of stained yellow teeth that jutted out like rotting tombstones in a derelict graveyard.

JJ tried to shake her off, but Valerie held fast, refusing to let go of his arm as her eyes continued to bore into his.

"I see you..." she rasped. "I see all of you..."

JJ wriggled and squirmed, but like her stare, Valerie's grip was unbreakable.

"There's no place left to hide from me now...not for you, or your friends." Biting his lip to suppress a scream, JJ tried desperately to prise her bony fingers away, but they wouldn't budge.

"The darkest corners...of your mind...that is where I'll be. Watching...waiting. Tonight, no one sleeps..."

With her last gasp threat, Valerie let go. Her scrawny arm fell limp, dangling awkwardly from the edge of the bed, as her piercing stare retreated behind dark, saggy eyelids.

"What the!"

JJ reeled back in shock, unsure what had happened, as Valerie lay lifeless on the bed, just as she had done before. The droning beep of her cardiac monitor softly serenading her back to sleep. Had he imagined the whole thing?

Flustered and even more eager to get away, JJ fumbled his way through the folds of the curtain and staggered into the corridor. He was panting now, craving air that wasn't tainted by this god-awful place. Why did he feel so terrified?

He didn't understand. She was a bedridden old woman. Nothing like the monsters he faced in Crooked House. Yet something about her scared him shitless. He remembered Meridia's words.

"This one scares me more than the last." They all experienced it, eyes which moved within the photo, watching them as they sat around Kane's dining room table. Was it an early premonition?

He needed to get back to Peter, and fast.

29

Squeaking his way down the corridor, JJ anxiously spammed the elevator call button until its doors opened. Selecting the ground floor, he slumped against the far wall and removed his cap. Sweat drenched his head, so he mopped his brow with his face mask and then stuffed it back into his jacket pocket.

He didn't care who saw him now, he just needed to get out. JJ watched the lights begin their countdown and replayed his encounter with Valerie to decipher her ominous warning. He was more perturbed by her talk of sleep than anything else she said. Did the cult know where they were hiding?

"*Ding!*"

The elevator came to an unexpected halt on the first floor, interrupting his thinking. JJ felt a sudden surge of dread swell within the pit of his stomach, rising all the way to his throat as the doors slowly parted.

"Phew!" he breathed a heavy sigh of relief as a young mother with a buggy entered the lift.

"Going down?" She sniffed tentatively.

Her eyes looked weary and red as if she'd been crying, whilst her daughter lay comatose in her cosy pink bed on wheels. JJ nodded, shuffling further into the corner to make more room.

Once inside, the woman pushed the button for the ground floor and stood with her back to JJ as they both waited patiently for the lift to respond. Letting out another deep sigh, he watched the sterile hospital ward slide away behind the dreary metal door. He was almost home and dry.

"Clunk!"

Someone snuck a hand through the last remaining sliver of light coming from the first floor, forcing the doors to reopen, and putting JJ's freedom on ice.

"Sorry!" the man apologized as he slipped inside and swiped an ID card, then pressed the green button for the basement level.

"You almost got away from me there!" Grady directed a wry smile at JJ, who was now trapped in the lift's corner.

With a theatrical double take, Grady glanced back at JJ and studied him.

"You're Alice's son, aren't you? I've heard all about you...and your friends..."

JJ glanced nervously at the woman with her back to him. There was no way Grady was going to do anything to him in front of a witness. He sensed the lift judder underfoot as it resumed its descent and decided to go along with whatever game the nurse was playing.

"Yeah, my mum works here. It's funny though, I've not heard her mention you before." JJ did his best to maintain eye contact as he tried to get a read on him.

Up close, he was a little taller than JJ and wiry.

There were traces of definition beneath his loose-fitting scrubs, so JJ guessed he might be a gym rat. Great, he thought, as he weighed up his chances of getting past him if things turned ugly.

"Oh, your mum works different shifts to me these days... just like today, in fact. So, what brings you here, James?" The tension was brewing between them now as Grady's smile slithered into a sneer while he stared JJ down.

He looked like a vampire under the elevator lights, pale skin, slick black hair and glistening blue eyes. Peter was right, there was something creepy about him for sure.

"I was looking for someone...a priest. He came in earlier, but I can't find him now. Have you seen him anywhere?" If Grady was wrong-footed by JJ's gumption, then he wasn't showing it.

Cool as a cucumber, he responded without batting an eyelid.

"Nope, can't say I have. I've had my hands full all afternoon with two very special patients, a married couple in their forties." The corner of Grady's mouth curled into a smirk as he waited for the penny to drop.

"They didn't make it sadly...left behind a couple of sons too, I hear. Tragic really...I mean, what's going to come of those boys now, with no one left to protect them?"

JJ's blood boiled. Did Grady just brag about murdering the Jacksons? JJ wanted to lash out and punch him right in his smug mouth, but then he noticed the scalpel in his hand. Its razor-sharp blade flickered ominously by his side.

On his finger, the ring, gold and onyx, sparkled on his tightly clenched fist. It was now beyond all doubt. White knuckled like a ticking time-bomb ready to explode, the nurse's mask finally slipped and revealed the maniac beneath, hiding in plain sight.

Grady shot a sideways glance at the mother and her child, then playfully raised both eyebrows at JJ, licking his lips as if to taunt him. Relishing the jeopardy of their silent standoff, he twirled the scalpel around in his hand and feigned a step toward the unsuspecting bystander and her child.

The sudden move turned JJ's legs to jelly as Grady continued to revel in their deadly game of chicken. Barely able to contain his excitement, his face twitched and quivered under the weight of the snicker he was trying so hard to suppress.

"Ding!"

The lift arrived on the ground floor and the doors parted ways, but Grady didn't move an inch as the woman heaved her pushchair out into the corridor behind him.

Instead, he remained embroiled in a petrifying deadlock with JJ. There was no way round him, and with the knife at his side, any attempt to barge past was only going to end one way. Still, JJ couldn't go down without a fight.

He clenched his fists and changed his stance, ready to charge, but before he plucked up the courage, Grady took a measured breath, placed the scalpel back in his pocket and calmly stepped aside.

JJ could tell it was taking every ounce of the maniac's self-control to back down, but he wasn't going to stick around long enough for him to change his mind. He warily sidestepped his way around him and backed out into the corridor.

"I'll be sure to keep an eye out for your priest, James," Grady said with a creepy grin. "I have a feeling you'll be seeing him again real soon though..."

The elevator doors closed between them, and JJ ran for his life towards the exit.

30

Peter was on edge. He'd been nervously clock watching ever since he lost contact with JJ and now found himself in a quandary. Having already given him an extra 5 minutes to get out, he was now second-guessing his next course of action.

There were countless reasons for JJ to still be inside and not all of them were bad. He might have found Father Alexander, or bumped into a member of staff his mum knows. For all Peter knew, the lift might be out of service and JJ was busy trudging up and down ten flights of stairs.

But on the other hand, someone could have abducted him, or worse. The longer Peter waited, the heavier the shackles of guilt hung around his neck. This was a stupid idea, his stupid idea.

In his stubborn pursuit of answers, he had recklessly put a 14-year-old boy in harm's way. Sure, they both discussed the risks, but how much can any 14-year-old really comprehend such things when blinded by a sense of adventure? A sense of obligation.

By the time they arrived at Chase Side, the whole harebrained idea felt like it was JJ's all along. Enough was enough now, though. Peter had no choice but to go in after him.

"Bang!"

His heart leapt into his throat as something clattered the passenger window. It was JJ, distraught with eyes like pools of sheer panic. Peter unlocked the car, and he bundled his way in.

"Go! We need to get out of here! Now!" He panted, fastening his seatbelt as he anxiously watched the hospital exit.

"Wh...what is it? What happened?" Peter asked, pressing the ignition button and reversing out.

"It's all true! Everything you said about this place... about my mum...I didn't believe it until now...until that nurse threatened to stab me!"

"WHAT?!" Peter hit the brakes, stopping outside the main entrance.

"Don't stop! Not here!" JJ pleaded. "We need to get back to the others...I saw Valerie too...she spoke to me. She's not a victim like the others...she's one of them!"

Peter's mind was abuzz with a million different questions, but JJ was right. There would be plenty of time to answer those later. Right now, he needed to get them back to safety.

Whatever JJ saw in there left him a nervous wreck. He looked petrified, squirming in his seat as Peter pulled away and put the hospital firmly behind them.

"It's ok JJ, you're safe now. We'll go back to St Peter's and you can tell us all what happened. Just try to breathe... you're safe now." Peter tried his best to reassure him as he made his way out onto the main road, but JJ continued to fidget as he rocked back and forth in his chair.

"I think I know who killed Kane's parents...it was that nurse! I think he's done something terrible to Father Alexander too...and it's all my fault!"

<h1 style="text-align:center">31</h1>

Silas Grady was already in need of another rush by the time he stepped out of the elevator and into the basement. Reserved only for staff with the highest security clearance, this floor was a graveyard for unused equipment and beds, but tucked away down its gloomy corridor was also a modest sized morgue.

It proved a useful go-between whenever he needed somewhere to stash a body or two before transporting them to the pit. Unlike the rest of the building, this level had undergone very little in the way of renovations over the years, apart from the occasional lick of paint.

With white breeze-block walls and an insipid grey asphalt floor, it appeared more like the basement of a prison than a hospital. Its raw, industrial aesthetic was reflected overhead via an exposed ceiling, crawling with thick grey metal pipes.

Silas closed his eyes and took in a deep lungful of the hot, sticky air. The distant aroma of paint fumes and fresh plaster enveloped him like a warm blanket of nostalgia, transporting him back to when he was still a student, learning his deadly craft and dragging his bloodied victims along the washed-out corridor.

He wondered how many cadavers these walls had witnessed, aside from his own personal body count. Thousands, he guessed. Despite the humidity, Silas liked it here. The silence and the solitude soothed his troubled mind. It offered him space to breathe as he straddled two very different worlds.

The one above where he was made to hide behind a mask, and the one below where his master kept him on a tight leash. In many ways, this murky limbo was the only place Silas ever felt truly free.

His leash, however, was a small price to pay to satisfy his bloodlust, and one he would not be paying for much longer, particularly now the Jordan boy crossed paths with Valerie. Silas contemplated the ramifications of that encounter and felt a smile creep across his ashen face.

Opening his eyes, he gazed into the darkness gathering at the opposite end of the passageway and walked towards it.

When he reached the morgue door, he couldn't resist the urge to take another peek at his handiwork from earlier that day. Upon entering, the room was chilly and dazzling, like the inside of an enormous heavenly refrigerator.

Furnished floor to ceiling with individual glossy white fridge doors, the fluorescent lighting overhead bounced off every single fixture and fitting, including the two surgical steel tables at the centre of the room. The air, whilst minty cool, still carried the distinct eggy aroma of rotting corpses.

It wasn't the Jacksons he could smell, though. They were far too fresh. No doubt it was an unclaimed patient, one that was old and contaminated so of little use to him.

"*Click!*"

Silas opened the latch on cabinet number four and pulled the slab out so he could see its occupant. Tim Jackson now looked a lovely shade of lavender beneath the mortuary's harsh lighting. The deep gash severing his carotid artery had congealed, so Silas delicately traced his thumb along its crimson ravine.

He took great pride in his work. The speed and precision with which he could end another human's life. Usually he would take his time, toy with his prey a little before slaying them, but occasionally, the thrill of a quick kill offered its own sweet release.

Seeing the warm river of blood suddenly erupt from a freshly cut throat was akin to watching fireworks on the 5th of November, or riding the Waltzer at a fairground. A moment of pure, unadulterated exhilaration as his victim bled out all over themselves, coughing and spluttering in their final throes of death.

But inevitably, the moment would pass, and the emptiness would return. Such intensity always left Silas hungry for more, so no one was more surprised than him when he spared the Jordan boy. If not for Valerie, he would have seen to him right there in the elevator. He would have cut his chubby little head clean off and then dispatched of the mother and her child just for good measure.

"Clunk!"

Silas condemned Tim's body back into its icy tomb and closed the door.

The Jacksons were traitors, betraying the temple and jeopardizing everything the Children of the Shadows had spent centuries working for. Their murder was as much a message to the others as it was a punishment for their treachery.

He was desperate to dispose of their youngest too, the

boy called Zach. Like those before him, the prophecy required that snivelling little weakling to enter Crooked House of his own volition.

So, what better motive for him to return than revenge? Their plan to systematically kill everyone who the boy held dear and drive him back to Crooked House was sure to ramp up now that Valerie had intervened. They were flying blind now, without their priestess, but Silas remained faithful to the cause.

With Valerie's help, this would all be over soon, making everyone else fair game, starting with the priest. Silas succumbed to another wry smile as he stepped back into the clammy corridor. He needed to go below and inform the Grand Master of this latest development.

Meridia was about to find out she wasn't the only girl in town with a gift.

32

Izzy swiped away the eleventh missed call from her mum and tucked her phone back in her pocket.

"Still no word on the group chat." She mumbled. "Something's wrong, I know it."

Feeling a little suffocated by her mum, Meridia had convinced Izzy to join her in Father Alexander's office.

It was a thinly veiled attempt to carve out some thinking time, away from all the fuss. Meanwhile, Zach and Kane took the keys to the rectory to raid Father Alexander's cupboards of any food he might have lying around. They were all tired and starving now.

Izzy felt guilty leaving Emily to make up the rest of their beds on her own, but didn't want to let Meridia out of her sight after she'd already gone missing once in the short time they were there.

"I can't sense anything, if that's what you were wondering." Meridia replied curtly. "Sorry...I didn't mean that the way it came out. I'm just feeling useless cooped up here. I should've gone with Peter, not JJ."

Meridia's shoulders slumped in defeat and Izzy knew she

needed a comforting arm of reassurance, but Izzy had her own stuff to deal with. Ever since leaving Zach's house, the slightest glance in her direction, or remotely snarky comment, now took on an entirely different meaning and struck right at her heart. She grew accustomed to being stared at, feeling like an outsider even with her closest friends.

Now, she felt paranoid, judged. To make matters worse, given the current circumstances, she also felt unable to share her feelings with anyone. Her attempted abduction paled into insignificance when compared to the brutal murder of Zach's parents and Meridia's latest brush with death.

Besides, what would she even say given the chance? That her parents, the two people in the world she trusted more than anyone, were members of an age-old murderous cult?

That was one can of worms she didn't want to open, particularly while emotions were running sky-high. Perhaps she could talk to James about it when he got back. He might be the only one who could understand how she was feeling.

"At least James knows his way around that place...that might be of some help, I guess." Izzy shrugged, avoiding all eye contact.

"That's true, but I still think I'm the one who should be there...My mum will never let me out of her sight now! What use am I going to be as a seer if I'm handcuffed to my mum the entire time?!" Izzy wasn't sure what to say.

At least Meridia still had a mum she could see and speak to. She sensed her phone through the fabric of her trousers. It was burning a hole in her pocket as she wondered how many more missed calls she'd accumulated since the last time she checked.

It was getting late now, and if her parents really were the monsters everyone thought they were, they would be suspicious now rather than concerned, particularly since Izzy disabled her 'Find My Phone' app. She wondered if JJ had done the same after finding out about the rings.

What a tangled mess this had become. A few months ago, everything in her world was perfect, and then they visited that wretched house. Now everything she ever poured her faith into, logic, science, her family, was turned upside down. The rug had been pulled out from under her and all she felt now was lost and alone.

Izzy glanced at Meridia, who was deep in her own thoughts as she sat behind the rustic oak desk in the middle of the room. Looking around, Izzy couldn't tell if Father Alexander's office was small or crammed with too many books.

To her right were oak shelves, floor-to-ceiling, which were overpopulated by encyclopaedias and history books, whilst to her left was a matching dresser cabinet, also filled to the brim with books. Unlike the rest of the church, this room was warm and cozy.

On another day, the subtle aromas of leather and sandalwood mingling in the air might have made for a much more relaxing environment. Dimly lit by a solitary brass desk lamp, the only other source of light was a tiny lead-paned window over Meridia's shoulder.

Nightfall tainted the glass, refashioning it into a black mirror. Izzy shuddered as she locked eyes with her own murky reflection. As she looked away, she spotted the brass photo frame resting on the corner of the desk, intentionally turned outward.

Mrs Alexander, she mused. A beautiful smiling

brunette left a lump in Izzy's throat as she reminded her a little of her mum. What a mess this was.

"*Beep!*"

Meridia's phone buzzed on the desk just as she felt her own phone vibrate in her pocket.

"The group chat!" She blurted, as Meridia started reading the message. "Is it James?"

"No...it's Kane. He's found something and wants us next door."

33

Kane rubbed the tiredness from his eyes as he scanned the montage of paper strewn across the living room floor. He was still waiting for the Mars bar he found in the fridge to work its magic and give his brain a boost.

"Is that everything?" Zach asked from the doorway behind him, still chewing his way through a Milky Way.

Luckily for them, Father Alexander had quite the sweet tooth, with more than enough chocolate bars to go round in his secret stash. They both felt awkward until then, unsure of what to say to one another as they timidly looted the kitchen.

"It's all I could find that makes any sense," Kane concluded, still in awe of the sheer volume of new information they had uncovered in the study.

"I think this must be Archie's murder board...the one JJ saw on Father Alexander's phone. See how the handwriting differs from the rest?" He pointed at the centrepiece, an A3 page from a sketchbook jam packed with information on Cold Christmas and Crooked House dating back centuries.

"We totally half-arsed it, didn't we?! Bowling over there

like a bunch of amateurs. I was such an idiot!" Kane took a slow blink of frustration, still blaming himself for every terrible thing that had happened since that fateful day.

"We didn't know...how could we?" Zach tried to pull him away from the edge of another meltdown.

"Archie did! He found so much stuff! All I did was look at one missing person's article before dragging us all straight to hell!"

"But where's Archie now? He knew all this and still went inside! At least we came back alive..." The very suggestion of mortality sucked all the air out of the room and plunged both brothers back into stony silence.

"*Click!*"

Out in the hall, the front door opened and Meridia announced her and Izzy's arrival.

"Hello? Where are you guys?"

"We're in here!" Zach replied, eager to jumpstart the flailing dynamic.

In a matter of seconds, both girls gathered behind Zach in the living room doorway.

"What is all that?" Izzy was the first to ask, peering over Meridia's shoulder at the hotchpotch paper carpet taking up most of the floor space.

Father Alexander's lounge was surprisingly sparse and modern compared to the cluttered and chaotic nature of his study. A smattering of recessed lights bounced off the empty magnolia walls, with little in the way of furniture to get it their way. Having dragged a glass coffee table over to the bay window, Kane had ample space to piece every scrap of information together for all to see.

"It's everything Father Alexander has on Crooked House, and there's quite a bit we didn't know..."

"Like what?" Meridia probed, her bright blue eyes foraging for a place to start.

"Sit down, guys, and I'll share what I've found." Kane gestured towards a comfy looking royal blue sofa whilst he leapt over the mishmash of scribbles and onto a narrow strip of carpet opposite.

Aside from a token picture of his wife, the lounge felt far less lived-in than the other parts of the house and felt more like a show home. A plug-in air freshener busily pumped the air with the scent of fresh cotton, but that only added to the pretence.

Based on what he'd learned, Father Alexander dedicated most of his free time to his study, and if he wasn't there, it was likely he would be in his kitchen indulging in chocolate. The entire house smacked of loneliness, and Kane wondered if anyone outside of the group would worry about his whereabouts.

"So? What did you find?" Meridia's impatience showed as she glared up at him from the sofa, where she sat sandwiched between Zach and Izzy.

"Sorry, right...by the way, there's chocolate in the kitchen...enough to open a sweet shop. I forgot to mention it when you got here."

"It can wait. This is more important." Izzy concluded on behalf of everyone as she continued to scan the mass of paper laid out in front of her.

"Right. So, I think the piece in the middle is what Archie found before he...went missing. Remember JJ said he saw a photo of it? At least I'm guessing it's Archie's, based on the handwriting."

"I can hardly read the rest of it!" Izzy grumbled in annoyance.

"I know, it's like Mr Seth's writing at schoo..." Kane trailed off mid-sentence.

His attempted reference to St Swithun's seemed awkward and out of place the moment it left his mouth, as if he was rubbing salt in the wounds of a past life everyone longed to return to.

"Anyway, I'm guessing that's Father Alexander's handwriting...because...well...it looks like my grandad's." Kane knelt so he could point to specifics as he covered them off.

"So, these bullets here list the different reports over the years and include some stories we uncovered in the files we found inside Crooked House. See, they mention the kids that were murdered in the seventies, and there's even something about a missing soldier which ties in with the echo in room 3. Check this out. It's an old extract from the Herts Gazette," Kane read the scrap of paper verbatim for the benefit of the group.

Local hero, private William Spencer, was declared MIA in 1944, however since then, there have been numerous rumblings of a government conspiracy, and subsequent coverup, following various sightings which occurred in the weeks after he went missing.

Our source, who wishes to remain anonymous, claims private Williams was in fact on compassionate leave around the time he disappeared owing to the sudden death of his sister, and was using that time to investigate the mysterious circumstances of her untimely demise.

A rambler discovered Jessica Spencer's body in the Cold Christmas woods during the early hours of February 12th, 1944. A promising nurse at Chase Side Hospital, the official line is that young Ms Spencer was found still in uniform from her previous shift and curled up beneath a great oak deep in the woods.

With no obvious signs of foul play, her cause of death was reported as hypothermia, and after speaking to close friends and colleagues, local police concluded she had somehow lost her bearings on her way home and ended up freezing to death.

However, local gossip differed, claiming they found Ms Spencer cowering instead of curled up, with a look of absolute terror etched on her face as if someone or something had scared her to death. This rumour was further substantiated when the town embalmer, Jeffrey West, claimed that despite his best efforts to correct it, her expression remained so disturbing the church ultimately deemed her condition inappropriate for an open casket funeral service.

When her brother William discovered this startling revelation, he took matters into his own hands and began asking questions around town and at his sister's place of work. Although the exact findings of his private investigation remain a mystery, it is said he was last seen alive checking into the recently renovated B&B Crooked House, not far from the spot his sister's body was found. Private William Spencer was never seen or heard from since...

"How did Archie figure all this out without the files? We couldn't find anything about him online when we looked." Izzy was invested now, her eyes wide behind her tortoiseshell glasses as she searched for an answer.

"Exactly!" Kane exclaimed. "As far as I can tell, it all comes from this guy here."

He traced his finger back to the top of the column labelled 'Cold Christmas'.

"Retiarius?!" Meridia exclaimed. "Who's he?"

"This is where it gets interesting. So, I looked it up and Retiarius is the name of a Roman gladiator. It's Latin, but its literal translation is 'net-man', so I'm thinking he might be someone Archie found online. Only problem is, whenever I search his name, all I come up with are dictionary definitions and wiki-links so it's a bit of a dead end. Whoever this guy is, he knows tons of stuff we don't. Look here, he even mentions the cult in a roundabout way, linking Cold Christmas to all sorts of historical events, the plague, the crusades. There's even talk of parliament being moved there at one point, and a series of secret underground tunnels! Retiarius knows his shit!"

"So how did Archie find him?" Zach asked the obvious.

"If I knew that, I'd be on the phone to him by now. I think Archie must've rinsed Google one evening. I know we've all done that too, but maybe he just got lucky and clicked on a link we didn't see?"

"I wonder if he's someone local...or some kind of historian?" Izzy was thinking aloud as she absorbed Archie's research. "And why didn't Peter know about him?"

"He could just be some crackpot conspiracy theorist." Meridia quipped, playing devil's advocate.

"I don't think so, M." Kane tried to bring them all back to the point he was building up to.

"See the notes, Father Alexander added. They all spin out of Archie's, like he was validating them. This isn't stuff you just find online or in a history book. We all saw the old journal Father Alexander brought to the hotel with him. He told us it wasn't online anywhere, yet Archie already had it covered...See!" Kane pointed halfway down the page.

"That says witch! He even talks about a witch finder in the area...that means he knew about Molly before any of us did. It's like an evil timeline of all the shit that's gone down in the area. If everything on here is true, which it looks like it is, then I reckon Retiarius might be more than a geeky local historian. I think he might be a member of the cult, or perhaps he was..."

"That's new!" Izzy pointed at another item on Archie's list and read it aloud. "An epidemic of people mysteriously dying in their sleep? What's that about?!"

"I saw that too. It sounds like A Nightmare on Elm Street!" Kane picked up a page of Father Alexander's scribblings and held it under the light.

"It looks like whatever it was it started sometime in the sixties, but it's sketchy at best and judging by the number of question marks, it doesn't look like Father Alexander could find any answers. Man, I can't read half of what's written on here! It's the same with this bit about people going missing in the area." Kane swooped down for another page and frowned as he struggled to decipher the handwriting.

"I guess Helen Ashfield could fall into this category. No one has found her yet, and she's not haunting any of the rooms in Crooked House. Maybe that's the pile of bodies you saw under Crooked House M?" Kane shrugged and placed the pages back on the floor.

"I know this doesn't give us a ton of answers, but I really think Retiarius is a lead we need to track down. Who knows, he could even help us end this fucking thing!"

A swell of hatred rose to the pit of Kane's throat, so he clenched his teeth to suppress it. His anger was all-consuming, and as much as his little presentation had provided a brief distraction, he knew he couldn't rest until he made everyone pay for what they did to his family.

He watched the group bury themselves in their phones as they hastily searched for Retiarius and knew he should probably do the same, but his head was fizzing. All he wanted to do was tear the room apart. He wanted to scream and kick and punch its walls until his knuckles bled. Anything to take his mind away from the pain he felt inside.

"Guys! I think I've found him!" Meridia burst his rage-fuelled bubble as she sprang to her feet, phone in hand.

"I think I've found Retiarius!"

34

"Wai...what!" Meridia sensed Kane peering over her shoulder as she tapped the link to Retiarius's profile.

"He's a troll." She said, flicking through his posts. "He's got beef with the Herts Gazette, by the looks of it."

Meridia switched to WhatsApp and pasted a link to the group chat.

"I've just shared the link. The Gazette wanted to do a piece on my mum after everything that happened with my dad. She said no in the end, but that didn't stop people gossiping online. I remember her crying about one troll who said she most likely deserved it. He wouldn't leave her alone in the end and when she called the police, they said it would be impossible to find him. Turns out all you need to make someone's life a misery is a keyboard and a VPN. Anyway, he had a dumb handle on there and Retiarius reminded me of him, so thought I would run a search on their blog."

"Shit! I would never have found that in a million years!" Kane blushed.

"His profile is blank, but judging by his posts, it looks

like he's been active on here for a couple of years." Meridia continued to scroll through the preview lines of all his comments.

"This is definitely where Archie got his information from. It's all here, including a threat to the local college about some underground tunnel they found. Listen to this... *'There is a reason those tunnels have been a secret for centuries and are still in use to this day. Some mysteries are better left unsolved. I would recommend anyone looking to poke their noses in places they are not welcome to make sure their life insurance is in place. You have been warned!'* ...he kinda sounds like he's trying to keep people safe, but the Gazette used his comment to promote their story and said it was a death threat!"

"What else does he say?" Zach stopped googling and put his phone away in favour of Meridia's narration.

"Er...he goes on about being initiated in those tunnels and then...here... *'The children are everywhere, walking among you, watching from the shadows. Their time will come again. The temple will rise from the ashes when the count reaches ten. Unless you want to die a hideous death, you will cease meddling in matters your tiny brains cannot possibly comprehend!'*...ok, so that might have sounded more like a death threat." She conceded.

"He's one of them. He's got to be!" Kane stepped away from the others and paced the room with his eyes glued to his phone.

"Children watching from the shadows? When the count reaches ten? He's talking about the rooms of Crooked House for sure! We need to find him!"

"How?! There's nothing in his profile, so we have no idea who he is." Meridia still felt irritable. "Maybe it's time for that chocolate, Zach."

"I'll get the bag." Zach skulked out of the living room as Kane countered.

"What if we reply to him online? Maybe we could flush him out somehow? Show him we know stuff too? It can't be that hard to set a profile up on there, can it?"

"Already on it," Meridia replied, without looking up. Her fingers were a blur as she typed away on her phone. "We need to come up with a name...something only he would recognize."

"Grand Master?" Izzy suggested. She was diligently reading Retiarius' greatest hits on her own phone.

"Nah, that could just as easily be a Marvel geek." Kane vetoed. "We need something only we could know. What about Molly's full name? What was it?"

"Harding," Zach reemerged, carrying a big bag of sweets in one hand, and a half-eaten Twix in the other.

"Your memory never ceases to amaze me, spud." Kane cracked a rare joke, and for a split-second, it felt as if today's tragedy didn't happen. "How about that, then? Molly Harding."

"I dunno. It might be too specific. Plus, there could be dozens of people called Molly Harding in the area, for all we know. How about MollyTheWitch?" Meridia's suggestion received unanimous approval from everyone.

"Done. Now all we need to do is get his attention. His last post was a couple of days ago, so at least we know he's still active. I'll see what it says. It doesn't look like it's had any bites yet." Meridia felt the colour drain from her cheeks as she read Retiarius's latest outpouring to herself.

"What is it M?" Zach quizzed, sensing something was wrong.

"It...it's a story about the demon of Cold Christmas...it's

coming up to 50 years since he murdered all those children..."

"What does it say?" Kane was chomping at the bit.

Meridia took a beat and then read the article aloud to the rest of the group.

50 Years On: Infamous Child Murderer Still Haunts Sleepy Village of Cold Christmas

Half a century has passed since the notorious Demon of Cold Christmas terrorized our community, but the scars still remain.

Despite the best efforts by local law enforcement, the killer remained an enigma, evading capture and tormenting the families of his victims during his year-long reign of terror. Claiming the lives of at least 5 children, whose bodies were never recovered, the Demon continues to cast a long shadow over the village of Cold Christmas, serving a haunting reminder of a dark past many are desperate to forget.

Detective Inspector Jason Richards, whose father Albert was a police constable assigned to the original task force, is among those looking to move on and has expressed his reluctance to revisit the case.

'While the passage of time has brought about significant advancements in the field of forensics, reopening a case as horrific as this would also require opening old wounds that have never truly healed. With little likelihood of any new leads materializing, the toll it would take on the families and the community make this a deeply challenging decision. But in the spirit of transparency, I can say with absolute certainty there are no plans to reopen the case at this moment in time.'

DI Richards' decision not to reopen the investigation

highlights the frustrating reality faced by police and victims alike when grappling with cold cases, along with the trail of unresolved grief and lingering questions they often leave behind.

As the 50th anniversary of these grisly unsolved murders looms, survivors of the victims intend to stage a poignant memorial to pay tribute to those loved ones whose lives were tragically cut short. Meanwhile, the Demon's legacy continues to serve a stark reminder to us all about the enduring impact of violent crime.

Meridia paused for a moment to allow the others to process what they just heard. Like her, they knew the demon still lurked somewhere in the shadows of Crooked House, but if their encounter with Molly was anything to go by, perhaps his reign of terror had never truly ended. That's what made Retiarius' comment on the post all the more ominous.

"50 years! Shit..." Kane was the first to break the pensive silence.

"That also means old man Richards was on the force when all this was going on." Kane resumed pacing the room as he searched for dots to connect.

"Which means we were right not to go to the police if his son is now a detective. I still can't figure out how Valerie fits into all this, though. Is she one of them too, or just another victim?"

"Judging by her picture and what I saw at the hospital, I still think she's one of them." Izzy had a steely look in her eyes as she added her tuppence worth.

"So, wait, what did Retiarius say about the article?" Zach was the first to realize Meridia was still holding something back.

"You're not gonna like what he had to say, guys..." Meridia gave a solemn shake of her head as she stared glassy eyed into her phone then resumed reading.

There is a reason the Demon was never caught, and it is the same reason Richards will never reopen the case. So many wolves and so few sheep, you never know who you can trust. Beware the night of the blood moon, for 50 is a milestone which carries more weight than gold. Regeneration and release.

Demons never die, they are simply reborn, so be sure to lock up your children if you know what's good for them. Soon the monster will rise again.

Meridia couldn't conceal the ice-cold shiver scurrying up her spine as she read the last sentence. Unbeknown to the group, she had seen the demon in action. She watched him brutally dispatch Izzy and JJ with ease while the world ended around him.

Would that terrifying vision soon come to fruition? Had all their blood, sweat and tears only given them a brief stay of execution?

The emergence of another seer filled Meridia with self-doubt. She needed Peter to return. He always knew how to raise everyone's spirits. Looking at the worried faces surrounding her, she knew the gravity of their situation wasn't lost on any of them, but they hadn't seen him with their own eyes.

"We're going to lose aren't we..." Kane spoke, choking on tears of dismay as he stared down at the potted history of Cold Christmas laying at his feet.

"Look at this shit...just look at it all...there's nothing good here! No survivors who lived to tell the tale, no saviours coming to anyone's rescue. All there is death and destruction. There's no way we can win!" It was as if he read Meridia's mind, and his outburst threw a wet blanket over everyone else in the room, cloaking them in nihilism.

"*Click!*"

Before anyone could fill the void left by Kane's damning tirade, the front door opened beyond the living room and a series of footsteps clattered their way along the hall.

"Hello?" It was Peter and JJ.

They had returned from Chase Side unharmed, and their arrival had come at precisely the right moment.

It was time for them to kick another hornet's nest, and this one went by the name of Retiarius.

35

Having reconvened in the cold church hall, the group huddled under musty old blankets as they took turns in swapping stories to make sure everyone was up to speed on the evening's developments.

Their world was closing in on them all, and Peter wondered how much longer the magnolia walls and quaint stained-glass windows of St Peter's would keep them all safe.

The reach of the cult seemed endless and insurmountable. With centuries of violence and manipulation laid out across various scraps of paper pieced together from Father Alexander's study, the group were all-too aware this remained the tip of a malevolent iceberg. There was still so much they didn't understand.

The priest's absence was a sobering reminder of what was at stake now, and everyone knew there was little likelihood of him still being alive. The burden of guilt weighed heavily on Peter, as he had ultimately been the one to deliver Father Alexander straight into the hands of a homicidal nurse. That's if the crazed lunatic even was an actual nurse.

Whoever he was, he was clearly not someone to be trifled with, and was directly responsible for at least one of the broken families in the room.

Thankfully JJ agreed to omit the madman's gruesome boast when recounting his confrontation in the elevator, but it made little difference as Kane was quick to make a mental addition to the vengeful list, which was now tattooed on his broken heart.

The dramatic change in Kane's temperament was yet another tragedy. All that rage he was wrestling with, but his painful loss was still fresh, and Peter remained hopeful that in time he would see a return of the Kane of old. That was if they had any time left.

"The pizzas will be here soon, guys." He watched the shivering children munch away on the last of the crisps they had scavenged from the missing priest's cupboards and wondered if their delivery driver would be yet another knife-wielding maniac. The cult's influence seemed to know no bounds.

"Thank god! I'm starving!" JJ did his best to smooth over the cracks in the room, but nobody was buying it.

Tensions were high, and trust was at an all-time low within the group.

"So, now we are all up to speed. What do we do about Retiarius?" Despite her obvious exhaustion, Meridia was still keen to put their newfound authority on the cult to the test, and Peter agreed with her.

Having read all his comments during their edgy sharing session, the mystery blogger was clearly in the know and his constant warnings perhaps made him a potential ally, although they would need to tread carefully.

"I think the message we send is less important." Peter concluded.

"You've come up with the perfect profile name and should be enough to open up a dialogue if he is as knowledgeable as he claims. I say we just ask him to elaborate on his last post. If there is a danger the demon in room 4 is about to be reborn, then I'd like to understand exactly what we're up against."

"I don't know, it doesn't feel safe to me." Emily had been quiet until now, with no news to bring to the table aside from finding a stack of foldable z-beds in a storage cupboard at the rear of the church.

"We have no way of knowing who Retiarius is, or who he might be working with. For all we know, it might be a trap. Is there no way we can go to the police? Maybe call a department in a neighbouring town?" Her freckled face was fraught with worry.

"It's too risky. We don't know how far any of this goes. Archie's notes even talk about parliament, for Christ's sake!" Kane dialled up the paranoia by an extra notch and Peter was quick to seize the opportunity to address the elephant in the room and try to unite them all.

"Kane's right. Outside of this room, we don't know who we can trust. I say outside of this room because the people inside are all people I trust with my life. I mean it, guys." One by one, Peter forced eye contact with those around him before continuing.

"I know I can't speak for anyone else, but trust me when I say this, nothing we've uncovered in the last 24-hours... nothing...has changed a single thing about my feelings towards any of you. I want you to think about that for a moment. Our friendship, our bond, or whatever you want to call it, is what has gotten us this far. Now I know there may still be some doubts about me after what happened before, and I accept that. Hopefully, you can all see I'm trying to fix it. But I promise you I have zero doubts about anyone in this room. We need to be strong now, stronger than ever, if we're going to get through this. So, I just wanted you to know I'm here for you all. As I hope you still are for me, and for each other." Peter hoped his words were enough to break through the various barriers in the room and rally the group somehow.

"Peter's right." Izzy was the first to unburden herself, although Peter could tell from her wobbly voice she was struggling before she even started.

"I know I've not been through what some of you have. Nowhere near. But ever since my dad tried to take me, I've felt on the outside of everything, like nobody trusts me anymore. I don't know how much our parents are involved. But my dad was wearing a hood when he drugged me, so I guess that makes him pretty involved..." Tears seeped out from beneath her glasses as she searched for the right words.

"I just want you all to know whatever they've done. It's on them, not me. I never asked for any of this, and neither did JJ. I know our parents are on the wrong side of it all, but I'm not. We're not. You guys...you're my only family now... *sniff*...and families should talk, even when things get hard... *sniff*..." She trailed off into a whisper, overcome with emotion as she continued to wrestle with her composure.

"I'm sorry...*sniff*...this isn't easy...but I have to say it. I have to tell you. I just feel like I'm drowning...I feel like we all are...in our own way, and all I want to do is help, but I can't because I'm on the outside. I'm sick of being on the outside...I just want things the way they were between us.

We're all we've got now..." Meridia gave Izzy a huge sisterly squeeze as she broke down, followed by JJ, and the three of them sobbed together in a huddle.

"I feel it too," JJ whispered into her ear as he broke away, cuffing his tears.

"I still don't know how deep my parents are into all this, but you all know me. I'm not like them. I keep wracking my brains for reasons they might be involved. Like there's some perfect excuse none of us have thought of yet, but there isn't. Ever since I went to the hospital, my mum keeps ringing me." JJ pulled his phone out for all to see.

"Twenty missed calls, guys! I'm lucky if I get one usually...and this ain't late for me. So, I know that's not the reason she's calling. Truth is, I'm scared to answer her. I don't wanna know what she's got to say. I don't want to hear it. I guess there's nothing she can say to justify all this shit! All these twenty missed calls tell me is she's been talking to someone, that scumbag Grady I bet! Grrr.... this whole situation is a total mind fuck! Haunted houses, monsters, dead little girls. Crazy-arse people in cloaks with knives. Whatever Valerie is, and now the fucker in room 4 is due to make another appearance! I feel you, Izz, really, I do, and I'm sick of it, too. Whatever this awkwardness is, we need to hug it out or something and move on." JJ looked at Kane and Zach, then corrected himself.

"I don't mean move on and forget. I mean, move on with whatever plan we have to end this. Like Peter said, there will be time to grieve later. At least I hope there will be, and trust me, we all have plenty to grieve right now. But the only way we're going to get to that point is if we stick together." He glanced at Kane again as he finished his rant, and Peter could tell he was trying to encourage him to open up.

Although Kane's fury and appetite for revenge were

clear for everyone to see, nobody knew what else might be going on inside his mind, or how he felt about those who had now been tainted by their parents.

Aside from Meridia and Emily, he had plenty of motive to resent them all, but such speculation was about to end as Kane cleared his throat to speak.

36

"You should see what they want. Both of you." Kane looked at JJ and Izzy earnestly.

"We might learn something more about what's going on here." He feigned calmness on the surface, but beneath it, his anger raged on.

As conflicted as he felt about everything that happened, he knew deep down his grievance wasn't with JJ or Izzy. He had known them for most of his life, and although he could say the same about his parents, he wasn't about to let his anger impede their friendship. Not when he already lost so much.

"I know I'm angry. I can feel it, even now. It's constant. Eating away at me. I can't even think straight most of the time, not like I used to."

"It's ok," Peter interrupted. "The way you're feeling is perfectly normal. In fact, given everything that's happened, I'd be more concerned if you weren't angry. You just need to let it out if you can."

"I don't know how. I'm scared. Scared of what I'll do. Earlier, next door, all I wanted to do was smash everything.

I just wanted to lose it and go crazy. I'm worried if I do that...if I lose control, then I might never get it back. I'm scared I'll end up just like them, a monster. I want you guys to know, no matter what I say or do...no matter what's going on with me, none of it is about you, ok?" Kane's voice splintered, so he paused a moment, closing his eyes to steady himself.

"I know you've all lost everything, too. I just can't believe they're gone, you know?" He continued, eyes-closed, to preserve the shred of composure he was clinging to within.

"Last night we were all laughing and eating pizza, but I wasn't there...at least not really. Even though I knew it might be our last meal as a family, I wasn't listening...wasn't watching as much as I could, as much as I should've been." He shook his head in despair.

"I didn't know what was going to happen! How could I? I just wanted to make sure we all came back alive. I didn't think they were the ones in danger...*sniff*...I didn't think it would all turn out like this. I just wish we had the time back...*sniff*...that day...I dragged us all there...*sniff*...it was me. If I hadn't, then...then maybe...*sniff*..." Kane broke down in tears as the weight of guilt and grief he was carrying became too much for him to bear.

All he wanted was to go back in time. To scream at them all to stay home that day. Tell them to make do with all the silly, trivial things they did every other weekend. Back when they thought they had all the time in the world.

The hopeless realization it was all too late, feeling like a dagger lodged in his heart, and with each new wave of regret, his own seething rage twisted the blade.

As his sobs rippled through the heartbreaking silence, the others leaned in to comfort him, but he was quick to wriggle free, shrugging them off before anyone could get their arms around him.

"I'm sorry guys, it's not you...I swear...I just can't right now. I need to keep going. We all do." He looked down at his dejected little brother and desperately wanted to hug him.

To tell him everything was going to be alright, but he knew it wasn't. Not now. Not ever.

Peter was right when he said there would be time for this later. When it was all over, he would stop and allow himself to collapse into the arms of those who loved him, but right now, the anger was all that was keeping him going. If he was to be any use to anyone, he had to lean into it. Embrace it.

As much as he knew Zach needed comforting, he also needed his big brother to be strong, so that's what Kane had to be, no matter what.

"We need a plan. I think we should send the message to Retiarius and see what happens. Like Peter said, our username should be enough to get his attention..."

"Just did it." Meridia interrupted, tucking her phone away in her pocket. "I've turned the alerts on, so we'll wait and see if he bites."

"Cool, so that leaves us with your parents." Kane turned his attention back to JJ and Izzy. "You can't ignore them forever, and we've all got school tomorrow, so we need to think about that too. Maybe the longer we stay quiet, the more likely the cult is to think we've run?"

"I'm not so sure about that," Peter speculated.

"Given everything else that's happened today, I think we need to assume the worst, as far as Father Alexander is concerned. The Children of the Shadows seem to have eyes and ears everywhere, so it will only be a matter of time until they figure out we're here. My guess is Father Alexander got too close to them before he met us, and that's why someone paid him a visit. It won't take them long to realize his keys are missing. I expect we'll have a night here, tops, and even then, I'll have to keep watch. This place only has two exits, so we're vulnerable if they arrive in numbers."

"Shit! I thought we'd have longer." JJ flipped the visor of his cap and rubbed his brow.

"They have resources, remember?" Peter continued. "There's nothing to stop them from involving the police and having us all arrested! We've no right to be here, and if something has happened to Father Alexander, who else can corroborate our story?"

"BANG! BANG!"

Everyone jumped at the loud knocking on the church door.

"It's ok, that'll be our dinner." Peter reassured them all as he wandered over to investigate.

"Wait!" Kane followed, handing Peter one of two wooden pillar candle holders he'd swiped from the end of the aisle.

"Just in case." He shrugged.

Whoever killed his parents had masqueraded as an internet repairman to get in the door, so a cult member on a pizza delivery bike wasn't as far-fetched as it sounded.

Kane pressed his face to the glass next to the door as Peter gripped the handle. It was too dark outside to see any detail, but the shadowy figure on their doorstep was definitely cradling something in his arms.

"BANG BANG!"

The knocking came again, startling them both.

"Do it," Kane whispered, raising his makeshift club behind his head like a baseball bat.

He felt his temples throbbing at the prospect of a confrontation, and tightened his grip in anticipation. The varnished wood squeaked in his palms while Peter cautiously turned the handle and peered through the slender opening he made.

"Pizza for Mr Johnson?" Peter opened the door a little wider to receive the large stack of bright red pizza boxes and sat them down on the floor behind him.

"Thank you." He closed the door and let out a sigh of relief.

"Mr Johnson?" Kane asked, confused.

"We can't be too careful now, and I thought Seymor Butts might be a bridge too far."

Kane loosened his grip on his weapon and felt an unexpected twinge of disappointment that he wasn't given an excuse to use it.

"Just a teen, by the looks of it. No ring." Peter concluded, locking the door as Kane carried dinner back to the others.

They resembled a pack of ravenous hyenas, perched on the edge of their seats and ready to pounce as they waited for Peter to give them the green light. The aroma of melted mozzarella fused with piping hot pepperoni was intoxicating.

"Dig in!" He declared, and for the next twenty minutes, the only sound to be heard in St Peter's hall was five hungry children munching their way through seven extra-large, deep-pan pizzas.

"So, what do we do now, guys?" JJ asked, as he collapsed the last empty pizza box and dusted his hands of cornmeal.

Kane spent the entire mealtime contemplating the same question. The quiet indulgence of his favourite comfort food had calmed his mind a little, giving him time to reflect and gather his thoughts.

For the first time all afternoon, he felt more in control of his emotions and was ready to focus on the task at hand. As they often did, the group looked toward Peter to get the ball rolling, but Emily was the first to pipe up.

"I know I sound like a broken record, but I really think it's time we go to the police. Not the local police, but someone on the outside. Higher up...like Scotland Yard. This isn't a game! We've already lost too much, and now it looks like Father Alexander is gone, too. Who's next? What's it going to take to make us realize this is way beyond us? If you ask me, we should get out of Shawbrook and head for the city. We'll be safe there and let the authorities do their job rounding up whoever's involved." Emily seemed more on edge than before, and Kane guessed the day had finally caught up with her.

Her suggestion made perfect sense. Had it not been for his thirst for revenge, he would have happily packed his bags and run for the hills.

"That's definitely one option available to us," Peter accepted.

"We need to remember what we're up against. Getting out of Shawbrook, or Thundridge for that matter, is not as simple as it sounds. Despite being outnumbered, we are still a threat to the cult's plans, and the longer we evade capture, the greater threat we pose. The last thing they'll want is attention from the outside, so they will aim to keep us contained. It's what I would do in their shoes. As a small town, we only have a couple of roads leading out of here and based on the numbers we've seen, it wouldn't be difficult for them to cover all our exits to keep us from leaving. We can't simply call Scotland Yard and expect them to investigate on our say-so either. What would we even tell them? That the police in Shawbrook are part of a centuries-old cult hellbent on the world's destruction? The only people they would lock up are us. The same hurdle also prevents us from going to the press. No one in their right mind would believe our story."

"What if we posted something online?" Zach suggested.

"Nobody is gonna take us seriously after what happened last time." Kane pricked himself on his own observation and wondered if the cult had played any part in discrediting their last YouTube post.

"Kane's right." JJ affirmed. "We have zero credibility online, so I doubt anyone would see anything we put out there now. Even Peter doesn't have the number of followers we'd need to make an impact...no offence."

"Well, we can't just sit here and wait for them to find us! For all we know, they might be out there right now!" Emily snapped, frustrated everyone had picked holes in her suggestion.

"Look, it's been a long and gruelling day, so for now, I suggest we stay focussed on getting through the night." Peter's voice was jaded.

"The best use of our time right now is to rest. God knows we can all use some, and I don't know when the next opportunity might present itself. Tomorrow is another day, and we can gather our thoughts in the morning, with clearer heads. The problems we face aren't going anywhere, and will still be here when we wake, so it makes no sense driving ourselves crazy when we're all exhausted."

"What about school?!" A creature of habit, Izzy was desperate to cling onto at least one pillar of normalcy.

"That's the least of our worries, I'm afraid, dear." Peter

replied, then, realizing he was being dismissive, quickly backtracked.

"I can square that away with the headmaster in the morning. There's no need to fret. Suffice to say, though, none of you will be going back there anytime soon."

As Peter got to his feet, Kane pondered his reply. Was this the new normal? Being on the run.

Living day-to-day, never knowing where they would sleep from one night to the next. He cast his mind back to the first time he met Peter and how he'd explained the prophecy they were all so desperate to avoid.

Once again, over the course of 24-hours their world had changed radically. Was this the beginning of the end?

"Peter's right." Emily added. "I can call the school in the morning and tell them you've all got food poisoning or something...I can lay things on pretty thick when I have to, so I'm sure the headmaster will understand. Don't worry Izzy dear, it'll be fine. I promise."

"Excellent! Now, can someone fetch me a couple of extra glasses and a tea-towel from next door please?" Peter made the strange request with his face pressed to the window as he surveyed the grounds outside.

"I'll go." Meridia was quick to volunteer.

"Thanks M. JJ, perhaps you can go with her? The street looks deserted, but as a precaution, I think we need to start doing things in pairs from now on. We need to bunker down for the night, so I want to safeguard some of these windows. The building is pretty old, and although it may look like a fortress from the outside, it still has its flaws." Peter rapped his knuckles on the flimsy pane of glass to emphasize his point.

"We must do all we can to keep any unwanted visitors at bay."

37

The crisp night air offered a refreshing reprieve from the heavy smell of pizza that lingered inside the church, and Meridia breathed it in as she and JJ crept out the back door.

They could've heard a pin drop once JJ pulled the door close behind them, so Meridia paused, worrying it might be too quiet. Hereford Lane was devoid of the usual suburban sounds. No distant hum of traffic, no gentle breeze. No sign of life.

"Jeez! This place is dead!" JJ broke the silence with a whisper, then ushered her forward. "Let's get this over with, shall we?"

Father Alexander's rectory backed onto the church and was accessible via a poorly lit side alley containing an assortment of plastic wheely bins.

Across the narrow passageway, and directly opposite them, was a wooden side-gate which allowed entry to Father Alexander's garden. It was a convenient setup, which meant Meridia and JJ could move from the church to the house in under a minute if they entered through the backdoor, which they did.

"*Click!*"

Meridia unlocked the white UPVC door, and they both scurried into the kitchen. Having pulled all the curtains and blinds on their previous visit, Meridia turned on the light and started rifling through drawers.

The room was small, yet functional, with all the mod-cons one would expect, bar a microwave. A continuous cream speckled work surface traced two adjoining walls to form an L-shape, leading to a shiny stainless-steel sink in the furthest corner. Above and below the clutter-free worktop were a handful of pine cupboards which perfectly complimented the vanilla colour-scheme.

"I know where the glasses are," JJ declared, opening the cupboard closest to the sink. "So now all we need to find are the tea-towels."

"My mum keeps ours in a drawer next to the sink, so you look over there and I'll work my way through these." Meridia pulled the last of four drawers to find a selection of neatly folded checkered towels.

"Found them!" she added, grabbing a handful and placing them on the counter.

"Awesome! Maybe we should take a quick look in some of the other cupboards, in case there's anything else that could come in handy?"

"You mean more food?" Meridia chuckled.

"No...well, yes..." JJ blushed, as he started working his way back along the wall, one cupboard at a time.

"I noticed a fruit bowl in the living room earlier. We could take the bananas back with us?"

"Perfect! Pretty sure pizza doesn't count as one of my five-a-day, so I'll go grab them while you check the fridge." JJ made his way out as Meridia wandered over to the silver,

American-style fridge-freezer on the opposite side of the kitchen.

She sensed a pang of guilt flutter in her chest at the thought of looting the poor priest's food and wondered if there was some slender chance he might still be alive.

Her mum was right. This had all gone far enough. With the Children of the Shadows now baying for their blood, they wouldn't be able to stay hidden much longer. Perhaps it was time to cut their losses and walk away.

"Argh!"

Meridia opened the fridge door and gasped in terror at the grisly phantom waiting on the other side. A putrefied corpse, riddled with centuries of decay, greeted her with outstretched arms swathed in desiccated flesh. With a sallow, skeletal face, staring at her through hollow sockets, it unleashed a howling scream from its withered lips.

The haunting wail carried the musty aroma of wet soil which washed over Meridia's face and made its way deep into her lungs. It was as if the fridge was a window into an open grave.

Trembling in shock, Meridia's legs turned to jelly, buckling at the knees as she clung onto the door handle to stay on her feet, but her efforts were in vain. Icy fingers, covered in dirt and muck, clawed at Meridia's shoulders until they found their grip and yanked her into the frosty tomb.

BANG!

The fridge door slammed shut behind her, and Meridia vanished without a trace.

38

JJ WANDERED BACK INTO THE KITCHEN CARRYING A plastic bag full of fruit.

"I found some apples, and a bunch of grapes, too. Result!" He paused when he found the room empty.

"M?" At first, he assumed she took their scavenger hunt into another room, but when he spotted the muddy smear on the floor in front of the fridge, he wasn't so sure.

"M?! Where are you?" He raised his voice above the wave of panic now crashing down on him.

He'd only been gone a matter of seconds, and there was no way Meridia would return to the church without him.

JJ marched over to the fridge and opened its door, half-expecting to find her hiding inside.

"Idiot!" he muttered to himself, staring at the half-empty bottle of milk and jar of Nutella.

"This isn't funny M! Where are you?!" He called out once more, but the silence that followed left him no other choice.

JJ charged out the back door to tell the others.

Meridia was in trouble again.

39

Meridia's screams were futile. Swallowed by the dense, suffocating mud that was slowly drowning her. Deeper and deeper, she was dragged down into the mire by her ghoulish captor, its scrawny fingers refusing to let go.

All Meridia could do was close her eyes and hold her breath as the deluge of muck and dirt continued to bombard her, clogging her airways, and starving her body of precious oxygen. The back of her throat and nasal passage tingled as her lungs drew close to bursting, but there was no room to exhale.

Buried deep beneath a mountain of earth, Meridia's limbs wilted, and her resolve waned until all she could hear was her deafening heartbeat, reverberating like a drum inside her head.

Louder and louder, it grew, labouring in its desperate pursuit of air, until it eventually faltered and faded into nothing. In the final depths of her despair, the darkness expanded like a pool of black ink, bleeding into every corner of Meridia's brain, until she ultimately lost consciousness.

"*Argh!!...*"

A cacophony of screams tore through Meridia's mind like a tornado of pain and suffering, jolting her awake. The agonizing cries continued, a chorus of torment, swirling and twirling around her as she scrambled to her feet. Meridia felt sluggish as she moved, grounded by a thick black tar weighing her down.

Wherever she was, it was cold and dark. A cave dipped in blood, filled with murky red shadows that flickered and danced on the wall in front of her. The musty smell of ripe soil interlaced with the coppery stench of death and decay.

"*Is this hell?*" She wondered, as the unrelenting screams persisted.

Meridia swiftly found the answer to her question when she turned to face their source. A crimson river, littered with bodies, rippled and splashed its way onto the muddy bank at her feet.

Thousands of faces, all twisted in anguish, crying out for mercy as they bobbed up and down on the turbulent current. Among the hordes of corpse-like casualties languishing in the gory waters, she caught the sound of someone screaming her name.

"*Meridiaaaa! Please!! Help meeeee!*"

She recognized the voice instantly and searched the odious sea of tormented faces for its owner. There, close to the shore, was JJ. Soaked in blood, his throat was agape, and he was missing most of the fingers on his outstretched hand. Waving his crimson stumps above his head, JJ beckoned for her to come closer. Meridia burst into tears at the sight of him.

Was this another glimpse of their bleak future? There was more than despair in his splintered cries. There was excruciating agony as he thrashed about, begging to be saved.

"*Don't move!*" A whispery voice wormed its way into her ear.

It belonged to a girl, and although unfamiliar, it was enough to stop Meridia in her tracks.

"*They will see you if you move.*" The voice came again, nestling inside Meridia's mind.

Nervously glancing around, she found there was nobody else with her as she stood on the river's edge.

"*My name is Beth.*" The invisible girl continued. "*I felt you once...long ago...when they condemned me here....*"

Somewhere beneath her gooey veneer, an ice-cold chill scampered its way up the back of Meridia's neck when the penny dropped.

"Elizabeth? Elizabeth Cooper?" Meridia murmured.

"*Yes...you remember! It was so long ago...an eternity.*" Beth's voice was soft and melancholy.

"Where am I?! Why did you bring me here?!" Meridia's temper flared at the prospect she'd been abducted by another lost soul in need of help. She had enough troubles of her own right now.

"*Ssh...you must be quiet.*" Beth pleaded. "*They might hear you.*"

"Who?! Who might hear?!" Meridia found JJ again in the crowded canal, but this time noticed Kane and Izzy flailing beside him.

Both were brutally mutilated. Kane's neck had been violently hacked, almost to the point of decapitation. As he battled against the tide, his head slumped flaccid on his shoulder, held on only by a sliver of serrated flesh that looked on the verge of snapping.

Meanwhile, Izzy bore a deep gash down the centre of

her head, slicing her glasses in two. Coagulated blood and fragments of her skull glistened from the wound as she struggled to stay afloat. Meridia wobbled at their gruesome appearance, devastated by the latest in a long line of grisly visions.

The pit of her stomach gurgled as bile bubbled its way up into her mouth. It was all too much to take. She had watched her friends perish before, and until now, had always averted it, but this felt different. Whatever this was, it went beyond the grave.

"You must see with your own eyes." Beth broke the ghastly spell Meridia was under. *"You must see what is waiting for you and your friends if you fail. You are the last of us...the best of us. You must do what we could not!"*

The desperation in Beth's voice was palpable and echoed Meridia's own frustration.

"WHAT?!" she bellowed. "Please! Just tell me what I need to do! I'll do anything!"

Tears streamed down her cheeks as Meridia implored her unearthly host to explain herself, but it was too late.

"Click-clack...click-clack..."

The spine-chilling sound echoed directly overhead, and Meridia froze in terror. Something was crawling on the ceiling. Something so big that despite the piercing screams of her suffering friends, Meridia could hear it scurrying toward her from above.

"Click-clack...click-clack..."

"Weavers!" Beth cried. *"They've found you!"*

As Meridia dared to look up, she sensed the ground beneath her tremble. A swarm of rotting, withered hands sprouted from the muddy bank and clawed at her calves, dragging her back into the earth.

"Argh!"

Sinking into the marshy ground, Meridia glanced up at the cave's ceiling and let out a blood-curdling scream.

The weaver was the stuff of nightmares. A vile and monstrous arachnid with gigantic sinewy legs, swathed in thorny bristles. Its brawny, egg-shaped torso was covered in greasy black hair that remained matted to its back as it hung upside down just a few metres from Meridia. Pulsating with an insatiable hunger for human flesh, its barbed legs rattled the rocky terrain like the staccato cracking of old bones being ground together.

"Click-clack, click-clack…"

Two flaming orbs of amber burnt through the gloom as the mammoth creature scampered toward her at ferocious speed.

"Argh!!"

Meridia screamed again as the army of undead hands continued to pull her into the ground. There was no escape. In a frenzied flurry, the grisly mutant scurried across the rugged clefts and crags until it was right on top of her.

Sizing up its prey from above, the weaver let out a spine-tingling shriek, revealing row upon row of jagged, shark-like teeth that glistened in the shadows of its cavernous mouth as it soured the air with its sulphurous breath.

Meridia, up to her waist in mud, felt petrified and trapped between two evils as she strained to evade the weaver's searing, hate-filled glare. In the depths of its throat, she could see a milky globule of slime forming, forcing its way up in readiness to vomit all over her.

The stench of sulphur intensified as steam seeped through the gaps in its razor-sharp teeth and its body retched like a cat coughing up a fur ball. Up to her neck now, Meridia closed her eyes and braced herself.

"Kaff! Splat!"

The dull and distant spattering of slime sounded above her, but she was safely submerged.

Spared from whatever fate the evil weaver had in store, Meridia was once again buried alive under a mountain of suffocating mud.

40

Meridia landed heavily on all fours, gasping for breath. The bitter taste of mud still lingered in her mouth, as if she was chewing on topsoil. Eyes firmly clenched, she plucked up the courage to peek at her surroundings and found herself knelt on an overgrown patch of grass.

Wherever she was, it was late evening, and the waxy blades beneath her palms looked more blue than green under the night sky. In front of her, a crumbling gravestone covered in moss reflected the moonlight overhead.

"Elizabeth Cooper!" Meridia read aloud. "1716–1728...she was the same age as me!"

Upon reading the ominous discovery, Meridia sprang to her feet. She was in the church graveyard, alone, or so she hoped. There was no sign of the weaver or her grim abductor anywhere, nor was there any sign of her friends.

The stained-glass windows of St Peter's were completely dark, its hall empty. Exasperated, Meridia could almost feel her precious life being cut short. Years snatched away from her with each new, harrowing vision.

"How can anyone expect to live like this?!" she bleated. "No wonder she didn't make it past 12!"

As she raged, a gentle breeze skimmed past her face, prickling the tears of frustration rolling down her cheeks. The air seemed warm, like a summer's evening, and something about it smelled different, clean. Gazing up at the sky, the moon looked glorious in its midnight haunt, brilliant and well-defined, as if she could see every crater.

"*Crack!*"

The sharp sound of a twig breaking underfoot snapped Meridia out of her astral trance. Someone was coming. Ducking behind the gravestone, she held her breath and listened to the footsteps as they approached. It was a woman, or so she thought. She could smell the floral notes of her perfume on the gentle breeze.

What was the mystery woman doing at St Peter's now, and who had turned off all the lights? The footsteps came to a halt at Elizabeth's grave, and Meridia sensed the hairs on the back of her neck stand to attention.

"I just came to thank you." The woman whispered. Her voice was soft and hesitant, as if crippled by shyness.

"W...we couldn't have stopped him without you, Beth. I hope you can find peace now..."

"*Chink!*"

Meridia rolled her eyes as the zip on her puffer jacket clattered against the headstone.

"Wh...who's there?!" the woman stammered.

Meridia stayed silent whilst considering her options. She had no idea who the woman was, or if she might be a member of the cult, but her instincts were telling her she wasn't a threat. After all, she'd come here to thank Beth for something, so perhaps that made her an ally.

"I...I mean it...I...I know you're there." The woman

spoke again, backing away this time. Meridia figured she would take a chance and trust her gut.

In the absence of any zombies trying to bury her alive or colossal spiders with fireballs for eyes trying to eat her, she figured it was worth the risk.

"Ok. You got me," Meridia said, as she emerged from the shadows of Beth's grave with her hands held high.

The woman on the opposite side of the plot was not much taller than Meridia and was somewhere in her early thirties. Beneath her round, gold-framed glasses and curly, strawberry-blonde bob, she had a pretty face, with high cheekbones and a delicate cleft chin.

Under the glare of the full moon, Meridia noticed a cluster of freckles peppering her slender, upturned nose. She was wearing a cream, cable knitted cardigan over an orange paisley summer dress, with an oversized brown belt loosely tied around her waist. Its gold buckle glistened as she took a step backwards, away from the grave, and Meridia saw the woman was svelte underneath her layers but broad shouldered, like a willowy catwalk model.

"Meridia! What are you doing here?" The woman asked. "I told you to wait for me at the hotel..."

She seemed every bit as confused as Meridia.

"Wait, what?! How..." Meridia didn't even finish her sentence when a man's voice bellowed out across the graveyard.

"I see her! There she is!"

"They've found me!" the woman screeched. "Run Meridia! RUN!"

Meridia spun back towards the church and clattered headfirst into the arms of someone lurking behind her.

41

"I'VE FOUND HER! SHE'S OVER HERE!"

Meridia screamed hysterically as her mum clung onto her for dear life.

"It's ok hun…I've got you." She whispered. "We've been looking everywhere for you!"

Glancing over her mother's shoulder, she saw the dim lights of St Peter's hall in the distance, and the warm summer breeze that had caressed her cheeks just moments ago was now hostile and bitterly cold.

"But the woman…" Meridia turned back toward the grave, but there was nobody there.

Peering up at the sky, the moon was now a murky grey, barely visible beneath the evening mist. The air was thick again, sticking in Meridia's throat, weighed down with pollution.

"What woman, hun?" Emily asked.

"There's no one else here but us." Sure enough, the graveyard was empty, all except for her friends now gathering around her.

"You need to warn me next time you do that, M." JJ

joked, trying to ease the tension. Meridia turned and gave him an enormous hug.

"Whoa! What's this for?!" He asked in surprise, but Meridia stayed silent as she choked back tears.

Overwhelmed with relief, she let him go and moved on to Kane, then Izzy.

Whatever horrors Beth had shown her, she needed to cling onto the terrible memory of them. There was no way on earth she was going to let that happen to anyone she loved. Not while she had air in her lungs.

She drew another breath of the chilly night air and followed the others back inside.

42

Having heard Meridia describe her latest encounter with the underworld, Peter felt even more bewildered. The shadow cast by Crooked House was as twisted as it was long, and the further they made it into the night, the muddier everything became.

He recognized the hellish place Meridia visited from his own nightmares, courtesy of Molly the witch, although he was grateful he was spared any run-ins with weavers.

Were the creatures real, or were they symbolic of something else? Who was the strange woman who recognized her in the graveyard?

Meridia wasn't alone in wrestling with her gift, and the more her premonitions played out, the more Peter tied his brain in knots, trying to fathom them.

"Now it really is time we all get some rest." He announced to the others, who were still fussing over Meridia whilst she got ready for bed. He could tell she loathed the extra attention, even from her mum.

At his instruction, the group grudgingly dispersed, each wandering back to their z-beds and climbing under the covers. Peter had dragged all the beds, but one, to the furthest corners of the hall, arranging them on either side of the altar and well away from the main door. The girls congregated on the left, and the boys gathered on the right.

Meanwhile, Peter assumed the role of protector, positioning his bed a few yards from the main door. Having spent hundreds of nights in haunted locations around the world, he was accustomed to going a night or two with little sleep, so would keep watch.

Once the children were all tucked in, Peter wrapped one glass JJ fetched for him in a tea-towel and smashed it on the floor. He then sprinkled the fragments in front of the windows he deemed susceptible to a break in.

"I saw this in a spy movie and thought it was a genius idea. I figured it wouldn't do us any harm, given how old some of these window frames are. Try to stay away from this side of the hall from now on if you can."

"Cool!" JJ approved, removing his hat and fluffing up his pillow as Peter continued.

"I know tonight will be tough for you all, but we need to get some sleep if we're going to figure out this mess tomorrow. Just try to be respectful of everyone else and keep noise to a minimum. I'm here, and so is Emily, if you need us. Do your best guys, ok? That's all any of us can hope for." Peter switched off the lights and climbed on top of his own bed.

He blindly felt around on the floor beside him for the wooden candle holder and gripped it like a baseball bat. If they were going to survive the night, the next few hours would be critical.

43

JJ's mind was abuzz as he lay staring up at the church's dome-shaped ceiling. Every attempt to lose himself in the maze of elaborate shapes carved above resulted in him being dragged back to a series of unanswered questions.

Like Izzy, his phone was full of unread messages and voicemails from his parents that he was too scared to open. A lifetime of lies now teetered precariously like a game of Jenga in its final throes. He intended to open them after dinner, but when Meridia disappeared for the second time that evening, the opportunity passed him by.

No good would come from reading them now, though, so JJ and Izzy both agreed to look first thing in the morning. That brought him to the next question on his list: Meridia.

It was quite the hug she gave him, and he knew she was holding something back when she shared her latest vision. Did she see something terrible in store for him?

It wouldn't be the first time, but somehow this seemed different. Meridia was spooked more than usual, and he caught her staring at him several times after telling her story.

"*Secrets and lies,*" he thought to himself as he let out a deep sigh.

"Psst," Kane whispered. "You still awake, mate?"

"Yeah...can't stop thinking about stuff."

"Same." Kane replied.

"I thought if we stayed away from that damn house everything would be ok...but now look at us!" JJ's guilt resurfaced as he wondered back to the day he turned up at Kane's with a box of donuts and a bright idea.

"It's bigger than the house now, mate, always has been. Those fuckers are everywhere! Sorry, I don't mean..." Kane trailed off.

"It's cool. I get it. I'm going to look at my phone tomorrow...maybe that will give us some answers." JJ doubled down on his promise, but remained scared of what answers his parents might offer.

"I feel like everything has changed. I know it has, but I mean between us all. When this started, it felt like we were a team...we used to tell each other everything. It's all such a mess now and I don't know what to believe anymore." Kane's voice cracked, and JJ couldn't tell if he was upset or simply struggling to keep the noise down.

"I still tell you everything, mate. You can even listen to my messages with me tomorrow if you like?"

"That's ok. I don't mean it like that. I dunno what I mean, really. Just paranoid, I guess."

"Do you think Meridia is holding out on us?" JJ blurted. "I mean, the way she hugged me, and the way she kept looking at me after."

"Definitely!" Kane's voice crept over the parapet, prompting a groan from Zach, who was on the other side of him.

"Definitely," he repeated, whispering softer this time.

"She kept looking at me, too. I think she saw something awful, and it's left me wondering if I'm gonna make it through this."

"We will mate. We've got this far, haven't we? Witches and monsters, now lunatics in hoods. We'll get out of here in the morning. Peter will come up with a way. He always does." JJ shuffled down in his bed and thought about his trip to Chase Side. "What do you think Valerie meant?"

"What do you mean?"

"Her whole 'tonight no one sleeps' spiel. I keep wondering what she meant. Do you think they know we're here?"

"Peter seems to think they won't catch on until tomorrow, so I'm hoping he's right. I guess the first thing they'll do when they realize Father Alexander's keys are missing is look around the hospital for them. That's if they even notice they've gone missing in the first place."

"I guess..." Another crushing wave of guilt washed over JJ at the mention of Father Alexander's name. "Do you think he's..."

"I don't know. For all we know, he may have escaped and is lying low for the night like we are."

"I hope so, man. We wouldn't be here if it wasn't for him." JJ closed his eyes to stop himself from crying, and for the first time that night, he felt as if he might succumb to sleep.

A solitary tear trickled out from beneath the tangle of eyelashes, weaving a warm salty path down his cheek and onto his pillow. Within a matter of seconds, Kane's inaudible whispers faded into the night and JJ drifted off...

"Ding!"

JJ's eyes sprang open as the narrow band of light expanded across his face. Dazed and confused by the blue haze of the fluorescent bulb creeping in, he wobbled and realized he was now on his feet.

"Huh?" He mumbled, squinting as he adjusted to his new stainless-steel surroundings.

Before he made sense of where he was, the sickly sweet, chemical aroma of lemons gave him the answer he was dreading.

He was back in the hospital elevator, but the long empty corridor beyond was unfamiliar. Glancing up at the tiny LED numbers above him, JJ shuddered when he saw the number 4 was burning red.

"Valerie!"

44

Father Alexander winced, awoken by an excruciating stabbing pain in his forearm, accompanied by a dull ache in the side of his neck. Still strapped to his wheelchair, he had no clue how long he was unconscious, but it was long enough for his body to have seized up.

Straightening himself as best he could, he tried to make a fist with his right hand and get the blood pumping through his damaged wrist. Hampered by the cast on his arm, what little grip he mustered only resulted in more pain, but Father Alexander cracked a smile, nonetheless.

He could feel again, which meant whatever drugs he was pumped full of had worn off. Looking around the dank, musty prison cell, he was certain he was alone, so took his time assessing the gravity of his predicament.

There were no windows in sight and he surmised the dim yellow glow skimming his shoulders was coming from either a dingy bulb or a small window behind him. He hoped for his sake it was the latter. Turning his attention to the floor, he noticed the ground was stony and hard, much like the walls.

He considered rocking himself onto his side to break the wheelchair, but such a move was loud and risky if it failed. As he worked his way up from the floor, he was buoyed by the fact his restraints were made of leather and fastened with flimsy looking buckles.

Finally, something he could work with. He twisted his left wrist back and forth, up, then down, to loosen the strap. If he could stretch the leather enough, he could pop the pin out of its hole. With one arm free, he could undo the other restraints and at least give himself a fighting chance of escaping.

Back and forth, up and down, he continued to writhe and wriggle. As the leather slowly yielded, each new creak carried him closer to freedom, until *'pop'*, the pin finally broke free. Giddy with excitement, Father Alexander made quick work of his restraints and gingerly rose to his feet.

His knees creaked as he stood, still weak from his ordeal, but at least he was mobile. As he hoped, the light streaming in was coming from a tiny square peephole at the top of a sturdy-looking oak door.

"This is a dungeon!" He muttered, shuffling to see what was waiting for him in the corridor beyond.

From what he could tell, the passageway appeared empty. Similar in style to his prison cell, the hall was dark and dingy. Its mottled walls were made of limestone, discoloured by mould, and decades of water damage for as far as the eye could see.

Wherever he was, this place was old. Maybe as old as St Peter's, but he knew somewhere at the end of the corridor was an elevator, and with it, a way out of this nightmare.

Making sure the coast was clear, Father Alexander drew a deep breath and clasped the door handle in front of him. Now for the moment of truth.

"*Click!*"

By some minor miracle, the door was left unlocked.

"Thank you, God!" Father Alexander sighed as he pushed the door ajar.

A waft of warm, musty air forced its way in through the gap which suggested he was deep underground and peering down the corridor, he saw a handful of doors just like his. At the very end, some hundred yards away, was the elevator he'd arrived in.

"*Could there be others locked away down here?*" He wondered.

"*Clap...clap...clap!*"

The sudden interruption startled him, and he spun round to see who else was in the room.

"Bravo priest! I'm impressed..."

In contrast to the Grand Master, this voice was soft but assured. Crouched in the shadows, Silas Grady had ditched his nurse's costume for something far more befitting of a medieval dungeon.

Wearing a thick, brown hooded cloak, he looked like a mad monk from the dark ages, squatting on the balls of his feet as if ready to pounce. Old and clearly well-worn, his robes were crudely shredded from his waist down to the ground. The ragged strips of fabric lay twisted and tangled on the stony floor like a plague of poison oak stretching out across the room. Although only his mouth was visible beneath his cowl, Father Alexander recognized him instantly.

"You! You were at my window last night!" He felt his temper flare, which triggered another shooting pain in his wrist, reminding him he was at a severe disadvantage.

"*Clink!*"

Grady tossed a laminate card across the room, which landed at Father Alexander's feet.

"You'll need that to operate the lift." He said nonchalantly.

Father Alexander's eyes stayed glued to Grady as he picked up the hospital ID card.

"What is this?!" He asked, confused by the man's offer of help.

"Your services are no longer required, priest." Grady snickered as he pulled a hunting knife out from under his cloak.

The serrated blade shimmered like a phantom in the dim light as he flipped it playfully from one hand to the other, leaving behind an ominous afterglow with each new flick of his wrist.

"That means you belong to me now." A cold sweat broke out across Father Alexander's brow as he fumbled for the door handle behind him.

"You've got to the count of a hundred, then I'm coming for you...ready or not."

Father Alexander hesitated like a rabbit in the headlights, torn over what to do next. Was this a bluff? A trap? A smug sneer snaked its way across Grady's mouth, then he covered his eyes and began counting like a child starting a game of hide and seek.

"One-Mississippi...Two-Mississippi...Three-Mississippi..."

45

JJ EDGED TOWARDS THE ELEVATOR DOOR AS HE TRIED TO get his bearings. There was no way out to his left or his right, just an endless corridor ahead, twitching under the trembling cobalt light. Its lustreless walls and glossy floor brought to life as they convulsed beneath the eerie strobe.

Reaching the threshold of his metal silo, an unnatural chill stung the back of JJ's throat and he watched his breath condense in the icy atmosphere. Despite bearing all the hallmarks of Chase Side, the passage was strange and unfamiliar. It had to be a dream. Abstract remnants from his run-in with Grady still percolating in the back of his congested mind.

"*Click!*"

JJ flinched as the hall lights went out. All that remained was the crimson glow of the tiny number '4' above him, its menacing glare bleeding into the darkness. Bullied by the mounting silence, he held his breath and listened to the void, but all he heard was his own rapid heartbeat ringing in his ears. He needed to get away from this place, distract himself with happier thoughts, but all he could picture was Grady's menacing grin.

"*Buzz...*"

In the distance, a single bulb fizzed back to life, painting a tiny section of the hallway blood-red, and from the gloom, a man stepped into its juddering spotlight.

"Grady!" JJ gasped in horror. Still dressed in his scrubs, the nurse lingered under the light's sinister glow, statuesque, as JJ shuffled back inside his steel cubicle.

With murderous intent, Grady marched toward him, scalpel in hand, like a man possessed.

"*Click!*"

No sooner had he begun his approach, the light cut out again and Grady disappeared in the darkness.

"Hell no!" JJ shrieked, frantically spamming the button for the ground floor. Staring into the abyss, he braced himself for a fight as he waited for the lift door to close.

"This is just a dream...it's just a dream." He muttered, fists clenched and his heart still beating ten-to-the-dozen.

Adrenaline coursed through his body as, once more, the oppressive silence mounted around him.

"*Buzz...*"

A couple of yards from where JJ was standing, another bulb flickered to life and bathed the hall in pink and burgundy. Beneath the baleful glare, Grady was still fast approaching, relentless, but this time something about him was different.

Sputtering and glitching with each new stride, the nurse was transforming into something else. Something far more terrifying. Each shimmer and flicker shrouded him in static, like a trapped soul clawing to escape from within. Consumed with rage, they radiated a vibrant red, piercing the gloom like tiny beacons of hate.

Twisting and twitching to a series of bone-crunching snaps and pops, the rest of his smarmy façade crumbled to reveal his fiendish nature. JJ watched on helplessly, gripped by terror, as Grady's mouth violently cracked and split in each corner, stretching his malevolent grin from ear to ear.

Sharp, thorny fangs forced their way out through his gums, pushing his teeth out by their roots and peppering the floor with their bloodstained shards.

Another series of sickening cracks echoed down the corridor as Grady's skin turned a deathly shade of grey and his sinewy frame expanded and hardened beneath his clothes, splitting his scrubs at the seams until all that remained were tattered rags.

As he continued his march toward JJ, Grady took on a guise of a barbarous gargoyle carved from granite, filling the corridor with his colossal presence and hungry for blood.

"Grr..." The monster formerly known as Grady growled like a wild animal as his forehead cracked wide open and knotted horns corkscrewed their way out of his skull.

Like crimson war paint, blood streaked down his wicked, unrecognizable face, and his grisly metamorphosis was complete.

"C'mon...c'mon!" JJ furiously hit the elevator button over and over as the demonic nurse drew closer.

He was drenched in sweat now and on the verge of a heart attack. Dream or not, there was no way he could take on the hulking mass alone.

Backing away until he bumped against the elevator wall, JJ slumped down to its floor in defeat. There was nowhere left to run. As the demon's shadow towered over him, JJ closed his eyes, desperate to avoid his evil gaze.

"Please wake up...please!" He pleaded with himself as the demon closed in for the kill.

Warm, clammy breath so close that it tickled JJ's ear, and then...

"*Click!*"

JJ flinched, opening his eyes to total darkness. An unseen force snuffed out all the remaining lights, rendering him blind to whatever unspeakable horrors the demon had in store. Heart in his mouth, JJ cowered in the corner, paralyzed by fear and listening to the creatures rasping breath, as he waited for the first blow to land.

"*Screech!*"

In the distance, he heard metal scrape against metal as the elevator door slowly closed and sealed JJ's fate.

46

In the serenity of the church hall, Peter glanced at his watch and let out a deep sigh. Only an hour had passed since he sent everyone to bed, and it was shaping up to be a long night. There was no sign of trouble since setting up camp by the main entrance, but he hardly expected the cult to broadcast their arrival should they decide to make a move.

Luckily, the icy draft billowing through the gap beneath the door was enough to carry even the slightest of noises in from the cold, so Peter remained confident they were safe, for now. Surveying the z-beds at the opposite end of the aisle, it seemed everyone was getting some much-needed rest. All but him, that was.

Although his body still felt weary, he didn't mind being the nominated lookout for the night. Along with Emily, he was the responsible adult, after all, and most experienced in listening for phantom noises.

For his own sanity, he would need something to help pass the time, but not something too distracting. As safe as they were right now, he couldn't afford to be complacent.

Not with an army of homicidal hooded maniacs baying for their blood.

Their situation sounded so absurd as he mulled it over in his head, and Peter wondered how it came to this, sleeping rough in a cold church hall whilst on the run from a sinister cult. The more he weighed up their options, the more it made sense for them all to flee Cold Christmas in the early hours and go find help. With the best will in the world, they were unlikely to topple the Children of the Shadows alone.

They had a stranglehold on this town spanning centuries, killing or corrupting anyone who got in their way. The idea of corruption ignited a spark in Peter's mind, and he quickly reached for his phone. If the mysterious onyx ring was the mark of a cult member, then it made sense that anyone without the ring had the potential to be trusted.

Unearth enough allies and they might just find a way out of this insidious bubble. If the police were indeed mixed up in it all, then it made sense to begin his search somewhere above them in the town's hierarchy.

"I can't sleep." Izzy startled Peter, sneaking up on him from behind.

"Sorry, I didn't mean to make you jump." She added, as Peter fumbled to keep a grip on his phone.

"Phew! It's ok dear, I was just immersed in thought. I didn't hear you get out of bed." The realization left Peter wondering what else he might have missed, and so he straightened up and did his best to look more alert.

"Meridia and her mum can sleep anywhere. It's a Wilson thing, apparently. Emily told me she even fell asleep at a bus stop once when she was standing up! I love them, but it's infuriating. I just can't switch my brain off." Izzy looked dejected.

"Sleep can be a tricky old thing. Sometimes the more we chase after it, the more elusive it becomes." Peter tried to console her.

Despite the age gap, he regarded Izzy to be the smartest in the group, in academic terms at least. Her fastidious nature was an enormous asset, but it also left her prone to suffering from a restless mind. After their first encounter with Crooked House, she went weeks with broken sleep. She craved logic and order.

Unlike Meridia, who led with her heart and was quick to blow a gasket in the face of adversity, Izzy was more cerebral, which meant she internalized her discontent. Instead of blowing off steam, she would bottle up her issues until such time she could work through them, and therein lie the problem. There was no rationalizing or working through what they were up against now.

"What are you doing?" she asked. Peter reasoned his little epiphany might be just the distraction she needed, so he shared his idea.

"Here, I'll show you." He patted a space beside him and opened Google on his phone.

"I had a thought about the ring Kane showed us. Until now I've been thinking of it as a way to identify cult members. JJ said Grady was wearing the same ring when he encountered him at the hospital earlier, so I've been wracking my brains to recall if I've noticed anyone else with one since I arrived in town."

"Me too." Izzy interjected. "But rings aren't something I usually pay attention to."

"Me neither, sadly. But it got me thinking...it may also be a way to identify people who aren't involved." Izzy's eyes widened as she pieced together Peter's reasoning.

"That means we could figure out who we can turn to for help!" She exclaimed.

"Exactly! Now, it's a long shot, but I figured if the police and the hospital are both compromised, then the next logical place to look for help would be the local council. My gut is telling me the cult has already recruited them. They have power and influence, which makes them desirable to the Children of the Shadows, and might explain how they have remained undetected for so long. But, there will also be opposing political parties operating in the area, and they might be our best chance at finding an outlier. I figured we could start at the top and work our way down."

"The mayor?" Izzy asked.

"He's as good a starting point as any." Peter shrugged.

"Chances are the same mayor presides over Shawbrook, Thundridge and Cold Christmas, which again would make him an ideal candidate for the cult. However, there would have been other candidates when he was elected. People with different agendas, and that's where I'm hoping we might find someone who can help us." Peter searched for the mayor of Cold Christmas and was presented with a range of articles from the Herts Gazette covering everything from his appointment two years prior, to a hospital wing he declared open to patients a couple of weeks ago.

"Chase Side!" Izzy declared.

"Let's see if there are any pictures of him, shall we..." Peter clicked on the link and waited for it to load.

Despite confirming his suspicions, he still found the instant connection between mayor and hospital deflating. Each new revelation they uncovered about the cult reinforced how much he had underestimated them.

"There!" Izzy pointed at the headline picture. "Zoom in!"

"Mayor Naidu. Can't say I've had the pleasure." Peter did as Izzy asked and expanded the image until the mayor filled his screen.

Vamsi Naidu wasn't your typical mayor based on his picture. All smiles beneath his full, bushy beard. He looked more hipster than politician as he casually posed for the cameras in the staged hospital ward.

His hair was thick and wavy, combed back in a loose side parting with the odd fleck of grey around his temples. Tall and slim, he was dressed in a trendy brown tweed suit and open collar sky-blue shirt as he shook hands with the beaming doctor beside him.

"Zoom in on his hands!" Izzy was chomping at the bit for answers, and clearly not as quick to write him off as Peter had been.

Once more, Peter obliged as much as his phone would allow. With his right hand firmly clasped by the doctor, it was difficult to discern if the mayor was wearing a ring or not. He had, however, cemented the shake by placing his left hand on top.

"Just a wedding band, by the looks of it." Peter clarified.

"Let's see if we can find a closeup of his other hand." He went back to the list of articles and clicked the next in line.

"Mayor Naidu and wife spotted cycling in Jubilee Park...perfect!" Peter beamed.

The last picture rekindled a sliver of hope inside him that the mayor might not be involved after all. Peter disregarded the fluff news article and expanded the image.

This time, mayor Naidu wasn't posing and seemed to be unaware of the camera altogether. Dressed in all black cycling gear, with a matching helmet, he was again all smiles, but this time accompanied by his wife.

In contrast, Mrs Naidu was decked out in purple Lycra, also with a colour-coordinated cycling helmet, and was pedalling a fraction ahead of him. Peter zoomed in on the mayor's handlebars in search of a ring, but the results remained inconclusive.

"Damn it!" He grumbled.

"It's a slideshow!" Izzy tapped the arrow icon to the right of the picture and skimmed through the accompanying images.

As she did, the mayor and his wife seemed to jostle for position in their private race, smiling and laughing as they made their way around the park's cycling path. They looked at a picture of wedded bliss, and the more the photos flashed past, the more Peter found it hard to reconcile the mayor could have any involvement with a murderous sect.

"Wait!" Peter interjected. "Go back one!"

Izzy hit the back button, relinquishing control to Peter. Zooming in, he got a clear shot of the mayor's right hand.

"No ring!" He whispered.

"Let's try another!" Izzy blurted.

Buoyed by the glimmer of hope they had uncovered. They excitedly went back to the list in search of more proof. After going through another six articles with a fine-tooth comb, they were both convinced mayor Naidu was a potential ally worth reaching out to.

Originally hailing from Enfield, the only son of a self-made entrepreneur, Vamsi was a second-generation British-Indian. He met his wife Reah whilst studying politics at North London University and the two of them now lived in Welwyn, some twelve miles outside of Cold Christmas, with their young sons aged 3 and 7. They were both relative outsiders, with no previous ties to the area.

"This could be just the bit of luck we need!" Peter declared. "We still need to figure out the best way to approach him, but it means the cult might not be quite as entrenched as we've been led to believe. I was convinced they held a position in office, but maybe they are limited to the police and hosp..."

"Uaah...grr..." Peter was interrupted by someone mumbling in their sleep.

"Sounded like James." Izzy speculated. "If his dreams are anything like mine, then I'm surprised we haven't heard from him sooner." She let out a deep sigh.

"We're going to get through this, Izz." Peter could sense she was still troubled, despite their findings. "If the mayor is someone we can trust, then he could be the perfect candidate to help us all get out of here."

"Is that the plan? To run?"

"The plan is to survive. If we can get out of the area, our chances of survival increase dramatically. All we need to do is buy ourselves enough time to come up with a proper plan. Not something we've cobbled together on the fly whilst constantly looking over our shoulder."

"Grr...gah!" JJ's unrest was getting louder.

"Should I go check on him?" Izzy asked.

"Give it a sec. It sounds like he's dreaming. Tell you what, let's see what's going on in the real world, shall we? Maybe it'll help take our minds off things a little before you go back to bed." Peter searched the latest news on his phone.

"What do you want to look at, Izz? Celeb gossip? The latest Marvel speculation?" He passed his phone over to Izzy so she could scroll the list of options.

She bypassed all the pop culture tabs and skipped straight to the subject of world news. Peter chuckled to himself as Izzy found an article on the US President's recent trip to London and clicked on it.

"Nuh...pl...nuh..." JJ groaned again, and Peter worried he might wake the others.

"I'm just going to check on JJ." He whispered, but as he rose from the edge of the bed, Izzy clung onto his wrist and stopped him in his tracks.

"What's wrong?" He asked, looking down at her. Izzy's tear-stained face was aghast as she stared at Peter's phone.

"What is it?! What's wrong?" Peter traced her look of dismay to an image and slumped back down on the bed beside her.

The photo was obviously staged, featuring the UK prime minster and US president tucking into a traditional bag of British fish and chips as the caption boasted about a rekindling of the 'special' relationship between both countries.

"C...can you see it?" Izzy mumbled. "Wh...what do you think it means?"

Sick to his stomach, Peter was lost for words as he gaped in silence at the disturbing image on his phone. Plain as day on the prime minister's greasy finger was an onyx ring, identical to the one Kane had recovered from his house. The startling revelation twisted Peter's brain like a pretzel as he grappled with the grim implications.

"It...it can't be..." He stuttered.

Peter scrolled through the article in a daze, unsure of what he was hoping to find. Anything to avoid looking at the terrifying truth they just uncovered, but what he found next was infinitely worse. As he soaked up the second photo, another bout of nausea stirred within, warm and bitter at the back of his throat.

The two middle-aged world leaders were posing in an

old British pub, indulging in another national pastime: drinking. Grinning from ear to ear, each man held aloft a pint of freshly pulled draft beer, and there, on the US president's ring-finger, was the same indelible mark of the cult.

The onyx stone, black as night, sent a deathly chill down Peter's spine, as the flicker of hope he thought they found in mayor Naidu was cruelly snuffed out.

The illusion of the free world shattered in an instant. Revealed to be nothing more than sleight of hand performed by an orchestrated evil, operating at a level beyond all comprehension.

Once again, the Children of the Shadows delivered a gut-wrenching sucker punch, but this one left Peter wondering if it was now time to throw in the towel.

Then he locked eyes with Izzy, an innocent in this whirlwind of corruption, desperate for him to offer her a glimmer of light at the end of this long, bleak tunnel. He did what most adults do whenever a child seeks reassurance the world isn't a dark and deadly place: he lied.

"We're going to get through this, Izz, I promise. It's always darkest before the dawn." Peter's words felt empty to him, as if he was going through the motions, but Izzy nodded regardless as she turned her attention back to the devastating image glowing in the dim church light.

There they sat, shrouded in uncertainty, without uttering another word. They were both so shellshocked by their ominous discovery they forgot all about JJ whimpering in the background.

<h1 style="text-align:center">47</h1>

Cowering in the darkness, JJ felt the floor beneath him shudder as the elevator ground to a halt.

"*Buzz...*"

Sensing the light above him crackle back to life, he peeked through the slender gap between his forearms as he continued to shield his face. The lift was empty. Its stainless-steel husk glimmered dismal grey, and the blood-curdling demon previously penning him in vanished without a trace.

JJ emptied his lungs of the breath he was holding in grim anticipation and replaced it with the thick, tasteless air now flooding the elevator. Gone was the acrid scent of Chase Side Hospital, although its icy chill remained.

"*Ding!*"

The crimson letter "G" illuminated overhead, and the door slowly opened.

JJ scrambled to his feet, still quivering from his heady cocktail of adrenalin and fear. As the metal curtain opened on the second act of his chilling nightmare, his heart plummeted to the depths of his stomach.

A sheet of old, tattered newspaper danced to the tune of a gentle breeze, twirling and fluttering its way into the elevator until coming to rest at JJ's feet. Its sepia headline silently screamed of a missing girl, but it was the least of his concerns.

Beyond the confines of his steel carriage, another horror loomed, all too familiar. A tatty green sofa, frayed at the seams, and the bones of a grotty yellow armchair were all that stood between him and a room branded with a brass number 4.

Its neighbouring rooms formed an orderly line to his right, whilst to his left, a pair of tall glass tumblers ogled him from the sidelines, perched atop a mahogany service bar gathering dust. JJ returned to Crooked House.

Filled with dread, he reached for the elevator controls, only to be met by a smooth metal panel where the buttons once were. The sallow light overhead flickered and died, leaving him at the mercy of the shadows lingering outside.

"*Hehehe...*" A childish giggle bounced around the lobby, chased away by the pitter-patter of tiny invisible footsteps.

"Jessica?" JJ whispered, stepping closer to the elevator door.

"*This way...*" the voice echoed back. "*This way...come quick...*"

The ghostly command gave him the creeps, stirring unwanted memories of Meridia's ordeal in room 6.

"It's just a dream..." He asserted, inching further forward.

"None of this is real!" Although JJ's rational mind believed this to be true, a niggling part of him, the same part which felt the beads of sweat gathering beneath his cap, begged to differ.

"*Quickly!*" The phantom child grew impatient, imploring him to come, and this time JJ answered the call.

Taking in another deep breath of sour, dust-infused air, he stepped outside of the elevator.

"*Crunch!*"

Shattered glass crackled underfoot as a wintry chill snaked its way around him, nipping at his ears.

"It...it's just a dream..." he mumbled again, turning back to the elevator for reassurance.

As he did, its heavy metal door juddered to a close and JJ glimpsed the contour of his own reflection on its cloudy surface. Wedged from floor to ceiling in the entrance of Crooked House and with no lift shaft to support it, the metal cubicle looked as if it had crash landed from outer space.

"Definitely a dream..." he breathed and waved at the reflection staring back at him.

"Wha..." JJ froze, dumbfounded, as the murky mirror image continued waving after he was done.

Slow and sardonic, the mysterious shape persisted with a mind of its own, as if it was mocking him.

"*Thump!*"

JJ flinched as the shadowy figure's languid wave shifted gears and turned into a punch, rattling the shiny surface as if it was trapped behind the reflection.

"*Bang!*"

It pounded on the door again with a supernatural force, shaking Crooked House to its foundations. Plaster and brick dust fell from above, peppering the floor with orange and white, as the malevolent reflection continued to spiral, lashing out like a caged animal, desperate to escape its steel prison.

"*Bang!...Bang!...Bang!*"

The metal door rocked and buckled under the tirade of ferocious blows, each one striking fear into JJ's heart, as dent upon dent appeared before him.

"*Hehehe...*" More infantile laughter erupted over his shoulder, and JJ turned to catch sight of his tormentor. Nothing.

Was this another of Jessica's games? His head was spinning now, besieged by the nefarious denizens of Crooked House, or perhaps his own inner demons.

"*BANG!*"

JJ jumped out of his skin as another almighty crash boomed behind him. An eerie hush followed, filling him with dread as he turned his attention back to the elevator.

"Shit!"

The door finally succumbed, ripped wide open to reveal a cavernous void that was inky black, as if something had punched a hole through reality. JJ backed away. His eyes darted around the crumpled metal carcass in search of the malignant spirit.

"Dumb-arse brain!" He grumbled. "Why can't you think of nice things...like pizza...or donuts..."

"*Click...Click...Click!*"

One at a time, long, bony fingers with razor-sharp nails emerged from the breach and clinked against its edge. Carved from the shadows, the sight of its translucent skin sent shockwaves of terror rippling through JJ's body. The horsemen had returned.

Rooted to the spot, he watched in horror as two shiny orbs awoke deep within the darkness and glistened like stars on a clear winter's night. Within seconds, he sensed his body surrender to their intoxicating afterglow, melting away whatever resistance he could muster.

Emerging from the dense twilight of its metal tomb, the

ghoulish creature closed in on its prey. Eyes ablaze, hissing through teeth cut from glass, the harbinger of doom crawled into the hallway on all fours like a fierce predator set to pounce.

Any urge to run was lost in translation between brain and body, swallowed by the impenetrable fog coalescing in JJ's mind.

Slinking ever-closer, the creature was almost within striking distance now. Ashen robes ebbed and flowed amidst the icy undercurrent, embroiled in a macabre tango with the elements, but try as he might to run, all JJ could do was watch as the monster closed in.

Thoughts of friends swirled around in his addled mind; nameless faces of people he loved but couldn't recall. Two brothers and a girl with red hair. He had to find a way through the fog. He needed to regain control.

"Dooon't...looook..." His inner voice slurred as it wormed its way through the static in his head.

"Don't look!" The voice came again, louder, clearer, and this time it sparked a tremor in the corner of his eye.

"Fight it, JJ! You've gotta fight it!" The tremor turned into a twitch, and then a wink, as somehow, he found the strength within to wrestle his eyes away from the horseman's gaze.

Cold, rancid breath prickled his flesh as the barbarous creature loomed over him, thirsty for blood. It was now or never. Teetering on wobbly legs, JJ spun away from the monster and flopped awkwardly over the back of the yellow armchair.

"Oof!" He landed in a crumpled heap on the other side.

It wasn't perfect, but it was enough to buy him some time.

Clambering back to his feet, there was only one

direction left to run, and that was deeper into Crooked House, and so run he did. A chorus of nails scrabbling against stone clattered over his shoulder as the horseman bounded after him.

The chase was on.

48

Father Alexander squeezed his way through the elevator door the moment the gap was wide enough and stumbled out into the empty corridor.

Drenched in sweat from the searing pain in his arm and still woozy from being drugged, he had to find a way back to the others. He needed to warn them. But first, he needed to escape the deranged lunatic he left counting to a hundred in the hospital's secret dungeon.

"*Kaff kaff...*"

The sterile aroma of disinfected lemons collided with the lingering taste of anaesthesia and triggered his gag reflex. Coughing and spluttering, he guessed a direction and headed off down the insipid blue hallway in search of civilization.

Despite its homogeneous appearance, this section of Chase Side looked unfamiliar to him. There were no signs overhead, or colour-coded breadcrumbs to follow on the floor, and the empty halls suggested visiting hours ended some time ago.

If he could only find an exit, he might stand a chance of

getting back to St Peter's under the cover of darkness, but first he had to navigate the hostile maze ahead.

Father Alexander approached the first intersection with trepidation. Keeping his back pressed against the wall, he craned his neck to see around the corner, only to find another deserted corridor.

Considering Grady's thirst for blood, and the hospital's underground dungeon, there was no telling who he could trust now. Anyone working at Chase Side was almost certainly an accomplice, so Father Alexander needed to sneak out undetected.

He figured a fire exit would be his best bet, and that was exactly what he found some fifty yards ahead. Readying himself to make a dash for it, he wondered if Grady had made it to the count of a hundred yet.

If it wasn't for his injured arm, he would have been tempted to stand his ground, but now he'd wondered if he played right into the psycho's hands when deciding to run. This was, after all, Grady's home turf. An icy shiver escaped from under his collar at the thought of being caught by the knife-wielding maniac. He had to get a move on.

"Ding!"

Father Alexander heard another elevator arrive over his shoulder and it was all the motivation he needed to bolt. If Grady was hot on his heels, his only chance of survival lie somewhere beyond the perspex door.

He shoved the panic bar and bundled out into the frosty night air. The sudden icy blast snatched his breath away, crushing him with its biting embrace, and Father Alexander winced as another shooting pain soared up his forearm.

In the distance, a row of streetlights signposted a narrow path snaking its way around the building, but beyond it was nothing but dense hedges at least 8 feet tall. He had no choice but to follow the path. But which way?

"Crunch, crunch, crunch…"

He gambled left, racing across the shingles as fast as his trembling legs would carry him. Each laboured step inflicted more and more pain as the stony ground clung to his feet like quicksand, sapping what little energy he had left. It was as if the hospital itself was conspiring to slow him down.

Glancing over his shoulder, there was still no sign of Grady. All he needed to do was make it to the front of the hospital. From there, he could disappear into any number of side roads or alleyways and give his stalker the slip.

Gasping and wheezing for air, he made his way along the winding path. The bitter chill seared his lungs with every breath, but he continued, forcing one foot in front of the other as fast as he could.

To his left, Chase Side remained eerily quiet. Shards of light seeped through closed blinds, casting shadows on the ground like prison bars, incarcerating his silhouette as he hobbled along the pavement.

As the path curled its way around the corner, Father Alexander was buoyed by the faint glow of headlights combing the roadside up ahead. His gamble paid off and gave him a second wind.

As he got closer, the rhythmic pulse of a siren soon joined the meandering rays of hope. Slicing through the darkness with its vivid blue beam. He was so close to freedom, he could taste it.

But as he arrived at the building's edge, the faint glimmer of light guiding him home was cruelly snuffed out.

49

JJ's heart was beating out of his chest as he sidestepped the grubby emerald sofa and hightailed it down the gloomy hallway.

"It's just a dream...it's just a dream..." He panted, glancing over his shoulder at the beast in hot pursuit.

A flurry of claws and teeth, the horseman tore its way along the stony path behind him. Its eyes like malevolent headlights illuminating its way through the murky B&B.

"BANG!"

All at once, the doors to JJ's right burst wide open, perforating the dark with dusty beams of light. Tangled in the jagged web of incandescence, JJ watched with relief as the criss-cross of daylight saturated the hall and offered him refuge from the horseman's wrath.

"Hisssss!" The monster skated to a halt, infuriated by the sun's poisonous rays. There it paced back and forth, eyeballing him from the confines of the shadows.

"Ha! Fuck you!" JJ gestured at the creature as he backed away and immersed himself deeper in the light's protection.

His celebration was short-lived, however, when he

realized he was blindly walking towards the wide-open rooms of Crooked House. Hesitating alongside room 1, JJ created a safe distance and peered inside. It was the only doorway shrouded in darkness.

Upon closer inspection, he found the room unnaturally black. Impenetrable, as if he was staring into the depths of space.

Spellbound by the mysterious void, he inched a little closer. The hairs on the back of his neck tuned into the growing sense of dread in the air as the clickety-clack of the horseman's claws scraping on the ground gently drifted into a distant hum.

"*Murderer...*" The whispery voice slithered its way out of the ether. A man's voice, rich in timbre but wrapped in pain.

"*Murderer...*" It came again. Beneath its melancholy, the voice was rhythmic, enchanting even, and JJ sensed himself being drawn to it.

"*Murderer...*" Curiosity piqued, he shuffled even closer, losing himself in its melody.

"*Murder her...murder her...murder her...*" The sudden change in emphasis brought JJ to a halt.

The voice was faster, more controlling, as it adopted a commanding tone.

"*Murder her...murder her...*" Louder and louder the voice became, bellowing out into the hall and reverberating in JJ's mind.

"*Crack...creak...*"

He baulked as the doorframe started rotting in front of him. Black mould skulked along the woodwork, corrupted by the darkness of the room. The infection spread, spilling out into the hall, cracking the plaster, and stretching across the floor towards JJ's feet.

Within seconds, the entire corner of the building deteriorated beyond repair, buried beneath centuries of putrid decay, and all the while, the voice continued.

"Murder her...murder her." From the depths of the screaming abyss, a fist emerged, white-knuckled and dripping with blood.

Held tight in its grasp was a familiar tuft of wavy red hair. JJ stood rooted to the spot in grim disbelief, brimming with tears, until his worst fears were finally confirmed.

Out from the void swung the blanched and bloodstained head of Meridia Wilson, her face etched in anguish. Like a macabre pendulum dangling from the length of her hair, her severed head swayed back and forth, speckling the floor with claret dripping from her serrated wound.

"It's just a dream. It isn't real...this isn't real..." JJ closed his eyes, desperate to wake from his nightmare, but his brain refused to release him.

Instead, he remained marooned in Crooked House, forced to confront its horrors, whilst gagging on the coppery stench of his friend's freshly spilled blood.

"It's all your fault!" Meridia's rasping voice crow barred his eyes open again, and he was met by her contemptuous scowl.

"You did this to me...to all of us. Murderer!" Her freckled face was awash with blood and hatred as she continued to berate him.

"You brought us here...you! I hate you for what you've done...we all hate you! You'll burn in hell for this James Jordan..."

The accusations sent him reeling. Deep down, he knew this wasn't Meridia. It couldn't be, but still her words cut him to the bone. He had to run.

If he was going to survive this nightmare, then he had to make his way out of the house and do it now. Shooting a sideways glance toward the horseman, he gasped in fright when he found it gone!

"Shit..." He mumbled, spinning away from the gruesome apparition in room 1 and bouncing down the hall like a pinball in search of the backdoor.

As he stumbled his way past room 2, JJ caught a glimpse of Molly's silhouette lurking in the doorway. Her malevolent eyes burned white in the shadows and rocked him to his core.

Gone was the grotesquely carbonized, spider-like phantom that chased them through the woods. Now she stood tall and svelte as her petticoat rippled in the gentle breeze, billowing in from the window behind her.

"*Back so soon?*" She cackled and snapped her fingers.

The surrounding doorframe erupted in gold and amber flames that lapped at the air as they skipped and danced along the walls outside her room.

"*Hahahahahaha....*" The witch's cynical laughter circled him, taunting him, as the fire continued to spread. Brushing his cap off, JJ cuffed away the sweat on his forehead and tried to escape.

How could this be a dream? The heat was so intense, the smell of smoke so real. He felt it sapping his strength as he plodded down the hallway, dizzy on fumes.

After a couple of leaden strides, the corridor grew dim, swallowed by thick black smoke from the witch's fire as it devoured everything in its path.

Through the thick charcoal plumes, he saw a man hanging from a noose in room 3, eyes bulging as he swayed back and forth to the subtle creak of a rope. A wooden chair was overturned beneath his swinging corpse and JJ was certain it was the ghost of Private Spencer, but the time for sightseeing was over.

He needed to stay focused and make it to the backdoor before the whole house went up in flames. Then he realized which room he would need to pass in order to get there.

50

As JJ approached room 4, he guessed he only had a matter of seconds to take stock of his surroundings before the fire caught up with him. In the rightmost corner of Crooked House, the room was home to its most fearful resident. The demon of Cold Christmas.

Dream or not, JJ didn't make it this far, only to stumble into his murderous lair.

Peeking to his left, doors 5 through 10 were all wide open and leaking light along the rest of the corridor like a haunted landing strip. A sea of shimmering cobwebs quivered beneath their gaze, and somewhere between them was his only way out.

"C'mon man, wake up!" Despite the fire nipping at his heels, JJ couldn't summon the nerve to carry on.

The demon absolutely terrified him. A brute of a man responsible for murdering countless children in the area when alive, and god knows how many more since.

For a moment he considered allowing the fire to swallow him whole in the hope it might force him to wake, but with nothing ever as it seems in this wretched place, he decided it was a risk he could ill afford to take.

It was now or never. JJ tucked his chin in and started sprinting, past room 4 and room 5, without so much as a sideways glance. As he reached the narrow passage leading to the back door, he slumped to his knees in despair.

"Noooooo!" He whimpered, wearily thumping the solid brick wall, denying his escape, then snickered in abject defeat.

"The house always wins..." It was something his dad once told him about the futility of gambling, and going up against this house was no different.

However, as the witch's flames crackled and hissed their way around the corner, they seemed to lose their appetite for destruction, as if even they were afraid of the monster in room 4.

Somewhere over his shoulder, a woman's desperate screams exploded into the hall, but JJ lost all desire to unearth whatever dark secrets lurked in room 5. Now wasn't the time for exploring, he just wanted out.

Scanning the rest of the corridor, his thoughts returned to Jessica and he remembered about the window in room 6. He broke it during an early encounter with the house when rescuing Meridia. A glimmer of hope flickered inside his chest, and it was enough to haul him back to his feet.

Still, the flames hesitated at the foot of room 4, but there was no sign of the demon yet, so JJ cautiously backed away towards Jessica's room. When he reached the edge of the door frame, he peered inside at the window. It was missing, just as he hoped, and beyond it he saw nothing but crisp, blue winter's sky.

"Finally..." JJ breathed with a sigh of relief, but

unfortunately, the escape hatch turned out to be yet another false dawn.

The moment he crossed the threshold of room 6, the towering oak wardrobe in its corner skated across the floor at supernatural speed and blocked his exit.

Its heavy doors flew open to reveal a trellis of ghoulish dolls and creepy puppets. The myriad of maniacal porcelain faces gawked at him from the shadows of the closet. Red-ringed eyes sparkled with demented glee from the depths of their cavernous sockets as they tittered through toothy grins like a gaggle of gremlins itching to wreak havoc.

JJ instantly withdrew, staggering back out into the blistering hall to find the fire rediscovered its verve. Trapped in a twisted pressure cooker of terror, he was rapidly running out of options, but before he could retreat any further, a bevy of bendy marionette arms burst from the wardrobe, carpeting the room with gaudy pinstriped sleeves.

Dozens of sinister white latex hands snaked their way towards him, snapping at the air like Venus flytraps in search of their next meal.

"Leave me alone!" He cursed, batting away their relentless advances as he wrestled his way towards room 7.

JJ only managed to stagger a couple of yards when, from the corner of his eye, deep within the advancing fire, he saw a shadow streak across the hall and his blood instantly turned to ice.

Immune to the blaze, and wearing a sinister smile, the demon stepped into the chaos, ready to unleash terror.

51

Overcome with exhaustion and pain, Father Alexander's knees gave way the moment he clapped eyes on the ominous welcome party waiting for him at the hospital's entrance. He was so preoccupied with making his escape, he foolishly waltzed straight into a trap.

Coming to a complete stop, he leant on the corner of the red-bricked reception building to catch his breath and collect what would surely be his final thoughts. There was nowhere left to run, and even if there had been, he now lacked the strength.

The bitter evening air burnt his throat as he gulped it down whilst deliberating his next move. There was no reasoning with Grady, that much he knew, and whilst on a good day he might stand a chance facing him one-on-one, this was clearly not that day.

A mere thirty yards ahead of him, the horde were fidgeting in anticipation, as if they were waiting for the headline act to arrive on stage at a concert. There must have been at least fifty of them, everyday people from all walks of life. All part of the murderous cult. The sight of them was every bit as sickening as it was demoralizing. Doctors, nurses, patients, old and young, were gathered together much like his own flock in St Peter's, although the congregation staring him down now worshiped a very different god.

"Nice of you to finally join us, priest..." Grady emerged from the pack to greet him, cloak flapping in the breeze and knife still in hand.

"For a minute, I thought I might have to fetch your wheelchair from the basement." Beneath the shadow of his cowl, a slimy grin snaked its way across his face, and he closed the gap between them both.

"Wh...what is all this?" Father Alexander wheezed as he tried to make eye contact with the onlookers closest to him.

Perhaps if he could reason with just one of them, there might still be a way to escape this madness, but the sea of stony faces staring back chilled him to the bone.

"Oh, you won't find any pity for you here, priest. Isn't that right, brothers and sisters?" Grady raised his arms like a conductor, his serrated baton glistening as he basked beneath the hospital spotlights.

Meanwhile, the crowd remained silent, watching and waiting for the late-night entertainment to begin.

In an impulsive act of defiance, Father Alexander edged forward and reached for his neck in search of his crucifix, only to remember it was now gone.

"Your god can't help you now," Grady mocked.

"He's long gone, I'm afraid...abandoned his sinking ship. You belong to us now..." the crowd responded, fanning out to form a ring around them both.

Was this the plan all along? A public execution? Father

Alexander's heart started thumping as his fight-or-flight response wrestled for control of the wheel.

Dog-tired and trembling under the evening's icy spell, he made a fist with his good hand and surveyed the fanatics surrounding him. Their flinty faces were unyielding, almost as if they were in some kind of trance.

Meanwhile, their sadistic emcee had a victorious grin plastered across his face as he playfully flipped his blade from one hand to the other. Father Alexander saw the anticipation bubbling inside him, his palms itching to dispense pain and suffering.

"What is this madness?" He pleaded.

"Have you all forgotten who you are? Just stop and think about what you are about to do here...I beg you! It's not too late...you can still walk away, put an end to this lunacy." His appeal was met with a ripple of contempt which swept its way around the circle.

"Oh, we're going to put an end to it alright." Grady was now giggling with excitement. "It's time, priest. An eye for an eye...you took our priestess, so now it's time to pay the price."

Until now, Father Alexander had never believed in the existence of evil. Ignorance and stupidity, most certainly, but not the evil often spoken of in the bible. Now, as he stared into the face of death, he realized he was wrong all along.

The horde of people gathered around him were neither ignorant nor victims of mass-manipulation. There was genuine conviction in their eyes, not fear or surrender. Conviction in doing terrible things.

The Children of the Shadows were far more than an old urban legend kept alive to scare children around the campfire. They were very real, and hungry for blood. What he found most chilling was the fact they were no longer in hiding.

The angry mob gathered around him now wasn't skulking in the shadows. They were standing in plain sight for all and sundry to see. As the terrifying revelation sank in, he felt what little wind he had mustered drop from his sails, and for the first time since his wife died, he felt alone.

In front of him, Grady adopted a crouching stance and twirled his knife into a reverse grip. The maniac was right, it was time, but Father Alexander wasn't about to go down without a fight. Planting his feet, he primed his weary body to make a stand.

"Argh!" He didn't even see the first attack coming, just a flash of steel as Grady's blade sliced through his cheek.

The wound was deep, and he was sure he felt the knife's serrated edge scrape his teeth on its way past. Cold air seeped in through the gaping wound, confirming his fear and amplifying the stinging, tingling sensation coursing through his jaw. The moment his nerve-endings relayed the trauma to his brain, Father Alexander's sight abandoned him.

Clouded by tears, and choking on the coppery taste of his own blood, he wearily raised his cast to protect what remained of his face, but it was no use.

"Argh!" Another blow, not as deep, ripped through his midriff and left him doubled over in pain.

Disoriented as he cuffed his eyes, he stumbled into the crowd, only to be shoved back into the lion's den. Floundering and dead on his feet, he battled to get his bearings as he searched for Grady amongst the sea of sneering faces surrounding him.

"Argh!" He was met by yet another assault, this time slashing his thigh and dropping him to his knees.

Grady was untouchable, a ghost, revelling in each cynical attack. Beaten and bloodied, Father Alexander prayed for a miracle, but the feeling of separateness only swelled within him.

How could God idly sit back and watch such brutality? Allow such evil to thrive? Each ferocious incision was delivered with pinpoint accuracy, but it wasn't just Father Alexander's flesh being stripped to the bone, so too was his faith.

As he knelt in a crumpled heap, the pain from his wounds rippled through his broken body and converged in his chest. He felt a tightness, as if his heart might give out.

"P...please..." He begged, palms raised over his head in surrender.

"Argh..." His scream reduced to a whimper as serrated steel tore open the centre of his left hand.

The sting was instant and agonizing, folding Father Alexander further into the frozen tarmac. He sobbed, peering down at the pool of blood collecting on the ground, and saw Grady's sneering reflection staring back at him from above.

"Please...st...stop..." He slurred, slavering thick gloopy blood into the expanding crimson portrait of his tormentor.

"*Kaff...kaff...*"

The warm coppery liquid filled his airways, putting further strain on his chest until Grady kicked him onto his back.

His head bounced on the unforgiving asphalt as the crowd fell away from view, and for a moment it was just Father Alexander and the night sky, pitch-black, without a star in sight.

The tension in his chest subsided, eclipsed by excruciating pain coursing through his body, and then

Grady stepped into his line of sight. Looming over him triumphantly, he lowered his hood and swept his greasy black hair from his brow. He crouched down, eyes wide with jubilation at his handiwork, and softly whispered.

"It's ok priest. It's over now...for you, and for your little friends..."

"Grr..." Father Alexander winced as he felt the blade pierce his chest.

Cold steel scraped against his ribcage as, inch by inch, Grady forced the knife deeper inside him.

"N...no...pl...please..." Father Alexander rasped, tears streaming down his bloodied face.

He sensed the blade trembling from exertion, pushed down to the hilt, and a cold tingling sensation washed over him, like the onset of anaesthetic. He felt the knife twist inside his chest, tearing through the coronary arteries of his skewered heart and sending a series of short, sharp tremors searing through his limbs.

As his mutilated body fell limp and the icy numbness crept across his face, he allowed his eyes to roll back, away from the cold-blooded lunatic lancing his heart, and into the night's welcoming arms.

The oohs and ahs of the satiated crowd faded into a gentle hum, and then into nothing, as Father Alexander silently bled out beneath the starless sky.

52

Grady waited, listening intently for the gratifying death rattle of his latest victim, and then watched with glee as a delicate trickle of blood escaped from the corner of Father Alexander's mouth.

Mesmerized, he followed the glossy crimson trail as it snaked its way down the dead priest's neck and seeped into his white cotton collar.

The complicit mob fell into a sobering hush as they ogled the bloodied corpse at their feet, and all that could be heard were the aeolian tones of the evening breeze circling above.

Beneath the crowd's rubbernecking, Grady pulled his knife from the dead man's chest, savouring every minuscule snag as the saw-toothed blade ripped its way free of Father Alexander's lifeless body. Still crouched, he took a moment to study his black cherry reflection in the blade and realized he was still grinning like a cheshire cat. This was a kill for the ages.

"Eye for an eye..." He murmured, still transfixed with his own image.

For the first time in ten years, he had broken his ritual of slashing his victim's throat. Perhaps it was the thrill of the crowd, another first for him. Or maybe it was the significance of who he killed. Whatever the reason, he felt different somehow. The reckoning was coming, and he was growing. Evolving.

He continued staring at his tinted reflection a while, looking for evidence of a change within him: a sign. Meanwhile, the crowd continued to loiter on the asphalt, backing away from the growing pool of blood at their centre.

"You can go now." Grady broke the silence, wiping his blade clean on his cloak as he rose from the ground. "I will take care of this. Our priestess has been avenged."

"What of the others?" A nameless voice echoed behind him from amongst the sea of onlookers.

"They are in hand, brother. We know where they are hiding and have eyes on them as we speak. The night walker will visit them tonight, and they will all be dead by dawn."

Waiting for the last of the stragglers to return inside, Grady leaned in closer again to get a better look at Father Alexander's eyes. Admiring his latest handiwork, he soaked up the anguished expression that had hardened on the priest's face as he stared aimlessly into the night sky.

"We're not done yet, holy man." He whispered.

Alone at last with his victim, he reached inside his cloak and pulled out an orbitoclast. Resembling a long, thin icepick made from surgical steel, the barbaric instrument from the 1950s was one of Grady's prized possessions. Once used to perform transorbital lobotomies, he discovered a much better use for it when carrying out the one kill ritual he would never deviate from.

Gripping the metal T-bone handle, he carefully thread

the needlepoint inside the inner corner of the priest's left eye and then pressed down until he heard a satisfying pop. Having reached a suitable depth in the dead man's skull, Grady crow barred the priest's eyeball out of its socket until it lay flaccid on his cheek.

Clinging on by a grisly optic nerve glistening red beneath the pale-yellow lights of the barren carpark, he took a moment to appreciate the bloody tears as they trickled down the father's face before moving on to the right eye.

"*Pop.*"

He repeated the gruesome process, freeing the last gelatinous orb from its almond-shaped prison cell.

"Hahahaha..." Grady snickered childishly at the goggly-eyed priest, as both eyeballs dangled from their hollow sockets.

Satisfied his trophies were undamaged, he set about detaching them with his hunting knife. This was always the fiddly part. Slicing through slippery, nerve fibres was like trying to cut overcooked calamari, but with a little perseverance he deftly removed both of Father Alexander's eyes and placed them in a brown leather pouch to go with the rest of his collection.

He followed this macabre ritual ever since he heard the expression that the eyes were windows to the soul. It gave him a sense of power, even after he claimed a life, as if he was robbing his victims of something much more.

"Time to go, holy man." He muttered, then hoisted the mutilated corpse off the ground and threw him over his shoulder as if he weighed nothing.

"You and I have a date with destiny."

53

JJ LOCKED EYES WITH THE DEMON THROUGH THE raging fire and struggled to break free from his nerve-shredding gaze. The hulking killer was even more terrifying in the flesh, and his towering frame filled the scalding hot corridor. Soulless eyes like liquid obsidian, devoid of any supernatural glint, bore into JJ's skull, rooting him to the spot.

It was a dark and malignant stare, made even more disturbing by the stark contrast of his ashen face and spiky white hair. Square-jawed and sinewy, the stone-cold killer radiated malice, while his brow loomed like a storm front, thick and furrowed with the weight of his murderous intent.

Wearing a fitted black t-shirt and matching jeans, the man-mountain was carved from granite and looked as if he could snap JJ's neck in a heartbeat.

As the demon took another step forward, his smile turned into a sneer and JJ caught sight of his teeth. Sharp metal implants made from stainless steel shimmered in the amber glow of the lambent flames and JJ stumbled back, trembling in fear.

"You're not real..." He whispered, but the truth was JJ wasn't so sure anymore.

He smelt the woodwork burning around him and could feel the heat radiating from the blistering paintwork, just as he could taste the bile in the back of his throat as he battled not to vomit. This was unlike any nightmare he ever experienced, and the longer it continued, the less he believed it was all a harmless dream.

The demon took another measured step forward, unperturbed by the fire's flickering embrace, and forced JJ deeper into the derelict corridor. He knew his only option was to turn and run, but where to?

So far, Crooked House had thwarted every effort to escape, and based on his knowledge of the building, the only conventional exits lay somewhere behind the approaching monster. Glancing over his shoulder in the opposite direction, all that awaited JJ was a dead end in every sense of the word.

"*This way...*" a childish voice snapped him out of his quandary.

He turned to find a ghostly little girl standing in the doorway to room 8, but it wasn't Jessica Adams. Incandescent blue, she was unlike the other sprits who walked the halls here. Her eyes appeared normal, for a ghost at least, and there was no sign of the strange soot that covered the other victims of Crooked House.

Instead, she looked more like a hologram or otherworldly projection, not quite flesh and blood like the fanged killer stalking him through the fire. With pigtails and a cobalt party dress, the girl gestured to JJ with a ruby-red lollypop she held in her chubby little hand.

"*Quickly! Before it's too late...*"

Weighing up his options between the mysterious girl in

pigtails to his left or the colossal serial killer to his right, JJ decided in a matter of milliseconds and raced towards her.

"*LEAVE ME ALONE!*" The coarse, bellowing voice boomed from the doorway of room 7 as JJ ran past and sent him careering into the opposite wall from shock.

Wearing nothing but a loose-fitting nightgown, a haggard old man stood hunched at the room's entrance, full of wrath, as he waved his bony finger in the air. A Dickensian nightmare, squinting at JJ through black starlit eyes, his wrinkled face was knotted in anger as he continued to rage.

"*I'VE CALLED THE LAW! BETTER HOPE THEY CATCH YOU BEFORE I DO BOY!*"

Scrabbling back to his feet, JJ galloped onward as fast as he could without daring to look back. As he hurtled towards the door to room 8, the girl ushered him inside with her lollypop and then gleefully skipped in after him.

"*BANG!*"

JJ shuddered as the door slammed shut behind them both and sucked the light out with it.

"H...hello?" He whispered into the gloom whilst fumbling for his phone.

"Damn it!"

He remembered sliding it under his z-bed before climbing under the covers. His brain continued to see-saw between dream and reality, never sure which state he was trapped in.

Surveying his murky surroundings, JJ saw the odd slither of light leaking in from cracks on the far side of the room. Blinds, or boards, maybe. Fleeting dust particles floated aimlessly in the pallid streams before drifting back into the gloom and vanishing out of sight.

Although his bleary eyes couldn't make out much, the

faint light gave him hope of a way out. Shuffling in its direction, he caught a waft of something sweet, like candy-floss or toffee-apples, the kind you get at the fairground. Usually, he welcomed any smell of food, but the sickly aroma was suffocating and left him feeling nauseous.

"*Hehehehehe...*" A mischievous giggle echoed from somewhere behind him as a chorus of tiny footsteps skipped past, right under his nose.

"Wh...where are you?" He stuttered, head in a spin.

Sensing he may have leapt from the frying pan right into the fire, JJ set off toward the light, feeling his way through the darkness.

"*Hehehehehe...*" Once again, he heard footsteps, circling him this time, and a shadow darted in front of the dim glow reeling him in.

"Stop playing and come out!" He fumed. "Where the hell are you?"

"*The darkest corners of your mind...remember?*" The little girl whispered from the shadows.

"*I told you I would be waiting, James...Tonight, no one sleeps. Tonight, you die!*"

54

JJ stopped in his tracks, unsure of what was circling him in the shadows of room 8. The ominous threat was Valerie's, word for word, although this time it was delivered to him by a childish brat.

Had Valerie died since his visit to Chase Side, or was she somehow straddling both planes at once?

A few yards away from the barricaded window, he made out its edges more clearly and saw heavy wooden slats nailed fast to the window frame. Without a crowbar, there was no way he was getting out that way.

"What's the matter James..." The girl's obnoxious voice crowed at him from the furthest corner of the room. *"...don't you wanna play?"*

JJ recoiled as the voice suddenly leapt beside him. He gagged on her warm, syrupy breath, thick like treacle, as it tickled his ear in the darkness.

"Shit!"

Trying to evade his pint-sized tormentor, he stumbled over something sturdy and sharp to his left and tumbled to the ground. Sprawled on his hands and knees, the chorus of tiny footsteps continued to run rings around him. Taunting him as he flailed around blindly in the dark.

"Why don't you call one of your friends for help, James? I'd love to meet them..." The girl snickered.

Her voice was everywhere, jabbing him from every conceivable angle like an elusive boxer toying with their opponent in the ring.

"Wh..." Punch drunk from her barrage, he staggered to his feet and started swinging wildly in the air.

"I'll knock that lollypop clean out of your mouth, you little sh..." But it was too little, too late. He's already given Valerie exactly what she wanted.

"Thank you, James. Feel free to invite the rest of them, hehehehehe..."

"Nooo!" As JJ raged at the malevolent spectre, the room trembled in response, like he triggered an avalanche.

Cracked plaster rained down from above, peppering him with dirty white ash, as the wooden boards holding him prisoner vibrated loose and clattered to the floor.

He glanced around him as murky daylight trickled in through the grubby window. The girl was gone, and he was now alone in the crumbling room.

"Chink!"

The grimy glass cracked, then shattered, as the window frame buckled beneath the weight of broken cinder blocks and cement, retracting the sun's afterglow.

As the dying embers of daylight streamed in, he watched Crooked House collapse in on itself, showering the room with dust and debris, breaking the bed and toppling the wardrobe across his last remaining exit. This was it.

The house he was inexplicably drawn to ever since his

first encounter was now about to seal his doom. Crushed beneath the bricks and mortar of a building steeped in death. As the fractured ceiling threatened to bury him alive, JJ slumped to his knees, accepting of his fate.

The house always wins.

55

JJ CLOSED HIS EYES AND BRACED HIMSELF FOR AN impact which never came. Although the ground beneath him still rumbled on, the smell of dusty rubble and mouldy plaster subsided, giving way to a foul new stench of smoky rotten eggs.

Braving one eye, he discovered the crumbling ceiling had mysteriously abated, and the collapse of Crooked House was put on ice. Flakes of plaster and paintwork peeled down the walls like a snake shedding its skin.

The room was mutating into something else, somewhere else. Chrome wall lights pushed their way through the crumpled remains of room 8, illuminating its splintered carcass to reveal traces of another torture chamber lurking beneath the surface.

JJ instantly recognized the navy-blue wallpaper and dusty-grey furnishings as the room continued to snap and crack around him, reconfiguring itself like a macabre Rubik's cube until its clunky transformation was complete. He was home.

Standing in the shattered ruins of his living room, the

house looked like a bomb had hit it. The grey corner sofa he spent so many nights alone watching his favourite movies on was now ruptured in two. Its ripped cushions were still smouldering from a rampant fire which stormed the walls and scorched the ceiling.

Coughing on the fumes, JJ rose to his feet, crunching on fragments of broken glass as he dusted himself down.

The house was silent, as it often was, with just him rattling around in its rooms, and he wondered what he was doing back here. Beyond the bay window, thick black smoke engulfed his street, billowing like a scene from a war-torn action movie.

Cracking and crunching his way across the debris littering the plush navy-blue rug, he noticed the family pictures somehow all survived the devastation. Lined up along the chipped wooden mantelpiece, JJ shuddered as he drew closer and saw the disturbing images on display.

Arranged in chronological order, JJ's face was crudely scratched away in each photo, exposing a layer of scuffed white paper beneath. His parents, on the other hand, resembled glossy mannequins, grinning maniacally as they proudly posed for the camera.

In stark contrast to their unhinged toothy smiles, their eyes were nothing but dark, soulless cavities, devoid of any emotion as they stared back at him from behind their waxy facades. Each abhorrent image made his flesh creep as he shuffled his way along the unnerving exhibition.

"What is this shit..." He murmured.

A family barbecue, football at the park, his first day at school. Someone morbidly recreated each of his childhood pictures in the same unsettling style. So many memories, now tainted by darkness. All that was, except his baby photo. It was conspicuous by its absence. Part of him was glad it was missing. The by-the-numbers picture of his former chubby little self, wrapped in a blanket, always made him cringe, especially on the rare occasion his mum was on hand to tease him over it.

"Waah...sniff...sniff...waah..."

JJ flinched at the mechanical sound of a baby wailing and cursed himself for tempting fate.

"C'mon man...wake up!" He grumbled, scouring the room for its source.

Crouching low, he held his breath to home in on it and sensed it was coming from somewhere beneath the scattered cushions. Amidst the carnage, he spotted movement under a rumpled blue throw blanket that lived on the sofa. Something was wriggling.

In any other similar situation, JJ would have run for the hills, but something inside compelled him to look. Ever since entering this muddled dream state, he hadn't once felt in control of his own destiny.

Every attempt to alter the path he was on failed, and this time was no different. Feeling compelled to peek under the blanket, he figured it was best to get it over with.

"Waah...sniff...sniff...waah..."

The muffled cries continued as he nervously reached down to grab the closest corner. Taking another deep breath, he snatched the blanket back and instantly peppered his Air Jordans in puke.

A porcelain effigy of baby JJ lay lifelessly staring up at him through vacant eye sockets. Its shiny, caramel-coloured head was brutally caved in like a smashed hard-boiled egg. Fatty globules of blood-spattered brains glistened on the carpet beside it, as a snake, black as night, slithered its way free from the gruesome wreckage and disappeared under the broken sofa.

"*Kaff...kaff...*" The stench was suffocating. A stomach-churning brew of blood and bile lay siege on JJ's nose and throat as the room seemed to close in on him.

"What do you want?!" He spluttered towards the heavens, disconsolate at the relentless onslaught of horrors he was being subjected to.

It felt as if his deepest, darkest fears were being systematically exploited and used against him. He hated creepy dolls. Even throughout the countless hours of horror movies he and Kane watched together, they were the one thing guaranteed to rattle him.

"Creepy dolls and poisonous snakes!" He snapped, throwing the blanket back down over the grotesque ceramic corpse.

"*Crack!*"

JJ turned on his heels to face the living room door and stumbled back in shock at what he found staring at him from the doorway.

His worst nightmare was about to get a whole lot worse.

56

JJ's blood turned to ice, freezing him in a moment of sheer panic. There, in the doorway, stood a hideous macabre doppelgänger of his father, complete with a demented grin. Head curiously cocked to one side, his eyeless sockets bore holes into JJ as he menacing loomed in front of the room's exit.

Up close, the sinister replica was enough to turn JJ's hair white with shock. What he had mistaken for wax was, in fact, caramel coloured porcelain like the mutilated doll rotting beneath the blanket. However, unlike the pictures lined up on the mantelpiece, his dad's face was now riddled with cracks like a grisly mosaic.

Between each piece of the gruesome jigsaw were glimpses of raw, bloodied flesh which made JJ wince. Dressed in a mouldy, royal-blue suit with rusty brown spatters at the seams, he looked as if he had just risen from the dead. His hands were every bit as fractured as his face and were dripping blood on the carpet, as JJ started backing away in fear.

"*Crunch!*"

Glass crackled underfoot, but this time JJ wasn't the cause. Spinning around in panic, he found his mum crouched in the opposite doorway like a wild animal ready to pounce. A spine-chilling patchwork of creamy-white, smashed ceramic held together by crimson clefts.

Her head twitched erratically from side to side, as if she was sizing him up. She wore full make-up, giving the impression a two-year-old applied it, with bright red lipstick smudged around her upturned mouth, and thick painted blue circles where her eyes should have been. Dressed in grimy cornflower scrubs, her light blonde hair, which was usually tied back into a tight bun, was now matted, tousled, and unkept.

Like his dad, she also appeared as if she clawed her way out of a muddy grave. With both exits blocked, JJ retreated towards the mantelpiece in terror while he weighed up his options. The porcelain zombies responded in kind, and with a revolting cacophony of crackles and pops, they lurched into the room like a couple of creepy stop-motion puppets, penning him in further.

With his back to the wall, JJ had nowhere left to retreat. Of the two grisly apparitions closing in on him, his mum was the most disturbing as she continued to crawl on all fours, grinning at him all the while like a crazed lunatic. Deep, cavernous sockets stared him down, unflinching, as she continued her approach, until suddenly she stopped in her tracks.

Cocking her head towards the ground, she sniffed the blue blanket, then whipped it away with her splintered hand. JJ's mum growled, an animalistic growl that rattled him to his bones as she found the doll.

In an instant, his dad swooped in, limbs jerking and twitching as if he was walking on hot coals. Together they huddled over their broken infant, cradling its tiny, fractured body as they groaned and wept.

Their grief was short-lived, however, as their wails turned to anger, and his mother hoisted the doll up in the air by its leg and smashed it against the nearest wall. The remnants of its cranium shattered into tiny pieces, splattering the wall with bloody fragments of gristle and bone.

"*Graar!*" His mother's spine-tingling roar reverberated around him, carrying the stench of death across the room, and JJ doubled over to vomit once more.

Heaving and retching his guts up, he wrestled to regain his composure while his parents inched ever closer.

"*Yooooou....*" His father's clunky rasp chilled him to the bone and reminded him of the horsemen in Crooked House.

"*Yoooooou diiiid thisssss...to all of usss...*" The accusation sent tears streaming down JJ's cheeks.

A mix of emotion and the eye-watering stink searing his lungs. There was nowhere else to run, and nothing left in the tank to try, even if there had been. His spirit shattered.

Whatever these creatures were, they were right to point their barbed fingers at him. This was all his fault and was from the start. Riddled with misery and guilt, JJ accepted he reached the end of the road.

There would be no more running now. He was done.

57

Izzy felt numb as she perched on the edge of Peter's bed, processing the implications of their devastating discovery. Just when she thought things couldn't get any worse, she learned the Children of the Shadows' insidious influence extended way beyond the confines of Cold Christmas and boasted at least two world leaders among their ranks. What good would mayor Naidu be now, she wondered.

Even if he could help them skip town, where would they go?

There was no telling how far the cult's duplicity spread or who they could trust in the outside world. There was also little chance of any sleep now, with that bombshell rattling around inside her frazzled mind.

Pushing her glasses back to the bridge of her nose, she watched Peter as he continued to scrutinize the offending article in disbelief.

As desperate as Izzy was to believe him when he said everything would be ok, she knew full well nothing would ever be ok again. In fact, right now, things couldn't be further from ok even if they tried.

Everything seemed so bleak and insurmountable, as if she'd been given a tiny glimpse of her future, only to discover she didn't have one. It left her wondering how much fight she had left.

After all, they were just a bunch of kids. The only worry on their minds right now should have been their predicted mid-term grades, not whether they would survive another day on the run.

Her fear and dejection were further compounded by the fact there was still so much she didn't understand. So many unanswered questions.

Sure, she had a vague idea of the cult's mission and Zach's importance to them achieving it, but why would anyone actively bring about the end of the world? What on earth made her parents sign up to such an undertaking?

There had to be more to it, if she could only find out what. Right now, however, they had a more immediate problem to solve: getting out of town undetected. The Children of the Shadows were not one, but several steps ahead of them, and for all they knew, they already had the church surrounded.

She looked over her shoulder at the others, sleeping in their beds, and imagined their reactions in the morning when they found out the extent of their predicament. That was when she saw JJ tossing and turning again in discomfort.

"Do you think we should wake him?" She asked Peter. "He looks like he's having a nightmare."

"I'm amazed he's the only one..." Peter murmured, having swivelled around to see for himself. "I'll go check on him."

"I'll come," Izzy declared, rising to her feet. Something was troubling her about JJ, but she couldn't fathom what or why. She had a niggling feeling she'd forgotten something important.

When they reached his bed, they found him drenched in sweat and thrashing around in distress.

"Nooo...noooo..." Eyes clasped shut, he was definitely in the grip of a bad dream, so Izzy quickly took the lead and crouched by his bedside.

"Ssh...James...ssh, it's just a dream." JJ continued to writhe.

She looked up at Peter for guidance and saw a wrinkle of concern across his brow.

"Do you think I should wake him?"

"It might be for the best, dear. He won't get much rest in this state, and tomorrow is going to be another long day." Izzy nodded and turned back to JJ.

He was grimacing now as he squirmed beneath his bedsheet and a pang of worry tightened in her chest. She gave his shoulder a shake and whispered in his ear so as not to wake the others.

"James...wake up James...you're having a nightmare." He remained oblivious, deep in the throes of whatever horrors were haunting his sleep.

"James..." She shook a little harder this time and felt a sense of dread brewing in the pit of her stomach.

"James!" She gave another firm shove before Peter swooped in and lifted JJ up from his shoulders.

"JJ? JJ wake up!" Suspended above his pillow, he gave him a forceful shake which would have woken anyone, even a Wilson, but JJ remained unresponsive.

"Something's wrong." Peter exclaimed as he lowered the convulsing teen back onto his bed.

"He's burning up! Quick, fetch some water, will you." Peter pointed at the bottle next to his bed.

"Argh!" JJ suddenly latched onto his outstretched arm and pulled himself up.

Trembling and dripping with sweat, his eyes snapped open, wide with terror, to reveal milky-white orbs drained of all their colour. It was as if he was blind.

The harrowing sight conjured up memories of the witch's metamorphosis, triggering an involuntary shriek from Izzy as Peter wrestled to break free from his ironclad grip.

Then, seemingly in a moment of clarity, the twisted tension drained from JJ's face, and he loosened his hold.

Still wide-eyed, he opened his mouth and rasped, "Meridia..."

58

Meridia was lazing on her favourite sandy beach without a care in the world. Eyes closed beneath her shades, she blissfully soaked up the warmth of the sun's golden rays whilst the soothing sound of the ocean lapping in the distance washed away all her worries.

For the first time in forever, she felt safe and completely at ease. A light breeze caressed her auburn hair as it sailed overhead, carrying with it nostalgic aromas of seaweed and coconut sun lotion.

"*Meridia...*" At first the whisper washed over her, vague and aloof, like the echo of a midsummer dream.

"*Meridia...*" The voice came again, louder this time, but still ethereal, as if being transmitted by a long-wave radio out of range.

The eerie intrusion was enough for Meridia to open her eyes, and as she did, a thick band of rain clouds swallowed the sun and shrouded the beach in gloom. As the temperature dipped, the breeze took on a biting chill, forcing Meridia to sit up and reach for her olive cable-knit cardigan.

Gazing into the distance as she wrapped it around her, she saw the once-calm waters thrashing beneath a sea of whitecaps and foam. The tide was approaching, and it was coming in hot.

With its newfound ferocity, the crashing waves shattered any remnants of serenity, and Meridia clambered to her feet. Then the heavens opened.

Torrential rain pummelled the beach, turning its gilded sands brown. Swept up in the monsoon of dread, Meridia turned and fled, trudging up the sludgy bank as fast as her feet would carry her.

Up ahead, she spotted the familiar outline of her nan's vintage caravan where she spent countless summers as a toddler. Its two-tone shell of strawberry and cream was a welcome sight, like a giant hard-boiled sweet with windows. Perched on top of the hill, it was exactly the lift Meridia needed to spur her on, and with a few long strides, she arrived at its door.

"Phew!" she wheezed, catching her breath.

Below her, the shore was now flooded, and the sweet smells she'd basked in only moments ago had given way to the earthy stench of rain.

"*Click!*"

She opened the door to the caravan and rushed inside, only to balk at what she found waiting for her.

"No... not now...not again!"

59

Nan's caravan always felt like a bit of a TARDIS when Meridia was younger, but now it was home to something way beyond its pint-sized frame. Turning to run, Meridia burst out the door, only to find herself thrust back into the same wretched lobby.

Despite the unfamiliar furniture and fresh lick of paint, there was no disguising where she was. The stone tiled floor and mahogany service bar between lounge and kitchen gave it away instantly, then, to her right, a series of rooms–one through five–confirmed her fears. She was standing in the gloomy entrance hall of Crooked House.

Trapped in some inescapable time loop, no matter how many times she ran out the door, she instantly wound up back in the jaws of hell.

"Grr...This bloody place! I thought we were done with this..." she muttered, shaking her head.

Had the witch somehow returned from the dead to haunt her dreams again?

Or perhaps this was the work of Archie, or Jessica.

Whoever it was, they were yet to emerge from the shadows of the empty, overcast room.

"*Creeeak...*"

She was about to go investigate when the office door opened behind her, and a young woman emerged lugging a retro vacuum cleaner on wheels. It clickety-clacked along the stony ground like an obstinate shopping trolly as the woman, a cleaner judging by her outfit, made a beeline for where Meridia was standing.

"Who are you?" Meridia asked, but the cleaner looked straight through her as if she wasn't there.

She appeared flustered as she wrestled with the odd contraption: a mass of wheels and grey, crinkly plastic tubing with a mind of its own. Wearing a mint-green apron, Meridia guessed she was somewhere in her late twenties. A little plump, she had mousy brown hair tied back in a bun, and a pair of maroon, thick-rimmed glasses in the shape of cat's eyes.

"Hello?" Meridia held her ground, waving to be seen, but the woman continued, oblivious.

With a sharp intake of breath, Meridia closed her eyes and braced herself for impact, but to her astonishment, the woman passed right through her like a ghost.

"Huh!" Meridia stood in the centre of the lobby, dumbfounded, as a melange of floral perfume and wood polish lingered in the woman's wake. Was this another of her visions or a dream gone bad?

"*Are you coming?*" The woman called back in Meridia's direction. "*I haven't got all day!*"

Perhaps she saw her after all. Meridia cleared her throat to answer, only to be interrupted by another tiny voice behind her.

"*Coming mummy...I was just talking to the man in the*

corner." A dot of a girl emerged from the office and skipped her way towards the cleaner.

She resembled a miniature version of her mother, minus the glasses, and instead of a bun, she wore her hair in cute little pigtails. The girl couldn't have been much older than five or six and was a sweet little thing, full of life as she bounced across the lobby in her frilly pink princess dress.

"*What man?*" Her mother asked, putting a pin in her wrestling match with the enormous bendy hose.

"*You know mummy...the man who lives in the shadows.*" The girl's nonchalant response released an icy tremor in Meridia's spine and sent it scurrying up to the base of her skull.

"*I've told you time and time again, there is no such thing!*" Her mother snapped.

"*But there is mummy, I swear.*" The girl's bottom lip trembled as she fought her corner. "*I can see him now.*"

"*Where?!*" The woman dropped the vacuum cleaner and tapped her foot impatiently. "*Well? Where is he?*"

"*He's behind you, mummy...*" Meridia followed the girl's stubby little finger and there, clear as day, lurking right behind the cleaner, was a horseman.

Meridia recognized its menacing sneer instantly. It was the same creature she sent packing beneath the old oak tree out front. Sheathed in translucent skin weaved from shadows, the monster silently loomed over the woman's shoulder. Its dusty robes cascading all the way to the floor like a murky waterfall.

Row upon row of thorny teeth glistened beneath the dim light, whilst its shiny black eyes sparkled like brilliant solitaires, beautiful and mesmerizing.

"Wait, no!" Meridia yelled as the woman turned in its

direction, but as she did, the horseman evaporated in a cloud of black mist.

"*See! I told you, there's no such thing.*" Unimpressed, the woman scooped the vacuum cleaner back up under her arm and continued walking toward room 1.

"*Hehehehe...*"

Meridia turned her attention back to the giggling girl and sensed her stomach churn. The horseman was now crouched beside her and whispering in her ear. Its voice crackled inaudibly as Meridia battled the urge to shuffle closer and eavesdrop.

"*What's so funny?*" The woman huffed, her patience wearing thin.

"*Nothing mummy...he said I mustn't tell. It's a secret.*" A wry smile crept across the creature's gaunt face as it remained glued to the girl's side.

"*That's enough now Valerie!*" The revelation caught Meridia off-guard and left her reeling.

"*Your nan will be here soon to take you to school, so no more silly talk. You know how she gets.*" Once again, the horseman cupped its hand to the girl's ear and whispered.

"*I don't like nanna...she's always mean to me when you're not around. I don't wanna go with her...I want you to take me to school.*"

"*I can't, honey. I need to work.*" The woman's voice softened as she knelt for a hug.

"*It won't be like this forever, I promise.*" She sighed.

"*We really need the money right now, and Dr Chapman was kind enough to get me this job so I can keep a roof over our heads.*" Meridia watched on, still shellshocked by the girl's identity, as the horseman rose to its feet.

With its back facing her, the creature stretched its arms out wide to form a barrier between Meridia and her gateway into the past. Then, without warning, it flopped to the ground, swallowing both mother and daughter to bring the curtain down on their puzzling re-enactment.

"No!" Meridia yelped, stepping forward, but she was too late.

Reduced to nothing but a crumpled pile of rags, Valerie, her mother, and the horseman all vanished beneath the creature's cloak. Edging closer, she gave the rags a tentative kick and backed away, but nothing stirred. They were gone.

"Noooo! I hate you nanna...I hate you!"

Meridia barely had any time to think before spinning on her heels at the sudden outburst. It was Valerie again, only now she looked a couple of years older. Still sporting pigtails, but this time wearing an emerald-green summer dress, she was being frog-marched across the lobby by an elderly woman with a face like thunder.

"Maybe we would both be in a better mood if you hadn't kept us up all night screaming! I dread to think what the neighbours must've thought! It's about time you grew up, young lady. Letting people fill your head with a load of nonsense...it wouldn't happen under my roof, that's for sure!"

The old woman was spitting feathers as she dragged Valerie along the floor by her elbow. With a short white bob framing her lean, wrinkled face, there was nothing warm and cuddly about the woman at all, and Meridia winced once she saw her nails were digging into Valerie's plump upper arm.

"Ow! You're hurting me..." she sobbed. *"Let me go!"*

But Valerie's resistance was all in vain as she was yanked ever closer to the B&B's door.

Again, they remained blind to Meridia's presence as they passed by, but the slipstream from their tussle caught the creature's robes at her feet and resurrected them from the dead. Dancing and twirling like a leaf blowing in the wind, the rags circled the two squabbling relatives as they stomped across the hall.

Around and around, they flew, growing and gathering momentum with each new lap, until Meridia saw flashes of the horseman's wicked face amongst the blur of black and grey. This time, the creature seemed to look straight at Meridia with its piercing black eyes, before swooping down alongside Valerie.

The petulant child stopped in her tracks, momentarily pegging her grandmother back as she listened to the creature's insidious whispers. In an instant, Valerie's temperament seemed to shift and a look of malevolence washed across her sullen face.

"*Ok nanna...*" she said, locking eyes with the woman as she continued to pinch her elbow.

"*But don't say I didn't warn you...*" Valerie smiled, a contemptuous smile full of scorn, as she followed her grandmother out of Crooked House.

The horseman escorted them part of the way, stopping short of the doorway, unable to venture into the sunlight, lavishing the courtyard outside.

"Why am I here?!" Meridia mumbled to herself, still unsure if she found herself shipwrecked in a vision or a dream.

The horseman whirled around to face her, as if it had overheard her mutterings. Frozen to the spot, Meridia did her best to suppress the scream pounding at the door to her throat as the creature skulked toward her. The monster's enchanting eyes narrowed as it edged closer, all the while sniffing at the air between them like a wild dog.

Meridia couldn't resist staring into the hollow of its skull as the cadaverous creature approached with its nasal cavity exposed to the elements. The darkness inside was endless, like staring into the depths of a black hole. Closer it crept, its bright eyes darting around the room in search of her, until Meridia sensed its cold, rancid breath on her cheek.

There was no easy way to get past it, and if she ran deeper into the house, it would surely catch her. Eyes clenched in terror, she prayed the horseman would simply pass through her like the other apparitions.

"I know you're heeere seer...." The creature hissed. "I can ssssmell your blood."

60

"Izzy?... Izzy!" Peter's voice reached inside Izzy's troubled mind and plucked her from her daze. "Fetch the water. We need to cool him down somehow."

Izzy sprang into action and raced back to Peter's bed at the front of the church. She grabbed the large, half-empty bottle and brought it back to him as quickly as she could. In a panic, Peter fumbled to unscrew the cap and emptied its contents over JJ's face.

"W...why didn't it wake him up?" Izzy stuttered.

"I don't know...it's like he's in some kind of trance. At least the water might help bring his temperature down. I'm no doctor, but it feels dangerously high." Peter gave JJ another shake, but he remained limp and unresponsive.

Placing an ear to the boy's chest, he signalled for Izzy to stand still. She didn't even realize she was anxiously shuffling on the spot.

"He's breathing and his heart is steady. We need to figure out what's going on here. Go wake Meridia, will you...perhaps she can help."

Izzy hurried over to where Meridia was sleeping. She looked so peaceful, snuggled under the charcoal blanket.

"Meridia...Meridia, wake up. There's something wrong with James." Izzy gave her shoulder a nudge, then a shake.

"Come on Meridia...we need you." Her lack of acknowledgment was worrying, even for a Wilson.

Izzy's anxiety swelled within her again as all her attempts to wake Meridia continued to go ignored. Something was very wrong. Desperate and out of ideas, Izzy resorted to peeling one of her eyelids open.

"Argh!" She flinched at the sight of Meridia's eye, milky and white, just like JJ's.

Whatever horrible thing was happening, it was happening to both of them. Adopting the same approach as Peter, Izzy placed her palm on Meridia's forehead, expecting heat, but her skin was stone cold.

"Oh, no...oh no..." she muttered, placing an ear to her chest. "Peter!" She screamed, tears streaming down her face.

"I can't feel a heartbeat! I...I don't think she's breathing!"

61

As the insides of Meridia's eyelids grew darker, an icy blast rattled her bones as if someone was tap-dancing over her grave. An eerie silence ensued, followed by the hollow sound of a woman sobbing.

Risking one eye, Meridia found the monster had indeed vanished, and she was now alone with Valerie's mother. Dressed in black, she was weeping beside a veneered oak coffin with three ornate brass handles on its side. Resting on a trestle stand, it made for a morbid centrepiece in an otherwise understated arrangement.

Surrounded by glass tea lights, a handful of flickering candles lay scattered on the floor around the closed casket, whilst the rest of the lobby was subdued by heavy teal curtains which covered its windows and entrance.

Despite the sombre nature of the occasion, there was a warmth to Crooked House that Meridia had not experienced before. The amber hues of its soft lighting were reminiscent of her favourite luna night lamp, whilst the cozy scent of vanilla and cocoa bean coming from the candles brought back memories of her own mum's famous hot chocolate. But regardless of the close resemblance to some of Meridia's creature comforts, all she wanted to do was scream in frustration.

She hated this miserable place, and all its twisted games. She hated the hold it had over her, dragging her back time and time again to share its gruesome history. As was often the case, none of this stumble down memory lane made any immediate sense. Why was her gift downloading Valerie's story, and why now?

Although she was an echo in Crooked House, she was also an old woman confined to a hospital bed and had been for some time now. As she tried to fathom her reasons for being there, Meridia sensed her temper simmering beneath the surface, flushing her cheeks with anger. She wanted answers, and she wanted them now.

Allowing her curiosity to get the better of her, Meridia edged over to the coffin to peer inside, even though deep down she already knew who it belonged to. As before, Valerie's mum remained unaware of her presence.

She stood there perpetually weeping, trapped in her own circular glitch. It was almost as if the house wanted Meridia to peek inside and placed everything else on a loop until she plucked up enough courage.

When she reached the head of the casket, she saw its lid was split into two halves, each accompanied by several tiny brass hinges. It reminded her of an old vampire movie she once watched at Zach's house, and for a moment she hesitated, wondering if this was all a trap.

If she couldn't even open a fridge without being dragged down into the depths of hell, then it stood to reason that opening a coffin in the middle of a haunted house might not be her smartest idea.

Once again, her thirst for answers outweighed her

better judgement, and Meridia felt along the underside of the lid with both hands until she had a good enough grip. The wood was smooth to the touch and heavy on her fingertips as she slowly lifted the lid.

"*Creeeak...*"

Shooting a sideway glace at Valerie's mother, she found the woman still crying at the foot of the casket, indifferent to the shameless intrusion.

"Oh god!"

Meridia gasped in horror at the corpse enclosed in the coffin's creamy satin entrails. Valerie's grandmother lay staring up at her with eyes white as snow. Her pale blue face was twisted and contorted as if she was scared to death.

Trembling, Meridia held the heavy lid aloft, unable to break away from the woman's ghoulish gaze. Her emaciated body was riddled with rigor mortis, freezing her in a moment of absolute terror with her mouth agape mid-scream.

"*Bang!*"

The lid slipped from her hands, sealing the spine-chilling monstrosity back in its wooden box.

"*Hehehehehe...*" A discord of baleful snickering erupted in response, reverberating around the lobby as Meridia reeled away from the coffin in shock. It was Valerie. It had to be.

She warned her nan, and now she was dead, but how? How does a seven-year-old murder an adult so horribly, particularly an old battle-axe like her grandmother?

As she searched her mind for answers, the laughter persisted, growing louder and louder until Meridia was forced to cover her ears. It was everywhere all at once, whirling and swirling around her.

She closed her eyes to block it out, but it was no use.

The intensity of each disturbing guffaw rattled her brain so bad she thought her head might explode. Then, as suddenly as it started, it came to an abrupt end.

Still shaking from the oral assault and the grisly cadaver, Meridia opened her eyes to a spinning lobby and reached out to steady herself on the coffin. It was gone, and so too was Valerie's mother.

The lobby's décor had also changed and now resembled an untainted version of the Crooked House she first encountered.

The tan leather sofas made way for softer seating and a much-needed injection of colour. Bold tones of green and gold chased away all the shadows except one.

At the far end of the lobby, close to the heart of Crooked House, an unnatural silhouette lingered. Impenetrable darkness in human form, it stood silently, watching her from afar.

"Wh...who's there?" Meridia stuttered, backing away toward the door.

The shadow maintained its distance, spilling into the lobby as it skulked along the floor toward her. Had the horseman returned?

The more Meridia stared at it, the more ambiguous it became, as if it was evading her scrutiny. Glancing over her shoulder, she saw the dwindling daylight trickling in through the glass patio door and knew it wouldn't be enough to offer any refuge.

"C'mon M, wake up..." she quietly pleaded with herself, desperate to control her tempestuous gift, but still Meridia remained landlocked in her own private nightmare.

"You can't wake up now, silly..." Valerie's condescending voice floated across the open space between them. *"This isn't your dream anymore. It belongs to me..."*

"Clank!"

Meridia felt the patio door at her back and reached for its handle. Locked. The window of light streaming in shrank around her as the sun accelerated its descent.

"No..." Meridia cried, turning just in time to catch the sun's final embers flicker and die behind the trees outside, and with it, her only hope of protection.

"Hehehehehe..." Valerie's menacing giggle rippled toward her from the depths of the gloom.

"There's no escape now Meridia..."

62

"Wh...what's going on?!" Emily sat bolt upright to find Izzy and Peter crowded around Meridia's bed.

"I can still hear a heartbeat!" Peter declared. "It's faint, but it's there..."

"Wai...wha....M?!" Emily flocked to her daughter's side as soon as Peter's words seeped in.

"Izz, go get as many blankets as you can find...we need to keep her warm." Peter barked as he persisted in trying to resuscitate Meridia.

Alternating between firm shakes and gentle slaps to her face, he was running out of ideas.

"I don't know what's happening." He turned his attention to Emily, who was wide-eyed in shock beside him.

"She's alive, but weak. She's cold, so we need to warm her up... whatever it is, it's affected JJ too, except he's burning up. It doesn't make any sense..." Peter's voice broke as he stepped away from Meridia and allowed Emily the room to swoop in and hold her.

"M...M, please..." she whispered. "Wake up...wake up M."

Emily continued to whisper in her daughter's ear like a mantra, pleading with her to come to.

"What's going on?!" Kane was standing confused on the periphery of all the commotion, watching it all unfold from the shadows of the dimly lit church hall.

Venturing closer to the hubbub, he felt Izzy breeze past him with a fresh pile of blankets.

"Guys! What is it? What's wrong with M?" No one answered.

They were too busy fussing over Meridia as she lay limp in bed. Standing on his tiptoes to see over the crowd, he could just about see her, pale and lifeless under the covers.

"We need to wake the others!" The panic was now palpable in Peter's voice, and it spread like a virus to those around him.

"I'm on it!" Kane replied, eager to help.

Turning on his heels, he darted back to the boys' half of the makeshift dorm, only to come to a screeching halt.

"What the..." He stood dumbfounded in front of his own z-bed, struggling to reconcile what he was seeing.

There, beneath the tatty rumpled blanket, Kane saw he was still curled up in his bed and sound asleep.

"I must be dreaming..." He glanced down at his hands, unsure what to expect.

They both looked and felt normal enough as he flipped them over and flexed his fingers. Shifting his attention back to the row of beds, he noticed JJ was dripping with sweat and his covers had all been stripped.

"What's going on..." He barely finished his sentence when he sensed a waft of warm air ripple through him, carrying with it traces of cologne, as Peter approached his dormant body.

"Kane's the same!" Peter bellowed. "His eyes are white

like the others, but his temperature seems normal, and he's breathing ok."

Was this an out of the body experience? It all felt so real and unlike any dream he ever had before. Kane watched, speechless, as Peter then scurried over to Zach's bed and lifted one of his eyelids open.

"Hey!" Kane protested, then stopped when he saw his brother's glistening, white eyeball staring up at the ceiling.

"Damn it! It's got Zach too…" Perplexed, Peter rubbed his forehead in search of answers. "What the hell is this, and why haven't the three of us been affected?"

Kane opened his mouth to speak, but the dwindling lights of St Peter's cut him short as everything around him condensed to form an impermeable darkness. The flustered exchanges of Peter, Izzy and Emily ebbed away on a wave of serenity as an ethereal light beamed down on him from above.

Its brilliant white rays were warm and soothing, like a sunny summer afternoon, and for a moment he relinquished all his worries and bathed in its splendour.

"This must be a dream…" He mumbled to himself, trying to quash the growing concern he might have died in his sleep.

"Hello?" He called out into the void beyond his celestial spotlight and his voice reverberated away from him, swallowed by the infinite expanse ahead.

"It's just a dream…" He asserted. "Everything's fine Kane…you can wake up now."

However, the dream persisted deluding him as it fanned the flames of doubt growing within. What if this wasn't a dream?

Another mysterious spotlight emerged a few yards in front of him and interrupted Kane's moment of uncertainty.

Dazzling and disorienting, it sliced through the darkness to reveal a man and a woman standing beneath its ivory glare.

"Mum! Dad!" Kane yelled once his eyes adjusted to the blurry figures up ahead.

A sight for sore eyes, their smiling faces opened the floodgates for a river of tears he was holding at bay since dinner. Dressed in white, they were wrapped in each other's arms and gesturing for him to join them. A picture of wedded bliss, just as they always were, they looked radiant and full of life. Kane wondered if he was dead after all, and this was his heavenly welcome.

The thought of leaving his brother behind made him shudder, tempering his urge to run to his parents with open arms. He couldn't abandon Zach. Not now. If he really died, then what more could he do?

"I'm coming!" He yelled, allowing his broken heart to take the wheel.

Cuffing his tears away, he bounded towards them. All he wanted was to be close to them again. To hear their voices, even if it proved to be the very last time.

The instant he broke beyond the barrier of his own light, Kane plummeted into the dark. Down he fell, tumbling and somersaulting away from his parent's loving embrace, deeper and deeper into the icy depths of the abyss.

63

"Uaah!" Kane flinched, bracing himself for an impact that never came.

He opened his eyes and was promptly blinded by the flourescent bulb flickering overhead. Wherever he was, he was lying on his back on a cold, hard floor. Climbing to his feet, he found himself at the centre of an endless white corridor with varnished concrete flooring as far as the eye could see.

Despite the celestial colour scheme, it was clear this was no divine passageway to the afterlife. Cracked paintwork offered little cover for the crumbling breeze blocks below, whilst overhead, a maze of raw metal pipes left Kane wondering if he'd landed in an abandoned factory.

The air was warm and stifling, with traces of fresh paint and turps clinging to his lungs. Wherever he was, it was somewhere completely alien to him.

"Squeeeak!"

Kane reeled around at the odious sound and immediately averted his eyes from the horrifying sight awaiting him. The sickening spectacle left him winded and doubled over in the corridor, searching for his breath. As the blood rushed to his head, a cold clammy sweat broke across his brow, tingling his face as he teetered on the brink of fainting.

"Squeeeak!"

Then the tears came, streaming down his nose and spattering the glossy grey floor at his feet. Clenching his eyes, he tried in vain to stop his stomach from churning as the spine-chilling sound reverberated in his traumatized mind, but it was too late. There was no way to unsee the grisly source as it cemented itself in his head and replayed on a continuous loop.

"Squeeeak!"

The sound came again, and Kane shuddered as his brain tirelessly filled the gaps in his mind with scenes of torture and suffering, flooding his senses with a river of blood.

He sensed his stomach gurgling beneath his sweater as the bitter taste of bile trickled its way into the back of his throat, sullying his tastebuds with its sour tang. The more he regurgitated the gruesome imagery, the more violently he reacted as nausea turned to anger, and anger turned to rage.

"Squeeeak!"

Each new gut-wrenching sound doubled down on the abhorrent display, searing it into his brain like a hideous tattoo. Spitting out the slimy remnants of vomit refusing to stay down, Kane needed to do something. He had to unleash the fury consuming him.

Glancing up through bleary eyes full of rage, he found the hooded silhouette shuffling away from him. Tattered robes snaked across the floor like a macabre mop soaking up the bloody mess he made.

"Squeeeak!"

With a meat hook in each hand, he was hauling the bodies of Kane's parents along the lustrous corridor. Robotic and workmanlike, the murderous disciple was devoid of all emotion as he dragged their mutilated corpses like he was lugging rubbish to a refuse site.

Harpooned faces, agog like prize fish, each meat hook punctured the underside of his parents' jaw, with its bloody point protruding from their gaping mouths. Their eyes were sadistically hollowed out, whilst their flaccid limbs sloshed about in the trail of blood left behind them in their wake, painting a dark crimson path along the insipid grey floor.

"Squeeeak!"

"Grr..." Kane exploded in a fit of rage, setting off after the killer like a man possessed.

"Squeeeak...splat!"

He slipped on the slick scarlet rivulet and landed face-first in his parents' blood. Gagging as its coppery taste stormed the back of his throat, he scrambled to get back to his feet.

"Squeeeak!"

The hooded figure turned right up ahead and slipped through a hidden doorway along the corridor. Soaked in blood, Kane watched in despair as his parents' legs slithered out of sight.

"This is just a dream..." He sobbed, staring down at his glistening ruby-red hands.

Once again, his anger took over and his hands became fists as he set off in search of retribution.

64

Skidding to a halt, Kane hesitated once he reached the secret doorway. Wiping his bloody hands down the front of his joggers, he surveyed the empty room of the corridor. There was no sign of his hooded tormentor, and no obvious hiding places either.

Everything inside was shiny and reflective, sparkling beneath the fluorescent bulbs buzzing overhead. A grid of glossy white doors covered the wall to Kane's right, from floor to ceiling, while a couple of heavy-duty ceramic sinks occupied the white-tiled wall to his left.

Two surgical-steel tables sat in the room's centre with drainage beneath them, which reminded Kane of the boys' showers at St Swithun's.

"It's a morgue..." He muttered, tracing the trail of blood all the way to a metal door on the far side of the room.

Deeming it safe to enter, he found the arctic temperature jarring, like stepping inside a giant fridge-freezer. As he tried to control his breathing, he noticed the air had a strange menthol taste that made his nose tingle.

Kane watched his breath form tiny clouds of white on white as he crossed the room, all the while keeping one eye on the wall of fridge doors that were no-doubt home to an assortment of cadavers. The chilly atmosphere cooled his temper, just enough for a splinter of caution to prick his mind and call for him to slow down a little.

As he tiptoed closer to the morgue's exit, his thoughts gravitated towards who or what might be waiting for him on the other side.

"*Click!*"

Kane turned the handle and gave the door a gentle pull. It led to a dark and dingy passageway. Creeping inside, he closed the door behind him and turned to get a better sense of his new surroundings.

Windowless and empty, aside from the remains of a dead bird a few yards ahead of him, the blood trail continued along the dusty stone-tiled floor a little way and veered off around a corner to his right.

"Shit..." He realized instantly where he was.

He was standing inside Crooked House. As he glanced over his shoulder, he discovered the door to the morgue was now firmly boarded up. Jagged slats of splintered wood were nailed haphazardly to its frame, as if to fortify against a zombie apocalypse.

"For fuck's sake!" He bleated, as once again the house had lured him inside, only to trap him

The narrow path ahead was eerily still, exactly as it was during his first visit, and Kane felt the hackles rise on the back of his neck in irritation. He needed to be more careful now.

If he learned anything from his previous exploits here, it was that nothing was ever as it seemed. Dream or not, whatever horrors lurked in these halls might prove deadly.

The realization he may be in genuine danger triggered Kane's knowledge of horror lore and left him questioning whether to follow the gory trail of breadcrumbs any further.

"That's what you want, isn't it..." He mumbled.

"You want me to follow, don't you? Well, screw you! I don't wanna play your twisted games anymore..." The second he uttered the words of defiance, he felt something bump up against his back.

The barricaded wall had closed the gap behind him, but it didn't stop there. It kept on pushing him along the corridor toward the blood. Turning to face it, Kane dug his heels in and pushed back to stop its approach, but it was no use.

Before he knew it, he was slipping and sliding in the blood as the advancing wall forced him all the way out into the lobby. Grinding to a halt, it stopped flush between rooms 5 and 6, like it always belonged there.

"*Hehehehehe...*" A ghostly giggle erupted, as if the house itself was mocking him.

"Jessica?" He whispered. "Is that you?"

The door to her room didn't stir, and all he heard was his own galloping heartbeat reverberating in the back of his throat. Taking in his surroundings, he found the house was exactly as he left it. Beyond the trashed coffee table and grungy yellow armchair, he could see the broken patio door.

There was a hint of daylight seeping in from outside and fragments of glass twinkled on the ground beneath the sun's gloomy afterglow.

The thought of making a run for it briefly crossed his mind, but he knew the house wouldn't allow it, so instead he conceded, reconnecting with the bloody trail which led him this far. Starting with his blood-spattered Nikes, Kane traced the gloopy red path all the way to room 8.

"Valerie?" he mused, before noticing another stain on the floor to his left.

An enormous scorch mark seared the stone tiles black.

"That's new..." He muttered, guessing it was all that remained of the terrifying horseman they had faced that day.

The sight of it sent an icy tremor scuttling to his tailbone as he remembered its rancid breath on the back of his neck when he tried to outrun it. He still didn't understand why the creatures had been in hiding since that day.

Were they still licking their wounds or busy plotting something terrible?

He recalled what Zach said earlier, that they were back. At the time, he dismissed his little brother, but now he wasn't so sure.

Could they be the ones responsible for dragging him back here? It wouldn't be the first time they reached out beyond the confines of Crooked House, but so far, Meridia was the only one ever to be abducted.

"*Creeeak!*"

Kane jumped as the door to room 8 slowly opened by itself. The trail of blood led directly to its entrance and then disappeared within. The ominous invitation proved just enough for the penny to drop, and Valerie's bizarre threat bubbled to the surface of his mind. He and JJ brushed it off as the senile ramblings of an ailing pensioner at the time.

What if she was more than that? What if she was like Molly?

Staring down at her room, Kane decided it was time to find out. With renewed anger, he marched along the hall to confront whatever might lurk in the shadows.

His suspicions of Valerie hardened with each step, and by the time he reached her room, he was convinced the old woman was behind all this.

Fists clenched, Kane stood at the threshold of her door and called her out.

<h1 style="text-align: center;">65</h1>

"*Valerie...*" Izzy leant in closer to Kane, unsure if she'd heard him right.

His eyes remained clamped shut as he lay motionless in his bed, but she saw movement beneath his lids.

He was dreaming. The sight of him revived the nagging feeling inside she failed to put her finger on earlier. She was missing something. Something important.

However, between her lack of sleep and the pandemonium now unfolding around her, she couldn't penetrate the fog surrounding her brain.

"What is it Kane?" She whispered, hoping he might hear, but he slipped back into his mysterious coma.

Beside him, Zach lay with a troubled expression etched upon his face, like he was in distress. He was the only one yet to stir. There had to be a pattern to this nightmare. She just needed to find it. This unfathomable condition started with JJ. He was the first to mumble in his sleep, then burn up.

Did he bring something back with him from the hospital? Some kind of superbug? Then she remembered his sketchy encounter with Valerie. Was she the cause? It couldn't all be a coincidence.

"Noooo!" Emily's cry from the other side of the hall jolted Izzy from her musings.

"Breathe!" she shouted, shaking Meridia violently in her bed.

"For god's sake, breathe!" Izzy and Peter flocked to her side in panic.

Meridia was deathly pale and languid in her bed. Brimming with tears, Izzy stared at her best friend's chest, desperate for proof of life, but there was none. Meridia was completely still.

Their efforts to keep her warm failed and now they were losing her.

66

Meridia shivered as the darkness engulfed her. Lost in an icy abyss of nothing, all she heard was the sound of Valerie's laughter snaking its way around her like a bower constrictor fixing to crush its prey.

The cold was suffocating, sucking all the air from Meridia's lungs like an ice bath as it swallowed her whole. She had experienced this sensation once before, when she witnessed the end of the world.

They survived that day, her gift somehow snatching them all from the fire. Since then, they fought off the horsemen of the apocalypse and conquered a 300-year-old witch. She was damned if she was about to lose to a spoiled brat in pigtails and a Disney princess dress!

"This is just a dream. It isn't real...it's just a dream...it isn't...real..." Meridia repeated the mantra over and over in her mind as she tried to focus on something else. Something real.

Her thoughts wandered to her cozy box room, her haven, and she tried to picture her luna night light. Its warm amber glow was always there to guide her home, no matter how bad her dreams were in the past. This was no different.

Meridia relaxed her shoulders and allowed her body to succumb to the cold. She couldn't fight Valerie if she was too busy fighting her surroundings. She needed to regain control. Meridia exhaled slowly, on her own terms, as she tried to recall every tiny bump and crater of her beloved lamp.

"This is just a dream..." she repeated, "...and I am in control. This is MY dream."

The more Meridia believed, the more she relaxed and the warmer she felt.

In her mind's eye, a familiar orange glow emerged, illuminating the darkness as it had so many times before. She imagined its warmth caressing her face as she stood firm in her conviction.

"This is MY dream..." Brighter and brighter, the light grew around her, chasing the shadows away, until all that remained were her and Valerie.

Meridia opened her eyes to find the brooding little girl scowling at her from across the lobby of Crooked House. Her furious eyes were pure white and aglow, like fresh snow on a winter's morning. Around them, the house had returned to its current state.

Gone were the remnants of its former glory. Now only dust and dirt decorated its ramshackle walls. However, amidst the grime and muck, its fluted-glass wall lights now burnt amber in rebellion, as if fuelled by Meridia's imagination.

Although she remained trapped inside the malignant B&B, Meridia's show of power was enough to give her a glimmer of hope. Once again, she had staved off death. Now all she needed to do was find a way out.

"You can't win," Valerie sneered.

Her chubby little face was seething with rage as she teetered on the brink of a tantrum.

"I have them all now...all your annoying little friends." The girl's voice took on a more mature tone as she gloated, croaking like her older self.

"Let them go!" Meridia growled, her temper taking the wheel.

As she felt her cheeks flush, the lights fizzed and flickered in sync with her indignation, and a wrinkle of concern flashed across Valerie's face.

"It's almost over Meridia. The reckoning is coming and there's nothing you can do to stop it..." Valerie backed away towards the rooms.

As she did, the shadows returned around her, reclaiming her territory and snuffing out the lights on the far side of the lobby. Like blackened branches rising from the ground, they embraced her as she retreated, cradling her in their sinewy web, until all that remained were two burning white orbs glaring at her from deep inside the darkness.

"There's no escape." Valerie's unearthly voice echoed around the room as the shadows wilted and withered away to reveal the desolate halls of Crooked House and its many doorways into hell.

Meridia surveyed their innocuous brass numbers with a heart full of dread. Whatever Valerie was, Meridia had seen enough to know she delivered on her promises.

Once again, her friends were in real danger and she needed to find them before it was too late.

67

"HUH!" ZACH SAT UP WITH A JOLT AND THE LINGERING sensation of falling.

He couldn't see a thing, so he figured Peter must have turned the church lights off to help everyone get some rest. Wiping the crusts of sleep from his eyes, he felt around on the floor for his phone and recoiled in shock.

"Carpet?" He whispered.

Straining to see in the dark, he noticed a faint beam of light drifting in over his shoulder and followed its trail, hoping it would guide his bearings. Zach hated sleeping in unfamiliar places at the best of times and was never one for sleepovers with his friends.

As he followed the pale narrow ray on its path to dilution, he became flummoxed when it settled on the thick pile of ocean-blue carpet. Zach took a deep breath and noticed the subtle floral scent of fabric softener replaced the musty aroma of old dusty sheets he wrangled with when climbing into bed.

"It can't be..." He muttered, reaching out into the gloom to his right.

Again, he recoiled as his fingertips grazed the cold metal base of his bedside lamp. He was home. Cautiously reaching out again, he tapped the lamp's base to wake its light.

An opaque yellow haze flooded the room, and Zach gave his eyes another rub in disbelief. He was sitting in his own bed, in his own room. Scanning his new surroundings, he found everything was in its rightful place, exactly as it was before this nightmare started.

His laptop and gaming monitor were both poised for action atop his desk. His collection of Marvel and DC heroes were standing guard on the shelf above, all untainted by the horrors he endured last time he was here.

"Zach?" He jumped as his dad's deep voice boomed through the door. "Son, are you awake?"

"Dad?" he croaked in dry-mouthed surprise.

"Don't forget, we're out most of the day. I've left some money for pizza on the table, and we'll be back around half-nine, ten." Zach bolted out of bed and ran to the door.

He found his dad still loitering and about to move on to Kane's room. Making a tall and sturdy target, Zach launched himself at his dad's waist and clung on tight.

"Woah, what's going on? We're not leaving the country. We're only going shopping and then out for some dinner..." Zach remained silent, taking in a lungful of his dad's signature scent: tobacco and bergamot.

"I...sorry...I had a bad dream, that's all." Zach grudgingly relinquished his grip and looked up to find his dad smiling down at him.

He loved it whenever his dad showed off his dimples, although these days they were hard to see beneath his salt and pepper beard.

"Hey, I'm not complaining. I just thought you'd

outgrown hugs like your brother. Why don't you go brush your teeth and get some breakfast. I'm sure your mum would like one of those hugs too, before we leave. I'm going to check in on your brother..." Zach's dad ruffled his hair like he was petting a dog and wandered off down the hall.

He felt a sudden wave of déjà vu as his dad knocked on his brother's door. Although he watched him do it countless times, there was something about the mention of dinner and pizza that stirred up a distant memory.

Was this a tragic prelude to something terrible, or just the remnants of a bad dream?

He plodded into the bathroom, doing his best to recall why he felt so ill at ease, but the more he grasped at the images whirling around in his mind, the more elusive they became. Slipping through his fingers and falling into the cracks of his memory.

By the time Zach finished brushing his teeth, he forgot all about his nightmares, and it seemed like any other Saturday morning in the Jackson house. Still, something inside of him was craving a hug from his mum before they left. Following his dad's advice, he sought her out downstairs.

"You ok spud?" Kane grabbed Zach's shoulders from behind as he dawdled in the kitchen doorway, making him jump.

"I posted a new video when you get a chance. It's a reaction video to *It's Behind You 6*...I watched it last night."

"Cool, I'll check it out. Have you seen mum?"

"She was here a minute ago...maybe she's out front. Do you want cereal?" Kane squeezed past him and made a beeline towards the kitchen cupboards.

Since his growth spurt, he didn't stop eating. Their mum reckoned he must have hollow legs.

"Thanks, I'll have a bowl of Coco Pops...I'm gonna go see if I can find mum. Back in a sec."

Zach opened the street door to a sudden blast of cold air that whooshed clean through his pyjamas and froze him from the inside out. It was a bright and crisp winter's morning, and the glorious blue sky illuminated traces of frost still lingering on the doorstep.

In the distance, he heard birds singing along with the gentle hum of traffic from the neighbouring streets. Using the door as a shield, he peered around its edge onto the drive and was surprised to find a gunmetal grey transit van parked up in his dad's usual spot. There was something familiar about the van as he studied it from afar, but again, the memory felt fuzzy and out of reach.

"Mum?" He called softly, but no one answered.

A tiny seed of dread sunk to the bottom of his stomach, and for a moment, he felt like he was back in his nightmare again.

Slipping into a pair of sliders waiting for him behind the door, Zach shuffled out to take a closer look.

"*Click!*"

As he approached the van, the metallic click of the back door unlocking sent a shiver down his spine, freezing him in his tracks.

"Mum? Dad?" He whispered again, trembling in the bitter chill.

Something nagged at him to open the van door and peek inside, but he felt scared. The seed of dread in his gut had taken root and now, as he ventured beyond the threshold of his family home, he felt strangely anxious and insecure. He thought about going back inside and fetching his brother, but his feet had other plans, urging him on with a mind of their own.

"*Creeeak...*"

Zach's heart skipped a beat as one side of the van's back door opened and leisurely drifted toward him. He hesitated once more. The sweet, nostalgic scent of candy wafted past on the breeze, reminding him of the fizzy cherry cola bottles his mum used to bring home from the local sweetshop.

Despite its alluring smell, something felt off. Even the birds seemed nervous, bringing their cheerful chirping to an abrupt end as they watched Zach push on toward the rear of the uninvited vehicle.

The unnatural silence was deafening, with the slow monotonous scraping of rubber soles on the tarmac the only sound for miles.

Drawing level with the open door, Zach's heart plummeted, and his legs threatened to collapse beneath him.

"Mum! Dad!" He cried, rushing to the van and almost tripping over his flip-flopping footwear.

He found his parents propped up, side by side, in the van's cargo bay. They were holding hands and staring up at its ceiling like two love-struck stargazers, but up-close Zach discovered there was nothing heartwarming about their pale and lifeless pose. Gaunt, cadaverous faces gazed glassy eyed to the heavens while their gaping mouths collected flies.

"Noo!" Zach sobbed, shaking his dad by the shoulder in the foolish hope of waking him.

"KANE! KANE!"

Warm tears met the ice-cold air as they poured down his cheeks. How could this be?

He hugged his dad just moments ago, and now he lay dead in the back of a stranger's van without so much as a mark on him, and his mum, his poor mum. He was so eager to see her without truly knowing why.

Was this the reason? Had he somehow known this was going to happen?

"Argh!" Zach withdrew in terror as a tiny black spider the size of a ten-pence-piece crawled out of his dad's open mouth and then scuttled away down his sagging chin.

Before he could call for his brother again, his parents' eyes were sucked violently back inside their skulls at ferocious speed. Crimson tears bled from the corners of their barren sockets, snaking their way down across the waxen terrain of their pallid faces.

Traumatized, Zach stumbled further backwards, his voice trapped in his throat, as another spider leaked out of his dad's mouth and disappeared into his shirt collar.

Another swiftly followed it, then another, as a sea of inky black arachnids oozed out from both bodies, scrambling free from their mouths and sockets, before skittering onto the driveway.

"Argh!"

Zach forced the scream up from his gullet and raced back towards the house as fast as his trembling legs could carry him.

The rapid patter of bristly legs on the tarmac chased him all the way inside as he slammed the door shut behind him, but it wasn't enough. Spiders poured through the gaps in their droves, scampering up the walls and scurrying toward his feet.

"KANE! KANE!" He shrieked, turning to look for his brother, but what he found instead was a dark and familiar corridor that doubled down on the shivers playing his spine like a xylophone.

No longer in the safety of his own home, Zach had somehow wandered back through the gates of hell.

68

ZACH TWITCHED AND CONVULSED HIS WAY DEEPER INTO
the heart of Crooked House, convinced he was crawling
alive with spiders, but when forced to slam on the breaks
outside the grubby burgundy door of room 4, he realized he
was alone.

Glancing back down the murky hall, there wasn't a
spider in sight. Just a collection of wilted silk traps gathering
dust in its corners. Zach's memories all came flooding back
to him as they rode the slipstream of a sickening gut punch
that left him in a crumpled heap on the stony ground.

Sobbing uncontrollably, he tried in vain to catch his
breath. It was as if he had lost his parents all over again.
Coughing and snorting, he floundered in his grief, unaware
he was being watched from the shadows.

"This way..." Kane's voice grabbed him by the scruff of
the neck and dragged him out of his anguish.

"C'mon spud...it's time." Bleary-eyed, Zach followed his
brother's voice and found him standing at the opposite end
of the corridor.

Cuffing away his tears, he squinted through the gloom

and balked when he saw Kane's eyes. Like polished onyx, they sparkled in the shadows as he beckoned for Zach to follow him.

"We need to get out of here..." He whispered. "We lost Zach, just like you said we would... But it's ok now. It's over. Come on...mum and dad are waiting..."

To his surprise, the revelation triggered a tingling wave of relief, and Zach staggered back to his feet.

"Wh...what happened? *Sniff*...I...I thought this was all a dream...everything was ok. Mum...dad...you. Then I ended up here again...I'm so tired...*sniff*...I'm so tired." Zach broke down again, casting his eyes to the floor as his body swayed back and forth like a tree about to fall.

"Is it really over?" When he looked back up, he caught the tail end of his ghostly brother disappear around the corner of the hallway.

"We were never going to stop them..." Kane's voice echoed back down the hall as Zach stumbled on in search of its source.

"Wait up!" As he turned the corner, he came face to face with room 10.

Door ajar, its brass number shimmered beneath the solitary light raining down on it like a sinister spotlight. The sight of it made Zach's blood run cold, leaving him frozen in the dingy hall. Again, he caught a glimpse of his brother as he vanished into the shadows of the dreaded room.

"C'mon...the others are waiting." Kane's voice slinked its way out of the darkness and hooked Zach towards it.

"What others?" A crease of uncertainty formed on Zach's brow as he stopped short of the room's doorway.

Propped against the frame, he tried to see inside, but the darkness was unfathomable.

"Kane?" He whispered, leaning in a little.

Before he could call out again, an invisible force shoved him from behind into the void. Zach dropped like a puppet whose strings had just been cut. Instead of landing sprawled on all fours and at the mercy of room 10, he kept on falling. Down he tumbled, into the never ending dark.

"*Hehehehehe...*" Ghostly laughter gave chase, taunting him, as he continued to plummet.

His futile screams, swallowed by the infinite abyss.

69

Kane entered room 8 in search of answers, but what he discovered hit him like a thunderbolt. Instead of the B&B's familiar sparse layout, he stood in the doorway of his own dimly lit, blood-smeared living room.

Still resembling the set of a violent slasher movie, it was exactly as he left it. Only now his parents' bodies had returned to the scene of the crime in a sickening reconstruction of their brutal execution. The overwhelming stench of death was devastating, clogging Kane's airways with a disgusting cocktail of copper and rotten eggs.

Cupping his nose and mouth to prevent himself from gagging, he couldn't help but stare at the bloodied corpses strewn around the room. Held prisoner by his own morbid curiosity, he needed to know what happened to them, no matter the cost to his sanity.

His dad was closest to him, head lolled backwards over the headrest of his favourite yellow armchair. It was a pose Kane saw countless times when his dad succumbed to his afternoon nap, except now his eyes were gruesomely hollowed out. Their cavernous, blood-filled sockets staring up at the ceiling above him.

Below his ashen face, his throat was agape like a gory smile, exaggerated by the crook of his neck. Blood saturated his grey sweatshirt and jeans, while tiny crimson droplets clung to his fingertips, dripping like a leaky tap as his hand hung lifelessly over the chair's padded arm.

Kane watched the blood seep into the thick beige carpet and sensed his stomach churning, like a pot of warm slimy broth, as he swallowed down the urge to spew. Shifting his teary gaze, he was greeted with open arms by his mum, who lay sprawled out on the royal-blue sofa.

Her head cocked back and to the side as she paraded a violent gash of her own. Sliced from ear to ear, her slender neck glistened cherry-red beneath the room's hazy glow. Her face, once so beautiful, was now frozen in a moment of sheer terror, unable to let go of her silent scream.

"*Clang!*"

The sharp clatter of metal on wood broke Kane from his odious enchantment and he whirled round to see the culprit. The killer was behind him, cloaked in shadows beneath his cowl and looming over the dining table as if he was preparing to serve up dinner.

With a blood-stained hand, he placed a large, serrated-steel blade down in the centre of its polished mahogany surface. Dry-mouthed and trembling from adrenalin, Kane surmised the weapon was a ceremonial dagger of sorts. Akin to a sword, the blade was razor-sharp and covered in mysterious cyphers, whilst its brass hilt was fashioned in the shape of an ornate figurine.

Intricately crafted, it appeared as if it belonged behind a glass case in a museum. Beside it were the two meat hooks used to drag his parents' bodies, the barbs still dripping blood. The man seemed oblivious to Kane as he went about meticulously arranging his deadly instruments. A cold-blooded hatchet man with a touch of OCD.

"I'm gonna fucking kill you for what you've done!" Kane roared.

His tears tainted by rage. Riled up and ready for a fight, he marched towards the murderer, keeping one eye on the dagger as he drew closer, but instead of making a move for his weapon, the man raised both arms to lower his hood.

The sudden motion made Kane flinch at first, pausing as he waited for him to reveal himself. He already knew it was Grady, the psychotic nurse from Chase Side, but he wanted to see him with his own eyes. He was about to make him pay for what he had done.

"Wha..." Kane gasped as the hood came down.

Grinning at him from beneath a mop of wavy chocolate brown hair was a sinister doppelgänger. Jet-black eyes glistened under the dim yellow light overhead as Kane stood immobilized by fear and bewilderment. The likeness was uncanny, causing Kane's entire body to tingle as his blood turned to ice.

"*You did this...*" His evil twin rasped, holding his crimson palms up for Kane to see.

"*This is on your hands, Kane. You killed our parents... butchered them. Zach's parents. And now you've killed all your friends too. All for a few measly likes on YouTube. Take a good look around you...see what you've done...*"

Kane found the stomach to look back at the bloodbath in his living room.

"Nooo!" There, gathered in the centre of the room, among the gutted cushions and broken picture frames, were the bodies of all those he cared about. JJ, Meridia, Izzy and Peter. All brutally slain, like his parents.

Their pale, bloodless corpses lay straggled across the carpet as if embroiled in a gruesome game of twister.

"Nooo...this can't be...this is just a dream. This isn't real..." Broken and in tears, Kane slumped to his knees in defeat.

His eyes glazed over at the horrors in front of him as the guilt he had carried for weeks came crashing down at once, crushing his chest like a ten-tonne weight.

"*Kaff...kaff...*"

Winded, he tried to catch his breath but couldn't grasp it.

Wheezing and gasping for air, he spiralled into a state of panic. This was more than the effects of guilt and shock. He physically couldn't breathe.

"*Kaff kaff...kaff...*"

Clutching his throat, Kane's eyes bulged as he writhed around on the floor in search of oxygen.

"*Kaff...kaff...*"

With his strength waning and his body becoming limp, he rolled himself onto his back, only to find the victims of his vanity looming over him.

Heads curiously titled, and each wearing a demented, toothy grin. Their grisly wounds slavered over Kane's face, filling his gaping mouth with blood and spittle as they watched dead-eyed from above. Choking on their putrid goop, he was powerless to stop the deluge snaking down the back of his throat.

Wide-eyed and distraught, Kane begged for mercy from his slow suffocation until a precocious little girl with dark brown pigtails heard his pleas. Dressed in a shimmering, bright blue party frock, she was sucking on a lollipop as she crouched down beside him with a smug smile plastered across her face.

"You can let go now, Kane..." she whispered. *"Mummy and daddy are waiting for you..."*

Her voice was older than her years with a rasping timbre, as if she was a heavy smoker.

Bewildered by her appearance, Kane felt his body go numb as a coldness washed over him. His throat was closing steadily, and he could no longer muster enough energy to cough. All he wanted to do was close his eyes and go to sleep.

Then all this pain and suffering would be over. As death tightened its grip, he tried to blink his way free from his paralysis, but all it did was make his eyelids feel heavier.

As the light dimmed around him, he saw the girl's eyes glow white and her smile become a greedy grin.

70

"She's stable...thank god!" Peter's words buzzed and crackled through the static in Izzy's mind.

Meridia was alive. They were not out of the woods yet though, as she remained in the grip of the mysterious condition sweeping through St Peter's and decimating her friends. Weren't they supposed to have some kind of protection here?

Perhaps holy ground only meant something in the movies she heard Kane talk about.

"*Kaff...kaff...*"

No sooner had the wave of relief finished its lap of the church hall did Kane stir.

What started as a tickle soon turned into a full-blown, whooping cough as they rushed to his bedside. Blue in the face and barely able to breathe, they found him writhing in his bed, clutching his throat.

"Kane! Kane, wake up!" Emily's futile pleas cut no ice with him as he continued to thrash from side to side.

His eyes were open, milky white, as if full of the same fog clouding Izzy's brain. Quick as a flash, Peter darted in and hoisted him up onto his bed. He frantically slapped Kane's back in the hope it would dislodge whatever he was choking on.

"Check his tongue!" Peter barked at Emily. She responded without hesitation, squeezing Kane's jaw and then feeling around inside his mouth with her finger.

"I can't...th...there's nothing in there." She stuttered, bobbing her head from left to right as she tried to get a look inside.

The chronic coughing persisted, unrelenting as it filled the hollow church hall with raucous rasps. As Izzy watched Peter and Emily's futile attempts to save Kane, she realized her jaw was clenched the entire time. This was her chance to help, and right now, she was blowing it.

Fired up, she marched back to Meridia's bed. She looked serene as she lay under her covers and the colour returned to her freckled cheeks. Izzy knelt beside her and swept her auburn waves aside so she could cup a hand to her friend's ear.

"Kane needs you Meridia...we all do. None of us know what's going on. We all feel useless and don't know what to do..." Izzy's plea transcended into a rallying pep talk that was as much for her as it was Meridia.

As she released all the fear and frustration bottled up inside, her whispers grew louder, firmer, until she was practically shouting.

"He's going to die unless you help him! Kane needs you...can you hear me? Meridia Wilson! Wherever you are, you need to use that gift of yours and you need to use it right now! Do you hear me?! MERIDIA!"

71

Meridia's name reverberated throughout Crooked House, shaking its very foundations.

"Izzy?" she probed, recognizing the thunderous voice at once.

It was a sign. Her friends needed her. Emptying her lungs, she closed her eyes for a moment and tried to concentrate, doing her best to push aside the infectious panic in Izzy's voice and the creeping chill of her desolate surroundings. She couldn't wait any longer to master her gift. She needed to find a way to move the needle, and fast.

Clearing all the clutter clouding her thoughts, Meridia looked within and tried to visualize her friend's faces. Imagining each of them in isolation felt far too contrived and unnatural, so she conjured up a cherished memory of where they were all together. A summer barbecue.

It was a milestone moment in Meridia's renaissance following the incident with her father, and for a couple of hours, thanks to her friends, she was able to forget her troubles.

They all were far too busy enjoying themselves to give

her any special attention that day, and Meridia welcomed the rare moment of anonymity. She could've watched them all afternoon as they fooled around shooting each other with water guns whilst Zach's dad cremated the first pack of burgers on the open grill. Happier times.

Emerging through the inky blackness of her mind's eye, she watched them all take shape, forged from the shadows of her imagination. They were blanched and hazy to begin with, blurred around the edges like smudged chalk drawings left out in the rain.

The more Meridia let go of the impulse to force things, the more vibrant they all became. Soon she could smell the sweet, smoky aroma of sizzling meat and feel the sun's blistering rays beating down on her back in the Jackson's backyard suntrap. It was all so real, so vivid, that she was convinced if she took the slightest step forward, she would join them all in the past.

Meridia swallowed the temptation to call out, doing her utmost to remain passive, just as she had during her tangle with Valerie. She observed from afar as Izzy chased Kane and JJ around the garden with a super soaker, all to the squealing delight of Zach, who was stuffing his face with handfuls of pretzels from a few bowls his mum laid out on the garden table.

It was the perfect tonic for her latest run-in with Crooked House, and Meridia soaked up every nostalgic drop as she bathed in her technicolour fantasy.

Oh, how she longed to return to their old life. Before, they all became ensnared in the cult's deadly web.

The summer sky dimmed, ever-so-briefly, then flickered like a faulty lightbulb as her concentration succumbed, unable to relinquish the urge to join in the fun. A shadow crept across the sumptuous lawn as Meridia's momentary lapse welcomed in a band of raven-coloured storm clouds, choking the sun on its bright blue perch and plunging the garden into lustreless gloom.

The memory continued to unravel as the garden fell silent and everyone within it froze with their backs to her. Icy tendrils of dread slivered up Meridia's spine as the ominous tension mounted, and she braced herself for what was to come.

"*Argh!*"

A cacophony of screams erupted, jagged and inhuman, that clawed at the air and curdled the blood, as one by one her friends turned to face her. Powdery white, with eyes snapped open in terror, the gang of ghoulish effigies stood motionless except for their mouths, which continued to stretch freakishly wide.

Each twisted expression was riddled with a unique brand of torment as their tortured cries rattled through the air like a death knell and burrowed beneath Meridia's skin. Her treasured memory was forever tainted, and now all that remained was the stark reminder of their bleak reality.

"Where are you?" she begged, shuffling toward the harrowing vision.

As she did, Kane broke free from the pack and charged right at her, coughing and sputtering. Limbs flailing like he was in the throes of a violent seizure; his eyes were now bulging and rolled up toward the heavens.

Desperate to comfort him, Meridia's emotions took over, and she reached out. Kane's hands slipped through her fingers like a ghost's as he evaporated into thin air.

"No..." She reached out to the others, but it was too late.

Their screams abated, and her connection was severed. They were all gone. In the blink of an eye, she was back where she started; marooned in the lobby of Crooked

House with no clue where her friends might be. A solitary tear escaped from the corner of Meridia's eye, snaking its way down her cheek, and then she finally understood what Valerie had meant and said it aloud.

"This isn't my dream..."

She raced off down the hall towards room 8. If Valerie was holding the rest of her friends prisoner, it was the first place she needed to look.

72

When she arrived outside Valerie's room, Meridia realized this was the furthest she ever ventured into Crooked House. To her relief, all the doors were closed along the way, and room 8 was no different.

Since fending the brat off in their last encounter, the house remained dormant, almost as if it was shunning her. Not that she was complaining.

If she inexplicably wound up inside Valerie's dream, then she hoped she would find answers on the other side of her door. With time being of the essence, Meridia couldn't afford to second-guess her instincts now, and stepped to it. The brass door handle felt warm in her palm as she gave it a squeeze and nuzzled her way inside.

"*Creeaak....*"

Remarkably, it opened without a hitch, although Meridia could have done without the noisy announcement of her arrival.

"What the..." Upon entering, she found an endless empty corridor with a series of closed doors on either side.

With a style attuned to the rest of Crooked House, the

stone-tiled floor stretched as far as her eyes could see, and its dilapidated walls were covered with the building's trademark chipped plaster and a light dusting of cobwebs.

Each burgundy door featured the same brass handle as the room she just entered, although here there were no numbers to guide her. Ornate wall-lights, identical to those scattered throughout the lobby, illuminated the long path ahead, and a heavy stench of ammonia hung in the air.

Edging a little deeper inside, Meridia felt a sudden burst of warm air waft over her, and with it, she detected the citric undertone of an industrial strength cleaning agent. Was this where her friends were being held?

Gathering her nerve, Meridia reached for the first door on her right and turned its handle.

There was no creak this time, and the door seemed stiff as she pushed it open. A faint blue glow escaped through the crack, followed by a burst of fresh air that smelled of daisies and freshly cut grass.

Meridia glanced down at her feet and saw what was impeding her access, as a plush green lawn gripped the underside of the door.

Pressing her face to the opening, she peered inside and let go of the handle in shock. The room led to a vast garden, framed by a brilliant blue sky and an assortment of vibrant summer flowers.

In the centre of the green, a man sat playing catch with a little girl. Wearing a blue and white striped polo shirt with beige chinos, he had a thin moustache and coiffed dark brown hair which shimmered like satin in the sun's glorious rays.

The girl, who looked like his daughter, couldn't have been a day over two. Rotund with bobbed brown hair, she wore a pretty pink summer dress and matching sandals.

The toddler was a picture of happiness as she sat giggling and clapping each time her dad caught the shiny red ball after she launched it at him.

"Valerie, catch..." the man chirped encouragingly, tossing the ball back, and the mere sound of her name made Meridia shudder. This was the little monster's father. Somehow, Meridia wandered into another memory.

In fact, she might have wandered into all her memories, judging by the length of the corridor behind her. Lingering in the doorway, she watched as Valerie continued to fumble with each throw, caught in an endless replay of a cherished childhood memory.

Meridia recalled hearing Valerie's mother say her father abandoned them both when she was a baby and wondered if it was because he knew what he brought into the world. Piecing together the snippets of Valerie's life, a small part of her could relate. She, too, knew how it felt to be betrayed by someone she idolized.

Even now, she wondered if there was a similar room to this in her own memory banks. A time when her life was better. Meridia dragged the door back through the grass and sealed it shut. As much as she would have loved nothing more than to unravel Valerie's origin story, she was running out of time to save her friends.

Meridia decided if the next room along housed a memory from a similar era, she would try a door on the opposite side of the corridor. She needed to get some sense of order and fast, otherwise she would get lost searching for a needle in a haystack.

As she grasped the handle, Meridia recoiled with a start. The brass felt freezing to the touch. Dragging the sleeve of her cardigan down to protect her hand, she opened the door to find a dark and dingy kitchenette beside a neatly made double bed.

The yellow and brown décor was kitsch, to say the least, and Meridia guessed she was encroaching on another defining moment from Valerie's childhood. About to close the door and move on, a woman's sombre voice interrupted her.

"It' won't be like this forever...it's just until we get back on our feet."

Peering back around the door, Valerie was now perched on the edge of the bed, head down, while her mother stood over her, trying to console her. It was a heartbreaking image, and Meridia remembered having a similar conversation after all the trouble with her own dad. As she eavesdropped on Valerie's sniffles, she wondered how much separated the two of them.

Was this how monsters were made? Just an impressionable young child, down on her luck, who made a handful of bad choices. Or did Crooked House nurture an evil lurking within her all along?

"What are you doing here?"

Valerie's ill-tempered accusation made Meridia jump, and she rattled the door handle in surprise.

The sullen little imp glowered at her from the edge of the bed with burning white eyes. Meanwhile, her mother glitched and flickered beside her like a movie paused between frames.

"Who do you think you are?!"

Valerie's voice deepened to an echoing rasp, as if possessed, and she swung her legs around to stand up.

"Get out! Get out!" She yelled, limbering up to attack.

As she charged towards Meridia, Valerie jerked and stuttered, jumping through the decades until she was a fully grown, formidable woman. Meridia slammed the door shut, trembling in fear as the handle rattled violently in her hand. Valerie wanted out.

"Bang...bang..."

The door yo-yoed back and forth, almost bowing in its frame, as Meridia pulled on it with all her might to keep her assailant contained.

"You're going to die for this bitch!" Valerie raged from inside. Glancing over her shoulder, Meridia's only hope was to hide in another room.

The corridor was narrow, and if she let go at the right time, she reasoned, she might make it to the room directly behind her. Leaning back full-tilt to keep Valerie at bay, Meridia risked letting go with one hand in order to grasp the opposite door handle.

"Bang!"

Her fingertips brushed the edge of the handle as it slipped beyond her reach. Stretching again, Meridia latched onto it and twisted it open in readiness. All the while, she sensed Valerie growing in strength on the other side of her, yanking her back and forth like a rag doll as she tried to break out.

"Bang!"

With one last heave, Meridia used her momentum to slip inside the opposing room, closing its door behind her in one smooth motion. Quivering and gasping for breath, she pressed both palms on the door and braced herself for the next attack.

73

As the silence mounted, Meridia contemplated releasing her grip on the door. Perhaps Valerie couldn't move from room to room after all. Perhaps she was already standing behind her.

Taking a deep breath, Meridia turned and pressed her back to the door as a precaution. She had no idea if she just jumped out of the frying pan and into the fire.

"Kane!" she gasped, rushing to his aid.

Grey sinewy tentacles covered in vile yellow mucus cocooned Kane, leaving him completely incapacitated. Pinned to the wall opposite her, he was barely visible beneath the sea of writhing, pulsating slime. All Meridia saw were his bulging eyes, as he choked on a grotesque appendage coiling itself around his throat and forcing its way into his mouth.

Frantically clawing at the swarm of tentacles slowly strangling him, Meridia tried to loosen their grasp on his throat, but they slipped and slithered through her fumbling fingers.

"They won't budge!" She screamed, gripped by panic.

As the weight of Kane's eyelids became too much for him to bear, she saw the life ebbing away from him as his body fell limp beneath the mountain of slime. If she didn't do something drastic, he was sure to die.

Without a moment's hesitation, she bit down hard on the slug-like limb that was throttling him. Sinking her teeth into its oily, soft tissue, she felt it flinch and retract. It was hurt.

Gooey yellow puss dribbled down her chin like raw egg yolk, but she didn't let go, not right away at least. She held on like a pit bull as she dragged the tentacle away from Kane with clenched teeth.

"*Kaff...kaff...*" suppressing the urge to vomit, Meridia watched Kane cough up the long, glutinous appendage nestled deep inside his gullet.

Acting on instinct, he somehow found the strength to wriggle against his hideous restraints, and the more they both battled, the more the wall of glistening tendrils loosened their hold on him.

With one arm free, Kane pulled and kicked at the remaining tentacles until he flopped onto the floor in a crumpled heap of exhaustion. He was free.

"*Kaff...kaff...*"

His lungs still heaving, Meridia let go of the revolting abomination between her teeth as Kane crawled clear of its grasp.

Spitting and cuffing away the foul remnants of its viscid blood, she watched in awe as the horde of convolving limbs withered and turned to ash. All that remained was a putrid looking, white-bricked wall peppered with hundreds of tiny black mould spores.

"What in the world of fuck was that?!" Kane growled, shattering the shellshocked silence between them. Despite looking deathly pale and being covered in slime, at least he was alive.

"I...I think this is some kind of dream...." Meridia stuttered. "I think Valerie has us trapped somehow...in a nightmare."

"You mean the sick old woman JJ saw lying in a hospital bed, is some kind of Freddy Krueger foot soldier for the cult?!"

"Huh? Freddy who?" Meridia faltered, unsure what Kane meant.

"Nothing..." He waved her question away as he wearily clambered to his feet. "It's a movie ...before your time. Before mine too, come to think of it."

"She's not old in here," Meridia continued, realizing it was Kane's horror knowledge which might help them get out of this hellhole. "She's young. A little girl..."

"With pigtails!"

"Yes...so you've seen her too."

"She came in to gloat at the end...phew!" Hunching over, Kane rested his hands on his knees while he took another breath.

"At the end of what?" Meridia pushed. Anything Kane knew could help them find the others.

"A nightmare...ha! I knew it wasn't real! I should've taken that lollypop and shoved it up her..."

"Kane!" Meridia shouted over him. "What happened? The others are here too somewhere...we must find them before it's too late." Kane quickly abandoned his rant and gave Meridia his full attention.

"Here? Right, ok...er...it was just a load of horrible stuff...stuff about my parents and you guys. By the end, I couldn't breathe, and Valerie came in and told me to let go. The whole thing was surreal...like one minute I was in a long white corridor thinking I was about to die, then the next I was choking on my living room floor surrounded by zombies. I closed my eyes for a second and then there you were...and I was in here." Kane's eyes darted from left to right as he tried to make sense of what was happening.

"Mine was similar. I started off on a beach. It was like Valerie took over somehow...like she forced her way inside my head..."

"I know you haven't seen it, but trust me, this is some proper Freddy Krueger shit..." Kane paced, as if Meridia's horrid revelation gave him a boost.

"Wait...before my dream...or right at the start of my dream, I was still in the church hall. I could see everyone in their beds...something was wrong with you and your mum and Peter were trying to wake you up. I saw Izzy grab a load of blankets to throw over you...shit, that might have been real, like an out-of-body experience or something...that's wild! Now I know how you must feel."

"That might be why I heard Izzy call my name earlier!" Meridia sensed they might be getting closer to the truth now. "What about Zach? And JJ?"

"They were both in bed asleep...my guess is anyone who fell asleep is in here somewhere." Meridia let Kane's theory sink in for a second.

If that was the case, then how come her mum was ok? It was a well-documented fact the Wilsons could sleep through anything.

"What? What is it?" Kane probed, sensing something was up.

"Nothing...we can figure it out later. Right now, we need to search the other rooms."

"Rooms? What rooms?" Now it was Kane's turn to look puzzled.

"Follow me." Meridia walked over to the door and gripped its handle. "Let's find out what your horror archives have to say about this..."

74

Kane hobbled after Meridia and found her loitering in the doorway, looking bewildered.

"Oh, no..." she gasped, staring upward.

"What? What is it" Kane opened the door wider so he could see what she was gawking at. "Holy shit! Where are we?"

"I...I don't know. It's all changed ..." Beyond their room was a gravity defying marvel of intricate architecture.

Like a never-ending pretzel carved from sandstone, the outlandish construct was an elaborate maze of mysterious dark archways and winding staircases spiralling away from them in every imaginable direction. Endlessly folding in on itself like a hall of mirrors, there was no beginning and no end.

"She's done this! She knows we're here...now we're never going to find them!" Meridia looked dejected.

Dwarfed by the insurmountable labyrinth standing between them and their friends.

"There were doors before...all in a long line. That's how

I found you so quickly. It'll take us forever to find Zach and JJ now..."

Kane surveyed the dizzying spectacle and didn't know where to start. He wasn't even sure which door they had just stepped out from anymore.

"Why doesn't anyone in this shit hole of a town ever play fair!" He fumed.

"Where do we start?" Meridia's bright blue eyes were wide with wonder as she traced the meandering web of archways skyward. "There must be thousands of doors here. We need to split..."

"Not a chance!" Kane interjected.

"Everyone knows you never split up in a horror movie. We need to pick a door and hope for the best. How about this one?" He pointed at the door closest to them.

"That's where we just came from!" Meridia snapped.

"Here, let's go for this one." She pointed at one a few yards away, up a short flight of stairs.

They both scampered up to the archway in question and hesitated at its entrance. Beyond the threshold was an impenetrable black void emitting icy cold air like a fridge-freezer.

"How do we know it's safe?" Kane asked.

Still weary from his brush with death, he wasn't sure how much fight he had left in him should things go south.

"We don't...but we've got to try. The others need us." Meridia reached out and thrust her hand into the abyss.

To their astonishment, it completely disappeared, as if it had ceased to exist. After a second or two, she snatched it back out and wiggled her fingers.

"See! C'mon, let's go..."

Taking a deep breath, Kane locked arms with her and they both stepped into the unknown.

75

"What just happened?" Emily asked, still cradling Kane's face in her hands.

"I've got no idea...he...he just started breathing again, the same way Meridia did. He seems fine now." Puzzled, Peter swept Kane's hair away from his brow and checked his temperature.

"He feels fine, too." He lowered Kane back into his bed and rubbed his stubble in deliberation.

"I think it was Meridia..." Izzy blurted from the sidelines. "I think she helped him somehow."

"But how? They're both asleep..." Emily was quick to challenge her bold claim, but before Izzy could counter, Peter piped up in her defence.

"Izzy may be right. We mustn't rule anything out. The laws of physics don't seem to apply to your daughter, as you've already seen tonight. She's saved us many times now, and in various ways. If there's any way to battle this mysterious condition from the inside, then I'm certain Meridia will find it. In the meantime, all we can do is keep them comfortable and hope they pull through."

The adults' exchange gave Izzy the eureka moment she was searching for, and her mind flew out of the traps like a greyhound, demoting the rest of Peter and Emily's conversation to a background hum.

She remembered one of Archie's threads had touched on a series of unexplained deaths over the last few decades. Each victim had died suddenly in their sleep! It had to be connected.

Kane was quick to dismiss it, as there was little evidence linking any of the deaths together, but now, with four of her friends in a mysterious life-threatening coma, it couldn't be a coincidence.

"Retiarius..." she mumbled to herself, as she retreated to the other side of the hall.

The phone signal was better there, and she wanted to be sure before spouting any half-baked theories.

It didn't take Izzy long to find the blogger again online and start skimming through his cryptic posts. She needed to act fast, as although things seemed calm now, there were still four ticking time bombs laying in their beds and it would only be a matter of time before the next one threatened to go off.

The first thing she noticed was a post less than an hour ago. It was in response to Meridia's. She realized Meridia had never divulged what she posted. They were all distracted by the return of Peter and JJ at the time.

Izzy scrolled down the feed to read the exchange in the right order.

@MollyTheWitch: *How do we stop the prophecy?*

Izzy chuckled to herself. It was classic Meridia to get

straight to the point. Whoever Retiarius was, they took the bait, so Izzy scrolled up to read their reply.

*@**Retiarius:** It's not safe to talk on here. If you want to learn more about the secrets of Cold Christmas, you can reach me at retiarius@proton.me.*

Izzy's finger hovered over the email address as she contemplated her next move. With nothing to lose, she tapped the link, taking her to her email account. Meridia was right in her approach. Now was the time to be direct, so Izzy feverishly composed her plea for help.

Subject: *Molly the Witch*

Retiarius, you don't know me, but I really need your help. Four of my friends are in a strange coma and I cannot wake them. I'm sure it's connected to a string of unexplained deaths in the area, and I need to know how to save them. A woman is also involved somehow, and I think she may even be responsible. Please get back to me. This is a matter of life and death.

Again, Izzy hesitated before pressing send. She knew the moment she pressed it, Retiarius would have her name, and she had no way of knowing whose side he was on.

Glancing back at the two rows of z-beds where her friends were fighting for their lives, Izzy decided it was a risk she must take, and so she hit the send button and watched eagerly for a reply.

76

Meridia sensed Kane loitering over her shoulder, but she lacked the vitality to speak or move. Rooted to the spot, she was unable to tear her eyes away from the disturbing landscape that lay waiting for them beyond the door.

"Oh, no..." she gasped.

"What? What is it" Kane pulled the door away from her and peered around its edge. "Holy shit! Where are we?"

"I...I don't know. It's all changed ..." Enveloped by an unfathomable edifice that corkscrewed and spiralled around them whichever way she looked, Meridia felt the wind drop from her sails.

Made from sandstone, the labyrinthine construct was a hotchpotch of acutely angled staircases and dark archways, endlessly twisting and unfolding away from them as far as their eyes could see.

"She's done this!" Meridia fumed. "She knows we're here...now we're never going to find them!"

Dizzy from the impossible, gravity-defying terrain

ahead of them, Meridia tried to come to terms with their new surroundings.

"There were doors here before...all in a long line. That's how I found you so quickly. It'll take us forever to find Zach and JJ now..."

She watched Kane's eyes glaze as he surveyed the task at hand.

"Why doesn't anyone in this shit hole of a town ever play fair!" He seethed.

"Where do we start?" Meridia lilted, looking up at the meandering mountain of archways. "There must be thousands of doors here. We need to..."

"Split up?" Kane finished her sentence with a puzzled expression.

"Not a chance!" They both said in unison.

"Déjà vu..." Kane asserted. "I think we've done this before..."

Meridia slowly nodded in agreement as she scrutinized their surroundings.

"Everyone knows you never split up in a horror movie..." she mumbled, piecing together the splinters of their conversation like the fragments of a forgotten dream. "What's going on?"

"I think we're stuck in some sort of loop..." Kane concluded.

"Valerie! She must be in our heads again!"

"Maybe... or maybe it's the door we went through last time we were here..." He stepped ahead of Meridia and looked skyward at the infinite options above them.

"So, let's pick another door this time. Won't that break the loop?" Meridia shrugged.

"I say we go down." She pointed at a staircase to their left spiralling downwards into the shadows.

"Didn't we go down last time?" Kane's reservation sewed a seed of doubt in Meridia's mind and brought her to a complete standstill at the top of the stairs.

"I...I thought we went up?" She stuttered. A sobering silence befell them as they both tried to untangle the knots in their brains.

"How long do you think we've been going round in circles like this before we realized?" Meridia's heart sank as the seed Kane had planted suddenly blossomed into a jungle of uncertainty.

The more she studied the myriads of archways around her, the more they seemed familiar, until she was no longer sure if they were wandering the meandering halls of Valerie's mind for five minutes or five hours.

"Let's go down two levels." She concluded. "Then you pick the door we go through."

"But what if that puts us back in the loop?" Again, Kane contested her, and Meridia felt her frustration boil over.

"Well, we have to try something! We can't just stand here listing reasons not to do anything. The others need us!"

"Sorry, you're right...but what if we forget again, and end up going round in more circles?"

"What ifs are phantom thoughts...isn't that what JJ always says? We need to pick another door that doesn't look so familiar and walk through it. Either that or we break your precious rule and split up."

"I've got it!" Kane declared. "I go through the door first, and you hang back a minute or two. If it is a loop, then I'll most likely wind up right back here again. But if I don't, then you'll know it's ok to follow." Meridia mulled over Kane's plan with one eye on the clock. His logic seemed sound enough.

"Ok, let's do it. At least this way I should remember

we're stuck, even if you don't, and we can try something else...although right now I have no idea what else we can do."

"We'll think of something, we always do..." They both trotted down the winding staircase until they reached an archway they both agreed on.

Staring into the icy abyss that lay beyond its threshold, Meridia felt a knot of dread form in the pit of her stomach. Was this her gift warning her this was a bad idea?

"Now remember, don't follow me too quickly. As soon as I go through, we'll both count to a hundred, and if I don't come back out, then you follow me in, ok?" Meridia nodded reluctantly.

Regardless of what her gut was telling her, they were running out of time.

"See you on the other side..."

"Dick!" Meridia shook her head at Kane's theatrics as he bravely disappeared into the void.

"One-Mississippi...two-Mississippi...three-Mississippi..."

77

"Buzz...buzz..." Izzy didn't have to wait long for a response to her email.

A trembling wreck of fingers and thumbs, she fumbled her way through her Gmail app and opened Retiarius' reply. She barely made it past the first sentence when she felt the colour drain from her cheeks and the room spun around her.

> It's good to hear from you, Izzy, although I wish the circumstances were better. I'm afraid you and your friends are in grave danger. I've had my eye on you all for some time now, watching over you from afar, and whilst I know how that must sound, you must believe me when I say I have your best interests at heart.
>
> Until today, I lived in exile, but now, thanks to all of you, the witch has fallen, and I have finally returned home; or what is left of it. The Children of the Shadows grow stronger by the day, and if they learn I am here, I'll be done for. That means you cannot breathe a word of this to anyone. I still don't know who can be trusted, but I know

with absolute certainty someone in your group is not who they appear to be.

There is much you need to know, but we do not have time right now. If what you say is true, then your friends may not have long. Can you tell me who is affected? And the woman you speak of, do you know who or where she is? Until now, only the inner circle has known the identity of the night walker.

If you have somehow found her, then I may be able to save your friends, but time is of the essence. I only hope this finds you in time.

Izzy's hands were trembling as she looked back across the hall at Emily and Peter. They were both gingerly carrying Meridia's bed to where the boys were sleeping, being careful not to tip her out as they navigated the church pews like two diligent removal workers.

"*Someone in your group is not who they appear to be.*" Retiarius' accusation rattled through her brain like a screaming locomotive.

Was Peter playing them all along?

Looking back, perhaps things had only gotten worse since his arrival, and he was extremely quick to take up sticks and move to Shawbrook in order to be closer to them all. Could it be he'd been part of this crazy conspiracy to end the world from the very beginning?

Izzy stopped pulling at the thread Retiarius dangled in front of her. After all, he could just as easily be talking about Father Alexander, and perhaps that's why no one had seen him since he was admitted to Chase Side. "*...not who they appear to be.*"

Was JJ duped by someone merely posing as a priest?

None of it made any sense, as both Peter and Father

Alexander helped to take the witch down. That said, she would be a fool not to find out more. After all, Retiarius was the leading authority on Cold Christmas and none of his previous posts showed any allegiances to anyone.

In fact, he just declared himself an enemy of the cult, so surely that made him a potential ally?

Izzy took a deep breath and cleaned her glasses on the hem of her grey Ralph Lauren sweater. She needed to take a beat. Retiarius' wild claims left her feeling hot and bothered, despite the cold, stale air of St Peter's hall.

There was just so much to unpack in his message, and what in the world was a night walker? Was Valerie secretly some kind of monster?

Head in a spin, there was only one person who could provide her with answers. It was time to press Retiarius for more information and see whose side he was on.

Who are you, and how do I know I can trust you?

Her reply was brief and to the point, so she hit send and waited for him to respond. Once again, she scanned the other side of the hall and found Peter giving Emily a reassuring hug, like two distraught parents watching over their children.

The sight of them brought all the confusion surrounding her own mum and dad flooding back to the forefront of her mind. So many loose ends, more than Izzy's brain could cope with right now, and so she shoved them all to the very back of her brain, burying them with the more pressing matters in hand.

"*Buzz...buzz...*"

Retiarius replied, which meant they graduated to a live chat of sorts. Why was he so keen?

Both are fair questions, Izzy, but there is no easy way to answer either of them. The fact is, there are very few people you can trust right now, and that includes your parents. But I'm guessing you already know that, otherwise you wouldn't be speaking to me.

The Children of the Shadows have their hooks in everyone. They even had them in me once upon a time. When I eventually wanted out, they took away everything that ever mattered to me, then threatened to kill my family if I ever returned. You see, everyone in their ranks owes them something important.

Something they cannot live without.

That might be their wealth, their partner, even their life. It's how it starts, fattening you up with all the things you desire, until one day you find yourself completely in their debt. That's how they got to your dad, Izzy.

Do you think he got all those rich and powerful clients on his own? This is what they do.

They own him now, and your mum too, just like they own most of this town. But not me. Not anymore.

With the witch gone, I can help, but I cannot tell you who I am yet. It wouldn't be safe for either of us.

You must tell me the name of the night walker before it's too late. She is the reason your friends are in danger. Unless we stop her, I'm afraid none of them will make it through the night.

The message sent a prickly chill skittering up Izzy's spine as she stood glued to her phone. She needed to return to the others before she aroused any suspicion, but not without replying first.

Whoever Retiarius was, he knew her, or of her at least. How else would he know about her parents?

A million questions buzzed around in Izzy's mind, like a hornet's nest of uncertainty.

The inner turmoil was deafening, cranking the dial up on her paranoia, but she needed to stay focused on her objective. She needed to save her friends. Any other answers she sought would have to wait, so again, she jostled her way through the noise in her head and drafted a reply. She had nothing to lose in telling Retiarius about Valerie, so that's exactly what she did.

> *The woman's name is Valerie Richards. She is a patient at Chase Side Hospital and can be found on the 4th floor. Whatever you intend to do, please hurry.*

Izzy hit send and pocketed her phone as she joined the others. Somehow, she needed to hold on to her nerve and hope Retiarius was as good as his word.

78

"Ninety-nine-Mississippi...a hundred." Meridia gazed up and down the colossal maze for any sign of Kane, but he was nowhere to be seen.

"Here goes..." She sighed, stepping up to the same archway he'd disappeared through minutes earlier.

Up close, the entrance felt bitterly cold and almost hostile as she readied herself to cross its pitch-black divide.

"This better work Kane..." she grumbled, before taking in a deep breath as if she was about to jump into icy waters.

After a second's hesitation, Meridia forced herself across the threshold. For a moment, she felt blind and numb, consumed by a deathly cold. Then the screams began.

A deafening cacophony of pain and torment swirled around her as she tumbled aimlessly through the dark, not knowing up from down. The disturbing sensation only lasted for a matter of milliseconds before all fell silent again.

"I told you to count to a hundred!" She opened her eyes to Kane.

He was standing with his hands on his hips and frowning at her from beneath his wavy brown mop.

"Now we have to start all over again..." Looking around, they were both back where they started, surrounded by endless archways of Valerie's mind, all leading to precisely nowhere.

"Wait! I did...I counted like we agreed. You didn't show, so I followed..."

"Shit! This means she's really screwing with us. I bet it doesn't matter what door we take, we'll just wind up here again. Fuck!" Kane's temper flared and ignited Meridia's as they both came within a hair's breadth of stamping their feet in protest.

"Grr...this bloody woman!" She fizzed.

"None of this is real...it can't be. We're all still asleep in the church. This is all just our brains playing tricks on us." There was a steel to Kane's voice now as he paced around Meridia, spit balling.

"You said before that you broke free...it's how you found me. How did you do it?" Meridia closed her eyes as she tried to explain what happened.

"I...I stopped fighting everything around me and tried to concentrate on something else, something good. I pictured my nightlight at home...every tiny detail, like I was drawing a picture in my mind, then I just held onto it for as long as I could. I imagined it getting brighter and warmer until..." Meridia opened her eyes, expecting Kane to tease her, but found him slack-jawed in astonishment at the amber orb now floating between them.

The light glitched and flickered momentarily before vanishing.

"Do it again!" Kane babbled, all agog. "But this time,

don't open your eyes until I tell you to. I think I know how to find the others..."

79

Izzy felt her phone vibrate in her pocket as she sat crouched beside JJ's bed. Whilst his temperature stabilized, he was still in distress.

His face was fixed in a pained expression, and his eyebrows furrowed together around the bridge of his nose. Quivering beneath the surface, his eyes darted left to right like the others. It was as if they were all embroiled in a horrible nightmare.

As Izzy reached for her phone, she wondered what the cult offered JJ's parents to buy their allegiance. It wasn't money, as they both still worked tirelessly around the clock, with JJ often left to his own devices.

Despite their differing home lives, she felt an affinity for him, particularly since uncovering the same wretched skeleton in each other's closets.

His condition was as terrifying as it was baffling, and although Izzy wasn't religious, she prayed to god that Retiarius could help them in their hour of need.

Valerie Richards. I know her and her husband. They were practically neighbours of mine when I lived here. The night walker has been a malleable weapon for decades now, eliminating hundreds, if not thousands, of obstacles to grease the wheels of the cult's expansion. It's crazy to think she was practically on my doorstep this entire time.

Legend has it she can infiltrate a person's dreams and kill them in their sleep without leaving a trace. That's why the string of unexplained deaths has been so hard to prove for all these years. I'm afraid, though, I am limited in terms of the help I can offer.

Chase Side is a fortress and sits on top of an underground network of tunnels. There is no way I will make it to the 4th floor without being caught. They will see me coming from a mile away. There may be another solution, however, but I'm afraid you're not going to like it.

Tell me, how much are you willing to risk for the lives of your friends?

80

Kane watched with bated breath as the pulsating ball of amber light reappeared in front of him as if by magic, fizzing and sparkling like a fiery plasma ball.

As before, the very fabric of the illusion which had them ensnared shimmered and glowed like the embers of a warm campfire. It was subtle when Meridia first attempted it, barely noticeable in fact, but Kane saw tiny fragments of Valerie's mirage break apart and flock toward the light, like glittering moths drawn to its magnetic flame.

Somehow, Meridia held the key to their escape, and whether it was her gift, or some other untapped supernatural power she possessed, he firmly believed their perseverance would lead them to the corridor they had both been searching for.

Just as Kane hoped, the more she focussed, the brighter the flames of truth burned, illuminating the bricks and mortar surrounding them until they resembled hot coals on an open fire.

Then, piece by piece, brick by brick, the unfathomable maze was stripped away like it was nothing but Lego and absorbed by the ever-growing light. Kane sensed the heat radiating in front of him as, inch by inch, Meridia ushered out the shadows and melted away the desolation they were sinking in.

"Keep going M..." He whispered, careful not to break her concentration.

The light was so bright now Kane had to shield his eyes, but he needed to be certain there was no way back to Valerie's twisted games.

Meridia needed to burn it all down to the ground if they were to ever save their friends. As the final fragments of Valerie's deception crumbled to iridescent dust and floated into the dazzling orb, Kane placed his hand on Meridia's shoulder and brought her out of her meditative state.

"It's ok M, you can stop now..."

"Wh...what happened?" Meridia opened her eyes, and for a second they flickered from brilliant amber to their usual blue and Kane wondered if she was about to shoot laser beams.

As before, the energy ball she manifested flickered and died in front of them, leaving them alone in an endless corridor with doors on either side, exactly as she described.

Whether it was a side-effect of the dream state they were in, or something more, Meridia's gift extended way beyond seeing into the future. For the first time since his parents' murder, Kane felt a glimmer of hope inside him.

"You did it M..." He beamed. "I don't know how, but you got us out. Now let's find the others and get the hell out of here!"

81

An icy, invisible hand brushed the back of Izzy's neck as she re-read the last message from Retiarius.

There was still no way of knowing for sure if she could trust him, but what other choice did she have?

Her friends were all teetering on the brink of death. Usually, she would have talked it through with them, and together they would have come up with an answer.

But since planting a seed of doubt in her mind about Peter, she couldn't even turn to him for help. Emily had too much on her mind as she staged a one-woman vigil at Meridia's bedside. It was time for Izzy to step up, just as the others had all done when their time came.

"Careful what you wish for..." she mumbled one of her dad's favourite sayings before drafting her response.

"*I would do anything. Please, tell me what I need to do.*"

It was short and to the point, but Retiarius held all the cards now, and Izzy knew whatever he had in mind she would need to go along with it. Based on everything he already divulged, she had an inkling of what his plan might entail. Waiting impatiently, she took her opportunity to check in with Peter until she heard back.

The tension was palpable at the other end of the church, but there was more than a touch of resignation in Peter's body language.

While Emily stroked her daughter's hand and whispered words of comfort, Peter watched over the boys with his hands on his hips and a look of utter dejection etched upon his face.

"Any change?" Izzy whispered.

"Afraid not, dear," Peter snapped out of his trance and forced a smile.

"They're not responding to anything I do, and although whatever you said to Meridia might have weathered the storm, as far as I can tell, they are all perilously close to the edge. Their breathing is shallow, and I still have no rational explanation for their eyes. I'm no doctor, but I've tried shining a light in Kane's and whilst his pupils are present, they are buried beneath a white film of fluid. If I didn't know better, I'd say the witch has a hand in this, but we both know it can't be her." A frown formed as his face let slip the burden he carried.

"I'm at a complete loss. The cult has cut off every reasonable course of action I would take, and short of kidnapping a doctor at gun-point and dragging them back here, I'm not sure what else I can do."

"*Buzz...buzz...*"

Peter heard Izzy's phone and glanced down at her pocket.

"Your parents again?" Izzy blushed as she nodded, knowing she was a terrible liar but hoping Peter was too distracted to suspect her of anything.

"If you need to talk, then you know I'm here. I can't

imagine how difficult this must all be, but just because the others are in danger, doesn't mean I'm not here for you. I'm sure that goes for Emily, too."

"Thank you. I've still not looked at their messages yet...I guess if I do, it makes everything real. James said we would look at them all together in the morning after a good night's rest." She shot a glance in JJ's direction, shuddering at the sight of him as he lay comatose in his bed.

He looked so frail and washed-out. There was also a sadness to him, one Izzy never witnessed before. It was as if Valerie's spell lifted the lid on his chirpy façade and given her a glimpse of the quiet desolation haunting him beneath the surface. The night walker needed to be stopped, no matter the cost.

"I...I just need the bathroom..." she mumbled, still shaken by his grim appearance. "I'll be right back."

Tucked away to the right of the main entrance to St Peter's, the public toilets would provide Izzy with the perfect opportunity to read Retiarius' latest message in privacy.

With only two banal, unisex cubicles to choose from, she entered the one closest to the external wall and bolted the flimsy, magnolia MDF door.

Once inside, she found it far cooler than the church hall, and the cubicle's woody scent reminded her of her grandmother's bathroom.

Imperial Leather, she recalled, spotting a half-used bar of the familiar beige coloured soap welded to the sink. It was an oddly fitting smell for a church toilet she thought as she scrambled to prize her phone from her pocket.

In theory, all you need to do is wake Valerie. She can't be in another person's dream if she herself is awake. As I explained before, Chase Side is a veritable fortress and home to some of the most influential members of the cult, along with arguably its most dangerous. Getting to her will be the tricky part. That said, I still believe there is a way you can slip in undetected, and that's where I come in.

I should be able to buy you enough time to get to the internal stairwell, but then I'm afraid you'll be on your own. Assuming you get out again, you'll find me waiting for you on the main road, ready to deliver you back to your friends.

Now, assuming you're still holed up somewhere in the area, I can probably pick you up inside of the next 10 minutes, but you'll need to tell me where I can find you.

Izzy, for this to work, you cannot tell anyone else what we're doing. I know this requires a tremendous leap of faith on your part, but you're running out of time. The longer you take to answer, the less likely it is we can save your friends.

Tick tock Izzy. You must choose and choose quickly.

Izzy slumped down onto the toilet seat with a loud thud. In her need to pull her weight within the group, she may have bitten off more than she could chew, leaving herself with a daunting decision to make.

This was one of those rare occasions she felt peeved by her own intellect. She already deduced Retiarius' plan included some thinly veiled ploy to lure her away from everyone else, and perhaps, on a subconscious level, it's why she read the message in the restroom.

Here, she was well positioned to slip out of the church with no one else seeing. It wouldn't take much effort, even for her, to crawl through the toilet window and out into the churchyard. She pressed pause on her racing mind and took a beat.

Was she seriously considering running off into the night with a potential psychopath? Was that really a better option than going to Peter and spilling the beans?

No matter how many ways she spun it, Retiarius was right about one thing. If Valerie was the night walker, as suspected, the only logical way of releasing her grip on the others would be to wake her.

But, what if she was wrong not to trust Peter? What if she told him everything, and he was the one to wake her?

Surely it would be far easier for an instantly forgettable looking 12-year-old to sneak in than a 6'4" celebrity heartthrob. Besides, if anything went wrong at the hospital, the others would be less likely to miss her than they would Peter.

It was time for Izzy to step up.

"*Ok.*" she tentatively typed. "*I will meet you on the corner of St Peter's Green in Thundridge.*"

With her thumb hovering over the send button, she made one last ditched attempt to come up with a better alternative, but with no one left to turn to and a renewed feeling of her own expendability, Izzy bit the bullet and sent her reply.

As she flicked the window catch open and climbed onto the toilet seat, she failed to hear the commotion stirring in the church hall.

Zach was in trouble.

82

Zach clattered to the ground face first and lay winded, sprawled on all fours, as he fought to catch his breath. Wherever he was now, it stunk. Glugging on a foetid cocktail of mould and mildew, he staggered to his feet and winced at the bloody grazes on his hands and knees.

The tingling pain felt like hundreds of tiny pinpricks, each wreaking havoc with his brain as he came to terms with the fact he might not be dreaming after all.

He was no longer in Crooked House, but would have gladly ventured back there if only to escape the eye-watering stench now suffocating him. Standing in the crevasse of a cave, all he saw was a jagged wall of damp limestone less than a yard from his face.

Bolted to it were a set of rusted chains with shackles at their ends, as if they were straight out of the dark ages. Coiled around themselves, they lay on the earthy ground at his feet, like copper-coloured rattlesnakes indulging in an afternoon nap.

Wiping away his tears, Zach turned to face the rest of

his dungeonesque surroundings and gasped in terror. Clamping his mouth shut to suppress the scream clawing to get out, he retreated under the cover of the shadows and surveyed the mountain of rotting corpses piled high in the centre of the room.

Stacked on top of one another like a grotesque pyramid, dozens of putrid remains, green with decay, lay twisted and fused together in a collective state of anguish. A jumble of adults and children dripping with slime–their decomposed skulls stared at Zach with mouths wide open in torment, filling the room with their silent screams.

Carved deep in the surrounding ground was the same star-like shape as Meridia's vision, delimited by flickering candles. Its trenches formed an intricate network of canals, slopping with blood from the mound of nameless victims above as they excreted whatever bodily fluids they have left.

It was all Zach could do not to vomit as he remained hunkered in the corner, searing his brain with grisly images of death and decay that could never be wiped clean.

The sound of footsteps abruptly awoke him from his gore-fuelled stupor, echoing beyond the room's only exit. A shadow stretched across the doorway beyond the towering ode to murder, followed by the sound of footsteps.

Someone was coming.

83

BEING CAREFUL NOT TO MAKE A SOUND, ZACH WORMED his way deeper into the corner until he could feel the wall's jagged strata pressing against the small of his back.

Beyond the dungeon's opening, the shadow drew closer, taking on a human form as it reached the room's entrance.

A cloaked figure entered, lugging the limp, blood-soaked body of a man over his shoulder. Behind him, a trail of crimson beads glistened in the gloomy candlelight. With eyes wide as saucers, Zach watched the cult member lay the body down on the ground with disconcerting ease, as if he weighed nothing.

Whoever he was, he was freakishly strong. From his limited vantage point, Zach couldn't distinguish the identity of either man.

His attention was immediately drawn to the body. Dressed head-to-toe in black, it didn't take long for Zach to guess its identity. Although he never met Father Alexander, he knew he was still missing and most likely dead.

When the body's head rolled over to reveal a

bloodstained clerical collar, Zach's worst fears were realized and a knot formed in the pit of his stomach.

"Grr..." Zach bit down hard on his fist to stop himself from screaming.

Father Alexander's bloodied face gaped at him through grisly, eyeless sockets. Frozen in a moment of heartbreaking futility, his haunting expression sent a torrent of warm, salty tears cascading down Zach's face as he wrestled with his composure. Heart pounding and sinuses overloaded, he opened his mouth to breath through the sudden surge of mucus clogging his airways.

With nowhere else to run, he watched the cult member disappear behind the mound of bodies and then reemerge with a full-length antique mirror tucked under one arm. Its ornate brass frame looked heavy and expensive as he propped it up against the wall closest to Father Alexander's head.

In the reflection, he saw the disciple's face. Blue eyed and clean shaven, the shadow of his cowl hid most of his features, but Zach saw enough to know exactly who he was. As Grady lingered at the foot of the mirror, Zach held his breath and agonized over the possibility he might spot him cowering in the opposite corner, but if he had, he wasn't letting on.

Scooting around Father Alexander's body, Grady pulled a large hunting knife from under his cloak, forcing Zach to bite down on his knuckles once more until he drew blood. Meanwhile, Grady took the dead priest's hand and held it up by his index finger.

"This little piggy went to market..." He chirped, wiggling the finger back and forth, before lowering it again and pushing the knife down hard like a chef chopping carrots.

"*Crunch!*"

Zach squirmed as he heard the knife cut through the bone, and Grady stood up with the severed finger clasped in his hand. With a menacing grin, he set to work, using the finger like a gruesome sharpie as he started drawing on the mirror.

Zach watched in horror as he occasionally stopped to squeeze more blood to the stub before resuming with his grisly creation.

Stepping back to admire his work, Grady gave Zach a chance to study the macabre symbol for himself. Although the blood had smeared and dripped in places, it was the same inverted star-shape as the one gathering slime beneath the pile of corpses.

However, Grady filled his interpretation with the head of a goat. Its horns occupied the upper two points, whilst the lower two housed its floppy ears.

The very base of the star contained the goat's nose and mouth. It made for a chilling sight and the illustration seemed to share Grady's unhinged grin.

Seemingly happy with his handiwork, Grady returned to Father Alexander's body and took another finger.

"*Crunch!*"

Swallowing down vomit, Zach battled the urge to make a run for it. He would gladly run all the way back to Crooked House if he could. Anything to get away from the maniac he was now trapped with.

He continued to watch as Grady stepped up to the mirror again and resumed his ghastly design. Each stroke was measured and meticulous. Backing away once more, Zach could now see letters inscribed between each of the star's points. In the top half of the image were the letters '*SA–MA–EL*', whereas at the bottom he wrote '*LIL–ITH*'.

None of the letters made any sense to Zach, but they did to Grady, who nervously backed away from the mirror as if something terrible was about to happen. He didn't have long to wait for a response to his gruesome ritual as a warm breeze swept across the room.

Blowing out most of the candles and wafting the rancid stench of death in Zach's face, the clammy gust of air seemed to come from the mirror.

Straining to see through the murk, Zach glimpsed a shadow drift past in the reflection. At first, he thought someone had joined him in his private little alcove, but on closer inspection, he saw it was something in the mirror itself.

"Click-clack...click-clack..."

The hairs on the back of Zach's neck stood to attention the second he recognized the ominous skittering motion. Paralyzed by fear, he watched the shadowy arachnid grow darker and larger as it drew closer, until it was looming over Father Alexander's reflection.

Judging by its silhouette, the phantom creature was enormous and powerfully built, like a giant spider on steroids. Dominating the lower half of the mirror, it lingered above the dead priest's head momentarily, then raised a sinewy leg.

"Chink!"

Zach gasped in horror as cracks zig-zagged across the face of the mirror like bolts of lightning. Whatever the shadow was, it wanted out of its glass prison.

"Crash!"

The creature's thorny leg came down like a hammer, smashing through the fractured mirror and spearing Father Alexander's temple with a sickening crunch.

With a mouthful of puke, Zach watched the priest's

face cave in, until all that remained of his head was a misshapen lump of bloody pulp leaking brain and cartilage onto the dirt.

From there, it slowly dragged Father Alexander's mutilated corpse into the black void where the mirror once was. As the priest's feet disappeared out of sight, an ominous hush descended upon the room and Grady hurriedly slipped out the same way he entered.

"*Clank!*"

A rusted iron portcullis came crashing down after him, sealing Zach inside the room, as Grady clung to its bars, watching and waiting from the safety of its grating.

Cuffing away the dregs of sick, Zach quivered in the shadows, suffocating on the strangling silence, until a cacophony of squelching and crunching reverberated around him. Shattering the silence, it filled the room with stomach-churning sounds of flesh being ripped apart and bones being ground to mush.

"*Click-clack...click-clack...*"

Two bright fiery orbs illuminated the gloom as they burned from deep within the abyss. Somehow, Grady's ghoulish ritual had punched a hole through the very fabric of Zach's world, and whatever abomination he summoned was now about to show itself.

The murderous nurse watched gleefully from the sidelines as, one by one, eight huge black spiny legs stepped beyond the confines of the brass framed portal and scampered into the room.

"*Click-clack...click-clack...*"

84

"*Grrrrr...Grrrrr...*"

"Zach! Zach..." Peter tried to cradle Zach's slender frame as his condition suddenly deteriorated.

Teeth clenched, and body stiff as a board, Zach twitched and tremored uncontrollably in Peter's arms like a pneumatic drill.

"What is it? What's going on?" Emily stepped across from Meridia's bedside as Peter wrestled to restrain Zach's arms.

"He's having some kind of seizure...I...I don't know what to do..."

Quick to react, Emily raced over to the vacant beds and rounded up as many pillows as she could get her hands on.

"Here...you need to let him go. The only thing we can do is try to prevent him from hurting himself." Emily set about cushioning Zach's head and neck with the extra pillows she gathered.

"You need to let go of his arms, Peter. I know it's hard, but if he is having a fit, then the only thing we can do is wait for it to pass before we can help him. My aunt is epileptic, and trust me, I know it sounds wrong and all you want to do is stop him shaking, but it can do more harm than good. You have to let him go."

"But..."

"Trust me, Peter..." She placed her hand on his and looked him in the eye. "You need to let him go."

Against his better judgement, Peter did as she asked and took a step back. Zach's youthful face was riddled with torment and dripping with sweat. With his covers now scattered on the floor, he writhed and convulsed as if he'd been plugged into the mains.

"They can't take much more of this!" Peter fumed, his voice close to breaking as he grappled with his own impotence.

Meanwhile, Zach continued to growl and shake like an earthquake.

"We need to stay strong..." Emily's voice soared above the unfolding chaos and self-doubt, pulling Peter back from the brink of collapse.

"Look! It's passing..." She took his hand and gestured toward the bed.

Sure enough, Zach's convulsions were subsiding, and his limbs relaxed. The moment he came to a complete stop, Peter swooped in to check his breathing.

"He...he's stopped breathing..." Peter trailed off as he started searching for a pulse.

"I...I can't find anything...Zach? Zach?"

Overcome with panic, Peter began performing chest compressions.

"Don't you dare die on me now! Please, Zach...please wake up!"

85

ZACH'S EYES GLAZED OVER AS THE TERRIFYING creature sent him reeling into a state of shock. Numb with fear, his thoughts scattered like autumn leaves in the wind as he starred at the monstrous arachnid scouring the room.

With a bulbous body covered in greasy black hair, it defiled the stony walls with its malignant shadow. On top of its towering frame, its brawny face looked as if it was plucked from the very depths of Zach's darkest nightmares.

Eyes fizzing with rage, the apex predator clenched its powerful jaw like a bear trap and hissed through jagged, blood-stained teeth.

Wedged in the farthest corner of the dungeon, Zach was utterly defenceless and could do nothing but wait for the hideous creature to spot him. Crouched stock-still, he held his breath and closed his eyes as he braced himself for the inevitable. A low whimper slipped between his pursed lips and he was certain it would prove the final nail in his coffin.

"*Click-clack...click-clack...*"

He heard the creature's breathing, laboured and raspy,

as if it was retching. Zach opened his eyes, hoping it was choking on Father Alexander's bones, but he found it skulking at the base of the putrescent stack of human remains. The fur on its body rippled back and forth as if it was struggling to regurgitate something from the depths of its gut.

"*Kaff...kaff...*"

Zach winced as the creature craned what little neck it had, projectile vomiting a huge globule of thick, green mucus at the very top of the pile.

"*Splat!*"

The disgusting blob, about the size of a football, struck its intended target, then slowly oozed and dripped downward, coating everything it touched in a revolting, creamy glaze.

Seconds after impact, the sticky spittle started to bubble and smoulder, flooding the room with a sulphurous stink.

"Acid..." Zach mumbled in a phobia-fuelled stupor, but the creature remained oblivious to his momentary lapse as it scuttled from side to side in fiendish anticipation.

Within seconds, the tangle of festering corpses smelted down into a liquid lunch for the eight-legged beast, and it wasted no time in lapping it up.

Somewhere between the revulsive slurping and Grady's snickering from beyond the gate, it all became too much for Zach to bear, and the room started spinning. Icy beads of sweat dripped down his back, and he teetered on his perch, kicking a stone across the room as he fought to keep his balance.

"*Crack!*"

The sudden ricochet got the creature's attention, and it turned to face his next meal. Dizzy on fumes and weak from exhaustion, Zach slumped down to his knees. Even if he wanted to run now, he couldn't. His legs had turned to jelly.

"*Click-clack...click-clack...*"

In a sudden burst of speed, the mutant arachnid set after Zach like a rabid dog, shrieking and hissing as it towered over him. Its slobber seared the earth at Zach's feet as he scrambled to get away, but it was no use.

Completely cornered, the creature had him within its grasp, and there was no escape. In the distance, he heard Grady rattling the gate in excitement, like a crazed fanatic consumed with bloodlust. Fearing the end, Zach reached up to shield his face and felt something tug on his elbow.

At first, he thought he snagged his sleeve on the rocks at his back, but then he felt a firm squeeze, followed by a yank. Snatched from the jaws of death, Zach hurtled backwards, through the wall behind him, then into an endless icy black abyss.

86

"Zach? Bro, can you hear me?" Kane gently slapped his brother's face to wake him.

Behind the first door they opened, they found him dangling lifelessly from a throng of vile tendrils, similar to the ones that had swathed Kane. Pale and covered in viscous slime, Zach looked so fragile as he lay with his head propped against Meridia's knees.

"I...I don't think he's breathing..." He stuttered, unsure of what to do next.

"C'mon Zach...breathe...please," Meridia pleaded.

Neither of them knew how long he was subjected to Valerie's gruesome torture chamber, but unlike Kane, he wasn't conscious when they first arrived on the scene.

"I don't know what I'll do if we lose him...we can't lose him, Kane...we just can't..." Meridia opened the floodgates and wept over her best friend's limp and lifeless body.

"Zach!" Kane's anger reared its head as he gripped his brother by the shoulders and shook him vehemently.

"*Kaff... splat!*"

Zach coughed up a mouthful of sticky yellow mucus and doused his brother's face.

Dripping in goo, Kane snatched his brother up from the ground and gave him a huge squeeze.

"Thank god…I thought I lost you!"

"*Kaff…kaff…*"

Still hacking and retching, Zach suddenly came alive in his brother's arms and anxiously wormed his way free.

"Argh! Get away from me…" Screaming hysterically with pupils dilated in terror, he lashed out at an invisible assailant and launched himself across the room.

Scampering away on all fours, he came to a halt in the furthest corner where he crouched, traumatized and trembling, like a wounded animal.

"Zach…it's ok…it…it's us." Kane tried his best to pacify him, but Zach's eyes continued to dart around the room in fright as he puffed and panted in search of his breath.

"Zach." Meridia stepped up to the plate, her voice low and tender.

"It's me Zach…you're safe now…" For the first time since he came to, Zach's petrified gaze softened, and his breathing mellowed.

"Is it really you?" He whimpered. "I…I don't know what's real anymore…" Meridia approached him with her palms up.

"It's us spud," Kane assured. "None of this is real…we're all trapped in some sort of dream…a nightmare."

"Like Freddy?" Zach sniffled, much to Kane's delight.

"Exactly! See…" He shot a smug look at Meridia, then turned his attention back to his brother. "Well, not quite. It's Valerie…we're all trapped in her dream somehow."

"But I saw them…mum, dad…I saw them die…" Zach broke down again.

"I saw them too...it's not real. None of this is..." Kane gestured at the run-down room they were standing in.

"Not even the giant spider?" Zach was calming down.

"Wait, you saw a weaver?" Meridia blurted. The tension in her voice threatened to send him spiralling again.

"It was Grady...he...he killed Father Alexander...and there was this huge pile of bodies in a dungeon. It was so gross...then he got a mirror from somewhere and...and..." Both Kane and Meridia listened intently as Zach babbled his way through everything he saw, including all the details of Grady's disturbing ritual.

It was no secret Zach was afraid of spiders and based on his own experience in Valerie's house of horrors, Kane wondered if she was accessing their deepest, darkest fears and then wielding them as a weapon. He abruptly cut Zach's story short, wondering what nightmare JJ might be trapped in.

"We need to find JJ...before it's too late. I need you to be strong now, spud, and come with us. There'll be time for swapping stories later." He hauled his brother up onto his feet and ushered him toward the door.

"It's gonna be ok mate. We're going to get out of this mess, I promise." Kane glanced back at Meridia, who was clearly still processing everything Zach told them.

There were several details that left her visibly spooked. As he grabbed the door handle to leave, the thought of a weaver waiting on the other side scurried across his mind and Kane sensed an icy hand reach inside his chest and squeeze his heart.

"R...ready?" He stuttered, shivering at the mental image and the worry he'd naively given Valerie some new material.

Meridia and Zach both nodded sheepishly as Kane turned the handle and opened the door.

87

"He's stable...I don't know how, but he's stable and breathing again." Peter remained perplexed by Zach's bedside.

The entire evening left his brain tied in knots, and now he found himself playing whack-a-mole with an unseen enemy as he hopped from bed to bed, frantically resuscitating the children one by one. It was utterly exhausting.

"Where's Izzy?" He asked, realizing he hadn't seen her since before Zach's gut-wrenching episode.

"I've not seen her," Emily replied, glancing around the empty church hall. "Last time I saw her, she was with you."

"Izzy?" Peter called out as he rose to his feet.

He was so preoccupied with Zach that he didn't notice if she returned from the restroom.

"She went to the toilet a little while ago...Izzy?" A hint of panic bled to the surface of Peter's voice as he wandered up the aisle, checking between each pew.

"Keep an eye on them, will you? I'll be back in a sec."

He gestured for Emily to stand watch as he made his way to the toilets.

When he arrived inside, he found one of the cubicle doors closed and showing as engaged. Breathing a sigh of relief, Peter called out to be sure nothing was wrong.

"Izzy? Izzy, is everything ok in there?" He sensed a chill circling the room, and beyond the flimsy white saloon door he heard trees rustling in the wind.

"Izzy?" He pressed, stooping low to peek through the gap at the bottom. No feet. Fearing the worst, he hurriedly took a coin from his pocket and used it to unlock the cubicle from the outside.

"I'm coming in Izzy..." He called, giving fair warning.

As Peter peered around the edge of the door, he felt his heart plummet like a lead balloon. The cubicle was empty, and the window was wide open. Izzy was gone.

88

Izzy stood shivering on the corner of St Peter's Green, having given her coat up for Meridia in her hour of need. All she had now was her phone and her wits as she waited for Retiarius to show.

The night air was biting at her ears as it whistled in and out of the surrounding trees, but cutting as it was, it offered a brief distraction from the endless river of doubt flowing through her mind.

Did she just walk into a trap? Was Retiarius about to hand her over to the Children of the Shadows?

Based on the location she chose to meet, she knew it wouldn't take a genius to figure out where the others were hiding, but desperate times called for desperate measures.

Luckily, the roads were deserted, and with only a smattering of light coming from the surrounding houses, she would have no trouble disappearing into the night if things turned ugly.

After a little over five minutes of tying her brain in knots, a midnight blue BMW turned into the street and dipped its headlights. Pulling up a few yards ahead of her, it sat with the engine purring, waiting for Izzy to make the first move. It was now or never.

Izzy jogged along the narrow footpath and cupped her hands to the passenger window to see inside. Behind the wheel, shrouded in shadows, was a young woman wearing a black baseball cap. She stared back at Izzy through the glass and directed her to the back seat with her thumb.

"*Click.*"

Izzy heard the doors unlock as she scrutinized the rear of the car for any hidden surprises. Satisfied the driver was alone, she opened the back door and slipped inside.

The car was a warm and welcome relief from the freezing wind as Izzy squeaked her way across the black leather interior to get a better look at Retiarius. Until now, she believed he was a man from their email exchange.

Staring into the rear-view mirror, she discovered a woman in her twenties, slight of build and wearing a dusty denim jacket. Beyond that, there was nothing much to tell, the shadow of her cap obscuring the rest of her features.

"Re...Retiarius?" Izzy stammered as the last of the cold rattled its way out of her tingling cheeks.

The woman said nothing and instead handed her a phone, then put the car into gear. As they pulled away, Izzy placed the phone to her ear.

"H...hello?"

"*Izzy Di Salvo. So glad you could make it.*" The voice on the other end of the line was distorted, masking the owner's identity, but Izzy knew at once it was Retiarius and felt her guard go up.

"*Sorry I can't be there, but it's just too dangerous to show my face. If the Children of the Shadows discover I have returned, we will lose our advantage.*"

"Who are you?" Izzy cut to the chase.

"Straight to business, eh? Haha...all in good time, child, all in good time. We have a unique opportunity tonight and it's important you know why. The witch you and your friends eliminated was their all-seeing eye, so with her now gone, and those who walk the shadows...those are the creatures your friends stupidly broadcast on YouTube...with them also sidelined, we only have one real bona fide threat to contend with at the hospital."

"The nurse." Izzy blurted, her head spinning from all the enticing titbits of information Retiarius casually squeezed into a couple of sentences.

"Ah, so you know about him, do you? There is more to that one than meets the eye. Not to be trifled with." Retiarius paused and let out a deep sigh.

"I'm not gonna lie to you, Izzy. If you see him while you're in there, the only thing you can do is run and pray to god you're fast enough to escape. There's no protecting you from him, I'm afraid."

Izzy's heart sank at the prospect of needing to rely on her running ability, as the last vestiges of the winter air she harboured in her bones snaked their way up and out of her spine.

"Where are the horsemen...I mean, those who walk in the shadows?" Izzy pulled at one of the many threads Retiarius had dangled in front of her.

"Horsemen? Oh, I see. Yes, I suppose that is partially accurate. My my, you know your stuff, don't you?" The more she listened, the more familiar he sounded.

Unlike his emails, there was a slight inflection when he spoke. Traces of an accent perhaps, but try as she might, she couldn't place it.

"Right now, they are in a dark and distant realm, waiting for a new path to emerge, but they won't stay gone for long.

That said, they are mostly all bark and no bite, for the moment at least. That will all change, however, if they fill the last room in Crooked House. You see, you and your friends have been a fly in the ointment...one which nobody saw coming, not even the witch. Tell me, how is it you've got this far? What is your secret?"

"S...secret?"

"Yes, you must have a secret...something you're not telling me. How else could you have survived this long?"

"Just lucky, I guess..." Izzy bluffed unconvincingly.

"Well, whatever it is, you've changed the path the world was on and given some of us a glimmer of hope."

"Us?" Izzy glanced up and locked eyes with her driver.

"Not all the missing people in this town are victims of Crooked House. Some, like me, have disappeared of their own free will. There is far more at stake than perhaps you realize Izzy...the cult's grip. It extends way beyond Cold Christmas..."

"The prime minster and the president?" Izzy couldn't resist a thinly veiled brag to balance the score.

"Aren't you the sharp one? Fascinating...you must tell me how you know so much...I insist." There was an air of menace in his tone that wormed its way through the voice distorter he was hiding behind.

"The rings," she conceded. "We found out about the rings..."

"Very clever. For a moment there, I thought I had another seer in our midst. Now that would be a stroke of luck..." Retiarius was fishing, but Izzy held firm. He was up to something.

If there were others working with him, then why not send one of those to stop Valerie? Of course, there was a chance they were all on the run, like he was, but why go to all this trouble? It felt overly elaborate and Izzy smelled a rat.

"What I don't understand is why so many people would want to start the end of the world." She shifted topics and tried pandering to his ego.

"Hahahahaha...Who told you that? Was it the historian? I bet it was...haha...perhaps you have simply ridden your luck until now. Seriously though, that's just like an academic to take things so literally."

"So, the world isn't going to end?"

"Oh no, the world is totally going to end...for sure. Just not in the way you might think. The whole fire and brimstone thing is only part of it."

"But Mer..." Izzy stopped herself from slipping up. "But Mr Higginsworth said if the Children of the Shadows fulfilled the prophecy, then we'll all die."

"Oh, you guys would definitely die. Me too, probably. If the prophecy is fulfilled, then people like you and me won't have anywhere to seek refuge. The cult, and I guess what you'd consider civilized society, are two different sides of the same coin. Truth is, they're both as bad as each other in their own way. I'm going to let you in on a little secret now Izzy, and that is we've all spent our entire lives being fed a big fat lie. Good and evil...they don't really exist, not in the way we're told, at least. After all, one person's right is another person's wrong. So, who's to say which side has the higher ground, really? It's up to whoever is in charge, of course. In reality, there is only order and chaos. That is what's really at stake here. We've spent our entire lives being spoon fed propaganda that chaos is bad. Something to be feared. Something from the dark ages...you see how even the word dark has negative connotations? We see it on the news every day. They've been brainwashing us all for centuries..."

"Who are they?" Izzy quizzed, unsure whose side he was on.

"Those pulling the strings, of course. The self-proclaimed good guys. They've been controlling us all from day one by whatever means they could. What do you think religion is? What purpose do you think it serves in our society? It's simply a primitive method of enforcing order. Control. Before science, religion was all we had, and war of course... and we all know who pulls the strings on that front. The bickering fractions we see battling it out for territory, they are all glimpses into our true nature. You need only look at the state of our planet to know the truth. We are nothing but a bunch of subservient savages masquerading as something more civilized."

"So, whose side are you on?" Izzy took a more direct approach as she wondered if she'd joined forces with a madman.

"I'm more of a pragmatist...a bit like you. I see both sides of the coin, but I'll be totally honest, I'm playing with the side that suits me best. We may all be savages at heart...deep down inside our lizard brains...but after centuries of being conditioned to be soft, we no longer belong in either world. Instead, we're condemned to this banal limbo, denying our impulses and keeping the peace. But at least we're alive. I suppose the perfect solution would be some sort of middle ground. Perhaps those Purge movies are onto something...but of course, you're too young to know what I'm talking about."

"I think I get the gist."

"The Children of the Shadows, they walk a very different path. Those within the inner circle, that is. There are lots of pretenders in their ranks, your parents included. People who've been promised a future when the time of reckoning comes, but they're no better equipped to survive it than you

or I. They are all puppets, strung along until they've played their part. I know, I used to be just like them. Pawns in a psychological war that has been raging for centuries behind the scenes, and now the war is all but won. The Children of the Shadows control the media now, you see. The ultimate kingmaker, whispering in our ears 24/7, sliding chess pieces around the board while no one is looking. Recessions, scandals, pandemics, conspiracies...even movements like the great resignation and the big reset...all elaborate stories, misdirection, concocted to break people's spirit. Pushing us all to the brink until we become so disillusioned with our lives, we'll welcome the devil himself in with open arms."

"Well, if that's the case, then what's the point of even trying?" Izzy countered.

Retiarius painted a bleak picture of the world, and his pessimism was infectious. Perhaps that was the point he was trying to make all along?

"I'm afraid if you came here looking for a hero, then you've climbed into the back of the wrong BMW. I'm just playing the percentages. If darkness prevails...and I mean that in the literal sense; then the sun will die, and I will inevitably die with it. As things stand today, we can live to fight another day, perhaps. Find that middle ground. Eliminating the night walker will only help tip those scales further in our favour and clip the wings of the cult."

The line went quiet, and Izzy mulled over Retiarius' ramblings. Was he a potential ally, or nothing more than a disgruntled ex-employee seeking revenge?

Glancing out the car window, she could see they weren't far from Chase Side now, and her stomach did a somersault with each new street they sailed past. The roads were eerily quiet, even for nighttime, and she still had no idea what was expected of her when they arrived at their destination.

"Wait, you said eliminate?" His choice of words finally registered as they turned the last corner and came to a stop.

"Don't play coy Izzy...you know just as well as I that your friends can't go without sleep forever. As things stand, the second one of them nods off the night walker will find them again and kill them. Mark my words. The only way to save your friends, and yourself, is to stop her once and for all. That's why you're here."

"Click!"

Izzy rattled the door handle, only to find the child lock was switched on. She was trapped.

"So, Izzy, this is what you're going to do for me now, and I'm afraid I won't be taking no for an answer..."

89

As they ventured back out into the corridor of Valerie's mind, they all breathed a collective sigh of relief. It was empty and unchanged, just as they hoped.

"This must be some kind of back door into her brain... like a hack or something," Kane mused, surveying the infinite string of doors on either side of them. "Do you think she knows we're still here?"

"I don't wanna wait around to find out." With no hesitation, Meridia rushed to the neighbouring room and turned its handle.

"He must be in this one..." she declared, pushing it open and disappearing inside. Kane followed, dragging Zach behind him like a rag doll.

"JJ!" Meridia rushed to the tangled mass of sinister serpentine tentacles that were piled high in the centre of the room.

There, among its mucus-coated coils, Kane saw JJ's hand poking out, limp and lifeless.

"Zach! Help..." Both brothers rushed to Meridia's side and tried to free him. Snatching and clawing at the swarm of slimy tendrils, they uncovered his face, and the sight of it sent shockwaves of terror rippling through Kane's body.

"We're too late..." Zach sobbed as they raced to prise the remaining slithering appendages apart and release JJ from their deadly grip.

Halfway out, Kane used all his strength to haul him clear, while Zach and Meridia kicked and stamped on the dying tentacles. As he saw with Zach, the second they lost their hold on JJ's body, the undulating members withered and turned to dust. With one last heave, Kane fell backwards onto the ground with JJ's lifeless body on top of him.

"JJ...JJ wake up..." He begged, turning JJ onto his side to help release the glug of mucus filling his airways.

"Please mate...please..." The desperation in Kane's voice spread like wildfire and soon they were each snivelling as they rocked JJ back and forth in a childish attempt to bring him back to life.

"Do something...please!" Kane pleaded with Meridia, who looked every bit as lost as he did.

"He's so cold...I...I can't leave here without him...I just can't...." He trailed off, still going through the motions, refusing to accept his best friend was gone.

Resting his head on JJ's cold, motionless chest, he closed his eyes and prayed for a miracle.

"None of this is real, mate...you need to come back. Please..." A sudden burst of warmth brushed against Kane's cheek and a hazy glow radiated somewhere beyond the darkness of his tightly clenched eyelids.

Meridia was channelling her energy once more, painting their stark surroundings a mesmeric amber. Backing away from JJ's body, Kane watched Meridia guide the pulsating orb towards their fallen friend with both hands.

The shimmering ball of light responded, hovering above JJ's chest, before diving inside him with a blinding flash of brilliant white. Meridia opened her eyes tentatively.

"The light..." Kane mumbled. "Where did it go?"

"I...I don't know. I wasn't even thinking about the light this time...I was just thinking about JJ, how he used to be before all this...his smile, his laugh. I was just trying to picture him alive..."

"Huah! *Kaff...kaff...*" JJ's sudden exhale made everyone jump as he hacked up a mouthful of yellow gelatinous phlegm.

"JJ!" Kane beamed, hugging him as he lay coughing and wheezing on the floor.

Dazed and disoriented, JJ flailed around beneath him like a beetle stuck on its back.

"Give him some space..." Meridia prized Kane off him and helped JJ sit up.

"Wh...whoa..." He flinched away from them all in fear as he adjusted to his new surroundings. "I thought...I thought I was..."

"You were mate." Kane blurted, still beaming. "M brought you back..."

"Back? Back how?" He mumbled. "From where? Where are we?"

"It's Valerie. We think we're inside her head...or she's inside ours. I can't tell anymore. All I know is, she wasn't joking when she threatened you at the hospital. She got to us in our dreams...turned them into nightmares."

"Like Freddy..."

"Yes! Just like Freddy." Kane shot a sideways glance at Meridia, who rolled her eyes in response. "Only Valerie's an obnoxious little shit running around in a Disney princess dress."

"I've seen her...I think I'd sooner take on Freddy any day of the week." He forced a smile and then looked beyond the crowd gathered round him. "Where's Izzy?"

"She must have stayed awake. I saw her with Peter and Emily...at the church. We need to find a way out of here and get back to them." Kane looked at Meridia again, hoping she had answers.

"Why am I covered in gunk? I can actually taste it...it's gross."

"Trust me, mate, you don't wanna know."

"I think I know the way-out guys." Meridia cut short their reunion and brought them all back on mission. "When we come out of here, there's a door to our right. That will take us all back the way I came in. Only trouble is, I came in through Crooked House."

"Fuck it, let's do it..." Kane was quick to snuff out any doubt amongst them as he marched over toward the door.

"I'm sick of this shit. Sick of running scared. All that place ever does is try to pick us off one by one. Divide and conquer...it's what the Romans used to do. It knows we're stronger together, so I say we go out there and kick it in the balls."

Wobbling up to his feet, JJ joined him at the door.

"Kane's right. I'm sick of running too. Let's make a stand, guys." One by one, they gathered around Kane and waited for him to lead them into battle.

It felt good rallying the troops, and he could see the belief in their eyes. It was time to take the fight to Valerie.

"*Click.*"

Kane turned the handle and peeked through the slender gap in the door. A savage growl burst through the narrow opening, rattling the walls and sending a jolt of terror coursing through each of their spines. White with shock, Kane slammed the door shut again and turned to face the rest of the group.

"Shit!" He declared with deadpan disbelief. "I think we may have a problem..."

"What is it?!" Meridia reached for the door handle, but Kane stood firm and held her at bay.

"Not yet." He explained. "I think our only option is to make a run for it and hope it doesn't see us."

"See us? Hope what doesn't see us?" Zach gulped.

"Er...well, I think it's safe to assume Valerie knows we're still here, and it's gonna take more than a nightlight to save us this time, M."

<h1 style="text-align:center">90</h1>

Retiarius's voice faded into the ether. Eclipsed by the high-pitched ringing in Izzy's ears as she battled to overcome the burden of expectation tightening around her neck like a noose.

"C...can you open the window...I...I think I'm going to faint..." she mumbled.

The sweet, sickly aroma of the car's creaky leather interior had become altogether suffocating and was making her queasy.

"*Breathe Izzy... Breathe...*" Retiarius' voice wormed its way back into her consciousness as the window opened a fraction and allowed the evening breeze to brush against her clammy forehead.

"*It has to be this way, Izzy. Valerie must die in order for your friends to live.*"

"B...but..."

"*But nothing Izzy!*" His creepy electronic voice boomed out of the speaker so loud she almost dropped the phone.

"*The more time you waste, the less likely it is you'll ever see your friends again. Perhaps you don't care about them as much as you say. You asked for my help, and I've upheld my end of the bargain. Now it's time you uphold yours."* Izzy's cheeks tingled as the cool air greeted her free-flowing tears.

"Tell...*sniff*...tell me what to do..." she whimpered. Retiarius was right. She had no other choice if she wanted to save them.

"Save your tears Izzy...she's evil, responsible for countless deaths, and right now she's trying to kill everyone you hold dear. To save them, you need to start by finding the second fire exit to the right of the patient block. Once there, you'll find its door propped open. That entrance will lead you into the emergency stairwell, and from there you'll have direct access to the fourth floor. You'll need to be quick though Izzy, so that means no dawdling. Although there shouldn't be anyone else using the stairwell this time of night, if you get caught, you won't have a snowball's chance in hell of explaining your way back out of there. Assuming you make it to the fourth floor, you'll arrive at the opposite end of the ward to the reception desk. Valerie is in cubicle 5, which you'll find halfway down the corridor and on your right."

"Wait...how do you know all this? Who's opening the door for me?" Retiarius was smart and formidable, but there was no way he could be this specific without someone already working for him on the inside.

"Never you mind about that, Izzy. The less you know, the better." He was protecting his asset.

If Izzy didn't know who had helped her, there would be no way of blabbing if she got caught.

"Once you slip behind the curtain, you'll need to wait for our signal."

"What signal?"

"Oh, don't worry. You won't be able to miss it. Once you

hear it, you'll need to count to a hundred, nice and slow, then switch off every bit of machinery in the cubicle. We should buy enough time for you to wait and make sure you've done your bit. You need to be certain Izzy...we can't afford for any mistakes. Then you'll need to make your way out the same way you came in. The carpark will be chaotic by then, but it should provide you with all the cover you need to sneak out and make your way back to the pickup point on Willow Road."

Izzy closed her eyes and took a deep breath as she rehashed the plan in her mind. She sensed her heart pounding against the inside of her chest as the breeze continued to whistle its way in through the window beside her. He made it all sound so simple, as if she was about to decommission a server.

Was she really about to commit murder?

"Oh, and don't even think about backing out once you're in there. All it takes is one phone call and you'll wish you died with all your friends." It was as if he read her mind.

Retiarius was one nasty piece of work and Izzy had no doubt whatsoever he would follow through with his threat if she lost her nerve. She was outmanoeuvred. It served her right to play with fire in the first place, but what else was she supposed to do?

As she conjured up images of her bedridden friends and their tortured expressions, she wondered if there was any truth in Retiarius' claim that someone within their group wasn't who they appeared to be. Unsure if she believed a single word he said, she asked anyway.

"Who is it that can't be trusted?"

The name he divulged sliced through her brain like shards of broken glass, tearing her reality to shreds. Every tiny detail he proceeded to share seemed to stack up, and

Izzy sat in stunned silence, listening to the rest of his story as she pieced everything together.

When Retiarius switched off his voice distorter and revealed his identity, she knew he was telling the truth, and whilst his earth-shattering revelation didn't alter her perception of him, it sent her into a tailspin.

Ignoring the multitude of missed calls and messages from Peter and her parents, she composed a warning for Kane and pressed send. As Izzy discretely tucked her phone back in her pocket, she cleared her throat and broke her pensive silence.

"Ok. I'm ready..."

91

Meridia braced herself to run as Kane seized hold of the door handle, as if his life depended on it.

"Remember, when I open this door you all need to follow M to the exit...and whatever you do, don't look back." He warned.

This wouldn't be the first time a monster has chased them, but nothing could have prepared them for what was waiting in the corridor.

As he swung the door open, Meridia couldn't help herself. She needed to know what had left Kane so spooked. Slowing to a jog the moment she entered the corridor, it didn't take long for the others to clatter into the back of her. Wedged in the doorway, they all got an eyeful of the hideous creature thundering towards them on all fours.

"Holy shit!" JJ's panic was swallowed by Zach's high-pitched screams as they collided into one another in their desperation to get away.

Their half-baked plan instantly descended into chaos, and all the while they tried to get out of each other's way, the bounding miscreation drew ever closer.

Its bloated head was a horrific tangle of fractured faces; each one a grotesquely distorted manifestation of Valerie, stitched together like a hideous patchwork quilt of pale, saggy skin.

With a dozen mouths full of broken, malformed teeth, and crooked eyes that were black as coal, it was a living embodiment of pure terror. Sprouting out of its gelatinous body was a horde of swarming, slimy tentacles. Covered in thorny spikes, they lashed against the walls as it galloped toward them in a flurry of flabby arms and legs.

"The door! Someone open the bloody door!" Kane yelled, as they all flocked to its handle at once.

Bundling through what was now their only way out, they spilled into the dark and dusty hallway of Crooked House, and Kane kicked the door shut behind him. Flat on his back, he pressed his legs to the door of room 8 to hold the monster at bay.

"*Bang!*"

The creature rattled his legs and the door's hinges as it vied to break out.

"*Bang!*"

Another vicious blow landed, sweeping Kane aside as the creature found a foothold.

"Help! I can't hold it..." He yelped, as a gaggle of spiky tendrils snaked through the gap, splintering the doorframe as they forced their way into the hall.

One by one, the others rushed to Kane's aid, pushing back with all their might whilst trying to evade the writhing mass of barbed feelers thrashing in the air.

"It's too strong!" JJ exclaimed through gritted teeth.

"M...now would be a great time to magic us up an RPG...or a tank..." Kane was only half joking with his wild request.

"All we can do is make a run for it...the plan hasn't changed guys. We just need to make it to the front door...if we can get through it, then hopefully, we'll all wake up."

"And what if we don't?" Zach countered.

"Well, then we're screwed either way." With that, Kane shuffled onto his side and got himself ready to run. "On three, ready? One...two...three!"

92

While inhaling a lungful of the crisp night air, Izzy watched the BMW disappear into the distance and questioned whether she was the one caught in a nightmare.

Marooned in the shadows of Chase Side carpark, she had no choice but to go through with Retiarius' diabolical plan. Assuming the hospital was the fortress he described, she skulked along the perimeter of the tarmac until she saw the fire exit he told her about.

Sure enough, a sliver of aquamarine was breaking through a gap in its door and mingling with the evening shade. Meanwhile, a silent symphony of light poured through the hospital's windows, illuminating the path ahead. If Izzy was going to make it to the entrance undetected, she needed to be quick and nimble. Two qualities that were not in her wheelhouse.

"Baby steps..." she muttered under her breath, egging herself on.

She would tackle whatever was waiting for her on the fourth floor once she got there, but to do that, she needed to get to the stairwell without being seen. Clinging to the last corner of cover, she scoured her surroundings one more time.

Despite the carpark being deserted, she could still see the odd staff member walking back and forth doing their rounds through the windows. Perhaps standing guard.

If one of them saw her, it would be game over. She pictured the thought of JJ laying pale and lifeless in his bed and it provided the last shot of encouragement she needed.

Staying low, she raced off toward the Lego-shaped building without so much as another glance around her. She couldn't afford to hesitate any longer. Her friends needed her.

93

Splinters of broken door ricocheted against the wall over Meridia's shoulder as she tried to flee the unrelenting abomination in Valerie's mind.

She sensed Kane pushing at her back and urging her on as he brought up the rear. While ahead of her, JJ and Zach navigated the scattering of grubby furniture in Crooked House's lobby as if they were competing on an obstacle course.

Regardless of whose imagination this was all a figment of, they knew the danger of not making it out alive was very real.

"It's locked!" JJ cried, rattling the patio door. "We need to break it..."

The glass door, which was smashed when Meridia wandered into this nightmare, had since been magically repaired and now stood firm as JJ gave it a lunging kick. Valerie was not about to let them leave so easily. Sensing its prey were cornered, the creature slowed to a slithering, self-assured crawl.

Its nightmarish mosaic of intertwined faces twitched

and glitched like they were on the verge of breaking apart as each hideous mouth licked their shrivelled lips in unison with a legion of slimy grey varicose tongues.

"It's not budging!" Zach joined JJ in the charge to break them all out, but nothing either of them did left so much as a mark on their bulletproof prison cell.

Before Meridia opened her mouth, Kane gave her one last shove towards the others, then faced their gruesome assailant.

"Get them out of here M...It's up to you now. I'll buy you as much time as I can." He turned and charged towards the monster.

Fists clenched and full of rage with his brother's desperate pleas to stay echoing behind him.

94

Gasping for breath, Izzy slipped through the fire exit door, and immediately glanced up at the mountain of grey concrete steps spiralling above her.

"Great!" she wheezed, knowing the longer she hung around at the bottom of the dingy, pale blue stairwell, the more likely she was to get caught.

Catching her breath, she noticed the hospital's signature scent of lemony disinfectant. Although here it had a damp, moldy undertone which supported Retiarius' claim, this section wasn't intended for public use.

So far, everything he told her proved to be true, but she couldn't afford to dwell on his most devastating revelation now. She had to keep moving.

There were two flights between each floor, meaning she needed to climb eight in total to reach Valerie. No matter how softly she tried to creep up each step, she couldn't seem to stop her trainers squeaking on the hard, greasy surface.

Each rubbery screech was amplified tenfold as it echoed up and down the stairwell, giving Izzy yet another reason to dread every step she took towards her ominous destination.

"Bang!...thump thump thump thump thump..."

Izzy froze halfway between the third and fourth floors as someone else burst into the stairwell below her. With her back pressed to the wall, she held her breath and listened as the thundering footsteps reverberated around her. They were getting louder and closer.

"Bang!"

A door beneath her clattered against the wall as the stairwell fell silent again. All Izzy heard was the beating of her heart until she emptied her lungs in joyous relief.

Squeaking her way up the last flight, Izzy's mouth went dry with dread as she delicately pushed the door ajar and peeked down the ward towards the reception desk. With all but one of its lights turned off, the corridor loomed, dark and foreboding, strangled by phantom shadows skulking their way up the cubicle curtains and along the barren ceiling.

Izzy grew to hate Chase Side over the last few days. Now, when it was at its most menacing, she would need to hide behind one of its curtains alone with a mass murdering monster. The gravity of her situation came crashing down on her like a ton of bricks as she ducked back inside the stairwell to compose herself.

Heart still racing, she slipped out of her squeaky shoes and took another deep breath.

"No turning back now Izzy..." she whispered, setting off down the ward in search of cubicle 5.

95

With no actual plan beyond throwing his first punch, Kane raced towards the vile kaleidoscopic nightmare, hoping its bark was worse than its bite.

"This isn't real, she can't hurt me...this isn't real, she can't hurt me..." he chanted to himself, but the second he came within reach of the creature's thorny tendrils he discovered the hope of landing any kind of attack was pure fantasy.

"Argh!" The monster's viscid tentacles lashed out and latched onto to Kane's limbs, ripping into his flesh with row upon row of spiny fangs.

A crippling tidal wave of white-hot pain engulfed him as the tentacles tightened their vice-like grip. Wringing the blood from his calves and forearms, they dragged him toward the gruesome, ever-changing amalgamation of hideous faces which lay licking their lips at its heart.

The more Kane wriggled and resisted their barbed embrace, the deeper the tendrils tore into him, until he felt their prickly enamel grinding against his bones. With his pain receptors overloading, Kane fell limp as he sprinkled his crimson-speckled trail across the stony floor. The room became a blurry haze of shadows and gloom as he teetered on the brink of passing out.

Somewhere in the distance, he heard the muffled screams of his friends as if he were underwater, and then everything around him went dark. He only hoped his naïve sacrifice wasn't in vain, and Meridia would somehow save the rest of them. Drowsy and numb, Kane ceased fighting and closed his eyes. He could do no more now. Valerie had won.

"Thud!"

The sudden impact jolted him awake as he clattered to the ground. A glimmer of amber light leaked in beneath his heavy eyelids, followed by the vague sensation of being dragged along the floor by his shoulders.

"Kane...Kane!" JJ's voice permeated the thick black fog clouding Kane's mind. "Stay with me...I've got you."

Try as he might, he couldn't stay awake. The pain was too much to bear. He rested his weary eyes and slipped back into the comfort of darkness.

96

Meridia stood aghast, as she watched Kane being manhandled and brutally torn to shreds by the nightmarish creature. His brother's traumatized screams echoed and swirled around her to the beat of a drum as JJ continued to pound against the unbreakable glass door. It was as if time was slowing down around her.

The unfolding chaos reduced to a snail's pace while she searched within for some kind of answer to Valerie's ruthless onslaught. But all Meridia found was her own blistering rage, bubbling like molten lava, ready to explode with the fury of a fiery volcano. She sensed its warmth making her skin tingle. All-consuming as it coursed through her body like a crackling wildfire.

Could that be her answer: to fight fire with fire? Was it time to stop running away from the one aspect of herself she feared most and use it?

She gazed at Kane's lifeless body, tossed to the ground like a bag of rubbish as it leaked blood into the crevasses of the stone-tiled floor. Looming over him was the myriad of mutating Valeries, stitched together like a macabre pantomime horse made from loose-fitting human skin. Her horde of tendrils lashing the air in search of her next victim. Each smug face snickering with glee at the pain and terror she was inflicting.

This was all her creation, that despicable, evil woman. From the perfect reconstruction of Crooked House to the grotesque monster staring her down, it was all Valerie.

Maybe Kane was right, and they somehow hacked their way inside her mind and this abomination was a defence mechanism, like antivirus software sent to eradicate some invasive malware.

Or perhaps this was just a glimpse of the real Valerie. The one who lurked beneath the Disney princess façade all along. Either way, Valerie was to blame for everything, and she was going to pay for what she did.

Meridia relinquished all control to the anger raging inside of her and the release was instant. Her dam of self-restraint splintered and shattered beneath the weight of her wrath, flooding her entire body with an energy the likes of which she never felt before.

Swathed in a radioactive orange glow, her feet lifted off the ground and suddenly she knew exactly what to do. Channelling every ounce of hatred she felt towards this wretched house and all its evil inhabitants, she unleashed hell, illuminating the room with an energy so fierce it threatened to burn everything in its path.

Whether her show of power was real or simply her own illusory contribution to a figment of Valerie's imagination, Meridia didn't care. All she wanted was to end their night of torture and save her friends. All of them. Even poor, blood-soaked Kane, who JJ now hauled to safety. She wanted to undo all the hurt Valerie's hideous alter-ego had inflicted.

As her newfound energy scorched the lobby, Meridia watched through amber-tinted eyes as the tentacled creature's advance faltered. A look of fear and confusion flashed across its multitude of flabby faces. This time, there would be no holding back. No mercy for the cult's latest assassin, sent to kill them. It was Meridia's turn to send a message. One that would shake Crooked House and all its monsters to their very core.

"This ends now, bitch!" She screamed at the shrinking creature.

"I'm taking my friend and walking right out of here and there's nothing you or any of you other fuckers can do to stop me!" Meridia's fire raged through the house, incinerating every insidious piece of Valerie's mind it touched, reducing it all to ash.

The screams of her friends made way for those of the creature as it blistered from the heat of the blaze. The air was thick with the stench of seared flesh, as each face bubbled and melted like wax in the roaring inferno of Meridia's fury, until all that remained was a grisly carbonized husk.

On the brink of losing herself to her rage, Meridia willed Valerie's charred remains to dust and watched them disintegrate, until all that was left was the burned ruins of her nefarious construct.

"M...M! It's over..." Zach tugged at her arm and pulled her away from the edge. His voice trembled, still full of fear. "Please M, we need to get Kane back or he'll die. You need to help us carry him across..."

Meridia touched back down onto the ground as the energy dissipated and her temperament returned. The orange haze clouding her sight cleared like an early morning fog and revealed the blackened fruits of her labour.

Crooked House lay in ruins, destroyed by Meridia, or at least this version of it. Still in a daze, she turned to the others, who were both distraught as they tried to lift their fallen friend. Behind them, where the door to their prison once stood, was now a shimmering celestial veil of translucent blue and purple light.

As if Crooked House now magically overlooked the northern lights. Beyond the soothing glow, through the lambent hues, Meridia saw St Peter's church hall. They were still in their beds while Peter and Emily paced around them in a state of panic.

"Quickly M, we need to get him through..." JJ sobbed, covered in Kane's blood. Meridia sprang into action, helping them lift his limp and bloodied body off the ground.

"How do we know this'll work?" Zach pleaded, desperate for reassurance he wasn't about to lose his last living relative.

"It'll work Zach. We just need to hurry." The truth was, Meridia did not know what lay ahead of them.

Nor did she have any idea what state Kane might be in when they eventually awoke, but they needed to at least try. So, with one eye on the uncertain reality they were about to enter, they tiptoed across the threshold and, one by one, vanished into thin air.

97

WHEN IZZY REACHED THE COARSE BLUE CURTAIN OF cubicle 5, she wasted no time ducking inside. Amazed she got this far undetected, she took a deep breath to steady her nerves before turning to face Valerie.

A frail bag of bones beneath her sagging grey skin, Izzy almost burst into tears the moment she clapped eyes on her. How could someone so weak and feeble be so dangerous?

To distract herself from the withered old lady she was sent to kill, Izzy focussed her attention on the surrounding machinery. Tracing the tangle of wires and tubes back to a power source on the wall at the head of the bed, Izzy reasoned she could shut everything down with a couple of flicks of a switch. Exactly as Retiarius promised.

She watched Valerie's shallow breathing go up and down beneath the bedsheet and questioned if she had the strength to go through with it all. Despite everything she saw at St Peter's and all the horror stories she heard on her way here, all she saw now was a withered old lady. Someone's wife. Someone's mother.

Even with all her smarts, Izzy knew she couldn't

possibly fathom all the implications of what she was about to do. Closing her eyes, she returned to the mental image of JJ for strength.

Struggling to block out the monotonous beeping of Valerie's heart monitor, she found it wasn't enough, as doubts continued to circle like vultures searching for their next meal.

What if Meridia already saved them somehow? What if she was about to kill Valerie for nothing? How would she live with herself knowing that?

"*BANG!*"

Before Izzy spiralled any further, an enormous explosion outside snapped her out of her futile deliberations.

The blast shook the entire building, rattling the windows in their frames, before a chorus of car alarms and muffled screams broke out.

Whatever Retiarius did to force her hand, it was big, as dozens of hospital staff pounded the laminated flooring in panic, looking for the nearest exit.

This was it.

Izzy had to the count of a hundred to decide what she was going to do.

Would she go through with cold-blooded murder, or risk the lives of everyone she loved?

"One...two...three..."

98

"Kane!" Meridia sat bolt upright in her bed and nearly butted heads with her mum, who was leaning over her.

Drenched in a cold sweat, she kicked the covers off and evaded her mum's attempt to hold her.

"Kane? Zach?" She cried, disoriented.

"I'm here...I'm ok." She heard Kane's voice over her shoulder. He sounded weary, but alive. Before she reached him, her mum snatched her from behind in a big bearhug.

"Thank god you're awake," she sobbed. "I thought I lost you..."

Despite the relief of being reunited with her mum, Meridia was quick to wriggle free, desperate to make sure her friends were all ok. She found Peter fussing over them as they sat perched together on the edge of one of the other beds.

"We woke up a little before you," Zach said, peering over Peter's shoulder as he had his temperature checked.

"Where's Izzy?" Meridia asked, combing the gloomy

church hall. She thought Izzy would have been the first to welcome them all back.

"She's not here," Peter answered.

"We think she left via the toilet window, but we don't know where she went and she's not answering her phone. Do any of you know where she might be?" Meridia's heart sank at the news.

Why would she have left the church alone at this hour?

"N...no...how long has she been missing?"

"Long enough to worry. It's important I...we find her." The slip up was out of character for Peter and instantly put Meridia's guard up.

Something was off, but she couldn't tell what. Doing another sweep of the hall, everything appeared to be exactly the way she left it, aside from some beds being shuffled around, and yet her intuition continued to nag at her.

"There's no fooling you, is there Meridia?" Peter's odd question broke the awkward silence and justified Meridia's inkling.

Glancing over to where he was standing, she saw the boys recoil in terror as they scrambled to get away from him. Turning to face her, she found out why. Peter's face was pale and gaunt, like an emaciated zombie. Wearing a smug sneer, his eyes were black as coal, sunken deep within their sockets and underscored by dark green shadows of decay.

"Is this more in keeping with what a monster should be, Meridia?" His voice took on an unearthly echo as he stepped away from the cowering boys and moved towards the church altar.

It was Valerie. It had to be. They were still trapped in her deadly deception.

"Don't look so surprised." Peter continued. "I know everything you know...hear everything you hear...even when you're sleeping. That's how I know Izzy is missing, you see. I heard the others talking about it when she first disappeared. I need you to tell me where she is...my master needs all of you..."

Meridia backed into the open arms of her mum, who was standing right behind her, except this time, there was no love in her embrace. Instead, her grip was unrelenting, threatening to squeeze the very life out of her like a boa constrictor crushing its prey. Wriggling and wheezing, Meridia glanced up and was greeted by the same soulless eyes as Peter.

"There's no escape from me." She said in the same hollow voice. "I am everywhere...Now tell me where the last of you is hiding and I promise I'll make this quick for you and your friends..."

Before Meridia uttered a word of protest, a swarm of slimy tentacles erupted from the ground and ensnared all three boys. Snaking their way around their arms and legs, the grey, sinewy tendrils shackled each of them to the spot.

"Don't tell h..." Kane's instruction was muffled by a tentacle, slavered in gooey yellow mucus, forcing its way down his throat.

His eyes bulged with terror as he gagged and choked on the gruesome appendage, while JJ and Zach stifled their screams in fear of meeting a similar fate.

"Shh..." Peter hushed the group of terrified boys. "Didn't your mothers teach you it's rude to interrupt...I hadn't finished talking."

Meridia felt her spine crack under the crushing force of her mum's grip as Peter walked toward her.

"When I was a little girl, my nan took me to a local aquarium. Ocean Odyssey, it was called. My mum was busy, you see, working two jobs after my dad abandoned us.

She said it would be a perfect opportunity for us to spend time together. My nan already knew I was afraid of octopuses, even though I'd never seen one in real life. My nan was good at uncovering what made people tick... or, more to the point, what got their goat. She asked a lot of questions. Nosy cow I called her once. I got a good hiding for saying it, but it's what she was. Nosy and vindictive. When we arrived at the aquarium, the first thing she did was march me straight to the octopus tank. I can still remember its tentacles ebbing and flowing underwater like it was moving in slow motion. I was too terrified to speak. I just stood there, paralyzed, pissing all over my patent leather princess shoes. All the while, my nan laughed and jeered. Spiteful bitch. She said it was punishment for keeping her awake at night. Depriving her of her precious beauty sleep. I suffered from night terrors you see...and that little stunt only made everything worse. I had nightmares for days after that, and all my nan kept saying was what a weakling I was...just like my mother. I was only 5 or 6 at the time." Peter looked lost in thought for a moment, reliving Valerie's harrowing childhood torture.

"It was the way they moved that scared me. So unnatural with all those legs and suckers...and don't even get me started on their big, fat heads. I kept dreaming I was being strangled in my sleep. I could feel its suckers at my throat as if it was real. Anyway, after wetting the bed for a few nights in a row, I decided to create my own monster. A big, bad octopus killer to keep me safe at night." Peter gestured to the boys.

"That's what you saw earlier...or a version of it, at least. It's changed over the years. My memory isn't what it used to be, but the essence is still the same. Imagine my surprise when I found out my dreams were real...imagine the temptation for a girl bullied and picked on by her nan every chance she got. Well, one night she got what was coming to her. I had my monster pay her a visit and return the favour, only I didn't stop at scaring her. I wrung the life out of the wretched woman and never looked back. Not long after, the Children of the Shadows found me and, well, here we are..."

"Why are you telling me all this?" Meridia coughed.

"I can tell you all want to know. I can hear the thousands of questions rattling around in your heads. Too many thoughts for my muddled brain. Oh, you all think you know so much...hahahahaha...you know nothing. But you Meridia, you I cannot read so well. It's like you have a private room inside your mind, a room I cannot get into. So, I'm going to ask you one more time. Where is Izzy?"

"I don't know...how could I?!" Meridia gave the only answer she could.

"Very well. You had your chance..." With a wave of his hand, the tentacles holding JJ hoisted him high in the air.

Grimacing in their grip, he writhed and squirmed, but they refused to budge.

"Don't worry..." Peter smiled at Kane, still gagging on the invasive tendril lodged inside his throat. "...it'll be your turn soon enough."

"Let them go!" Meridia yelled, but it was too late to reason.

"Argh!" JJ let out an agonizing cry as Meridia heard the creaking of tentacles tightening their grip around his arms.

As the noise continued to get louder, Meridia realized the creaking wasn't coming from the tentacles at all. It was coming from JJ. Grimacing and glistening with sweat from the unbearable pain.

She watched in horror as his shirtsleeves ripped at their

seams and hairline tears formed on the surface of his skin. He was being pulled apart.

"*Snap!*"

Meridia shuddered at the sickening sound of flesh being torn as JJ's arms came apart at the shoulders. A gooey mess of elongated muscle and tissue stretched across the gaping wounds, like melted mozzarella until it snapped and sprayed the floor with thick viscous blood.

"Noooo...." Meridia screamed, as she saw the ball and socket brutally separate.

JJ's arms flopped to the floor with fingers still twitching as another tendril coiled around his neck to steady his dismembered body. Beside him, Zach and Kane both wrestled against their slimy restraints.

Tears were now streaming down their faces, but it was all in vain. Valerie won, and there was nothing Meridia or anyone else could do to stop her.

"His head is next Meridia...last ch..." Peter trailed off, distracted by something elsewhere. Meridia felt her mother's grip loosen slightly.

"Yooou..." Peter rasped, his voice suddenly old and frail. The moment the word left his lips, the right side of his face wilted and sagged as if he was melting, and his hair turned white as snow.

"Deppots eb t'nac ehs dna gnimoc s'ehs...trebla em rof gnimoc s'ehs." The bizarre gibberish slurred from his drooping mouth as he collapsed to the ground in a heap.

Now was her chance. Feeling her mum's grip slacken completely, she shrugged her off and raced to the aid of her friends.

Meridia didn't make it more than a couple of yards when everything in front of her transformed, solidifying into a golden sand sculpture, with each gruesome feature intricately captured down to the very last grain. As she hesitated, she sensed the soft sand beneath her feet and the sound of lapping waves behind her.

Taking in her new surroundings, she realized she was back on her favourite beach, where this nightmare began. The warm sunshine was beating down on her back and the smell of fresh seaweed wafted over her, drifting on a gentle summer breeze.

Bewildered, Meridia glanced toward the sandy statues, a harrowing conclusion, cut short by divine intervention. JJ, viciously mutilated, with Kane and Zach forced to watch in perpetuity.

In front of them, centre stage and crumpled on the ground, a chilling amalgamation of Peter and Valerie, frozen mid-metamorphosis. Their features hideously knotted together to form a vile effigy forged from the depths of Valeries' twisted imagination.

As the wind picked up around her, it sent ripples through their sculpted remains, dismantling them piece by piece, scattering them across the beach like a fading dream. Once again, Meridia was alone.

The nightmare was over, and it was finally time for her to wake up.

99

"99...100..." Izzy reached the end of her count and rested her trembling hand on the power switches controlling the jumble of brightly coloured electrical cables below.

Trapped in cubicle 5 with the most notorious serial killer Shawbrook had ever seen, she had no choice but to go through with the rest of Retiarius' plan. If she didn't, her friends were sure to die.

"Argh!" She was about to summon the strength to flick the first switch when Valerie gripped her arm.

Staring up at her from the hospital bed, her baggy eyes were full of fear. Pleading for her not to do it. Somewhere beyond the throes of Izzy's inner turmoil, she heard the heart monitor gallop off like a racehorse at the Grand National.

"Yooou..." Valerie wheezed, her icy hand clasped tight around Izzy's wrist. Flinching to break free from the withered old woman's grasp, Izzy hit two of the switches, putting an abrupt end to the heart monitor's incessant beeping.

Despite her reasons for being there, it was an accident. But it started an avalanche of panic inside Izzy. and before she knew it, she had switched off every device in an angst-fuelled frenzy. Anything to stop Valerie's eyes from boring into her.

"Click-Click-Click..."

Each callous, staccato snap of plastic hammered another nail into Valerie's coffin as all the whirring and beeping subsided and gave way to a solitary patient alarm.

Hysterical and in floods of tears, Izzy remained inconsolable over what she had done and continued stroking the panel of switches in a state of shock. All the while, Valerie's dying gasps for breath went unanswered. Swallowed by the raucous discord of the unfolding chaos outside.

Nobody was coming to save either of them now, and there would be no way back from this. Closing her eyes to slow the deluge of tears streaming down her cheeks, Izzy focused on Valerie's fragile breathing as it rattled in and out of her sunken chest.

As each laboured breath grew further and further apart, she felt the old woman's arm flop down on the edge of the bed.

The night walker was dead, and along with her, so too was a part of Izzy's soul.

100

Albert Richards was suffering from the same terrible nightmare for about a week now, and no matter what he tried to do differently each night, it always came to the same heartbreaking conclusion.

It was 18 months since he last shared a bed with his wife. She always kept his bad dreams at bay. His personal dream catcher.

Dream scaping, she called it. Likening it to the way a landscape gardener would often re-shape nature to paint a prettier picture, she would do the same with dreams. When she first told him, he didn't believe her. Who would?

But when she recited his dream the next day over breakfast to prove her point, he had no choice but to concede. That was back when they were in their twenties, with their whole lives ahead of them.

Now, in their twilight years, Valerie spent most of her days in a dream state, although where she went on her travels remained a mystery. That was the nature of her illness. A wretched disease that had driven a wedge between them. The one battle he knew he couldn't win.

Tonight, however, he was determined to see her. Every day he sat by her bedside whispering instructions: targets for her special gift.

These days, she wouldn't listen to anyone else, not even Dr Chapman. Something to do with her condition, he was told. Her memory was deteriorating by the day, but each evening, before he said goodnight, Albert always delivered a special message of his own.

Painting a picture of their first date in her addled mind, he returned to his empty home and prayed she found him there. Waiting at their favourite table by the window, early as always.

After gurgling his mouthwash and rinsing it down the sink, he glanced up at the bathroom mirror and looked himself in the eyes. The years weren't kind to him as he scrutinized the liver spots on his balding head. A shadow of the fresh-faced beat cop who somehow caught his wife's eye.

Oh, how he longed to turn back the clock. Given their time again, he would take her away from this madness and keep her all to himself. He blamed them for her condition. Their relentless demands. Each time she did their bidding, he saw the toll it took on her. It started small at first. Misplaced keys, a pan left on the stove.

Little by little they stole her from him until one day she forgot who Albert was altogether. Almost fifty years of marriage, erased in a flash. He would never forget the panic in her eyes, confronted by who she thought was a stranger, but in truth, was the one man who loved her more than anything in the world.

Looking at the haggard reflection staring back at him, he found it hardly surprising she didn't recognize him. He barely recognized himself these days. Oh, to be young again.

Unable to look at his reflection any longer, Albert switched the bathroom light off and made his way to bed. Shortly after Valerie was admitted, he moved to their son's old room at the rear of the house, away from the main road.

He used the noise as an excuse, but the truth was he found it all too painful waking up next to an empty pillow each morning. As he wriggled his way down the single mattress, he closed his eyes and tried to picture Valerie's face. These days it was hard to visualize her without the tangle of tubes keeping her alive, so he kept an old photo by the bedside to ease the burden on his own ailing memory.

As he let go of all the tension in his weary old bones, a wry smile crept across his wrinkled face. Tonight, she would visit. Tonight would be different.

It didn't take long for Albert to drift off to sleep. His son's room was small and well insulated from the cold outside, so despite the initial chill associated with an empty bed, it never took long for him to warm up.

Over the months, he developed a technique for dreaming. Meticulously replaying the same scene over and over in his mind until he found himself there. It would work most of the time, but lately his mind had been hijacked by thoughts of that spoiled brat of a girl from up the road.

He still couldn't fathom how or why it started, as he never even laid eyes on her before. Until now. The moment he spotted her waiting for the Wilson girl, he was overcome with rage.

How dare she stand there and rub his nose in all the sleepless nights she gave him. It was a sign. It had to be. If that wretched child was alone and he was ten years younger, he might have walked across the road and snapped her scrawny little neck. Then to see her again at the hospital, where Valerie was.

Well, it was enough to make his blood boil. Albert tried to get his thoughts back on track, but it was too late. Once again, he allowed the irksome girl under his skin, and he was in for another night of torment.

101

No one was more surprised than Albert when he stood outside the door of The Old Mill Tavern. Even though he knew he was dreaming, he felt his heart flutter with excitement as he peered through the pub's sash window and found her sitting alone at their favourite table wearing a gorgeous royal-blue, halter neck dress.

Her chestnut hair was swept back into a tight bun, and she was sipping a glass of red, being careful not to smudge her cerise lipstick.

Albert chuckled as he caught her checking her watch, then realized he needed to get a wiggle on. It was their first date, and he'd been held up at the station that day, which meant he was running late.

Unlike their real first date, this time round, they had the whole place to themselves, with not another soul in sight. As he pulled on the polished brass door handle, he glimpsed his reflection beneath the light overhead and paused. He was twenty-two again. It was his first year on the force and before his hair started thinning. Straightening his collar, he gave his younger self a wink and went inside.

The tavern was the perfect venue for a first date. Nestled in the neighbouring town of Thundridge, it exuded rustic charm as its gently turning waterwheel created a soothing ambiance with the sound of splashing water.

The restored mill comprised a mix of cosy booths and traditional wooden tables, each topped with a mason jar filled with fresh flowers. Albert smelt their floral aroma as he walked across the polished hardwood floor.

"Sorry I'm late," he said, sliding out of his jacket and into his chair.

"That's ok dear. I'm sorry it's been so long." Valerie smiled as she took another sip of her wine. "I miss you Al...I miss this."

Albert reached across the table and took her hand in his. She felt so cold.

"I wish we had more time," she sighed, staring over his shoulder and out the window. "It's almost time now...I can feel it. Then we can be together again."

"I'd like that...I'd like that a lot." He gripped her hand tighter and tried to thaw the icy chill coursing through her veins.

Wondering how he would ever find the strength to let go again.

"*Ding-ding...*"

The bell sounded above the door and snapped him out of his daze. A visitor arrived, and a knot formed in Albert's throat as he realized he could no longer move. Glued to his chair, he watched Valerie's eyes fill with fear as she looked up at the trespasser, mouth agape.

"Deppots eb t'nac ehs dna gnimoc s'ehs...trebla em rof gnimoc s'ehs." The string of gobbledygook brought tears flooding to Albert's eyes as he remembered it from the night she was admitted. She muttered those same words at the dinner table one evening and followed it up with the same muddled expression.

Luckily, the paramedics had arrived just in time to witness her first seizure and took her straight to the hospital. When she woke a day later, the Valerie he loved was gone.

As Albert craned his neck to see who had entered, everything changed around him. A magical force transported their table from the cozy old tavern to the desolate grounds outside Crooked House, where their story began.

Surrounded by oaks and alders on a cold and cloudy winter's day, he watched as Valerie aged before his eyes. Her glassy brown eyes sunk deeper into their sockets, strangled by the baggage of time, as her pallid face drooped and wilted. In a matter of seconds, she returned to the frail old woman, it pained him to look at each and every day.

Glancing down at the table, he too, had aged. His hands were now emaciated, riddled with thick blue veins and liver spots. This was unlike any of his usual nightmares. The girl who haunted him of late was nowhere to be seen.

Tonight, a different intruder tiptoed into his thoughts, wearing a long brown hooded cloak just like his own. A brother or sister in arms, at least he thought until he saw the blade. Serrated steel and razor sharp, it glistened as the mysterious invader darted behind Valerie and grabbed her by the top of her wispy grey hair.

She didn't even struggle, couldn't. She just looked at Albert blankly as if the lights were on, but no one was home. It was a look he should've been accustomed to by now, but this one stung more than all the others. Her mouth sagged, as if somewhere deep inside she was screaming to be heard, but then her tormentor thrust the knife under her flaccid chin.

Albert squirmed and wriggled, but he couldn't break free of whatever spell was fixing him to his chair. Paralyzed and chained by fear, he was forced to watch as white knuckles pushed the knife in and slashed his beloved Valerie's throat from ear to ear.

"Nooo!" He screamed through clenched teeth as blood spattered, then gushed from her gaping wound, speckling him and her killer, before slowing to a steady pulse as she bled out all over her pretty blue dress.

"Nooo..." he sobbed, heartbroken and distraught, as a crimson pool oozed its way across the table toward him like a macabre mirror of death.

Trying to escape its path, Albert sensed a sudden and sharp pang in his chest, followed by a suffocating tightness as if the killer were squeezing the life out of his heart. Gasping for breath, he looked up at his assailant as they lowered their cowl.

There, across the table, stood Izzy Di Salvo. Her face aghast, she gawked at him from behind her blood-smeared glasses, and then, in the blink of an eye, she was gone. Left staring at the gloomy shadows on the ceiling, Albert clutched his chest as wave upon wave of searing pain rippled through his shrivelled body.

With his son's room spinning around him like a merry-go-round, he fought to find the picture by his bedside, locking eyes with it. One last glimpse of his beloved Valerie.

As he drew his final breath, he thought he saw his love smiling back at him from within the frame, and it was all the comfort he needed to let go.

102

Shellshocked, Izzy staggered out of the hospital fire exit in a grief-stricken trance. A blast of cold air hit her like a slap in the face the second she broke free from the suffocating stairwell, but it still wasn't enough to wake her from her daze.

She couldn't even remember how she had found her way out, but here she was, meandering in the shadows of Chase Side's patient block. Ahead of her, she saw a flickering amber light dancing on the frosty tarmac, and as she reached the corner and peered round, she came face to face with the raging fire, causing all the commotion.

A blazing row of parked cars pumped thick black smoke into the night sky, choking the handful of stars that had shown up to watch Izzy throw her entire life away.

She paused for a moment and observed the bedlam as a couple of orderlies tried in vain to douse the mesmerizing flames with their puny fire extinguishers while other staff and patients gathered at the front of the building to watch the dazzling show. Guzzling up their dry white mist, the insatiable firestorm continued to strive towards the heavens, bathing everyone in its pulsating heat.

Carrying her guilt like a lead weight around her neck, Izzy trudged around the perimeter of the carpark. All she needed to do was reach Willow Road. That was if Retiarius remained good to his word. Even now, in her stupor, she couldn't bring herself to think of his real name. Such was her disdain for him.

Creeping along the hospital's border, she reached a narrow break in the thorny shrubberies where she squeezed through in order to reach her extraction point. As she shielded her face from the onslaught of barbed branches, she heard the whoop of sirens announce a fire engine's arrival behind her. Surely, she was home and dry now. Even if Retiarius's driver stood her up, she knew she could find her way back to the church on foot if she needed to.

As Izzy stumbled out into the sleepy suburban cul-de-sac, she was met by the blinding headlights of a van. Another member of Retiarius' crew, no doubt. She wondered how many followers he had. The driver flashed the instant Izzy appeared and started up the engine. She'd made it.

Teetering forward as her eyes struggled to adjust, she tapped on the window of the passenger side and tried its handle. Staring back at her from behind the wheel was a face she recognized, although her usual chirpy disposition was replaced by something bordering on hostile.

"Mrs Hutson? What are you doing here?" Izzy mumbled, still punch drunk on shame and remorse.

What was the owner of Jubilee Park Café doing, getting mixed up with Retiarius?

Before she uttered another word, Izzy was grabbed from

behind and all the oxygen squeezed from her lungs as she was hoisted up in the air.

"Throw her in the back," Mrs Hutson barked. "We can deal with the bitch later. Retiarius was right, you're needed back at the hospital brother Grady..."

Izzy felt the blood in her veins turn to ice at the mention of his name. She was betrayed. Kicking and screaming, she tried to break free, but Grady was far too strong, scarily strong, in fact.

As he hauled her to the rear of the van and opened its door, Izzy scoured her surroundings for anyone who might help, but the street was abandoned, as was she. Its handful of unassuming, red bricked bungalows all turned the other cheek as she was vehemently tossed into the back like a rag doll.

"*Thud!*"

She winced as the back of her head bounced off the van's hard metal floor. Woozy from the force of the blow and nauseous from the overpowering aroma of cherries assaulting her airways, she tried to get back up, but was shoved down by Grady as he climbed in to join her.

Dressed in a dark hooded cloak, he wore a sinister sneer on his pale, chiselled face as it emerged from the shadow of his cowl. His bright blue eyes sparkled beneath the interior light as he stared at her unblinkingly.

Gripped by fear, Izzy flinched as he reached down and removed her glasses. His sneer turned to a demented smile as he studied her face intently.

"What pretty eyes you have..." he whispered.

His voice was soft and soothing, but with an underlying current of malevolence that sent shivers down Izzy's spine.

The interior light went out, plunging them both into

darkness as the van sped off to the sound of Izzy's petrified screams.

103

"Gah!" Kane awoke in his bed with the rancid taste of a tentacle still lingering in his mouth.

"JJ!" He muttered, quickly sitting up to look for his partner in crime. He found him perched on the edge of his bed, massaging his shoulder in disbelief.

"You're ok...thank god...where are the others?" Twisting round, he found Zach and Meridia looming behind him.

"Agh!" He recoiled, tumbling out of bed and onto the cold wooden floor with a loud splat.

"Shit...don't do that!" He said, blushing with embarrassment.

"I...I can't believe you're all here...are you? Really here I mean?" Peter stepped in and helped Kane get to his feet.

"All except Izzy," Peter said solemnly. Kane examined the cluster of empty z-beds.

"But we didn't see her in there...I thought she was out here with you. That means..."

"Valerie knew she had gone; she just didn't know where." Meridia cut across his rambling. "She was using our ears like hidden microphones, listening to everything that was being said in here while we were trapped in there.”

“There?” Peter asked. “I’m still not following where ‘there’ is…”

“We’ll explain it all later, but in a nutshell, Valerie has some kind of power that’s like mine, only instead of jumping through time, she jumps through people’s dreams and then turns them into nightmares. If you die in the nightmare, then you die for real. She’s like some movie character called Teddy, apparently. That’s where we’ve all been.” Meridia was trying to short-circuit any long debate to keep them all focused on Izzy, so Kane let her little faux pas slide on this occasion.

“I heard about Izzy while we were in there. I know she climbed out through the window, and it can’t be a coincidence we’re here and she’s not. I think she might have saved us all somehow…”

“The hospital…” JJ beat everyone to the punch.

“She must have found another way to stop Valerie. But how would she have got there? She must have had help…it’s too dangerous to go it alone, and why didn’t she tell anyone?”

“We had our hands pretty full,” Emily explained. “You kept sailing dangerously close to…well, let’s just say you had us all worried. Maybe she wanted to tell us but couldn’t…”

“Guys…” Meridia’s eyes were glued to her phone. It’s pale blue light illuminating all her worry lines for everyone else to see.

“I think I know who helped her.” She read the brief exchange between Izzy and Retiarius before they switched to email and triggered a groundswell of apprehension.

“Check your phones guys, in case she reached out to one of us…” Kane urged, pulling his phone from his pocket.

Before he even opened the message from Izzy on his screen, he noticed he was standing on something. At first, he thought it was a shadow, a trick of the light, but as he looked deeper, he saw it was a long black scorch mark tarnishing the church's herringbone floor. It seemed familiar somehow, but he was certain it hadn't been there before.

A knot of dread tightened like a clenched fist in the pit of his stomach as he realized where he saw it. It was the same marking he noticed at Crooked House.

Was this yet another illusion sent to pry information from them all?

He glanced around at the others with a newfound air of suspicion.

"What is it, mate?" JJ was the first to notice something was up, as Kane distanced himself from the rest of the group, backing away from the peculiar stingray-shaped stain at his feet.

"I...I'm not sure..." He stuttered, gazing at the tarnished wood.

Unsure if it was the criss-cross pattern of the tiles playing tricks on him, Kane rubbed his eyes and did a double take. He was sure he saw movement.

"Stand back..." He hollered. "Everyone, stand back!"

The others reacted unthinking, forming a circle around the mysterious shape, as Kane realized it wasn't a burn mark at all, but something far more sinister. The translucent, shadowy mass rose from the floor like a hot-air balloon, and the fist forming in Kane's stomach leapt into his throat and cut off his air supply.

The horsemen returned.

The creature's eyes sparkled with a menacing light, black and glittering like the darkest of nightmares, set deep within its skeletal face. As it continued to ascend above them all, it took on a more terrifying and familiar shape, filling out beneath its rippling robes and baring its jagged teeth.

Floating high now, out of reach and close to the church's arched ceiling, it looked down at them all and sneered. Its robes ebbed and flowed languidly as if treading water, then it opened its mouth to speak.

"The reckoning is nigh, and your time is almost up. Seer or not, nothing can save you from the demon...Consider this fair warning..."

Its clunky, rasping voice reverberated around the church like a preacher's thunderous sermon and every syllable rattled Kane to his bones.

Without uttering another word, the menacing phantom soared toward the rafters and melted into the shadows above. It was an ominous message, delivered on what was sacred ground. The horsemen were back and stronger than before.

Kane sensed whatever was left of their world closing in around them, and as he looked around the room, he knew it was a feeling shared by the rest of the group.

Peter was the first to break the mounting silence, choosing to rally everyone.

"This message changes nothing. If they were so close to winning, none of us would be here. Our plan remains the same guys. We need to find Izzy and another place to hide. Before Izzy left, we thought we found someone we could trust, but I'm not going to lie, the Children of the Shadows are much bigger than any of us first thought. The road we now find ourselves on is going to be long and hard, but I know we can do it. All we need to do is make it through the rest of the night. Grab your things quickly and get to the cars. I don't know how long we have until they arrive." With no time for chitchat, the group scrambled to collect their things.

They were on the run, for real now, and Kane knew there was no telling how close they were to being caught.

As he stuffed his bag full of anything he could get his hands on, Kane glanced at the message from Izzy again and opened it in private. There must have been a reason she reached out to him and not Meridia, and it didn't take long for him to realize what that was.

The moment Kane finished reading the message, his anger bubbled back to the surface. They had a traitor in their midst, a murderous fanatic, just like the ones who killed his parents. Izzy left it to exactly the right person to deal with them. He would make them pay for what they had done.

Kane, if you're reading this, it means I have done something terrible tonight and I am no better than the monsters we're running from. It was the only way I could save you all. I had no other choice.

I'm running out of time here, but there's something you must know before I go. Even though it might sound crazy, you must believe me when I say it's true.

Do not trust Emily. She's one of them, Kane. She's a member of the cult. She's been lying to Meridia this entire time. You must stop her, no matter what.

You need to get as far away from this place as you can. Retiarius knows you're at the church and he might come for you. He's dangerous, and if I'm not there with you all, then he can't be trusted.

I know who he really is now, Kane. It's Gregor. Retiarius is Meridia's dad. You need to protect her. You need to protect them all.

I'm sorry I can't be there, but there was no other way. I'm going to miss you all so much.

Please don't give up, Kane. Don't let what I've done be for nothing.

Fight them to the end.

Izzy x

EPILOGUE

"I...I don't think...*KAFF*... I don't think I can make it... *kaff kaff*..." Kane gasped.

"You...you need to leave me here. Otherwise, we won't make it..." Peter shone his torch on Kane's ribs and found blood seeping through his makeshift dressing.

The knife was driven to the hilt, and Peter did not know what major organs were damaged inside him. Drenched in sweat and covered in dirt, Kane dropped to his knees in the tunnel and coughed some more.

"I mean it Peter...*kaff*...I can b...barely walk now. You need to go..."

The trickle of blood leaking from the corner of his mouth told Peter his condition was grave, but there was no way he was going to leave him to die forty feet underground and alone.

He crouched at Kane's side and swept his matted fringe away from his forehead to check his temperature. He found him deathly cold and trembling. Fighting back tears, Peter put his arm around the boy's shoulder and drew him in close for a hug.

"I'm not going anywhere without you, ok...*sniff*...just keep talking while I figure something out...Kane...Kane!"

"S...sorry...I'm just so tired..." Kane was slurring now.

Peter knew he needed to seal his wound fast or else he would bleed out. He tried his walkie-talkie again, but all he heard was static. If only he knew where the nearest exit point was, he might manage to carry Kane above ground and radio for help.

Or perhaps Meridia knew Kane was in trouble and had already sent someone to find them? God, he hoped so.

Staring into the gloomy abyss, Peter listened for something, anything which might give him a sliver of hope. Nothing.

"Kane?" He gave him a gentle nudge.

"*Kaff...kaff*...I'm still here...but you need to go...*kaff*... there's not enough time..." Kane was sounding weaker by the second, but he was right.

They were all running out of time. With only a matter of hours before the blood moon, they had only one chance to stop the demon's resurrection and save Izzy. They had to reach the Crooked House before she was sacrificed.

Peter shone his torch along the tunnel's ceiling and traced the mould-infested, cobbled archway a few metres ahead. There had to be another exit somewhere, and then he saw it, a break in the wall up ahead. It had to lead somewhere.

"C'mon Kane, stay with me... I'm getting you out of here." Buoyed by his discovery, Peter lifted Kane to his feet and carried him along the damp and decaying passageway until they reached the opening.

Sure enough, he found another archway leading to a murky alcove. It had to be a way out. "Wait here while I go check it out," Peter whispered, propping Kane up against the nearest wall.

Torch in hand, Peter tiptoed toward the opening, not wishing to disturb any more rats that might be lurking in the shadows. As he crept closer, he heard a strange rhythmic pulsating sound, like a cat purring.

Hesitating, he searched for a better angle to shine a light inside, but whatever was making the unsettling noise was hidden around a blind corner. If he was to have any chance of saving Kane, he needed to push on, so Peter edged a little closer, taking the corner as wide as possible.

"*Squelch.*"

As he reached the alcove's entrance, he felt something sticky underfoot so directed his torch to see what he stepped in. He gasped in horror to find the ground was thick with glistening yellow mucus.

A vile, sulphurous stench wafted out from the shadows and Peter realized he made a terrible mistake, but it was too late now.

The moment his torchlight struck the back wall and illuminated the source of the ominous sound, he felt his legs seize up and a prickly cold sweat broke out beneath his shirt.

Trembling in petrified silence, his shaky spotlight surveyed the rest of the recess to see the full extent of the nightmare he had foolishly wandered into.

A cluster of crusty, slime-infested eggs the size of giant pumpkins lay scattered across the ground, each one twitching and throbbing like a ticking time bomb of terror. Weavers, dozens of them, just waiting to hatch.

The Children of the Shadows were assembling an arachnid army capable of crushing anything standing in their way, and Peter knew if just one of these monsters got loose, the war would be lost.

He glanced back at Kane, bloodied and barely breathing in the corridor outside, then he refocused his attention on the menacing brood and realized what he needed to do. There was no way he would allow a single egg to survive, no matter the cost.

AUTHOR'S NOTE

"The more you look, the more you see."

I don't follow mainstream news. I don't watch it, I don't read it, I don't listen to it. I dip in and out of sports and entertainment, mostly to check the latest scores, or to discover up-and-coming movies that might be of interest, but that's pretty much it. You might think that's ignorant or lazy, but I've been that way ever since I studied media in my early twenties and got to peek behind the curtain as it were.

I rely on the important stuff finding me via the people I trust, largely because it allows me to safeguard my sanity a little better. I've never quite understood why someone would choose to start their day by watching an endless conveyor belt of horror and injustice.

So, when I first came up with the idea of an evil sect hell-bent on marching us all towards the apocalypse, I knew I wouldn't need to look very far for inspiration. In fact, all I had to do was turn on the news. As expected, the more I watched, the more shocked and disillusioned I became. It seemed whenever I thought I'd nailed the tone for the Children of the Shadows, the world screamed "hold my beer" and showed me what real horror was. But what really terrified me the most about everything I saw was the way it left me feeling powerless to change any of it.

My little deep dive into futility got me thinking what if. What if everything I'd watched play out around the world was really the result of a coordinated evil? A secret society pulling the strings from the shadows. Steering us all towards Armageddon.

As a result of my 'research', it's fair to say this book took on a slightly darker tone than The Rising and Night of the Witch. It's also probably worth mentioning that book four is going to be even darker. Sorry/not sorry.

But, despite the increasingly bleak outlook faced by its characters, and the way their circumstances sometimes bleed into our reality, at its heart, the series remains a tale of resilience and hope. No matter what I throw at this incredible group of friends, they never give up fighting for what they believe in.

So, for those of you, like me, who find the mounting horrors of the real world a little too much to take from time to time, I hope you find solace in these pages and allow them to transport you to a place where evil has a name, and a group of ordinary people stand a genuine chance of saving us all from its grip. Or do they?

ACKNOWLEDGMENTS

First, I'd like to say a huge thank you to all my readers. I've been blown away the warm reception you've given the Crooked Tales series so far and I can't wait to find out what you think of this, the latest instalment.

I'd like to thank Ray and Adam at Wicked Ink Publishing for their incredible support and encouragement. I wouldn't be the writer I am today without you.

I'd like to thank my wife Nikki for keeping me grounded as I delve deeper into the dark side of my imagination. Your love and understanding means the world to me.

I'd like to thank my son Harry for being my biggest fan and a constant source of joy in my life.

I'd also like to thank my friends and extended family who put up with me prattling on about evil monsters and plot twists whenever we see each other. Your patience and humour are genuinely appreciated.

Lastly, I'd like to thank Winnie, the only dog I've ever really taken to, who always sat on my mouse whenever she came to visit and then refused to budge. Without you, Children of the Shadows might have been finished a lot sooner.

ABOUT THE AUTHOR

© Chris Harrison

Chris Harrison, born in North London, is not just a writer, producer, and author of the *Crooked Tales Series*; he's a storyteller on a mission. Graduating from Middlesex University with a degree in Film, Chris turned his fascination with the art of storytelling into a lifelong exploration of literary and cinematic horror. Having previously written for film and education, he's now dedicated to realizing a dream—crafting immersive worlds filled with spine-tingling terror for a young adult audience.

Chris's creations fuse classic supernatural themes with contemporary urban mythology, re-imagining our deepest fears for a new generation of horror enthusiasts.

www.chris-harrison.com

instagram.com/chrisharrison1975

threads.com/@chrisharrison1975

tiktok.com/@chris.harrison75

x.com/CHarrison22975